APOLLO BURN

PILLARS OF FIRE AND LIGHT BOOK 2

To Babs! Enjoy!

KEN BRITZ

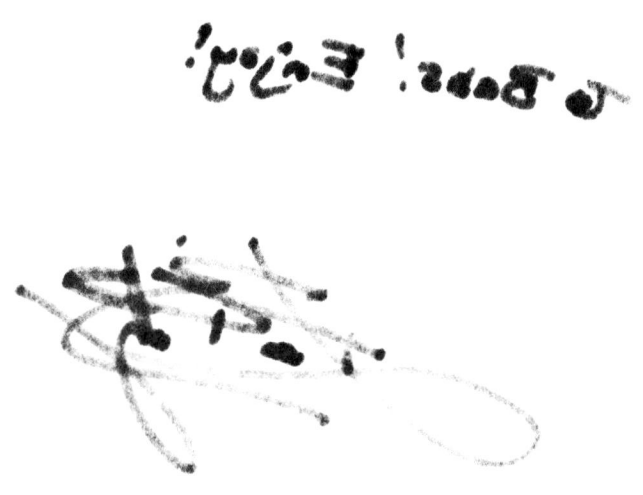

Copyright © 2017 by Ken Britz

All rights reserved.

No part of this book may be reproduced in any form or by any electronic or mechanical means, including information storage and retrieval systems, without written permission from the author, except for the use of brief quotations in a book review.

*For Karen and Carl.
I love you, Mom and Dad.*

APOLLO BURN

PILLARS OF FIRE AND LIGHT, BOOK TWO

Ken Britz

1

DEATH IN THE FAMILY

WASHINGTON, DC—
Isolde Marks stepped off the elevator, dropping the backpack from her shoulder to dig out her keys. The police tape was across the apartment door, marking it as a crime scene. Isolde frowned, pulling out a small knife. She sliced the tape and then opened the door. It was dark inside, an open floor plan of a modern apartment, with the kitchen and living room as one large space. On either side were rooms—her father's study on one and bedrooms on the other.

Sheets of rain fell against the floor-to-ceiling glass walls that overlooked Washington, DC's smudged skyline. The rooftop terrace was dark and gray like the room. *Is there something near the ledge of the terrace?* she wondered. It was hard to make out in the driving rain. She stood still, waiting for her eyes to adjust to the dark. She didn't want to turn on the light and see the truth just yet. The old Churchill, a round-shouldered leather-covered chair, was a black shape facing the DC skyline. She lowered her pack to the floor and went into her father's study. It was sparse—an ornate desk, some army mementos, and a few of his favorite military periodicals. She sat down at the desk and stared at the two photos in the room. On a shelf, four people within a frame were smiling—her father, Cornwall; her mother, Janine; her brother, Lance; and Isolde herself—years younger than she was now. She was maybe eleven in that photo, making it nearly a decade old.

Isolde pulled back the hood of her University of Washington jacket. She ran a hand through her wet hair and tightened the tie on her ponytail. On the desk was a single picture of Isolde herself, taken the day she left for college. She shook her head, unable to reconcile this image of her doting father with the driven monster he had been at Tintagel. *Tintagel,* Isolde repeated to herself. She'd almost forgotten that place. Of course, she would never really forget Tintagel and Project Avallach. Twice her father had almost left her for dead— once while on a mission gone bad and at the end, when he wanted to destroy Avallach. That was the day she had turned her back on him, and that had made him realize he only had one child left in the world.

Isolde's hackles rose at a sound. She slid her fingers over the inside of the desk and pushed the catch. A compartment slid open. She drew out the M9 Beretta. With the expertise of an army officer's daughter, she checked the clip, chamber, and safety in one smooth motion. She stood and edged out of the room, her gun close to her body and her senses on high alert. She moved back into the open part of the penthouse. The kitchen and living room were empty. She scanned and saw nothing out of the ordinary.

She stalked to the old Churchill chair in the center of the living room. Light from the rippling rain made the old leather waver as if it were a hologram. The chair faced the large windows and the balcony —toward the skyline. Except for this chair and the desk in the study, the furniture in the apartment looked new and unused. Her father hadn't lived here until he retired from his DARPA work and Isolde had left for university just a month ago. He'd planned to follow her to Seattle, or so he said. She wanted to believe his sincerity, but now it didn't matter.

She caressed the leather back of the chair. He'd loved to sit and read to his children when she and Lance were young. Then she saw the perfect one-inch-diameter hole through the high back. There were no burn marks, but there was a dark stain of dried blood. She raised the gun and aimed at the chair's damaged back. The geometry and result were wrong. She dropped the gun to her side.

A glowing man stepped from the bedroom hallway and her arm swiveled to target him, safety off. The man carried a helmet and his hair was a close-cropped blond, pale in the gray light. With the skintight n-suit he wore, she'd have recognized that powerful build anywhere. *Arthur MacGabran.*

"Jesus," she whispered.

"Why are you whispering?" Arthur asked.

"You scared the shit out of me," Isolde exhaled.

"Tough army girl like you?"

"I could've shot you. I should've shot you."

Arthur raised an eyebrow. He dropped his kinetic energy field and the halo surrounding his body winked out. "You can now."

"What're you doing here?" She raised a hand. "No, it's not as much of a surprise as it should be."

"Looking for clues."

"Clues?" Isolde lowered the gun.

Arthur pointed to the chair.

Isolde examined the hole in the light. "The police said a fatal puncture wound, but that's a peculiar statement. Not a gunshot wound or a stab wound."

Arthur held out a set of goggles. "This may help."

"I'm not a DAMSL anymore," she said. During her brief time at Project Avallach, Isolde had been trained as a DAMSL—Data Analysis Monitoring Synchronous Link. They were handlers to the Avallach subjects, controlling their manifest power input/output and feeding them mission information. Isolde had an aptitude for it. She'd been Indiana Beckham's DAMSL until Indiana was expelled from Project Avallach by the program director—Isolde's father, Brigadier General Cornwall Marks. *Indiana.* Another name she wanted to forget. That was a bit harder to do. Isolde had been the same age and temperament as Indiana and she'd gotten along well with the former Olympic fencing champion. *Indiana was not easy to get along with*, Isolde thought with a smile.

"It's not a job offer."

Isolde took the goggles. They were less like goggles and more like thick wraparound glasses. The technology had advanced even after the death of the project, the report of which had been greatly exaggerated.

She flicked them open and put them on. She tapped the power button and the lenses went dark, overlaying the room with augmented reality and artificial light. There were markers all over the room where Arthur had tagged interesting things or noted information pulled from police records. She saw the wound and the outline of her father's body in repose.

Arthur moved to stand where the attacker had been, close to the chair. Arthur raised his arm and roughly matched the distance and angle of the attack. The *Caliburn* rings on his fingers gleamed. Avallach candidates were a unique breed. Genetically and neurally modified humans, they could generate, or "manifest," power from an entropic collector grid into their bodies with the assistance of these focal rings. This power also created a kinetic energy field that surrounded and protected them from high-velocity weaponry. The focal rings—a set of rings worn on the index, pinky, and thumb—also allowed them to create blades of plasma-like energy called waveblades. They functioned loosely like swords, if a sword were made of an energy/matter matrix held together by the brain-wave pattern of the candidate. There had been only a handful of manifest candidates before Cornwall Marks shut Project Avallach down. Arthur was one, and its first. Indiana was its best. *Indiana.* Isolde shook her head and focused on Arthur's statement.

"He knew them," Arthur said.

"Them?" Isolde asked.

Arthur ignored the question, so Isolde studied the data from his position. His geometry matched, and as far as Isolde knew, there weren't many people who could use the weapon Arthur and his Avallach team had.

"The man had a waveblade."

Isolde raised her father's sidearm. "It could've been you."

Arthur nodded, raising his hands slowly and nonthreateningly.

Isolde flicked her hand through the information and saw a more precise time of death than the system had reported. It had been at 2:14 a.m., with a five-minute margin of error. She skimmed through the data feeds and found that Arthur had been recorded in Mumbai—countering an attack of some kind. He was rather good at thwarting key events before they happened. She examined the data carefully for editing, but the wealth of information was too great. She returned to the room itself with a flick of the wrist, examining the clues. "No fingerprints. No forced entry. Everything points to Dad expecting company."

Arthur nodded. "He knew his attackers. Someone he had given our tech to."

Her father had died in this room. *Dad.* Isolde had remained as detached as possible. After all, her father had ignored or used her for years until the fallout from Project Avallach. Tears blurred her vision but she held her aim steady. It hurt.

Arthur and her father had fought bitterly and in the crucial moment, Isolde had helped Arthur against Cornwall. Her father had been so focused on getting revenge for Lance that he nearly sacrificed his only daughter, and that she could not reconcile. "I quit Avallach for him, you know? He was wrong. I'd never overcome that I wasn't the first child, or even a boy. But you broke something in him—or maybe freed. I don't know the word, but he knew then." Isolde placed her hand over her heart, where a large diamond necklace rested. It was the last gift she remembered her father giving her.

"You didn't go to the morgue or here when they notified you?"

"My first thought was that he was playing me. He always manipulated me. Even when I turned on him, I suspected he would still use me, maybe wait it out until school's over. And Seattle's a long way from DC. Why rush if he's dead? The DAMSL data is good, but that could've been manipulated before you got here. I just learned to not react to him—even at his death."

"You left us without a word. So did T. S."

She missed T. S. and wanted to see him now. Another stab of emotion hit her. They had separated because of her father. Now, perhaps, the possibility of reunion had opened. *Not quite yet*, she thought. She pushed thoughts of T. S. away and turned her mind back to her dead father.

Isolde fingered the necklace. "I left Avallach and went to school. Things were different. He was done. Retired. We stopped talking about it." Isolde shrugged. "I got used to him being the father he should've been the first twenty years of my life. Then when I heard he was dead, I didn't want to burst that little bubble just yet."

Arthur nodded in sympathy with Isolde's plight. Arthur had never reconciled with his own father, not even in the days when both father and son had been at Avallach. Isolde never knew Aidan MacGabran. She'd just read his files. DAMSLs learned a lot about their candidates.

"Your father had security cameras?" Arthur asked.

Isolde sniffed, collecting herself. She pulled her snarky aura back around herself like a blanket. She brought up and waved through the data feed, accessing the camera outside her father's apartment door. The system had already pulled the relevant information from the feed and had marked that there was a 12 percent probability the data had been altered. She played the time-stamped stream. Two people walked to the door. A man and a woman were dressed in dark jackets and knit caps for fall. The man was Arthur's height and build, and the woman . . .

"This can't be right." She lowered her gun arm.

"If you assume only the Avallach candidates can manifest, then that should be me, and that should be her."

"That's impossible," Isolde said. She motioned, zooming in on the face, but it was obscured by a heavy scarf. Her long raven-black hair was unmistakable. *Indiana*.

"Is that me?" Arthur asked.

Isolde moved to the face of the man. "I can't tell, but it can't be;

the system says this bit of data is clean, which rules you out. You can't be in two places at once, can you?"

"So that can't be her."

Isolde pulled off the goggles. "Indiana burned up in the atmosphere. There's no way she's alive." She refused to believe that it was Indiana. There wasn't enough data to confirm it. "You said something about assuming only Avallach candidates can manifest. What did you mean?"

"If that's not me nor any of the rest of the Avallach team, then Avallach tech is out in the wild. We've suspected ever since Sam was kidnapped, but this just confirms that they've made it work."

In the wild? Had her father given Avallach's tech to someone else and they'd killed him over it? Anger shot through her sadness. "I'm coming back," she said.

"That's not why I'm here."

"I don't give a damn why you're here, and I'm pretty sure I know why. I want to be Conditioned, because whoever did this"—she pointed to the hole in the chair—"knows your tech, and I want to know it better. I don't care why they killed him. I just want to know who, and the playing field will be even when that happens."

"Does this mean you believe me?"

"I believe the data. You didn't kill him and you kept your promise." Isolde's eyes narrowed. "But you had a hand in Indiana's death. I'm never forgiving you for that."

"Nor should you."

"I brought luggage and left it downstairs at the doorman's desk."

They went to the door and Isolde scooped up her pack.

"Is that the gun he shot me with?" Arthur asked, opening the door.

"You're such a drama queen." Isolde looked at the gun. She clicked the safety back on and put it into her bag. "Yes, it is." She hooked her bag over her shoulder.

A woman on the other side of the threshold rammed her right arm forward and Tasered Arthur with fifty thousand volts.

2

JUMP-START

Anora stood at the threshold. She examined the police tape and saw that it had been compromised. She pulled out her contact Taser. In theory, it should have been the best option for her to incapacitate and apprehend Arthur MacGabran. Would it work on him? Reports on Arthur were inconsistent and lean on facts, and Maven was always particular about sharing details of his work before it was ready. *Maven.* He appreciated her work in refining the math in his psychogenetics theorem, and it was infuriatingly beautiful. Was Avallach the reason why he had been so quiet regarding his ongoing research? Had he found a way to finally prove his theorem? Her mind dialed back to the present.

"I should open the door," Simon said.

"No, if there's no one here, I want to look around. No point in alarming anyone." She reached for the handle to see if it was locked.

The door opened, and Arthur MacGabran was there. Acting on the instinct, Anora shoved the contact Taser into his abdomen and hit the button. Arthur fell back, the door slamming open. Behind him was a young woman Anora had seen before. Isolde Marks. Friend? Lover? Why did that definition enter her mind?

A heavy backpack struck her arm, knocking the Taser away, and

Isolde came at Anora in a rush. Off balance at first, Anora fell back on her decade of training experience. Isolde threw a right-hand palm strike. Anora grabbed Isolde's right wrist, leaned back, and twisted, opening her opponent's body to attack. Anora kicked Isolde in the solar plexus, pivoted, and threw the woman onto the floor. But with the girl's slippery jacket, Anora's grip wasn't sure, and Isolde rolled with the throw and out of Anora's grasp. She bounced off the hallway wall. Anora, adrenaline flooding her system, gave a short shake of her head to Simon.

Her bodyguard stood back, waiting for a more opportune moment while keeping an eye on the prone Arthur. He'd been working for his employer long enough to know she had some competence in martial arts.

Isolde struck out with a right kick to Anora's knee. Anora grasped Isolde's ankle with her right hand and lifted, then kicked Isolde in the groin, throwing her back against the wall she had just bounced off of. There were pain and anger in her deep-set eyes, but Isolde wasn't cowed.

Anora kept the woman off balance with her judo training. Every strike Isolde made, Anora countered by using Isolde's momentum against her. Anora was fluid despite being restricted by her leather jacket. Adrenaline dilated time by a fraction. Anora was a well-trained *kudan*, but this opponent was also trained in the military martial arts—an effective jack-of-all-trades. Isolde was young, fiery, and fast, but Anora kept her wits and let her training take over. The rush of combat was far different than the katas of the dojo.

Isolde came in low and Anora took the brunt of the strike to deflect some of the energy. Anora struck Isolde and she went down. Isolde swept her foot out and knocked Anora down, slamming her head onto the floor. Dazed, Anora wrestled with the woman, who jumped atop her. Isolde hit her in the jaw. Anora saw sparks. Anora grappled, trying to pin the firebrand. Then the weight was gone as Simon pulled Isolde off in a choke hold.

The bodyguard pinned Isolde's arms and kept her legs from striking a vulnerable point. Her face was crimson, and she gasped for air as he held her windpipe in a lock. Anora rolled away to find her Taser.

Simon yelped, dropping Isolde and then falling to his knees.

Arthur was behind him, glowing like a sun god.

Damn, Anora thought. Helping her had taken Simon's attention from Arthur. She should've let him deal with the girl.

Simon spun and swung, but Arthur was inside the swing and his hand drove into Simon's abdomen. A blinding blue bar of light appeared through Simon's back. Anora shielded her eyes from the bright light, and Simon convulsed if he were having a grand mal seizure. Bones popped. The pillar of light vanished and Simon slumped against the wall, twitching.

Arthur stepped over him. Anora got to her feet and into a defensive stance. She glanced at Simon. There was no wound, which meant the blue blade wasn't meant to kill. Instead of approaching her, Arthur helped Isolde.

"You okay?" he asked.

Isolde rubbed her throat. "Yes," she croaked, and gave Simon a kick.

Anora leapt at Arthur. Arthur leaned back but did not block her attack. *Stupid*, she thought, and the Taser made contact. There was a flash and the discharge shot up Anora's arm.

ANORA SHOOK HER HEAD, trying to clear it. Her jacket pocket felt warm, almost hot. Her right hand was numb and she held it close. *Yes, that was stupid*, she reminded herself. Her Taser discharged into the field surrounding his body, which reflected some of the discharge back to her.

Arthur and Isolde had returned to the apartment. Isolde had her bag on her shoulder, but she was hunched over in pain.

"... kicked me right in the holiest of holies," Isolde was hissing.

Anora rallied her strength and sat up. "Where are you going?"

Arthur turned to Anora. "You should go."

"Don't you know who I am?" Anora asked, standing. She waved her right hand like he'd struck her funny bone. Where was her Taser?

"I don't care," Arthur replied.

Isolde rummaged through her bag as they walked. She grimaced, trying to walk upright. "I'm gonna need some ice for my kit 'n' kaboodle."

"I'm Dr. Myrrdin," Anora said.

Arthur ignored her. "You didn't see anything out of place here, did you?" he asked Isolde.

Isolde shook her head.

Anora continued, "You had something to do with the death of my brother." Her hand went to her pocket. Her One terminal was hot in her left hand, overloaded from the Taser discharge somehow. She hoped it wasn't permanently damaged. She pushed through the open door. They weren't planning to stay. Escape?

"I had nothing to do with the death of your brother. As his sister, Dr. Anora Myrrdin, you should know he wasn't concerned about his death, but rather his work."

"That's what you are. His work." Anora kept a defensive stance but followed the two of them. She saw the halo surrounding Arthur. She had missed her opportunity with the girl there. Isolde was a dark silhouette in the gray light.

"I could just shoot her," Isolde said in the conversational tone of a bored teenager. "Kick to the groin, bullet to the boob. Seems like a fair trade."

"And what work is that?" Arthur asked Anora.

Anora processed the information but didn't respond.

Arthur shook his head. "You're going to have to look elsewhere for the cause of your brother's death. Have you looked in the Atlantic Ocean?"

"His body was never recovered. What do you know about it?"

"I'd really like to shoot her," Isolde said as she pulled up her hood and zipped up her jacket. She jammed the gun back into her backpack and turned to Anora. "Lady killer."

Arthur shook his head again and opened the terrace door. The dull sound of rain became a rushing peal.

Isolde shrugged and walked out onto the balcony. She pulled on her backpack. On the terrace sat a slick black machine that looked sort of like a motorcycle, if a motorcycle had no wheels.

"Do you know Veljko Rogošić?" Arthur asked Anora.

"Who's he?" Anora responded.

Arthur shrugged. "You're asking the wrong questions."

Anora saw the hole in the Churchill and looked away. Arthur hadn't stabbed Simon that way, so it was true. Arthur didn't kill if he didn't have to. Anora pressed on. "You're not leaving this building without me."

"You tried taking me by force. Are you going to try taking me by command?"

Isolde snorted at that.

Anora stared at him. "Building security's been alerted."

"Then I'll say adieu," Arthur said, stepping out into the rain. The raindrops did not touch his hair, but rather were suspended above him like a puddle and rolled around the field his body generated.

Anora ran to the terrace door.

"Another reason to be Conditioned: I'm tired of getting wet," Isolde complained.

"Just remember not to manifest if you want to take a shower," Arthur said, climbing onto the device. At his touch, it floated in the air. A kickstand retreated into the recesses of the device. To Anora, it was a cross between a mechanical bull and a high-performance motorcycle. Stirrups clicked out behind Arthur.

"What happened to my brother?" Anora asked. He was getting away. She could stop him, maybe. Feeling was coming back to her hand and she put it into her pocket. The back of her neck tingled, despite the cold autumn rain.

"You can't get that knowledge from me."

"Women throw themselves at you to find out what you're all about," Isolde said, climbing onto the back of the device.

"Recall how that's going for me."

"What's one more?"

"Not her," Arthur said, looking back at Isolde. He put on his helmet and handed Isolde the goggles for her eyes.

"Because she's a Myrrdin?"

"Especially because she's a Myrrdin." His voice had that filtered radio quality now.

"I'm not letting you go," Anora repeated. Rain pelted her hair and face.

Arthur turned back to her. "Dr. Anora Tajin Myrrdin, brilliant computer scientist. PhDs from MIT *and* Stanford. Pioneer in artificial intelligence and distributed network communications."

Isolde sighed. "And a genius? Didn't we learn our lesson the first time?"

"There's always something to learn," Arthur agreed. *Caliburn* gleamed as he gripped the handles of the machine.

"How do you stay on?" Isolde asked.

"New suits have electromagnets. You don't have a suit, so feet in the stirrups and hold on," Arthur instructed.

"You're nice and dry." Isolde hugged him close. "But I still hate you."

"You can be president of the fan club." Arthur turned to Anora. "I know who you are, Dr. Myrrdin. You're just not asking the right questions."

Anora shuffled through her options. Was he Maven's final project? She had to know. "Take me with you."

Arthur shook his head.

"Afraid of what you'll do to another Myrrdin?" she asked.

"I'm afraid of what you'll do to me."

"Is that fear? I thought Navy SEALs don't feel fear."

"All men experience fear. Well, all but one. Good-bye, Anora."

The machine rose soundlessly upward over the ledge and disappeared. Anora heard Arthur's voice. "Let's get to the Raven. We'll get to Kai faster that way."

"Yay, Kai," Isolde said with sarcasm.

ANORA CLEARED HER MIND. She'd been acting foolish. She couldn't restrain him, but she couldn't just let him go. Her chances of finding him again were remote and she'd worked too hard to fail at this point. She leapt onto the ledge and saw the black shape receding below. She only had a moment, but the calculations flashed in her mind. She wouldn't make it. Before she could let the lower brain functions of her mind stop her, she stepped back and then jumped into space.

"Holy shit!" Isolde said as the woman reached for her, falling far short of the steed.

"Hold on!" Arthur said.

Her lower brain functions took over. Anora screamed and her mind was filled with fear. Out of the corner of her eye she saw the steed. It pitched down toward her. Arthur's halo brightened and the steed rocketed faster than gravity to catch up with her.

"Reach!" he yelled to Isolde as they both grabbed one-handed for Anora's arms. Desperate, Anora grabbed both hands. It was slippery, but she held on and the steed rolled into a spiral.

"Fuck!" Isolde said, her arm wrenching, and lost her grip on Anora. Arthur reversed the roll and Anora floated, then slammed into the steed. Arthur's arm went around the woman's shoulders. Anora's stomach slammed into her feet as the steed yanked back and leveled, heading out over the streets. Isolde relaxed her grip and held on to Arthur as the steed sped up. She jammed her feet into the stirrups.

"Can you move?" Arthur said to Anora.

"I can," Anora said. He held her by the collar of her heavy Burberry raincoat. She spun her body until she could grab on to the steed.

"Just dump her into the river," Isolde said over the wind and rain. "About ripped my arm off."

"Or just take her where we're going anyway," Arthur replied.

"This crazy bitch? She jumped off a thirty-nine-story building!"

"You liked the last crazy bitch we knew," Arthur said.

"Good point," Isolde said, and pulled Anora onto the steed. "I can't believe you jumped."

"It was easy," Anora huffed, her mind regaining control over her fear. She settled in behind Isolde and wrapped her arms around Isolde's waist. Arthur let go and focused on guiding the steed out over the bay. "I knew he wouldn't let me fall."

"How did you know that?"

"I've been studying Lieutenant Arthur MacGabran for months."

"How is it you two know so much about each other but have never met?"

"It's complicated," Arthur said.

"You got some big balls," Isolde said after a moment.

"I'll take that as a compliment," Anora said.

3

LEVELING UP

WASHINGTON, DC—

"Fifty seconds," control said into the loudspeaker. Owen dodged low as Kara came high, her waveblade flashing blue. Owen kept moving as John came in low from behind. Owen blocked him and turned to Kara. She flicked her blade at chest level, so he brought *Nornian* to block, his strength pushing her back.

John lunged straight and low. Owen hopped away from them both, moving toward a wall to keep them within his peripheral vision. They swung together—a well-coordinated attack—coming in straight at him. He swung his waveblade down and blocked Kara, but John's blue blade struck his shoulder. Owen's arm spasmed in pain and he jerked back, hitting his head against the padded wall. *Nornian* winked out. His right arm was numb and in agony. He dropped to one knee as John came in for a second stab.

Owen launched himself at Kara. He got under her swinging waveblade and put his shoulder into her solar plexus, driving the wind out of her. Her blade blinked out and she hit the mat hard, her auburn braid whipping the air. Owen stumbled and then turned to face John.

John moved in like a jaguar ready to kill. Sweat poured down his face and his waveblade shimmered. Another bull rush wouldn't work, but until Owen regained use of his right arm, he'd have to be wary. John's control over his own blade was tenuous. *I can outlast him*, Owen thought.

"Twenty seconds."

John rushed in. Owen stepped back from the man's advance. John lunged. Owen grabbed John's wrist. John's waveblade winked out as Owen spun and threw him to the mat. Pain lanced up Owen's back as Kara's waveblade struck him. Owen collapsed to the mat.

"Time," control said.

"Damn, I can't manifest for another second," John wheezed. "Does it get easier?"

"Yes," Owen said through clenched teeth. He rolled onto his back. His team was getting good. They were anticipating his moves, which meant his training with them was getting limited. Their manifest ability was slowly coming along, with Owen in the lead with how long he could maintain his power as well as the amount he could pull from the grid.

"Thanks for the gut punch, asshole," Kara coughed.

"John got my arm."

"This is why we need two of these things."

John sat up. "Why do we need to do this sort of training? We're not finding a lot of opponents who can use these blades." Owen nodded and shared a look with Kara. John Pellam was coolheaded under pressure, but he was not as far along in training.

"Good point," Kara agreed. "There aren't more than ten members left of Avallach."

"That we know about," Owen pointed out.

"We have fifty more in the works, not counting our squad and Mara's."

"We're in the trial group and the only ones with useful focal tech. Those fifty have no way to manifest yet. The gauntlets aren't ready, so we're outnumbered two to one for now."

"Just a matter of time." John got up and wiped the sweat from his face. "Phasing is slippery with these focal rings. I can barely hold the waveform, let alone shift it."

Owen motioned to Safir and Hong Le, the two other manifest-capable members of his squad. They got up and joined the trio. Owen rubbed the feeling back into his right arm. He motioned to the observation deck. "Safir and Hong spar next. See if you can manage more than sixty seconds of manifest." The two men nodded sharply and went to the center of the mat. He turned to Kara and John. "Hit the showers."

Owen grabbed a towel, wiped the sweat from his face, and went to the control room as the speaker announced, "Five seconds to start."

Dr. Ogier Dane clapped Owen on the shoulder when he entered the control room. "Looking quite well."

"How're the waveforms?" Owen asked, peering over the data from the bout. He shook his arm as its nerves regained control.

"Stable at the level you're operating at. All three waveforms look excellent. We won't need to tweak the focal matrices any further than we've done. Do you have a moment?"

Owen turned to Ogier. "Something new?"

Ogier's hand held his shoulder, and he lowered his voice. There were only three other researchers in the control room. "I've compared your recent test results and those prior to your Conditioning."

Owen's alertness snapped into focus. He hadn't had a relapse since his Conditioning. In fact, he thought the condition had reversed itself.

"It's inconclusive. We see improvement, but I'm not certain there's a complete reversal of your symptoms. It's a bit more complicated than just a genetic change. We're also seeing some physiological changes. How do you feel?"

"Great. I fell once getting out, but I'd been in the tank for a couple of weeks. No incidents or problems since then."

"It's possible that was atrophy." Ogier did not sound convinced.

"If you're trying to scare me, doctor, you forget who my mother is."

"I've seen enough patients in my life to not be as optimistic as I was in my youth. I'm hopeful, son, but I'd like to wait until the changes have settled in your body before we call it a success."

Owen smiled and flexed his hand. "I'm glad you don't do motivational speeches."

"Do you plan on telling your cousin?"

Owen shook his head. "I'll tell Morgan only if I have to."

Ogier nodded. "Don't push your limits too far just yet. It could expose a problem before it's had a chance to resolve itself."

"I'll take that under advisement, doctor."

Ogier watched the spar between Safir and Hong. "Morgan wants to see you before you leave for the day."

Owen hit the showers. John was gone, but Kara waited for him under a scalding jet. Owen smiled. He was powerful and ready. Morgan was going to announce his promotion to head of the operations team. He just knew it.

OWEN SAT in Morgan's office. She was not there, as usual, but he checked her calendar. He was dressed in his customary black suit, crisp white shirt, and black silk tie. He had changed in the last few months of grueling training, so he'd had new suits made for his more powerful frame. He looked out over the city, examining the sand-bleached obelisk in the distance. Farther off he saw the lit white dome of the memorial. The evening's autumn rains had passed on to the northeast, leaving a starless, lead-colored sky.

Morgan entered, wearing an understated but expensive gray raincoat. She peeled off her gloves.

"Drink?" Owen asked, getting up to go to the minibar.

Morgan smiled and took off her coat. Beneath she wore a fashionably cut suit of dark gray with a thin skirt that showed off her long legs in gray hose. Her blond hair was unbound and coiffed perfectly to her shoulders. "Is that your haircut?"

Owen scrubbed his hair. It had grown out since his time in the tank, and it had changed to a lighter blond color. "It seemed appropriate."

"It looks like *him*," she said, and there was a curious note in that last word. Was it anger or pleasure?

"How's my mother?"

Morgan raised an eyebrow but did not reply.

Owen fixed her a gin and tonic. "Mother was in town. You were out of the office, presumably for dinner." Owen shrugged at the logic of putting two and two together.

She took the drink and sat in her high-backed office chair, facing away from the view. Morgan never relaxed as most people did after a taxing event. She perpetually held her poise. "I noticed Aunt Muire Ann was in town, but I had a rather more interesting meeting."

That was a bit of a surprise, and probably a misstep on his part. He was better at anticipating his mother's movements—it had been his job before he became a part of Brightwork. Owen sat back down, unbuttoning his jacket. The moment was coming. He'd earned it. "A political meeting?"

Morgan waved the suggestion away. The ice tinkled as she drank. "Too early to tell. I had an interesting call with Aunty CEO."

"Things are going well now that she's in charge of LaFayette Corporation," Owen said. He kept up with what was going on in the family business. "Not that your tenure was worse in any way," he added, trying to not stray out of bounds again.

"She's made drastic changes already, all to realign for changes in the market." She waved her hand. "I made some suggestions that she might not ignore this time around. I mentioned Brightwork and it was her turn to give advice, most of which I'll ignore since you and Richard are leading what we're doing here. I think she sometimes forgets you're here."

Owen nodded. He was the tip of their spear, or would be soon if all things fell into place. If Morgan's plans continued apace, the entire world would be transformed in as soon as five years. Owen frowned. "She doesn't return my calls."

"She's a busy woman." Morgan leaned back in her chair. "She did mention the triplets."

"How's Jeri?" Owen asked, referring to his sister, the only one of his siblings who had not joined the family business. *And me, now,* he added.

"She's done with NASA, I heard. A shame, really. That was her dream; what she's doing now is anyone's guess."

"Sometimes we must give up our dreams," Owen said. He was used to being out of his mother's thoughts. Muire Ann thought little of Owen—or anyone—these days. She was consumed with what she loved—being the CEO of LaFayette Corporation. Morgan had held that position before ceding it back to Muire Ann in exchange for Brightwork.

Morgan's gaze glittered green. "How very true."

Owen didn't know what to think of that. Morgan ran on a level of energy that was little matched by anyone else. After graduating early from all her schools, she'd climbed the LaFayette corporate ladder with a relentless march that led to her toppling Muire Ann inside of a decade. She was incredibly accomplished, and Owen could not help but admire her. "Do you want to talk about the mission?" he offered, hoping to spur things along.

"General Marks?" Morgan looked bored and touched a paper on her desk. "Last director with ties to Brightwork. Did you learn anything new?"

Owen shook his head. "I searched his apartment discreetly. Did you know he was suicidal? Our General Marks was not the person we knew a few months ago."

"That's what happens when people find a new religion. A weakness of spirit, perhaps." Morgan had little patience for people.

"There aren't any council fingerprints left, save the secretary's."

"I don't think we'll have a challenge any time in the future, and she'd like nothing better than to pretend Avallach and Brightwork never happened. In fact, there may be some new avenues to pursue with her..." Morgan drifted off in thought for a moment, then gave a short nod. "How did Mara perform?"

"Exemplary, considering it was a simple field trial."

"She performed excellently under your supervision, then."

Owen frowned. "Supervision? It was my field trial. She was backup."

Morgan drank. "Fix yourself something."

Owen tilted his head. "Morgan, I know a shit sandwich when I see one. You compliment me on my supervision. What's the 'but'?"

"I'm putting Mara in charge of the Operations Team."

Ice water shot down Owen's spine. "That's my job. I'm the most—"

"You're much too valuable to risk."

"What the hell does that mean?"

"It means what it means," Morgan said.

Owen clutched the chair arms. His stomach knotted.

Morgan smiled. "Cousin, did you really think I'd let you risk that valuable DNA of yours? You're the Alpha, the wellspring from which all things Brightwork emanate. Your job is to train the corps."

Owen's emotions switched from shock to anger. It was true he was key, but you didn't exactly need his DNA to create the nanovirus. Not anymore. "You think I haven't been doing that? I'm the best—"

Morgan tossed a newspaper across her desk. "Have you seen this?"

Owen picked up the paper. It read in bold letters, APOLLO STOPS SHOOTING AT FORT HOOD. "Apollo" was the new nickname for Arthur MacGabran. Once it had been "Archangel," after he was seen defusing a bank hostage situation. When later reports showed he had no wings, the twenty-four-hour media machine respun him as "Apollo." Below the title was a photo—a black blur of a man wrestling with a gunman. Owen didn't bother to read further. He met Morgan's penetrating gaze. She knew what he wanted more than anything in the world, and she was keeping it all from him.

"Have Mara deal with him," he suggested hotly.

"We don't have the resources to remove him from the board just yet, Prime," Morgan said, using the derogatory nickname Owen's mother had given him. Her eyes softened. "I know how you feel—"

"No, you don't," Owen interjected, standing.

Morgan tapped her fingers on the table. "You've got it backward, Owen. You're the keystone to this operation. Without you, none of this is going to be possible. You need to realize this."

Owen's jaw clenched. He pulled the mask of calm back down. What if she knew about his condition? What if Mara did? Owen had kept a small but significant piece of information and now he wasn't sure how much Mara knew—probably nothing. *Delphi.* Morgan was holding him back. For what? He buttoned his jacket and brushed away his thoughts. "It's clear, cousin."

"Stay focused, Owen. I don't want the Chevaliers affected by your actions. I need them as focused and sharp as you are."

Chevalier Corps. *Corporate rebranding of Brightwork*, Owen mused. Owen bowed his head. "Any other orders?"

Morgan shook her head. She had already moved on to other work.

I should've seen it coming, he thought. He went to the door.

Morgan looked up. "Leto asked for you. Go see him sometime when you're free. He misses you."

"Was that your closing compliment?" Owen asked, but shut the door before Morgan replied. His calm was paper-thin. He wanted to throw something. His fists were tight. The executive secretary peered up at him with interest. He forced himself to relax. He needed to find Arthur and take care of him. Then there would be no Prime. No derivative. Just Owen.

4

FLY TO CAMELOT

SOMEWHERE IN VIRGINIA—
"Come on, old man," Lamar said, chewing on his toothpick with nervous energy. The two of them sat in the lit interior of the Raven, a prototype stealth helicopter. A victim of cost overruns, it was picked up by Maven after it was canceled. It had been the workhorse of the Avallach field trials. Now it sat in a rainy glen, rotor idling while they waited. Birgitte was on the flight deck, monitoring communications.

Percy frowned. "Old man?"

Lamar's eyes swept over the chessboard, and Percy knew he was clicking through the potential strategies. The problem with Lamar was that he played speed chess, and for Percy that exposed a weakness. He only thought enough moves ahead to play well. He rarely thought the game through to the end.

Percy touched a bishop and considered the ramifications of the move. He'd taught Lamar chess when they were both quite young. Percy had learned from an upstairs neighbor. Old man Gorman loved the game but was homebound and had no one to play with, so he taught Percy how to play. Nathan Gorman never went easy on him and beat him two years straight. The old man played at his own level and expected Percy to rise to the occasion. Fortunately for old man Gorman, Percy didn't know losing could also be humiliation, and he learned from the old man. Percy grew beyond the basics into opening moves, strategies, and pattern recognition. He half expected that the old man would quit playing him when Percy won, but the old man was delighted to have someone who could teach him something for a change.

Percy studied his move, then shifted to his white knight, moved it, and sat back.

Lamar glanced at the board, then moved his own black bishop.

Percy concealed his pleasure. The old man had often told Percy that he telegraphed victory too early. "Let the man figure out he's been beaten himself. The good ones will know it."

Lamar sat back, satisfied with his move. "Damn, you move so slow," he complained jovially. "Like an old man in a four-story walk up."

"You're two years older than me," Percy said. He knew what his next move was, but he considered the possibility that Lamar might uncover the pattern before it was too late.

"You're confusing age with appearance," Lamar said, preening.

Percy chuckled and then moved a white pawn. "Lilly said you were as homely as a bovine."

"Bovines can be majestic," Lamar said. He snapped up his white queen and moved it to capture Percy's pawn. "How's Lilly? You talk to Mac?"

Percy shoved his hands into the pockets of his hoodie and studied the board. Percy and Lamar had known each other their entire lives. Lamar had been there when Percy was born. Aunt Drayna had the Polaroid to prove it and had shown it off until it became so faded that it was just two ghostly baby faces in a dog-eared frame. Their families lived in the same complex, and for Percy, Lamar was a big brother. For Lamar, Percy was an only brother among the many sisters he already lived with. Lamar was a wild child, defiant with everyone but Percy. Percy knew how to manage Lamar, how to engage his smarter side in just the right way. When old man Gorman took to teaching

Percy, Percy, in turn, taught Lamar chess on the days their mothers would leave them alone for hours while they went grocery shopping or off on some other adult activity. Back in the days when you could leave a child home—it was just the way it was. Lamar hated the game at first since it had nothing to do with transforming robots or action figures. One day they strolled through Washington Square Park and saw the chess hustlers playing. Some cheated, rigging the clock in their favor, but the good ones played with an admirable finesse. Soon after, Lamar played with them, picking up strategies born out of love for the high pattern changes that came with playing at speed. Percy knew he loved the illusion of motion that speed playing gave. Lamar rarely beat old man Gorman, but the old man enjoyed Lamar's style.

Percy moved the white knight again. "I don't know how Lilly is."

Lamar had reacted the way Percy expected, moving a pawn to block. "It's killing you, my brother."

"Not sure what to do about it, Lamar," Percy said, making his move.

Lamar slammed his black bishop in place. "Do you wanna quit?"

"Not while I'm winning," Percy replied, raising an eyebrow.

"I meant the team." Lamar frowned.

"No," Percy said, moving his white queen. Lamar should see the pattern now, he guessed.

"No one better than Lilly. Trust me," Lamar said, moving his own bishop to take the exposed queen. "You worried about disappointing Mac? Upsetting his plans?"

"Sometimes I don't think Mac knows what his plans are," Percy replied.

Lamar grunted and gazed at the board. "Mac has a plan, and we need to follow it through. We might not see the vision, but I see the pattern."

Percy knew his next move, so he let his mind wander, lost in thought. In his early teens, Lilly Blanc had been the new girl next door, and he'd visited her as often as he could get away with, much to the amusement of her mother and consternation of her father. They never dated in the official sense of the word, but they had always remained close, and Lilly had never dated anyone seriously. While Percy had gravitated toward Lilly, Lamar had drifted into the badlands gradually and then suddenly, as the saying goes. Lamar ran with a gang of punks.

Percy had been a young punk himself, all-knowing and full of that false sense of self that youth gave and wisdom later tempered. Percy always felt guilty when he thought of that time because it was one of his happiest in a childhood filled with the ups and downs of parental drama. Old man Gorman passed away and Lamar's visits were rare. Lilly played chess with him, but she didn't have the enthusiasm Percy had for the game and soon gave it up.

Percy observed Lamar from beneath his cowl. Lamar's face was clouded with thought. Did Lamar know how much he had changed Percy's life that day? He had to have known.

In his late teens, Lamar got into bad trouble with both the gang and the law. Percy remembered listening to Lamar's problems and they sat in his tiny bedroom until Percy thought through the best way out of the situation. In the end, he knew if Lamar stayed in New York, he'd serve jail time, be seriously injured, or worse. He also knew Lamar wouldn't commit to something without Percy to guide him. So, Percy marched with him to the Times Square recruiting station and enlisted them both in the United States Marine Corps. They scored well on their Armed Services Vocational Aptitude Battery. They never spoke of Lamar's problems, and things turned around when they went to Camp Lejeune as Percy again became the constant in Lamar's life. Lilly remained, but she had her own career path as a doctor.

Lamar smiled. "Come on, old man, time to lose."

Percy snorted and studied the board. Did he miss a move?

"You gonna write her back?" Lamar asked.

"What're you talking about?"

"Come on, man. Don't bullshit a bullshitter. I know she sent you a message. You've been wound up all day. We ain't in the field, so that means Lilly."

Percy raised an eyebrow at Lamar. "What makes you think that?"

Lamar leaned back with a big grin. "I'm not dumb. I know Mac gave her a JD because you asked him to. Now he did it, and she sent you a message and you look like someone gave you latrine duty."

"Damn, Lamar. How long did you know?" Percy was surprised Lamar knew Mac had given Lilly a Janus device—tech that looked like a phone but was a sophisticated AI and communications device. Communication via Janus was untraceable and secure. It also acted simultaneously like a personal assistant and data gathering powerhouse. Percy was sure Janus had functions they hadn't even scratched the surface of yet.

"Since forever, man. We're brothers, you and me. You having bad thoughts?"

"Just different thoughts. About family." Lamar saw right through him. Percy smiled at that.

Lamar shook his head. "You should think of yourself."

"Says the giant baby I've been coddling for years."

Lamar chuckled. "Your move."

Percy peered at the board. Birgitte leaned out from the flight deck. "Message from Arthur. Prepping for dust-off. We need to make the flight cross-country."

"They meeting us here?"

"No, going to pick them up in transit."

"Little risky."

"Always is." Birgitte smiled and disappeared. The hull of the Raven thrummed.

"You oughta figure out what you want, Perse."

"I know what I want," Percy blurted. Percy had missed Lamar's move. He'd been careful and focused and with one distraction, he'd missed it. Lamar had played him. Stupid. He tipped his king over.

"Checkmate," Lamar said with a smile.

Percy punched Lamar in the shoulder. "Good game."

"I got lucky. Wanna talk about it?" The lights clicked from low white to red. Percy reached over and slapped the door shut, closing out the damp night air.

"I'm not paying you for therapy sessions." He thought about the message Lilly sent. It had radiated shivers down his spine when he read those three words. They were imprinted in his mind and all he could think of was the serious risk it posed to the team. He also knew he was delaying. He wanted to be with Lilly. Even Lamar knew they belonged together, which was high praise from a man who thought relationships were a waste of time. Percy couldn't blame him. For them it was always about family. The family stayed together.

Lamar stood and patted Percy on the shoulder. "Work it out. Call her, little brother." He packed his chess set and strapped in. Percy nodded and sat there, frozen. He looked down at his Janus device. As always, Lamar was right. His Janus device pinged.

"Incoming message from Arthur," Janus said.

"Accept," Percy said.

THEY WERE IN THE AIR, the Raven ascending. All around them, the ship thrummed, but Percy knew that from the outside, the ship was invisible to radar and most sensors. Still, they practiced emissions control when going airborne and maneuvered around most flight traffic patterns. They were almost over the Atlantic before Arthur caught up with them.

"One mike," Birgitte said into Percy's ear.

"Roger," Percy said, standing and clipping his harness to the hull. The Raven was most vulnerable when her stealth profile was compromised, often only when any of her doors or weapons bays were open. This Raven, *Thought*, was unarmed, though she'd been recently modified for long-distance flight with Avallach tech enhancements. After a couple more flights, the next enhancement would be retrofitted, removing the need for rotors altogether. It would make her incredibly fast as well. They had a small window to expose themselves to radar detection. It was unlikely flight control radar would detect them, but a military installation might catch a sniff.

Percy thought about Lilly and being back with her. He'd lost track of time when he heard Birgitte's voice. "Opening now."

"Roger," Percy said. He hit the safety switch and the rear door opened. The red wall turned to black as it opened into the night. They were inside a cloud bank.

"I don't see him."

"He's close," Birgitte assured him.

"I'm here." Arthur's voice clicked on Percy's earpiece. He grasped the waveform and his vision snapped into clarity. Through the gloom, he saw Arthur's halo as he approached. The steed was behind and below them. It didn't fly like anything relying on lift and aerodynamics. It came on steadily. Percy's job was just cursory; Arthur knew how to bring the steed in. Arthur wasn't alone. Two more figures were riding with him, pushing the limits of the steed's capacity.

They floated up and out of the cold night. The kickstand came down as Percy hit the release to close the door. "Check," he said to Birgitte.

"Roger. Nothing from up here."

"Charge is good," Lamar said. He was in the propulsion chair, adding power to the new engine system.

Percy moved to give Arthur a hand.

"God," a woman said. "I need air!"

"Floating in air for the last hour wasn't good enough for you?" Isolde asked.

The other woman thrashed around.

"Hold on," Arthur said, taking off his helmet. The woman punched him in the face. "Percy, grab her!"

Percy dove for her ankles. She was caught off guard and landed hard on the carbon-fiber deck. "What's wrong?"

"She's freaking out," Arthur said. "Claustrophobia, I think."

"Fuck this." Isolde ran up to the flight deck.

Anora threw Percy from her and he landed on his back. Arthur rubbed his face. She was screaming. Arthur dove at her and managed to get his arms wrapped around her.

Isolde returned with something silver and shiny in her hand. She slammed it into the woman's shoulder. Anora thrashed around, giving Arthur a busted lip and knee to the groin, but he held on. After a moment, she relaxed, then her eyes rolled up into her head and she slumped against him.

"Christ, I think she is crazy," Isolde said. She smiled at Percy. "Hey, Percy!"

"Hey there, Izz. I thought you left." Percy gave her a hug.

"Circumstances," Isolde replied. "Caught some crazy woman on the way, too."

Arthur shook his head. "No, she's severely claustrophobic. Could've told us that when we got into a helicopter that doesn't have windows. She's tough." He wiped the blood from his lip.

"Who is she?"

"Percy, meet Dr. Anora Myrrdin," Arthur said.

"I told you to dump her in the Potomac, but no, you had to keep her," Isolde said.

"She's not a dog or a plant," Arthur replied.

"Damn," Percy said. "Let's get her onto the stretcher at least."

Arthur and Percy hefted her up. Arthur checked through her pockets and found a phone. "It's dead, but let Janus check it," he said, handing it to Percy.

"Did you find what you were looking for?" Percy asked.

"General Marks is definitely dead, but someone else has our technology."

"Just like you thought," Percy replied.

Lamar walked back, saw Anora and Isolde, and whistled. Lamar gave Isolde a hug. "Sorry about your dad."

"Thanks. He was a dick."

"Yeah, but he was your dick, or dad, or whatever."

"I get the sentiment, but let's not dwell on it, okay?" Isolde said.

Lamar turned to Arthur. "Drive's charged. I heard you saw some of our tech?"

"Looks like it," Arthur replied, sitting down. "Got that med kit you grabbed the elephant tranq from?"

Isolde tossed the kit to him.

"Then we got an arms race, Mac," Lamar said, and frowned. He didn't like that idea at all. Lamar sided with the late Dr. di Lago—the technology belonged to those who meant to do good with it.

Arthur patted the steed. "I don't have any idea if they have magnifier technology. Kai's taken steps with the Sisterhood to destroy all prototypes and our functioning magnifiers all have destruct systems integrated."

Lamar folded his arms. He wasn't happy with that answer either, but Percy knew the magnifiers were critical to the next phase of Avallach. Those devices allowed them to convert manifest energy into other forms or power engines only previously dreamed of. The Raven tested one of those drives now. This was its third field test—so far it had performed flawlessly.

"I'm not about to let the rest of our technology be stolen."

"No shit. Seems a bit late for that," Lamar quipped.

"Lamar," Percy said, warning him, and looked at Isolde. She stared off into space, her fingers toying with the large diamond necklace around her neck.

"We got a plan?" Lamar asked, strapping the steed down for transport.

"You'll be with me on the next trip to Dinas. Percy and Ed are on the next field mission."

Lamar frowned. "I don't want to go back to Dinas. It's still under construction, surrounded by water, and there are no women."

"Unless you count all the sisters and the Echo team," Percy said.

"I don't," Lamar grumbled.

"Marines are supposed to operate on or around water," Percy said. "Besides, you went to Dubai."

"Yeah yeah. Now I gotta train Echo recruits. They're so green, Mac."

"You were green as hell until Indy beat you into shape," Arthur said.

"'Beat' is such an appropriate word." Lamar smiled. "Who're we getting?"

"Birgitte. Prianna and Sahar are going with Ed and Percy."

"Goddamn it," Lamar said.

"I heard that!" Birgitte said from the flight deck.

"I mean that in a nice way!" Lamar went to the flight deck. "Women only hear you when you say something like that..."

Percy sat down across from Arthur. "Think we should be going out on these missions with our tech out in the wild?"

"I don't like wasting time chasing our tail."

"Anything we do could be a trap."

"Let me be the one to carry that burden."

"This isn't a monarchy, Mac," Percy said. "We all got a stake in this."

Arthur nodded. "You're right."

"You got this vision that will put us in the right place. We must trust that, but we check things out. And what about her? Izz I can understand. She's one of the guys—"

"I heard that," Isolde said, getting up. "I can pee standing up if I want."

"You know what I mean." Percy smiled.

Isolde put a hand on Percy's shoulder. "Thanks, Perse."

"You're always welcome on the team, kid." Percy patted her hand.

"I'm going to look for food."

"This is a stealth heli—"

"Freeze your balls off on a one-hour flight to umpty-fuck and see how hungry you are." Isolde waved and went toward the flight deck in search of food.

Percy shook his head and then turned to Arthur. "She hates your guts, you know."

"Yes. The enemy of my enemy—"

"No, she hates you because you let Indiana die."

Arthur glowered in the red light. "I know the burdens I carry, Percy. I know the prices I have to pay."

"Don't be surprised if she shoots you when your shield is down."

"Joke's on you. I already offered to let her do it and she didn't take me up on it."

"Was it at Marks's place?"

"Yes."

"Dumbass, she's not going to leave behind evidence."

Arthur chuckled. "I'll try to remember that next time I offer to let her shoot me."

"The next time she'll probably take it."

"Good thing she likes you guys."

Percy nodded. "I'm pretty sure she won't shoot me. She might shoot Lamar, but not fatally."

"She's going to be Conditioned."

"Sounds a little more dangerous for you."

Arthur set his jaw. "Isolde isn't vengeful. I'll not forget her help when I destroyed Tintagel, and I made a promise not to harm her father, which I kept to the end."

"Who do you think killed the general?"

"The question is, was it on orders above him, or is this new group severing ties with DARPA and operating independently? Marks was part of DARPA Black, but that entire branch went dark after Tintagel. As far as I can tell, both directors who headed up Black are dead or missing. Maybe the second director—de Vance—went rogue? I don't have enough information, and we could speculate all day long. We'll have to take another approach—maybe flush them out before they're ready. I just need to figure out how."

Percy motioned to the stretcher. "And Anora? We can't have people we can't trust."

"I didn't say she was on the team. Besides, I didn't bring her along for her looks, nice as they may be—"

"Focus," Percy reminded him.

"Kai wants to see her."

"Oh, since when do we let Kai tell us what to do?"

"Since she became the matron of the Sisterhood."

"Damn," Percy said, sitting down. That was a big deal.

"Yeah, but I'll take your advice. She's not on the team unless you say so."

From anyone else that might have sounded patronizing, but Percy saw the sincerity on Arthur's face. "I'll let you know, but my vote right now is no. Myrrdins are tough. Think Isolde's pissed someone offed her dad? This was her brother. If she's anything like him, we're in for trouble."

"I'll tread lightly." Arthur stood up and dabbed at his lip. He called to the flight deck. "Strap in, guys. Time to go to *Camelot*."

"'Tis a silly place," Lamar chimed.

"Seriously?" Isolde asked.

5
TRUST ISSUES

MV *CAMELOT*, SOMEWHERE IN THE ATLANTIC—
"You're not going to leave me, Anora!" Reince grabbed her suitcase.

"You're not stopping me!" Anora wrenched the suitcase free from his grip. She teetered backward at the top of the stairs but regained her footing, only to be slapped hard in the face. She reeled around, dropping the suitcase down the stairs. She collapsed in a heap.

"You can't," he said in that pleading plaintive voice. How could she? She couldn't make herself move. He took her hands and helped her to her feet. Her cheek was stung red. "You can't leave me," he said.

"I can't," she whimpered in response, falling under his spell. Inside she wrestled with herself, trying to make her body do what it must—to break free.

He gazed at her with his dark beautiful eyes, tearing down her defenses. Her willpower flagged, but she summoned her defiance, small now. "I can't, Reince," she whispered.

His face darkened with the rage of a beast. He shoved her away from him and back down the stairs. She fell into blackness.

Then a hand grabbed hers. Not forceful, but firm. She wrenched her arm to get away, but the hand was gentle, callused. The touch caressed, and the pain of memory leached away. Her heart thudded in her chest, but the claustrophobia lessened as she reconnected to her body. That dream self wasn't who she was now. How often had she had that same dream? Her senses came back as the dream faded. She wished she only saw Reince in her dreams, but ever since her treatment, things had gotten . . . worse.

She felt the gentle roll of waves.

Anora opened her eyes. Arthur held her hand and massaged it gently. He smiled.

"What're you doing?"

"Massage therapy. You were having a nightmare, so I thought I'd not wake you dramatically."

"I know what you're doing," Anora said. She willed herself to not jerk her hand back. It felt nice and calmness settled in. "I meant, why are you here?"

"I came to talk to you."

"Don't be stupid," Anora said.

"Like sister, like brother," Arthur said. "When I was recovering before Avallach, I learned a little about how massage therapy can help with trauma—"

"What trauma?" Anora's mind flashed hot.

"Crippling claustrophobia, I believe. Also, you jumped off a building."

"Oh."

He massaged Anora's hand and wrist. Anora had developed a strong connection with massage therapy. It reminded her of Roxanne, her employee and sometime massage therapist. Arthur was excellent at this and her emotions warred beneath the surface. She was in a small cabin and she lay on a comfortably appointed bed. She recalled the late-night flight to the Raven and landing on the yacht. She felt the thrum of a ship's motor. They were still under way and the ship rolled steadily. She reached over and pulled One out of her jacket. It had cooled after the journey, but it would not come to the diagnostics screen.

"Wondering where you're at?"

"How far out to sea, actually. How far from the Potomac?" Anora shoved the terminal back into her pocket. She made a mental note to have the next version shielded better, or have a secondary beacon with separate electronics in case she needed to activate it. "So, you're Maven's last project?"

Arthur frowned. "Second-to-last project, really."

Anora waved a hand. "*Archimedes* was a distraction."

She hit a nerve. Arthur stopped massaging her hand. "An awful lot of money for a distraction."

A small part of Anora had enjoyed the touch.

The door opened and Isolde entered.

"Hey, crazy's awake. Hi, crazy," Isolde said, then turned to Arthur. "Kai's on her way."

Arthur let go of Anora's hand. "Thanks for the warning."

"I'm going to get ready for the pod. How come you've only got one working?" Isolde asked.

"What if the yacht sank?" Arthur said.

"Uh, good point."

"Actually, we were testing a gimbal system that isolates the pod even more from its environment. It worked with the last occupant and test subject." Arthur stood.

"Who was that?" Isolde tilted her head.

"Jeri Brand."

"Never heard of her," Isolde replied dramatically. "Okay, I've heard of her."

"Ping me when you're ready," Arthur said.

"Going to give me last words of advice?"

"Something like that."

Isolde snorted and left.

"She doesn't like you. Or trust you," Anora said.

"She wanted to drop you into the Potomac," Arthur replied.

"Am I supposed to be grateful?"

"I rescued you from a four-hundred-foot drop."

Anora smiled. "You did what you were supposed to do."

"I'm inclined to rescue fair maidens—"

"I'm neither of those, but since we're talking, yes, you've always done the right thing as far as I can tell. It's in your programming."

"But you believe I killed Maven."

"You've killed in the past. Made a living from it. People who need to be eliminated get eliminated. I think my brother was one of them."

Arthur folded his arms, closing himself off from Anora. "Death has a purpose."

"Is that how you justify yourself?"

"Have you killed anyone, Anora?" Arthur's ice-blue eyes bored into hers.

Anora stared him down. "No."

Arthur stared at her. She felt her sympathetic nervous system responding. Her cheeks flushed and her anger rose. *This man is dangerous*, she told herself. She pushed the anger down.

"Need to call for help?" Arthur asked.

"No."

Arthur took a step toward her and she flinched. He shook his head. "You should learn the difference between friend and foe."

The cabin door opened and a tall, auburn-haired woman stepped in. She slapped Arthur hard in the face. She stared Arthur down with the same ice-blue eyes he had. *Kai MacGabran*, Anora thought. She wore a simple jacket, a T-shirt, jeans, and Top-Siders, and her hair was cut in a simple pageboy style. Everything about Kai said military efficiency without the uniform.

"What the hell is wrong with you?" Kai asked.

"Hi, Kai," Arthur said, rubbing his face.

"Fuck you. Investigate Marks, not bring back his daughter."

"I agreed to bring Isolde back if she ever asked. She asked. You asked me to bring Anora here specifically—"

"I'm right here," Anora said.

"Just a minute," Kai said, waving a hand. She turned back to Arthur. "You don't go on missions, Arthur. That was supposed to be Percy."

"I wanted to see for myself. It could've been me that killed him, you know. I do what's necessary."

"And the last time it was necessary? Remember the last person you brought into Avallach?"

That remark struck Arthur harder than the slap. "She's all yours. I'll be by to pick her up when you're done. I need to talk to the team."

Arthur left.

"You know how to work his buttons," Anora said.

Kai turned to Anora. "If you wanted to get in touch with Arthur, you could've just asked me."

"Why would I ask you? You're his sister."

"I guess you don't know as much about Avallach as I thought you did." She put out her hand. Rings sparkled on her fingers. Anora shook her hand. "I'm Kai MacGabran, Arthur's sister and—" She sighed heavily. "Matron of the Mare de Scientia."

Anora frowned. "The Sisterhood doesn't have a matron. Not since Donna passed away."

"Was murdered."

"For her ties to Avallach." Anora nodded. Kai gave her a questioning look. "I have some old notes from my brother."

"The three birds and I are the custodians of her technology now." Then Kai frowned. "Didn't you know? You surely voted in the election. It was very drawn out."

Anora frowned, trying to find the words. "I was very sick until recently. I haven't been in touch with the Sisterhood. You're matron?"

"I am," Kai said. "Grande Dame Li conferred the title upon me last night. Trust me, no one is as surprised as me."

Anora studied Kai's face. Except for her blue eyes, she shared little with her brother. Where Arthur was open, charming, and rugged, Kai was sharp, drawn, and smoothly refined. Anora inclined her head and offered her hand. "Mother."

With an air of solemnity, Kai took her hand. "Daughter."

"I am here to serve."

"It is I who serves you," Kai responded.

"This is all awkward."

"It's going to be more awkward when you find out you're being sent home."

"Why?" Anora stood. "I thought you asked me here."

"When Arthur reported who he had tagging along on his little excursion, I thought it best to have a nice little chat with you. Grande Dame Li agreed and wanted to meet you as well."

"I'm honored. I haven't spoken to the grande dame since she was matron when I was a child."

"That makes even me feel a bit old." Kai smiled, then her thoughts shifted to Anora. "You don't belong here, Anora."

"Arthur had something to do with the death of Maven, and I'm not leaving until I find out what."

"Do you really believe that?" Kai studied her face.

Anora did not like to be on the defensive. Not anymore. "I'll find him again."

"How did you do that, by the way?"

"I put together enough details to know that Marks was involved in a project that both my brother and Arthur were involved in. When Marks was killed, it was just a matter of waiting him out. For all of the media attention he gets, he's predictable— if you constrain the variables."

"And you're not satisfied with his answer?"

"How do you mean?"

"Cornwall Marks gave the order to down Maven's plane."

Anora folded her arms. "You have proof?"

"What more proof do I need? We know now that Marks built a second project on the technology of the first and when things went awry, he had it all shut down. Arthur kept Marks from killing the entire team."

"That sounds like so much bullshit."

Kai smiled. "You've worked for the government before."

"You've done your own homework, mother."

"So, you know there are deeper, darker parts than most people realize. So much bullshit? What explains Marks's actions? What about the singular piece of evidence that ties him to this other group? The fatal wound?"

"That no one has seen outside of your little Avallach."

Kai held up a hand. Rings glinted on her thumb, index, and pinky fingers. "Would you like me to demonstrate on you?"

Anora backed down. She knew she'd pushed just a little too far. "So, Arthur is involved in Avallach."

"Arthur *is* Avallach. He makes it all possible. Maven and Donna built the Avallach technology around him. From him."

"All the more reason for Arthur to take it away to suit his own purposes." Anora smiled. She was testing the waters. What did Kai really know?

"That's completely absurd."

"I don't think my brother knew what he was creating."

"And you're proposing my brother is some sort of Frankenstein?"

"Arthur has his own agenda and people that get in the way of that don't last long."

Kai stared at Anora.

Anora took a breath. "As much as I've studied him, I don't trust his motives. I don't trust him."

"I don't think you should," Kai agreed. "But that should be enough reason for you to not be here. You can't trust him and we can't have people with divided loyalty."

"And where does your loyalty lie, mother? What of your obligation to the Mare de Scientia?"

"They're one in the same now."

The cabin door opened and a wizened Korean woman smiled. Grande Dame Li wore traditional Korean clothing, bright and colorful on her small, bent frame. Behind her stood Sister Min-Ji, Li's closest friend and companion.

"Grande Dame." Kai bowed her head.

"My tests are all done." Li waved a hand. "I wanted to see the spitfire before we go back to land."

Anora stood and bowed deeply to Li, who placed a hand on her head.

"I heard you've been ill? You look well," Li said. She smiled at Anora, who smiled in return.

"I'm better. My treatment is almost done. What brings you here? Not just to see me?"

"I haven't seen you for almost two decades and you want to complain about my seeing you now?" Li tapped her fan on Anora's wrist in mock severity. "The Scientia wants to take precautions. Especially the new matron. She's not the nervous sort. A bit of a spitfire herself." Li eyed Kai.

Anora gave Kai a questioning look.

Kai smiled. "I was persuaded to have a sensor implanted that can monitor my life functions. I agreed only if Grande Dame Li would do so as well. I do not like the idea of an easily broken line of succession."

"Regression, you mean. I haven't been matron in . . . well. Let's not talk about how ancient I am." Li smiled. "We're in turbulent times. We haven't lost a matron to treachery in well over a century and a half. Did you know someone tried to poison me once?" Li sighed. "I'm still saddened by Matron Donna's passing. She was much loved by the sisters."

"I held her in high regard," Anora agreed.

"I know who it was," Kai said.

"Matrons may not act like military dictators," Li warned. "You must tread carefully, then strike when you must. Do you think Sun Tzu was a man?" Li tapped her chin with her fan.

Kai bowed her head, but Anora could see she ground her teeth.

Li made that sighing sound that said she'd won the conversation. She tapped Anora on the knee. "I'm going to see this young man we've been fighting over. This is all very exciting for an old lady like me. Reminds me of the time when I was at Ansan University with your brother . . ."

"My brother?" Anora asked.

"I'll tell you sometime. I'm getting queasy. Whose idea was it to have a boat? This cold weather is not good for my bones, you know. Drag me out here, stick something in my body, and various other old-person complaints. You can fill them in yourself." Li kissed Anora and Kai, then left, shutting the door behind her.

In the vacuum of the grande dame's wake, Kai and Anora stared at one another.

Kai pulled two devices from her pocket. She handed a badly beaten and damaged device to Anora. It looked something like a phone, but much thicker, heavier, and similar to her One terminal. It was, however, badly damaged.

"What's this?"

"That's a Janus device. It's our secure means of communication. It's an AI system."

"It looks like junk."

"It did survive atmospheric reentry, impact, and the South China Sea," Kai replied. "It was Indiana Beckham's device."

"Ah yes, *Archimedes*'s test flight. I was briefed when I took over Telemachus," Anora mused, then looked at the device. "Janus?"

"Arthur's not letting you inside the walls of Avallach, but I have a need for you. The Scientia has a need for you. Two needs, actually."

"This is one of them?"

Kai nodded. "The first is Central Augmentation Meeting Location and Negotiation Network—CAMLANN for short. It's a terrible name, but it's—"

"The new virtual meeting place for the sisterhood. I remember the proposal. That was some time ago."

"Avallach brought the technology, so we're going to implement it. That's the first. The second is that I want to know what's on that device. Indiana gave it to me, but I haven't been able to decrypt it and the system is completely packed with data as far as our technicians have been able to determine."

"And the other?"

"Scientia's building a secure virtucast system to replace our older, slower means of communication. Mixed augmented and virtual reality. It's built upon the Quantum Protocol."

"QP is my work."

"I know."

Anora chuckled. "There had to be a reason why I couldn't find or trace your communications. I thought QP had gotten buried in some unworkable government dead-end project."

"Janus and CAMLANN both use the Quantum Protocol. Janus can easily manage it but CAMLANN cannot manage the protocol. I assume it's a multipoint or bandwidth issue. I'm just a grunt."

"QP isn't meant to scale and remain secure. You want me to build you a secure virtual system for Avallach?"

"For the Mare de Scientia primarily. Avallach will use it as a sponsored project. I want the Sisterhood to be able to communicate more freely, yet securely. We have that ability now."

Anora turned the broken device over in her hands. "Secure communications is no longer my line of work, not since my dissertation days when I created QP. But the Janus AI. This is what you really want me to work on."

Kai smiled. "I don't know what's on that device, but whatever it is, it was worth dying for."

"Indiana died giving this to you?"

"No, she died saving me. She gave that to me just before she died. Something beyond Arthur drove her to sacrifice herself. She wouldn't sacrifice herself for just anyone or anything. Arthur, yes, but me? No."

Anora handed it back to Kai. "Any data jockey worth his salt can recover the data on this system."

Kai pushed it back. "Aren't you just the least bit curious?"

"About what?"

"About what a girl like Indiana Beckham would be doing with whatever is on that device?"

"It could just be porn or photo shoots. She had a pretty big ego."

"She gave up her ego before she gave up her life, Anora."

Anora considered the device. "For you, mother, I'll do this. I'll work on CAMLANN as long as you tell me what Arthur is up to."

"I won't have to do that." Kai handed Anora another device. "This is your own Janus. Feel free to take it apart and see how the AI works. But it's your means of contacting me now."

"Not through the Sisterhood?"

"No. Not until CAMLANN is done. I don't expect I'll be matron very long. There are . . . factions who believe my ties with Arthur are too strong. They're right. But once elected, I cannot refuse to be matron for the first few lunar cycles, at least. So, I must do what I can in the time that I have."

"Arthur can't know about this?" Anora held up Indiana's device. She didn't trust him, but it was interesting that Kai wanted something kept from him. It piqued her curiosity.

"He has enough problems dealing with Indiana's death. Deservedly, of course, but I'm not going to push him any more than I have to. Full Scientia resources are at your disposal."

"I won't need them and it's always best to keep the Scientia away from anything I'm doing."

Kai nodded. "You may want to be local to the DC area. I can set you up with facilities." Kai's phone chirped and she pulled it out to examine it. "Grande Dame Li will be leaving soon, so we'll talk some more on the flight back."

"I'll start putting my team together."

6

BROKEN DREAMS

WASHINGTON, DC—
"Coming up to threshold," Richard MacRossa said. He was heavyset, sporting a gray beard and clean but rumpled clothing. He sat in front of a bank of monitors and beyond that was a Plexiglas partition where Owen stood. On his left hand was a large gauntlet that reached his elbow and looked much like a robotic piece of armor. Lights illuminated along the gauntlet and a set of cables sprouted from the elbow, snaking to the bank of servers and electronics processing a raw data feed. "Hold it," Richard said. Scientists around and behind him worked, recording and reviewing the data. "Very good. Low delta."

Owen concentrated on the manifest waveform. His jumpsuit was rolled down to his waist and he was sweating through his sleeveless shirt.

"Bring it up to ten percent," Richard said, and watched the power levels transmitting through the grid increase.

Richard MacRossa was one of the lead scientists of Brightwork. His specialty was nanomolecular design. It was his work that had refined the genetic viral rewrite that gave Brightwork subjects the same attributes as the Avallach candidates. His work was also critical in replicating the focal technology pioneered by Avallach's lead inventor, the late Dr. Donna di Lago.

The focal technology was incredibly complex and not something Brightwork was prepared to create before the untimely death of Dr. di Lago.

"Excellent," Richard said. "Let's go to twenty-five percent."

"Easy for you to say," Owen panted. "This device isn't working properly."

Richard chewed on the stem of his unlit pipe. "That's a fine piece of machinery you've got there. The matrix is tuned to less than a hundredth of a percent to your waveform."

"Twenty-five," a scientist reported.

"Stable," Richard noted. "Fifty percent now."

"Feels like I'm pushing one fifty," Owen said, the nimbus around his body brightening. The lights in the chamber dimmed and instruments recorded the entire electromagnetic spectrum around him. He flexed the gauntlet, small servos within the device moving with the pressure of his muscles. "This thing weights fifty pounds."

"Forty-six point two pounds. Ready for waveblade manifest."

Owen flexed his hand again, then the gauntlet reached out as if to grasp a cup. The bar of white light sprang into being within his hand. Owen's eyes constricted to pinpoints. He felt incredible power. While it was difficult to manage, the waveform wasn't as slippery as the one generated by his focal rings.

Owen's mind clouded and he froze. He felt possessed, as if he'd lost control of his body. His mind was drawn to a place . . . he saw a cathedral somewhere. It was far away; he knew that somehow. He had to go there, but he didn't want to. He pulled against the force, but his mind was being ripped away, trying to drag him out of his body and to that place. He had to go there. He *had to*. A flash of her face—the young woman Indiana, only her eyes were a glittering blue like his own. What did—

"Waveform delta is increasing. We're losing the waveform,"

Richard said, and the waveblade flickered for an instant and winked out. Alarms chirped in the lab. "We've lost it. Power levels dropping."

Owen's mind snapped back; the force was gone with the power. It was incredible. He couldn't resist . . . Owen rubbed his eyes and looked around him. No one was looking at him. "What happened?"

Richard pulled the pipe out of his mouth and fussed with it as he examined the data. "It's a prototype. It's not finished."

They hadn't known or seen a thing except the data in front of them. Surely that had lasted more than an instant? Owen composed himself, lowering his arm. "I can't move my hand." Owen forced his hand open against the unresponsive micro-servo motors.

"Nonsense."

The lights on the gauntlet went out and more alarms chirped over the loss of data. "Oh?" Owen scowled. Should he chance it?

He held out the *Nornian* rings in his right hand and a waveblade snapped into existence. He waved it around and then cut a nearby table in half with it. The table collapsed, the energy plasma passing through it as though it were vapor. Owen continued to be impressed by the Avallach tech. The *Nornian* rings had once been called *Gram*, when they were possessed by the Avallach candidate Sam Brastius. Owen and Brightwork had acquired Sam and his rings in the mission that also killed the focal technology's inventor. *Gram* was tailored to be used by Brastius, as it was tuned to his brain-wave pattern, unique as a fingerprint.

Richard and his team had modified *Gram*, and other acquired Avallach focal rings, altering the matrix shape so that it accepted a different brain-wave pattern. Thus *Nornian* was born. Owen had been practicing with the rings for a month now, and manifesting the waveblade was becoming easier with each test. But never before had he felt—then the force grabbed his mind again, so strong; he let go and *Nornian* winked out. It was gone and he fell to his knees, panting. *Stupid*, he told himself. It wasn't the gauntlet. It was the manifest power. What was it and why now?

"Don't break my equipment," Richard complained, watching a

piece of gear collapse with the table. "Are you okay? You look like you shat a cactus. Or cacti."

Owen waved him away and got up. "We have plenty more gear." One effect of manifesting was the hyper clarity it brought to Owen—colors were brighter, shapes were sharper, the air felt more like water on his skin, and sounds were crisp and distinct. It was overwhelming at first, but when he stopped, the world became dull and ordinary. He would have manifested all the time if he could. The day he'd be able to manifest perpetually was not far off. But if this force returned, how could he use it? He was shaken to the core. Something was out there.

Richard tapped some controls, looking to restore the gauntlet's circuitry, and then sighed in resignation. "We're done for the day."

Owen got to his feet and collapsed onto the chair behind him.

Richard opened the Plexiglas door and entered. "You're looking more like Arthur every day, when you're not shitting cacti."

Owen's bright blue eyes flashed with anger. He lifted the heavy gauntlet and rested it on the arm of the chair. "Have something to say about it?"

"You think that was an accident? He was the prototype and the antecedent in many ways."

"What does this have to do with the damn gauntlet?"

"Absolutely nothing, although, it would be interesting to see how much better his *Caliburn* rings would work on you."

Owen hadn't thought of that. Brain-wave patterns were unique, but how much would they need to be altered? Would they need to be altered at all? He looked at his *Nornian* rings, which were thick. That was partly due to the fact that their original owner was a big man, but also due to the modifications to allow his mind to generate a matrix and channel energy. He imagined the glittering *Caliburn* rings there, unmodified, in an identical hand. His mind went back to the gauntlet.

"This test was abysmal."

Richard saw his expression. "I don't have to allow you to do the testing, y'know. I pick the test subjects."

Owen wiped the sweat from his face. "I know." He had to accept things as they were, for now. Morgan had denied him the role as leader of the Operations Team. So Richard had agreed to allow him to test the new gauntlets. Owen hoped it would show Morgan his desire to be more than just a trainer and blood sample. Why couldn't he make her see that he was better than Arthur? There was a creak as Owen mangled the chair arm with the gauntlet and realized how angry he felt.

"I'm going to have to dial back the servo responsiveness," Richard mused, unplugging the gauntlet from the systems and getting a wrench to manually open it. "And this prototype is much better than the previous one. I wish your cousin would stop taking my gear for no discernible purpose. It's damned hard enough just developing this tech, y'know."

"What about the part about it losing power?"

"I'm not a miracle worker. I'm also not an engineer. I'm a nanotechnologist." He patted the gauntlet. "What's built in here is partly the matrix we've replicated, but there's technology to tune the waveform to its wearer. It'll get smaller, but all these additions were to help compensate."

"I'll never be able to swing it fast enough."

Richard put the pipe between his teeth and continued to work. "Looking to get into some sword fights? I thought those went the way of Errol Flynn and the *Three Musketeers*. Or at least *The Princess Bride*."

"That's exactly what I intend to do." Owen frowned as he watched.

Richard unlatched the gauntlet. "This is just a prototype. Like the focal prototype your mother brought, this is larger than it needs to be. When we get it down to a manageable size, we won't need the servo systems. It's got issues, but the matrix tuned to you this time."

"Like what you did with *Nornian*?" Owen asked, flexing his right hand.

Richard shook his head. "At best, *Nornian* is aligned to a hundredth of a percent with months of work. This was a near-perfect tune and it took only a few hours." Richard released the final catch, and the gauntlet opened and Owen was able to slip his arm out of it.

"There we go. Once we get it right, we can tune the device to you or anyone who can manifest in a moment. Then the gauntlets can be produced in large quantities."

"You seem to think we'll have more candidates than gauntlets."

"We already do, and that's not going to change until we get these into production."

"It's a shame you can't get them into ring form."

"A gauntlet or glovelike form makes it easier to interchange. There are only a few glove sizes, but a lot of sizes for rings, and you have three of them—a different size for each finger. What a pain in the arse."

Owen rubbed his left arm. His arm felt like it was being constricted by the gauntlet, like a blood pressure strap squeezed a few times. "What if we made a whole suit like the gauntlet?"

Richard chuckled. "Iron Man? Completely impractical. Then you'd really be slow and cumbersome. You're already high KE proof. What more do you need?"

Owen smiled. "Augmented strength? Jet boots?"

Richard laughed. "You're already augmented, and flight in such a suit is fantasy. At least with the technology we have now."

Owen thought about it for a while, then seemed to agree. "What if you could cram a collector grid into it?"

"We'll get the grid into a backpack, but the field it will emit will be short and the power conduit will be limited. I got a version reduced to the size of a roll-away case. Decent range, but it's not perfect."

"Might be a good backup system."

"You're right, which is why we're working on it."

Richard disconnected all the leads and wires from Owen's face, chest, and arms. Owen stood and examined the mangled armrest of the chair and then the table with its overturned equipment. Richard hefted the gauntlet onto a workbench. "Power loss, size, weight. These are all surmountable. The real problem is that it's leaky as hell."

Owen rubbed his forearm. "Leaky?"

"These focal devices put out a particular energy signature. See, this is the beauty of Dr. di Lago's work—"

"Let's not get all googly-eyed."

"You have to appreciate the work of a master," Richard clucked. "Ogier combed through our test records on our man Brastius. There were small distinct signatures—not easily detected by most modern equipment, but if you aggregated enough disparate and mundane sensors, you could find the waveform. At least, that's how we think the Avallach bastards found it. I'll be damned if I know what they used to aggregate the enormous amount of data they had to sift through, but our own records and advanced sensing equipment found the signature easily. Incredibly small, really." Richard gazed at *Nornian*. "Such perfect tuning."

"I'm not sure what you're getting at."

Richard patted the gauntlet, which now looked like the robotic equivalent of a biology experiment. The guts of the system were spread wide open, revealing internal sensors and components. "As much as our system has perfected the tuning aspect, its signature leakage is strong and pronounced."

"So?"

"It's a signature. Not only is it traceable to where you are, it can even tell someone who you are."

Owen looked down at his rings. "So, I can be tracked by my rings?"

"If they knew what they were looking for, yes. The focal rings had a minimal signature until we modified them. Now they're a bit leaky. Not as bad as the gauntlets are now." He motioned around him. "We've shielded any signatures from leaking outside Brightwork. The thing is, with *Nornian*, if they do get a sniff of a signature, the chances are, they'll think you're Brastius, not... you."

"Because the rings are tuned to him?"

"They were, and the signature is close. You'd see that it was his signature, but garbled."

There were possibilities in that, but Owen needed to think. What did that mean for him? What did that mean for Avallach? Could he find out where Arthur was? Confront him? Take him down? The possibilities sifted in his mind, the compulsion all but forgotten.

∼

OWEN ARCHED HIS SPINE, his hands caressing her body and her curves. Long blond tresses swept down her back as she straddled him. She was lithe and athletic, and his body responded as much as his mind. They moved faster and faster, spiraling into pleasure. Owen closed his eyes and slid his hand along her hip. She felt like her, what she would feel like again. Her fingers clasped his. He moved his other hand along the small of her back, between her shoulder blades, and then into her hair. He grasped it and tugged, losing himself in the pleasure of the moment. She gasped and her hair became slack.

He opened his eyes and she looked back at him in surprise, the blond wig in his hand. He threw it across the room, the pleasure switching to anger, like a broken spell.

"I didn't like it anyway." Kara ran her fingers through her shoulder-length auburn hair.

Owen frowned. "That wasn't the point."

"And what's the point?"

Owen had lost the moment. He pushed her off of him and got up.

"Are you mad at me?" Kara called after him.

"Why would I be mad at you? I still fucked you."

"You didn't finish."

"Story of my life." Owen pulled on a robe.

"Want me to leave?"

"Do what you want."

"Come on, don't be mad at me," Kara said, getting up. "You have a thing for blondes. Maybe I'll dye my hair next time?"

"You can stay if you want." Owen closed the door behind him. His heart was racing and he felt cheated. *It should've been her*, he told himself.

IN HIS LIVING ROOM, Owen poured himself a tumbler of scotch. Even the buzz of alcohol had diminished in the face of the greater high that manifesting gave. He'd done cocaine before, and yet that hardly came close to what manifest power felt like. No wonder Arthur did not want to give it up when Marks tried to shut down Avallach.

Owen sat down at his desk, opened a drawer, and pulled out a small stack of black folders. He took another swig and flipped through the material. Reports on Avallach and Arthur that the former DARPA Black director Ryan de Vance had made. A lot of the information was on Brightwork itself, but there were investigations into Arthur's past, per General Marks's request. Both of Arthur's parents had been a part of an old project called Spartan, long since defunct. Arthur was a product of that project, and by direct correlation, so was Owen himself. Owen wondered if he was the only copy.

He read over what little was known of Spartan and concluded that it was unlikely. Cloning had been around for decades, though not taken seriously until Dolly the Sheep came along in the mid-1990s. Genetic experimentation was more avant-garde during that time, and Spartan was one of those projects. There was a long list of spinoff and branch projects; it was hard to tell if Spartan was a success or not, though none of the results had ever been released. DARPA had a habit of exploring vast avenues of science to see what was possible as well as abandoning unsuccessful endeavors.

He shoved that aside, not caring to know much about it. He read through a small file on Arthur's mother. Igerne MacGabran, a neurobiologist of some renown then, had moved from Spartan to an older project called Astrologer, which also spun out into a dozen side projects when it was dismantled or deemed as ineffective as its predecessor Nostradamus. Written in small script in the margin, probably by de Vance, was the phrase "Marks—Delphi? Shut down?" Owen considered that. He pulled out a file and read through some scant notes he'd found in Marks's study. They were mostly written in an oblique manner, referring to Delphi only twice. There was something in this, but what was the importance of it? It was a hunch, but he filed the information away in his mind. He'd be able to sort it out later. He put the paperwork together and pushed the file away.

He pored through files on Avallach. There was an after-action report on Indiana Beckham's encounter with a black ops squad. It made for interesting reading. He stared at the image of Indiana wearing a white bodysuit. Something about her stance and face spoke to Owen. This was the woman who was, by all accounts, the strongest Avallach candidate—stronger than even Arthur, the progenitor. If de Vance's reports were correct, Indiana had never peaked in power. After she had been expunged from Avallach, she fell of the radar. A few months ago, Morgan had found out through DARPA that Indiana was dead now, destroyed on the flight of a prototype shuttle stolen from its launchpad the very same day Marks tried to shut down Avallach. That was as much as was known.

Owen downed the rest of his scotch and sat back. The alcohol burned in his belly, but rather than dull his emotions, it made him tired. He stared at the photo of Indiana and imagined her with blue eyes.

He stalked through the woods, a young boy close at his side. He knelt and examined the soft forest floor and sniffed the air.

"Something?" the boy said.

"Spoor. He's close," the bronze-skinned man who was Owen said. He planted his spear, opened the sachet at his neck, and smeared the paste onto his skin. It was made from the urine of another boar mixed with the blood of a female and preserving mud. It stung his eyes. The boy made a face.

"The boar knows that man hunts," Owen said to the boy. "But if it thinks another male boar is rutting in its territory, it'll come to us." He picked up his spear and continued on, his dark eyes gazing at every patch and leaf for indications of passage.

"But we're hunting him."

Owen tossed the boy the sachet. "We're downwind and he can smell us. We're not hunters anymore—things to avoid and ignore. We're enemies now. He'll come to us."

"Wha—"

There was a sound. The man stopped and turned, squatting down. A snort or grunt. The boy followed suit. He searched the dappled forest, but the undergrowth was thick. Gods, this was a great hunt!

Owen stalked toward the sound of the boar, circling to make sure his scent was in the beast's nostrils. The rustling was louder and there was a squeal. Owen turned, and a flash of tusk came from the brush toward the boy. He shoved the boy out of the way with his shoulder, sparing him from the tusk and getting his spear in the boar's path. But the hunter wasn't set as the boar charged. The spear glanced off the hide of the beast. He shrieked in pain as the tusks of the great boar gored him and threw him back into nothing.

Owen snapped awake, his glass shattering on the ground.

"Shit," he gasped, the dregs of the dream wiped away with shock of being awake.

Kara came out of the bedroom, a kimono cinched around her waist. "Something wrong?"

Owen held out a hand. "There's glass everywhere."

She stopped, barefoot, then padded slowly over.

"Nothing's wrong," Owen said. He considered the dream. He rubbed his lean stomach, imagining his intestines in his hand. It was curious, but not all that disturbing. She placed her arms around his neck. "I'm sorry," he said automatically, lost in thought.

"I'm sorry, too," she said, running her hands down his chest and kissing his ear. He felt the coolness of her rings on his bare skin. He took her hand in his. *Eurfron*, her rings were called now, but before that they were *Joyous*, Indiana Beckham's first set of focal rings.

"Do you want me to clean it up?" Kara asked, looking at the shattered glass.

Owen made a fist. "Do you have plans today?"

Kara shrugged and smiled. "Just another day of training. Commander Holt is taking the team through indoctrination of new procedures. I could be persuaded . . ."

Owen kissed her bejeweled fingers. *Joyous*. "Can you come to the lab with me? I want to look over some logs and try something."

"Weren't you just at the lab today?"

"I want you to test something for me."

"That sounds vague and mysterious. What are you thinking about?"

He looked at the photo of Indiana again. The compulsion was a memory now, but it had imprinted something on his mind. "Just to test a theory. Boar shit."

7
PRIORITIES

ISTANBUL, TURKEY—
"I don't want to tell you what to do, but you need to shit or get off the pot," Ed said.

"What?"

"This game you're playing with yourself. Should I stay? Should I go? That kind of problem is really distracting."

"I'm not dis—"

"For us, not you."

"Oh."

"What're you thinking?"

Percy looked out the window, admiring the bustle of life. A warm breeze wafted through the opening, a far cry from the cold weather gripping the United States. He rubbed his neck. "Thinking about a family, I guess."

Ed yawned next to him, his black sunglasses reflecting the sunny day's glare. "Anything?" he asked, sounding bored. Percy knew he was alert and scanning the streets below. They were both in street clothes, their n-suits concealed beneath.

"Not yet," Sahar said in both their ears. She was plugged into their suit systems and Janus had worked its way into nearby monitoring systems.

"What kind of family do you have?" Percy asked, scanning the streets. It was hard to pick out someone doing something suspicious in a foreign city. Still, people had a way of walking and going about their business that felt routine. Only a handful of the people who walked beneath their window had no purpose, but most of them were tourists.

Ed shrugged, his eyes not leaving the streets. "I don't have much family. Dad retired out of the army when I got my commission in the navy. He figured two Tiwazes in the US military was too much. My sister Anna's a schoolteacher in Pennsylvania, married to some soft doughboy. I think Jim's a CPA, but who cares? He starts talking and I want to shoot myself. She's has kids and they're doing all right. Check it." He pointed to a man moving with just a bit more speed than the crowd.

"Could be."

"Okay, think that's him," Sahar said.

"Put me on intercept. Percy, you get ahead of him. Try to beat him to his target, whoever that is."

"Janus has the route."

Percy pounded down the stairs. He left Ed behind at the first turn as he worked his way down the winding streets of Istanbul. The smells of cooked food, perfumes, and musk wafted up from the street. He loped, not too fast. *Grall* was ready. He felt the trickle of power as he held it back. Sahar and Prianna were close by, blanketing them with the grid. He followed Janus's directions, which brought him along the main thoroughfare. He saw the shadowed face of the man up the street. Ed was behind him, moving through the crowd. Percy turned in the direction the man was heading. He saw a bus stop and headed toward it.

"Bus stop?" Percy asked. He rolled through the directions from Arthur in his head. *"Find a musician. Protect her from the suicide bomber. She'll be waiting."* Waiting at a bus stop?

"He's slowing," Ed replied. "Or lost. He's kind of big. Pack?" That last was directed at his DAMSL.

"Your suit sensors read faint traces, but nothing detectable at this range," Sahar reported.

"Moving again. To you," Ed said.

Percy was near the bus stop, where a clump of people waited for the next bus. He stood near the group; the trickle of power was like the edge of an adrenaline rush. He scanned to find the real target. The bus cruised down the street and most of those waiting made themselves ready. A woman marched toward the bus stop carrying a violin case. She was young, university age. Maybe a graduate student. Her hair was shoulder length and flowing with her hurried gait. She didn't look distinctly Turkish, but in such a cosmopolitan city, it was hard to say.

"He's almost to you. Damn it," Ed said, thumping the hood of a small car that tried to run him over as he crossed the street.

"It's the girl," Percy said, moving to put himself in between her and the approaching man.

The woman gave him a quizzical look as if he had just offered his place in line. Percy only smiled. The bus approached.

"I'm moving," Ed said.

About a hundred feet away there was a shout and then screams. The crowd parted and Percy saw the man struggling with Ed. Ed wrestled with the attacker and Percy saw the pack.

"Bomb. Alert everyone, Janus," Percy said.

"Clear the area! A bomb has been detected!" Janus's voice was emitted by every phone, radio, and television set in the local vicinity. The voice repeated the alert in Turkish as people ran away from the area. *Effective*, Percy noted.

The attacker was strong, but Ed countered his strikes. He shoved Ed away from him, drew a gun, and then fired at his opponent. The man aimed at the violinist. Percy ramped up his KE field to maximum and brought his arm up. He covered the shocked violinist with his body and shield, making himself seem like as large a target as possible. His KE shield flared with each shot, absorbing the kinetic energy of each bullet, stopping them completely until gravity exerted itself and they fell to earth.

The violinist threw herself into the bus shelter and cowered with the few people who'd chosen to freeze over fleeing.

"Ed, detecting an electronic signature," Sahar said.

"His bomb," Ed said, flicking *Grel* to life and cutting the man's gun barrel off. "Sewer below?"

"Two feet down," Sahar said.

Ed grappled with the man now, pulling his jacket down to pin his arms. He dragged him into the street among parked cars. Ed flicked *Grel* again, spinning his arm in a wide circle, and he knelt. A chunk of pavement fell in. Ed grabbed the man and threw him into the hole. "Fuck me," Ed said to himself as he activated his KE shield and threw himself over the hole in the ground.

The bomb went off and the world went crazy. The earth bucked, tossing people to the ground. Percy threw himself onto the violinist, protecting her from the shattering debris of the bus shelter as the blast wave hit. Manhole covers blew off, a section of the road collapsed around Ed's location, and he disappeared into the dust and debris. Cars parked along the road fell into the hole. Glass from the bus, cars, and windows shattered. Percy's ears rang and he froze for a moment, holding on to his manifest. Debris flickered on his shield and chunks of rock fell around him. After the worst of it, he sat up, his shield winking out.

He checked over the woman. "Are you okay?" he asked, realizing she probably didn't know English.

"Yes." She nodded, clutching her violin and checking it over. She had minor cuts but was otherwise all right. Percy looked over the rest of the people in the bus shelter. He heard sirens in the distance and Janus's voice still repeating through her tinny speakers and echoing down the street.

"Janus, you can stop now." The announcements stopped.

"Not seeing any major injuries up here. Ed, you okay?"

"Need a hand," Ed coughed.

Percy picked himself up and ran to the hole. He couldn't see anything through the dust. He tapped his sunglasses and they went to infrared.

"I see you," Percy said. He hopped onto one of the partially sunken cars and picked his way down the rubble. "Damn, you had to fall into a sewer. A wonderful smell."

"You're so prissy for a marine sometimes. Get your hands dirty once in a while."

"Wasn't planning on being immersed in a cloud of atomized sewage."

"Fucking car landed on me. Can you believe it?" Ed said. He was pinned against the inner wall of the sewer by another, smaller car. There was a red smear coated in dust. *What was left of the bomber*, Percy thought. He'd seen his share of these gruesome attacks in Afghanistan.

Percy got next to Ed and with leverage, they moved the car enough that he could get out. Percy grabbed Ed's hand and pulled him from the wreckage.

"What is it with tiny cars? They're like slow little bullets, trying to smoosh me," Ed said, following him as they worked their way out of the hole. "At least the bomber didn't succeed, unless you count turning himself into molecular components. How's the woman?"

"She's all right."

"Any other injuries?" Ed asked Prianna.

"Nothing major being reported yet," Prianna said.

"How's lockdown?"

"Janus and Prometheum are working to keep footage contained. There was only the usual tourist footage, but you're in a debris field," Sahar reported.

"I love really smart systems that proactively prevent data leakage," Percy said.

"You worry about leakage? I mean, I don't mind my handsome face on TV."

"Careful what you wish for," Percy said. "Aren't you used to clandestine operations?"

"Doesn't mean I don't love to be on TV. These two things aren't mutually exclusive."

"You're weird," Percy said.

"Let's get out of here," Ed said. "You DAMSLs close?"

"Two blocks over. Steeds are ready."

"Super. Rooftop?"

"Janus will guide you."

"So, before I was so rudely interrupted," Ed commented, "my ma and pa retired to the elephant-graveyard state of Florida to wait out the clock. That's all I got for a family really unless you count my sister's cute little rugrats."

Percy brushed the dust from his hair and set his sunglasses to normal view once they were clear of the cloud. He wrinkled his nose at the stench. "Smells terrible."

"Not every fight is as pretty as the movies."

"Good thinking on containing the bomb," Percy said.

Ed smiled. "It was that or jump on the guy, and I wasn't about to test the limits of my own ability just yet. Thumbs-up for the sewer being so close to the surface in an old city. Up here." He went up a set of rickety stairs. "You talk to Lilly yet?"

"Nah, I've been doing my part."

"Mhm, I've heard that one before. Sounds familiar."

"What? Everyone seems to be worried about me and Lilly."

"Look, man. You got plans. I can read it on your face."

They made it to the rooftop. Sahar and Prianna were there, standing next to the steeds. Both wore AR glasses, but the rest of their attire made them look just like all the other tourists in the area. Ed walked over to the roof's edge and peered over.

"Too bad we can't see all the hubbub from here."

"You were just there," Sahar said, pinching her nose. "You made a huge mess and smell like it."

"I didn't make the mess. I just contained it. Okay, I sort of made the hole, but I didn't blow it up. I know you're rolling your eyes at me."

Sahar looked at him with dark goggle lenses. "Whatever do

you mean?"

"I can feel them rolling right now."

"You're paranoid."

"That and my ginger powers are what keep me alive," Ed said. He put on his helmet, tugging it on over his scruffy red beard.

Percy tugged his own on, feeling the close fit and the audio switching on to filter out the background noise. He flipped the faceplate closed, and filters cleaned the air and sealed his suit.

"Can you hear me?" Ed said.

"Read you," Percy said, noting he was on the private channel with his helmet heads-up display.

"Look, you're dedicated. We all see that. But don't lose sight of what you want for what Arthur wants. They may not be the same thing. Did he send Lilly a Janus yet?"

"Yeah."

"If you have a dream of another life, don't give it up for someone else's dreams. That's how people become bitter."

"I think they're talking about us," Sahar said to Prianna as they put on their own helmets.

"Sounds like a lot of words of wisdom." Percy touched his steed and the focal magnifier activated. The steed floated from the ground and its kickstand recessed automatically.

"I have no dreams, really. Mac's my best friend. And Kai? She's in the same boat as me, I guess. Our loyalty is what keeps us where we are. You, though? There's nothing keeping you back from what you want. Lilly isn't in this fight, you know. You get to think about what she wants. About what you both want. Just don't distract the rest of the team with your hesitation."

"I'm used to it," Prianna said with a smile.

They activated the steeds and floated high into the air. Sahar wrapped her arms around Percy's back while Prianna held on to Ed. This was how they'd arrived in Istanbul and how they were leaving.

Percy channeled power, but his mind was elsewhere. He thought about Lilly and what Ed had said. "Thanks."

"I'm not bitter yet, but I got time. Damn shame to see you get that way, though. You're a helluva candidate, even if you are a marine."

"Ex-marine at this point."

"Details. If you were a knight, I'd say you were a paladin. That model of chivalry."

"Are you asking me out on a date?"

Ed laughed and did his best Oprah impression. "You get a date! You get a date! Everyone gets a date! Race you to rendezvous!"

"Hey, not so fast!" Sahar complained as the steeds rocketed across the sky like black streaks.

WESTERN ATLANTIC OCEAN—

It was night when the Raven touched down on the yacht, idling. Arthur met them on the deck wearing a heavy peacoat. The seas were rough, but *Camelot* managed.

Arthur radioed Birgitte. "I'll need another trip. You up for it?"

"Of course. Janus did most of the flying. You'll need to charge the engine," Birgitte replied as the cargo door opened. Ed and Percy walked the steeds off as Prianna and Sahar finished their onboard work.

"Good to see you," Ed said. "Miss us?"

"It's only been a few days," Arthur said. He signaled to Percy that he wanted to talk with a nod. "Kai's looking for you."

"Music to my ears," Ed said. "I can't wait."

"She probably wants to kick his ass," Percy said. "Where's Lamar?"

"At *Dinas*, training with Echo Series and Hector," Arthur replied. "Jeri just got her rings, so she needs her first round of manifest training."

"She'll be caught up with the Echo group pretty soon, I bet." Percy hoped Lamar was all right. The *Dinas* facility was far from land and from prying eyes. He looked up at the cloudy night sky. *Most prying eyes*, he amended. It was still under construction and was less like a training academy and more like a construction site.

"Need a DAMSL?" Prianna asked Arthur after packing and walking down the ramp of the Raven.

"We'll be all right," Arthur replied, boarding the Raven.

"Safe trip!" Sahar said, high-fiving Arthur on her way down.

"What's that smell?"

"Me needing a shower," Sahar replied.

Percy grabbed food from the galley. Sam was there, eating.

"You heading back out?" Sam asked.

"Touch and go," Percy acknowledged.

"Can I come with?" Sam asked.

"Quality time with Birgitte?"

Sam smiled. "Something like that, mate." They returned to the Raven. Sam walked into the flight deck, handed Birgitte food, and sat in the copilot seat. Percy ate and watched them out of the corner of his eye. Sam hadn't been quite able to manifest since his rescue early in the summer. Still, he had stayed on the project and Percy had a feeling it had a lot to do with Birgitte. They were both DAMSLs now, helping out candidates where they could.

We have more DAMSLs than candidates now, he thought morosely, but reminded himself there were more than a dozen Echo candidates in training. He thought of Lilly and how badly he wanted to be with her. Was that really it? Did he want something? Or was it that what he wanted was simply not what he was doing now? As a human being, he possessed incredible power, but all he thought about was being just a regular guy. It was funny. He'd never had these thoughts when he'd been deployed. A lot had changed, but what?

Percy grabbed a handhold as the Raven lifted off with a thrum of its body. He turned to face Arthur.

Arthur's arm was outstretched, *Caliburn* touching the focal magnifier that was mounted to the engine. His body glowed as he fed power from the grid through his body into the focal magnifier, converting the energy into a stored state. He had a pained expression on his face and snapped out of it when he let go of the power. His halo vanished.

"You okay?" Percy asked, walking past him to hit the door release and close them into the cocoon of the Raven's stealth.

Arthur collapsed against the bulkhead for a moment. "Yeah, just . . . something," he whispered. He pressed his hand to his forehead, then touched his ear. "Got enough charge, Birgitte?"

"We're good," Birgitte replied, and the Raven heeled over as they turned and rose into the night.

Arthur just nodded at that. Whatever was bothering him had passed as quickly as it came.

"Having problems manifesting?" Percy asked. As the first candidate, whatever problems might arise long term, Arthur would be the first one to feel any of their effects.

Arthur shook his head. "I don't know what it was. A vision, maybe? Something pulling at my mind. It was powerful, whatever it was. Did you feel anything?"

Percy shook his head. "I thought you were confined to the ship. You know, Kai's orders and all that."

"Don't worry, I'm not looking for a fight. Besides, Kai's distracted by her new job." He peered at Percy for a long moment. "You still thinking of leaving?"

Percy nodded. "Been thinking of it a lot. More than I should."

"Nothing wrong with that. I do have a confession, Perse. I lied to you."

Percy finished his sandwich and waited.

Arthur glanced at the cockpit and pulled out his earpiece. Percy got the hint and removed his device as well. "I do need you for something important. I can only trust you to take care of it."

"I'll do what I can."

"Strictly off the record. I can't have the sisters, Kai, or anyone know about this."

Percy's stomach tightened. It wasn't the first time Arthur had compartmentalized things, but he never hid anything from Kai. Except Indiana, but everyone save Arthur had been in the dark about that. Arthur needed loyalty, and had it in spades with his team. He'd helped select them, after all.

"Nothing counter to the project. Just something you need to do for me."

"And what's in it for me?"

"No more missions."

"It's that important?"

"Well, it's two missions, really, but this one is the big one."

Percy thought about that. "Two and I'm done?"

"That's the gist of it," Arthur said. "Echo group is coming up to speed and the god pods made it to *Dinas*. Truth be told, I'd rather Isolde be at *Dinas* than here, but it'll be a while before the pods there are online."

Percy wrung his hands. Now that he was faced with the possibility, he wasn't sure what to make of it. He wanted to go home, back to the way things were before he had left Lilly. "You said you lied to me before. About what?"

"About our tech being out in the wild. There's more than one group."

"What the hell?"

Arthur held up a hand. "When I explain it, you'll understand what it is."

"You better have a damn good excuse, like cloning yourself or the team or something."

Arthur nodded. "You see, it starts off with a list . . ." He pulled an envelope out of his peacoat and handed it to Percy. "Take a look at it when you land."

"Really off the radar to be using paper," Percy said.

Arthur gave a wry smile. "You might be surprised at what you find. It'll also bring you to your second mission."

"Written here, I take it?"

Arthur put his earpiece back into his ear and patted Percy on the shoulder. "You're one of the most important people."

"Well, I am pretty great," Percy said, trying Lamar's self-congratulatory tone. It didn't seem to come off as he wanted it to. "That can't be the only reason you're here on the Raven."

"Nope. I have a visit to make to Dr. Myrrdin."

"Would you really have dropped Dr. Myrrdin in the Potomac?" Percy asked. "Are you leaving one dangerous woman for another?" Percy thought of Isolde, still in the god pod aboard *Camelot*.

Arthur smiled and sat back for the ride. "You only see what's on the surface. Just like Maven, there's a lot more to Anora than anyone sees. I have a feeling if you're on her side, she'll bend over backwards for you. If you have to, you'll help her. It'll be the best course of action."

Percy pondered that for the rest of the trip.

8

SYSTEMS INTEGRATE

WASHINGTON, DC—
"Good gravy, I thought you died," Roxanne said when she entered the room. She hooked a thumb over her shoulder to indicate the large warehouse room outside Anora's glass-enclosed office. "Guys are here to run more fiber optics."

Anora sat up on her couch and pulled off her glasses. She rubbed her eyes. "Sorry, I was taking apart the existing system."

"Most of the team is here now, if you want to say hi," Roxanne said.

"How are they doing?"

"Mostly ready for this new project. You know how excited they get when you whisk them away from Binary HQ. Makes them feel special."

"They already know they're special." Anora stretched. "Of course, the COO wasn't too happy I took away the group again, but I authorized some head count, so Max is happy. It balances out and there's no shortage of work for Binary." Max Gentry was a great operations officer, so she had to smooth things over in person when she pulled her "skunkworks" team. There were plenty of harsh words, but after a couple of weeks, things had settled down by her last check-in with the company. In fact, he'd already hired three new researchers to plus up the teams Anora had pulled from. What could he do? Binary AI was founded and owned by her. With the addition of Telemachus to her responsibilities, it gave her even more reason to get away from the day-to-day running of the business. She'd also made some legal provisions that both the board of directors and Max would be happy about.

Roxanne sat down on the couch next to Anora and handed her a mug of tea. Anora exchanged it for her AR glasses. Roxanne put them on and looked around the room.

"This is your Quantum Protocol code. Why are you looking at that old stuff?"

"Found it in the wild, being used, including a secure virtual reality enclave. I might as well open-source QP at this point." Anora sipped her tea. "Besides the AR bottlenecks, QP wasn't designed to sustain multiple point connections. You have your work cut out for you."

"That's why QP is great, but I see what you mean," Roxanne sat back, her eyes delving into the virtual displays that lay beyond the physical world. "Oh hey, you got One operating."

"Hi, Roxanne," One's disembodied voice replied.

Anora nodded. "She's in a limited mode for now, but I got the localization system running diagnostics now. This was an interesting experiment from the lab and I'd like Heph to build a portable system for me."

"I like how you call your old office a lab. That reminds me." Roxanne pulled out a couple of terminals from her cardigan sweater pocket, which looked like giant autumn oak leaves. "Fresh off Heph's custom hardware shop."

Anora admired Roxanne's festive sweater. *Is it that late in the year already?* Anora thought. She shook the thought away and ran her fingers over the new terminals. They were thicker than the old model. Heph was a brilliant hardware engineer and was always working on a number of prototypes. These new terminals were probably just one of them. Still, it was as if he crafted hardware out of thin air. "All the new changes made?"

"Hardened shell and isolated beacon. What the hell did you do to the last One?"

"Punny." Anora ran her fingers through her hair. She needed a shower. She put the terminals on the workbench, cycling through the configuration system. Once she had them initialized, One would automatically inject and configure herself. It had become routine for Heph to give her bleeding-edge technology for her AI systems. "What day is it?"

"Monday," Roxanne replied absentmindedly.

Anora stretched a bit. She was wound up tight but needed to sleep. It had been a couple of weeks since Arthur brought her back to DC, but that wasn't what had her restless. Or maybe it just compounded things. How did she make it through her treatment without going insane?

"Trouble sleeping still?"

"I don't want to sleep," Anora said, pressing her palms to her eyes.

"You've been like that since you got through your treatment. What did the doctor say? You're not having a recurrence?"

Anora shook her head quickly. "Just still recovering. I don't wanna talk about it."

"Need a therapy session, Nor?"

"I'd love one."

"They're ready to roll the table up here. I'll get it done." Roxanne pulled up the glasses and tapped a message into her phone to someone on the team.

"God yes, please." Anora stretched and considered trying out the shower of her new office.

Roxanne was back to looking at her virtual code. "Are you thinking of multichain links?"

"QP isn't going to work as is, so we're going to need a central hub that establishes the individual links."

"Point-to-multipoint broadcast would work. How tight does it have to be? Government tight, military tight, or vestal virgin tight?"

"Impenetrable."

"Oh, so just like QP. That's an interesting problem."

"You're my net-com expert," Anora said.

Roxanne pulled off the glasses and smiled at Anora. "I've been here a long time, Nor. Is this what we're working on?"

"That's what you're working on. I've got a special project for myself," Anora said.

"You don't do special projects, so that's gotta be something good. Take a shower and I'll have the table brought up."

"Why do I hire pushy employees?"

"I'll talk to One while you're freshening up. We'll get some breakfast, and I'll pretend I understand your decade-old dissertation, you tell me what I'm supposed to do, and we can start doing it. I'll need to start ripping out some of this code, though. It's not optimal for low-bandwidth needs."

Anora took a long hot shower, but she felt drained rather than refreshed. She hated these periods, and this time she blamed Arthur. He had triggered emotions and memories she had worked hard to bury after her treatment. She estimated that she could work for a few more days before exhaustion did her in. Roxanne waited for her at the massage table when Anora stepped out of the bath.

"Frost the windows," Anora told One, and the floor-to-ceiling windows that looked down over the open floor of her specialist team's work area went translucent.

"Mm, you really got this place tricked out," Roxanne said, patting the massage table.

Roxanne, one of Anora's longest-serving employees and a close friend, had taken up massage therapy lessons after she had learned that Anora had sessions. Anora was sure that Rox had a pretty good idea why she was in therapy. *Some secrets should die with their owners*, she reminded herself.

She lay down on the table and Roxanne started at her shoulders.

Roxanne's touch was jarring at first, but it was firm and rhythmic.

Anora sighed and closed her eyes. She might be able to sleep after all.

"That's a good sound," Rox said. There was a knock at the door.

"No," Anora said, but the door opened anyway.

"Don't you know better, Joey?" Roxanne chided the man as she worked.

"I'm sorry, but there's someone here to see Dr. Myrrdin," Joey said.

"Someone unimportant," Arthur said as he stepped past Joey into the office.

Joey shook Arthur's hand. "Joseph Bertram. Joey. Do you work out?"

"It's a cross-training sort of thing. Military training."

"Nice rings. Is that a navy peacoat?"

"Yes," Arthur said, unbuttoning it with his free hand.

Anora breathed deep. She did not want to open her eyes just now. She'd already started her therapy. "Wait outside."

"Go on, Joey," Rox's hand left Anora's bare shoulder in what Anora knew was the shooing motion the short woman often gave. "Who's the hunk of beef?" Roxanne said to Anora.

"I call dibs!" Joey said from the doorway.

Anora held on to herself, keeping her emotions at bay. "Arthur, this is part of my software engineering team. Roxanne Hasan."

Roxanne shook Arthur's hand. She was dark haired and had big dark eyes, a contrast to Arthur.

"I'd die if I dated someone like you," Rox said, her hands back on Anora's shoulders.

"Stop drooling," Anora exclaimed from the massage table.

"I like this place. Red brick, very hipster start-up. Where's the foosball table?" Arthur asked.

"God bless the USA," Joey said, walking back down the metal stairs from the loft office.

"Aren't you Canadian?" Roxanne yelled after him.

"Half Canadian on my mother's side."

Arthur shut the door behind him. "Not a lot of people you have here."

"My core team. They're brilliant software engineers and most were students of mine when I was going through my graduate degrees."

"Their specialty is artificial intelligence?" Arthur asked.

"Most. Roxanne here specializes in network communications."

"She has good hands, too. Think you could work out this kink I have?" Arthur rubbed his shoulder.

"Old war wound?" Rox asked.

"Something like that."

"Want him to wait outside like the rest of the riffraff?" Roxanne asked Anora. "I mean, you are naked and all."

"No, but we'll need better physical security," Anora said, and turned her head to Arthur. "Something I can help you with?"

"It's personal." He glanced at her, then around the room, being polite. He was very much the Boy Scout still, Anora thought. While she wasn't a prude, she appreciated his discretion, then chided herself for it.

"Did you go on a date without telling me, Nor?" Roxanne asked.

"Jumped off a building. Thanks, Rox."

Roxanne squeezed Anora's hand. "Now you're pulling my leg. Let me know when I'm needed."

"You've already helped a bunch," Anora said. "Give him your glasses, please."

Roxanne took off her glasses and handed them to Arthur before walking out. "I'm going to go swoon now," she said to herself.

"Last time we talked, it was pretty clear I wasn't wanted," Anora said.

"What was clear was that you wanted answers from me. It had nothing to do with Avallach."

"It has everything to do with Avallach."

"You've researched your brother's plane crash?"

"Of course."

"Mind if I see?"

Anora indicated the glasses. "You know what those are?"

"More fashionable than what we have." Arthur put the glasses on.

"More advanced. One?" Anora asked.

"I'm here," One's young voice said.

"Can you instantiate?"

"I have sufficient capacity now."

"Visual representation, please."

"Yes," One replied. A small girl appeared next to Arthur. She looked like what Anora would have looked like as a child.

"Arthur MacGabran," One said.

"Nice to meet you," Arthur said.

One cocked her head slightly and smiled. "I'm One. You did excellent work at Fort Hood. Prevented over two dozen people from being shot."

"Thank you." Arthur looked to Anora, who had gotten up and gone to the bathroom. Anora was sure he got a glimpse of her backside.

"She's a work in progress," Anora said as she shut the door.

"I'm a functionally complete artificial intelligence program. I've been in operation for nearly a decade."

"Don't brag," Anora said through the door. "One, show him the research we put together from Maven's flight recorder."

Windows appeared in front of Arthur, showing logs reported by air traffic control as well as the reported flight path of Maven's Gulfstream IV. There was an ellipse placed over the last known trajectory, indicating a degree of uncertainty. Arthur studied the information. Anora had marked the major air force wings and naval air stations with projected flight paths.

Anora returned, dressed in black rocker tee and jeans.

"Quite a collection of data you have here," Arthur said.

"Yes, and it's mostly wrong."

"Oh?"

"The flight path doesn't just match the air traffic control logs. It matches perfectly."

"Too perfectly?"

Anora picked up the second pair of glasses on her workbench. The lenses went dark when she put them on and the data came up in her vision. She waved a hand and the marked logs appeared. "The variance and cadence are too regular."

"And the voice recording?" He took off his coat.

"I did a forensic analysis of the recordings they released based on the Freedom of Information Act. It's been expertly edited."

"Sounds like a conspiracy theory." Arthur smiled at her, then turned to One. "Is it?"

"There is a high probability that it's been doctored," One replied.

"Flight logs from the military?"

"None of note, but I found JP-8 fuel logs used during the time period. Correlated activity does not match logged fuel burn, even accounting for spillage and measurement accuracy."

"Classified flights aren't logged on normal systems, and there's sufficient variance—"

"Already accounted for."

"I see." Arthur spied Indiana's damaged Janus device. He picked it up. "From Kai?"

Anora shrugged. "Pet project. It's broken."

"Drive's intact and encrypted, though. Think you can crack it?"

"The passphrase lock is more complex than just saying 'Open sesame.'"

"You could hack—"

"You trying to tell me how to do my job?"

Arthur put the device back on the workbench and put his hands in his pockets. "It may not contain any useful information."

She saw something on Arthur's face. Doubt or hope? It wasn't fear, but it was something. She focused on his statement. "That's the same line the FAA gave when they failed to recover the flight recorder of my brother's plane."

Arthur nodded and looked back at the virtual map. "I see you—"

Anora waved her hand, wiping away everything. "Why are you here?"

"I thought I'd save you the trouble of coming to find me a second time. You were looking for me, weren't you?"

Anora was silent.

Arthur turned to One.

"Wasn't she?"

"Yes."

"I had nothing to do with Maven's death. He was important to me."

"As you said. You're just one of his pet projects."

"We're not at cross purposes here, Anora. I want what you want—to find out who killed Maven and Indiana."

"I don't really care about Indiana, but if you know something about Maven, we can talk." Anora made herself another cup of tea and gestured up another terminal. She saw that Roxanne had already started work on the CAMLANN codebase. Roxanne had also opened a channel to One in case she was needed. If they weren't the same age, Anora would have sworn she was being mothered by the petite woman.

Arthur gazed at the broken Janus device. "I can open that."

"And how would that help me?"

"I'm not saying it will help you, but if you want to solve that little problem, Kai would be happy."

Anora waited for the catch.

"Janny?" Arthur leaned over the device.

Janus's voice, tinny over its damaged hardware, replied, "Passphrase, please."

Arthur leaned over and whispered something to the device. He spoke to it a few times until there was a small chirp.

Anora steeped her tea while she waited.

Arthur shook his head and sat back while Janus decrypted. "How does One here know who I am?"

"I have a complete record of the information gathered on you over the last five months," One replied.

"One only has the data you've accessed?" Arthur asked Anora.

"You can ask her," Anora said.

"One?" Arthur prompted.

"There's little public information regarding you or the remaining members of your team on analysis databases or public Internet archives. It's difficult to obtain such records."

"That's the Prometheum Protocol. Don't let your internal systems be exposed. It has instructions to erase specific information, and if the protocol determines that you have a copy of the flagged information, it will try to break the system to effect the erase."

Anora nodded. "And you wonder why I don't like the idea of my artificial intelligence being used for military purposes."

"Prometheum isn't an AI, as I understand it. It's more of an intelligent system. I'm not an expert."

Janus pinged, finally coming to life from the passphrase decryption. "Confirmed. My systems are degraded."

"Status of memory?" Arthur asked.

"Ninety-nine percent intact. It looks like I had a bumpy ride."

"You're back on Earth. Anora Myrrdin is going to take care of you now."

"Awful nice of you," Anora said, picking up Janus and plugging it into one of her computer systems. "Janus, I'm going to download and unpack your storage systems. Please allow One to replicate your data."

"Understood. You have full access. Please call me Janny."

"Copying," One said.

"It probably feels less weird to you than to me to be talking to two different AI systems," Arthur said.

"They are easier to understand than meat bags such as yourself," Anora replied.

"I'll leave you to it, then." Arthur picked up his coat and went to the door.

"Off to save someone?"

"Probably."

"What about your proof about Maven?"

Arthur took off his glasses and handed them to Anora. "You wouldn't be interested."

Anora took the glasses and grabbed his wrist. "I could stop you. Make you tell me."

Arthur didn't move at her touch. "You can't make me tell you what you want to know, Anora. But I can give you the information you need."

Anora frowned. He was so calm, so damn sure of himself. It reminded her of Reince, and yet not. She let go of his wrist.

"Good luck, Anora. Nice meeting you, One."

"You as well," One replied.

Arthur opened the door.

"Are you doing anything tonight?" Roxanne said as Arthur walked down the stairs.

"No harassing the client!" Anora yelled, hitting the clear button on her window glass.

"Oh, he's a client now?" Roxanne yelled back.

"I'm sorry, I'll be quite busy," Arthur replied.

"That's a damn shame." Joey elbowed Roxanne in the ribs. "Do you have an army buddy maybe?"

"Actually, just my sister at the moment."

Roxanne laughed after Arthur left the office building.

Anora sat down and drank her tea. "That worked out."

"You may want to inspect the data streaming from Janny," One said.

"All right. Visual data please." Anora reached forward and expanded the data stream into a number of floating structures. She inspected the data.

"This is not a data stream or file."

One said, "I'm inspecting the data. It's tightly packed information and highly compressed. I'm unable to determine what resides in the information. It matches no known data structures. I've found some instructions to reassemble, but the directives do not make sense to my system."

"Let's see what the dependencies are," Anora said. The code blocks expanded and shrank in size, showing relational connections. "Okay, it's not source code, exactly, nor is it binaries."

"It's not a working system, but it may be a neural network," One offered.

Anora inspected the growing data. "What the hell is this?" It was like a punch to the gut. She might have been staring at a neural network that'd never been successfully created before and that she'd never heard of.

Anora stretched. She really should get Rox back up here to finish her session. Talking to Arthur had put her on the defensive again. "Okay, One, we're going to need some tools to restore this. Kai, this is an interesting problem you've handed me." She went to her office door.

"There you are, you little dickens," a heavyset programmer said. He was halfway up the stairs carrying a large laptop.

"Henry, can you get Simone? I need her to double our server systems today."

"I was just going to—double? It's possible." He rubbed his beard and trundled back down the stairs, his laptop still in hand.

Anora looked over the data that streamed on Janny, then moved over to what One alerted her to. She frowned at the location data and then took her glasses off.

"Have you initialized your devices?"

"Both are nearly ready."

Anora walked back to the door. "Rox!"

She wanted that massage. Things were going to get weird.

9

NEW DATA INPUT

"Upload complete," One said.

"Compile the latest build for me." Anora walked over and sat down on her couch. She debated another cup of tea but ruled against it.

"Just a few moments."

"Then run it against the data."

"That will take some time," One said. "John Cador is calling."

"Put him on," Anora replied.

"I thought I'd catch you this early, Anora," John said.

"You call me at all hours, John."

"And you always answer. That's never a good thing."

Anora hated to waste time, so she got to the point. "Did the transfer of Telemachus assets go through?"

"The board has approved and I'm sending papers to your office to sign by courier. Projections from the cash influx will accelerate our microsat R & D."

"You don't sound all that happy," Anora said. "The shuttle program, as fully vested as my brother was in it, was a failure." It had taken some doing, but she had managed to get the assets out of her hands and into the right ones to continue the work.

"I don't know if it was all that much of a failure," John said. "It was an expensive endeavor, to be sure—"

"John, let's be fair. If Maven favored anything, it was that project. NASA's been breathing down our necks about the issues on Platform 39 and the destruction in orbit. This will signal clearly that the program is shuttered and all assets are off the board. Do you want me to sink my company's value into my brother's company?"

"Absolutely not," John said. "You're right. None of us are like Maven, but we do have a tendency to cling to real hope. The *Archimedes* was a phenomenal attempt."

"Agreed. I just don't want to talk about it anymore. When can we clear out Warehouse One?"

"It can be cleared out in a month and we can reconfigure it for the new work in another two."

"That'll be good. Keep security tight on those assets. A breach in security protocol will void the contract."

"Of course," John agreed, and Anora could tell he was already done discussing this topic. He cleared his throat. "At the risk of sounding fatherly..."

Anora rolled her eyes. John was a capable manager, but he tended toward being patronizing. "Go ahead."

"How are you doing? I know you've been ill of late..."

"It's been almost a month, John. I've missed a few things, but I'm doing quite well now." She paused, then added, "Thank you for asking."

"We should do dinner sometime. We have a few items to go over. Transfer of assets. Some of your brother's possessions—his house in New York. Things like that."

"A social call?"

"Business first," John said jovially. "You've got some legal workings that we should iron out as well."

"Of course."

"I've transmitted a report on the new microsat to your inbox via Quantum. I have a physical copy also."

"You can dispose or store as you like. I'd prefer the former over the latter." Anora suppressed a yawn. "John, I'm running two companies now. My brother left things to your capable hands, and I don't plan on changing that. I want Telemachus to remain solvent and profitable. Telemachus has the brain trust to be able to build its own rockets now. Add that to the microsat systems and we can double profits in a couple of years. Let's keep moving in the right direction."

"Of course."

"I'll look over the report and send you my thoughts."

"Very much like your brother. Good-bye, Anora."

One hung up for Anora. She took her glasses off and thought for a moment. "I'm going to go for a walk."

"I'll alert Simon," One replied.

She grabbed her coat and both terminals and jogged down the steps. The lab was quiet. It was early morning and she'd been working on building the necessary tools to unpack and restore the system that resided on Indiana's old Janus device.

She buttoned up her coat and went out into the frigid winter air. A couple in cold-weather running gear jogged by, but otherwise, the street was deserted. In a few hours, there would be a bustle of activity as locals got up to be about their day. She'd worked on AI reconstruction since the beginning. She offloaded all of the CAMLANN work to Roxanne to solve and lead the rest of the team. With occasional guidance from Anora, the team managed just fine. They would be finished in a few months, after extensive testing.

Anora cleared her mind. She had a lot of research and correspondence to catch up on—John's call had reminded her of that. One managed most of her correspondence, only flagging things that required responses, but even that piled up. One was an incredibly useful assistant who probably knew Anora better than anyone in her life. That wound her mind back to Maven and what Arthur had left her.

She thought about breakfast and her stomach rumbled in response. She grew cold, so she called Simon to take her to her new flat. Simon, driving her personal car, arrived in short order. He was always alert to her movements. She had good people around her. That made her think of Arthur again. Why?

When they arrived at her new address, Anora got out of her car, and Simon followed her. She punched in the door code and entered the building. Anora steeled herself and got onto the glass elevator just as another man bundled head to foot walked in and veered toward the elevators himself. He charged onto the elevator next to her.

"Floor?" Anora asked absently.

"Whatever floor you're going to," the man said.

Anora's senses, already jittery in the enclosed space, jumped to alertness. Simon's body shifted. He was ready.

The man took off his heavy hat. He unwound the scarf and smiled at Anora. "Dr. Myrrdin?"

"Yes?"

"I'm Percy Jones. You might not remember me, but we met on board the Raven."

"Ma'am?" Simon said, sensing the tension in her voice.

"It's all right," Anora said. "MacGabran?"

"We need to talk."

"You should make an appointment," Simon said. Percy took off his gloves, and his fingers were bare. If he was Avallach, he didn't have his focal rings on. It was, Anora understood, a sign of trust.

Anora put a hand on Simon's arm as the elevator door opened. "Come on in," she said, opening the apartment door and walking into her spacious unused apartment. She tossed her keys on the counter. A man was seated at her dining room table.

"What the hell?" Anora said.

"I did say 'we,'" Percy said. His hands were at his sides, ready for a fight but not threatening violence.

"How did you get into my apartment?"

"It's quite secure, but if you have patience . . . ," the man at the table said.

"Want me to call security, ma'am?" Simon said. He stayed close beside her, ready to defend. He had a hand in his pocket, though Anora couldn't say if it held a gun or a panic button.

Anora shook her head. She turned to Percy. "You, I know." She turned to the other man. "You. You're not one of them."

The man at the table had short spiky hair and the air of a Tibetan monk. Anora flipped through her mental files, her fingers twitching to grab her terminal. In a second, she had the information. "Captain River Qilin."

The man named River inclined his head in assent.

"Military police and data analytics are your military occupational specialties. I see," she concluded, and regretted not having One's sensor suite installed before coming here. She was trapped. At least she had room and didn't feel confined. She glanced out at the skyline of the city, then back to these two men. "A bit convenient of you to show up just now." It was true. Anora had researched every thread she could find out about Avallach.

"I've been working on a case," River replied. He looked at Percy. "Percy tracked me down. He said you needed the information I have."

"Information about my brother's death?"

River nodded but looked confused. "Yes, I do. That is a bit of a journey if you want to take it. You weren't given any orders?"

Anora shook her head. "I've not been told anything by Arthur MacGabran."

River seemed to nod at that, satisfied. "That's good. I was afraid I was too late. Awaiting your orders, ma'am."

Anora placed a hand on the counter. "You have me at a disadvantage. You've come here expecting me to have commands for you. What for?"

"Whatever it is you need us to do," River said.

"You and Percy?"

"My group. Percy is not a part of that."

Percy's stance was closed and unreadable. He looked doubtful, but when Anora stared him down, he said, "I've been assigned to you, for the time being, ma'am."

"You're the highest-ranking officer?"

River chuckled. "We no longer hold military rank, ma'am."

"Then stop calling me ma'am. I'm not paying you."

"Yes, ma'am."

"What are you?"

"We're the people you're going to need when things turn very bad."

"This already sounds like one of those times." Anora regained her composure. Nothing had happened in the first few minutes. She took out her terminal and put it on the counter. She turned to her aide. "Simon, it'll be all right. If I need you, I or One will contact you."

"I'll check with building security." Simon was unhappy, but he nodded and left the apartment. Anora made herself tea, glad the apartment was appropriately stocked. At least One had gotten that right, though she couldn't exactly blame the AI for missing such a security breach. She should've expected it when she jumped into this morass. Everything should have been roughly where it was laid out in her home in California, so she only stuttered through the motions.

"Tea?"

River and Percy declined.

"Why are you here?"

"I explained it to you."

"No. You're a failed Avallach candidate. That doesn't explain why you're here."

"I'm here because of Arthur. I'm on your side."

Anora finished her tea and waited. No one spoke. She knew she had to drive this conversation. "I'm not on anybody's 'side.' I'm going to find out who murdered my brother and make them pay for it."

"You want to know who killed your brother?"

"That would be a start," Anora replied, sitting down at her table. "You said it would be a journey?"

River nodded.

"One, how much time do you need to compile and restore the data on Janny?"

"Current estimate is approximately two days," One replied.

Anora turned to River. "Is it far?"

"Just a plane ride to the Caribbean is all we need."

"And I'll know what happened to my brother?"

"I started in the military police but had an opportunity to move into the 'cybersecurity' side of things."

Anora sneered. She hated that word, 'cyber.' It made things sound more important or ominous than they were.

"When Arthur restored me—"

"Restored? You were discharged from Avallach and then medically discharged from the army."

"Yes. I thought about getting a job in the technology sector, but Arthur put me to an impossible task."

"Trying to get me onto a plane to the Caribbean?"

Percy snorted a laugh at that.

"The first impossible task," River corrected himself. "I investigated the loss of your brother's plane. I also found contradictory evidence that did not support the information provided in regards to the crash. Why was your brother's flight pattern routed over the ocean, for example?"

"And you found something that I haven't?"

River shook his head. "Not along that line of theory. There were too many dead ends and inquiries were not going to solve the problem. So, I went to the reported crash site and tried to find the plane."

"That's fruitless."

"It is if the plane was reported to be in the wrong location."

"Look, I know all of this. The area of uncertainty introduced by the contradiction is too large to search. I can't determine if the fuselage components they found were actually in the location reported."

River nodded. "I stumbled along another hypothesis while I was out there."

Anora leaned forward.

River folded his hands. "What if at least one of the passengers survived?"

"If the plane was struck by a missile, no one would survive."

River smiled. "I may have found the right contradiction that works in your favor then."

"You found a survivor?"

River nodded.

"In the Caribbean?"

"Interested now?"

"Yes, but why not bring him or her here?"

"It's an investigation and you need to be a part of the discovery. If I brought this person to you, would you believe them?"

"Reasonable. Yes, I'm interested."

"Then it may be two impossible tasks I've been able to accomplish."

Anora looked to Percy. "You could've led with that. Or Arthur could've." Percy spread his hands and opened his mouth. "I know, I know." It left Anora feeling uneasy. She didn't like this at all. But what choice did she have? "We're not taking your plane or helicopter or flying whatevers. If you're going to kidnap me, at least we can take my plane."

~

GRAND BAHAMA ISLAND—

Anora's private jet landed at West End in the warm early morning air. It taxied and parked. Anora, River, and Percy got out. An attendant was waiting for them and handed Anora a set of car keys.

Anora was dressed in a simple silk blouse and skirt. River and Percy were dressed in short sleeves and shorts for the warm weather. It was a large change from the cold weather of the DC area. Anora got into the waiting late-model Mustang.

"Don't trust my right-handed driving?" River asked as Percy hopped into the back.

"I don't think you've ever driven on the correct side of the road," Anora replied, emphasizing her normally light British accent. She started the car and it rumbled to life. In moments they were out of the airport and driving up the coast at a leisurely thirty-five miles per hour. "I hope this trip is worth it."

"It will be." River put on a pair of Ray-Ban Wayfarers and looked out over the blue ocean.

Anora thought about Arthur MacGabran. He was obviously working from a script that only he knew about, and she wondered if he might be who Maven was looking for to prove his theorem. She made a mental note to see how good of a fit Arthur was for the theorem—not that it would make him any more interesting, but it would lead her to understanding why her brother had been so interested in him.

Anora shook her head. She admitted he was a fine-looking man, and sharp, though not an academic. Why should that be important to her? She'd fallen for the academic/athletic mix before with incredibly disastrous results. She recalled all the intramural soccer games she'd attended to watch Reince play. Should she try something new with Arthur? She wasn't about to make one move toward him.

The warm, humid air made her blouse stick to her skin. She was glad she'd chosen to wear a bathing suit beneath her blouse. She was not about to miss out on a chance to enjoy a bit of sun, even if for a few hours.

She glanced back in her rearview mirror. Percy had put his rings back on and he clearly did not trust Anora at all. Anora had a thick enough skin to not let it bother her. From their small talk on the plane, she understood that Percy was doing this more as a favor to Arthur than out of any sort of real desire to protect her. *I don't need protection*, she reminded herself. She'd left Simon and his small cadre back in the States. If she could manage to show trust to these Avallach people, it would give her an edge when she needed it. She smiled to herself—Arthur surrounded himself with trustworthy people. Could she use Percy in some way?

She drove along the northern coast of Grand Bahama Island toward Xanadu Beach. River motioned for them to park, and Anora nosed the Mustang into a spot. She pulled on a pair of fashionable white-framed sunglasses that matched her wardrobe. She expected to walk toward Xanadu Beach, but River turned away from the main beach and walked along the shoreline. Percy hopped out. He had his tech glasses on, darkened for day. The sand was already warming but not yet hot from the morning sun.

"Have you read the reports on the Avallach candidates' abilities? I spent some time studying what Arthur had archived," River said.

"Stop bullets, enhanced senses. Superhero stuff?" Anora bluffed. Truth was, she knew little of what had been done at Avallach. Only what she had experienced firsthand. She shivered despite the warm breeze.

Percy spoke. "Maven did a lot of tests at Avallach—strength, endurance, speed, all of that. Not just comparing what they could do with manifesting, but looking at how the genetic manipulation changed us. Those of us who made it, that is."

"Most of the Avallach team is already in peak physical condition."

"Which makes it all the more interesting that we achieved considerably higher gains," River said.

"I don't think they'll be participating in the Olympics any time soon," Anora quipped, then remembered the former Olympian who was a part of Avallach. *Indiana Beckham.* It was annoying how often the dead woman came to mind.

"We made large gains in endurance. You could run farther than previously thought, with and without manifesting. They found that even just after manifesting, you could reach beyond your previous limits. It was as if the body had stored extra energy that you could tap into. Normally without the field, the waveform was useless, but this was an interesting effect."

"How long do you think that energy could last?"

River shrugged. "I don't think they explored the true depth of it."

Percy shrugged and shook his head.

River looked out over the ocean. "Good day for surfing, I think."

"Do you surf?"

River smiled. "No chance to, and the army isn't exactly a place where you spend a lot of time near water. There was the navy for that. Too bad, though. I'd like to go to Hawaii."

"I spent all my time in sandy places," Percy added.

"You should go there sometime, it's incredible," Anora said. She had a house on Kauai, though she hadn't been there in years. She loved to swim and surf, but her claustrophobia made snorkeling and diving too difficult. Her treatment had made it worse, it seemed.

River watched the ocean. There were a few surfers out on the early morning waves. A surfer rode a wave neatly to shore and then hopped off of her board. She had long black hair and dark skin and she wore a one-piece of sunset hues, like fire upon the water. Anora frowned. *It couldn't be her, could it?*

The surfer picked up her board and planted it in the sand, unstrapping her ankle strap and pulling the wet strands of hair from her face.

River headed toward her, and Anora saw that his gait had shifted to something determined. She sped after him and Percy trailed after.

The woman was powerfully built. Every bit of her frame was muscular—the frame of a bodybuilder. Her black hair was slicked back on her head. The woman considered another trip into the waves but sensed their approach. She turned to face them, and the startled expression on her face was unmistakable. She grabbed her board reflexively, wanting to run, but then froze in place.

River made a noise of surprise himself. His hands were shaking. He drew close. "It's you."

The woman stared at River for a long time, then said, "It's me." And they embraced each other, like long-lost lovers.

Anora watched the exchange, perplexed for a moment. Her logic took hold and she sorted through the right information. *Not her*, Anora thought. *But someone useful. Someone dead.* This was Captain Priya Ellen Noire, USAF.

After a moment, River and Ellen parted, holding hands.

"I've been looking for you," River said.

"I've been trying to not be found," Ellen said. She had refined Indian features and was about Anora's age, perhaps a little older. She looked strong enough to crush that board beneath her arm. "I didn't think he'd send you. Goddamn Arthur." Ellen shook her head with a rueful smile. "Always doing the impossible."

"He said you needed me."

Percy's face was dark, but she could see the look of surprise. Ellen stepped to him. He smiled at her. "Damn, Cap. It is you."

"It is." Ellen returned the smile. "What does Arthur want to do with me?"

River stood there for a moment looking at Ellen, then looked back out at the ocean. "I'd like a drink."

Percy nodded. "That's a good idea."

"At ten in the morning?" Anora asked.

"Nothing prepares you for the shock of finding someone you've been told a hundred times is dead," Percy said.

"I run a bar." Ellen hooked a thumb over her shoulder, then squinted at Anora. "Who's this?"

"I'm sorry. This is Anora Myrrdin. Maven's sister."

Ellen's face went gray as she moved to shake Anora's hand.

Anora shook her hand anyway. It was strong, powerful, but trembling.

"You look nothing like your brother," Ellen said.

"Half brother. My father's Korean, not Arab like Maven's. You are?" Anora asked, but already knew the answer.

The woman hesitated. "*Koee nahin.*" I sounded Hindi to Anora.

"Bullshit," River said. "Anora, this is Captain Priya Ellen Noire. Ellen. She blew up the *Archimedes* and was the pilot of Maven's plane."

"You're dead," Anora said.

"Yes to all of that," Ellen said.

"You killed Indy?" Percy said, the disbelief plain on his face.

"And Kai."

"Kai's alive," Percy said. The dark anger on his face was barely controlled rage. Ellen had betrayed them.

"Kai's alive? And Jeri?"

"Yeah, you bitch," Percy said.

Anora stepped between them. "Stop. Your job is to watch over me, right?"

Percy glared at Ellen, then at Anora. He clenched his fist.

"Listen to me. Let's find out what happened, then I get to say what we do next."

"The fuck you say," spat Percy.

"The fuck I say." Anora poked him in the chest. Percy stared at Anora and then backed down. *This guy can keep his cool*, she thought, and filed that away.

Anora turned back to Ellen. "Let's get that drink and hear all about it. Now."

10

NO-FLY ZONE

OFF THE EASTERN COAST OF FLORIDA, FIVE MONTHS AGO—
Ellen set the autopilot and leaned back in her seat. They were in for a short flight up the coast. The approved flight path took them out over the Atlantic and then hinged westward toward the small regional airport where they kept Maven's plane. She thought of Indiana and emotion welled up inside her. She rubbed her hands together, feeling *Asi* cold against her skin. She pushed the thoughts away.

Analisa sat next to her in the copilot seat. "You all right?"

"Just thinking of my family for a moment," Ellen lied.

Maven entered the cockpit.

"Should be home in a couple of hours," Ellen reported automatically.

"Is it home?" Maven said, surprising her when he spoke. "I rather think we'll have other things to contend with."

"What do you mean?"

"When these kind of people make mistakes, they start to correct or erase them."

Maven left the compartment.

Ellen looked at Analisa, who gripped the controls and nodded. She'd been traveling so much with her that Analisa had taken flying lessons. *The girl is like an information sponge*, Ellen thought.

Ellen pulled off her headset and went after Maven. "What do you mean?"

Maven turned back to her. "Sam escaped. Do you think that'll pass quietly when we find out who was behind his kidnapping?"

Ellen had a dark pit in her stomach. "It'd be nice to know."

"Cornwall wouldn't take that lightly."

"You're saying he did it?"

"Use your brain, Noire." He saw her forlorn look. "Marks was useful to a point. Distracted by other problems. Working with someone like that's quite dicey, but we've got to deal with it now. We've no other choice."

An alarm buzzed in the flight deck and Ellen returned to it just as an angular black fighter jet rocketed past the Gulfstream. "Shit!" Ellen exclaimed.

"Something on the headset," Analisa said.

She put her headset back on. "Golf Lima Seven Three, alter course to one three five immediately or we will be forced to take action." The voice was the pilot of the stealth fighter.

Ellen keyed the mike. "This is Golf Lima Seven Three, our flight path has been approved—"

"Golf Lima, alter course to one three five."

She snapped on the intercom. "Take a seat everyone. Going to get bumpy."

"What's going on?" Millicent asked from the passenger compartment.

"Someone coming to correct a mistake," Ellen replied. She saw it now. She was a collaborator, and Marks could not have it known that she was the one who'd sabotaged *Archimedes*.

"Analisa, get the portable pack," Maven said. "Emergency power up."

Analisa got up from the copilot seat and stumbled into the main cabin.

Ellen disengaged the autopilot and pulled hard on the controls. The routine procedure would be to alter the flight path to a course that was not dangerous. They were directing her out to sea. She didn't have the fuel, which meant they intended to shoot them down once they got far enough out to sea. Altering course to comply wouldn't help, but staying steady wouldn't help either. *Let's see about that*, she thought.

She throttled up the engines and nosed into a steep dive. The Gulfstream IV wasn't designed to pull hard maneuvers, so its turn and dive felt interminably long to a combat-trained pilot like Ellen. She heard shouts from her passengers.

"Golf Lima, do not accelerate or change altitude—"

Ellen ignored it. They'd be weapons hot now, coming around to fire a missile at them. She had nothing though—no countermeasures or counterfire. She raced against time with no way out. She leveled the plane at a couple of thousand feet above sea level. If she was lucky, the radar flight pattern would make it obvious. Someone might notice, but then again, this was probably a Homeland Security response. *Fucking Marks*, she thought bitterly.

Maven stumbled into the cabin. "Put this on," he said, shoving a large backpack into her hands.

"I'm busy flying for our lives!"

Maven fell into the copilot seat and grasped the controls. "Do you think we'll all make it out alive? The system's active. Use it."

Ellen did feel the prickle of the field in the back of her neck. She seized the waveform and energy trickled through her body. Everything snapped into bright clarity. *Asi* glittered. "If we can get low enough—"

"Put the bloody pack on," Maven said. The fighter roared overhead. "I'll keep the plane straight now."

"They'll come around, go hot, and that'll be it," Ellen said. She pulled on the pack, strapping it quickly to her body. This was a carbon-fiber design, built with a hard shell. They'd been testing it as an emergency solution since the portable pack in Geneva had worked out well. "I have a shield. If you all get close—"

"Just do your job and survive. You owe me." Maven locked his eyes on Ellen. The proximity alarm buzzed again, then blared.

Heat seeker. Ellen turned to face the back of the plane and manifested to her maximum. She snapped the KE field on her left arm just as the plane exploded.

In movies, when a plane, car, or train exploded, it was always through some demolition device that blew it to smithereens, or a CGI trick. In the real world, pieces and parts of the plane blew apart but weren't obliterated by the blast. This was why black boxes and wreckage survived. If the movies were believed, you'd be lucky to find something larger than a toothpick after a plane was destroyed.

Ellen was thrown back into the cockpit and slammed against the windshield. Her KE shield and field absorbed a lot of the blow, but everything went topsy turvy. She saw night sky and dark water through seams breaking apart. The wreckage of the plane, no longer one cohesive unit, was still traveling at speed and now blowing outward from the explosive force of the heat-seeking missile. Ellen closed her eyes and felt gravity take immediate effect. She opened her eyes. She was pinned inside the wreckage of the cockpit in free fall. With adrenaline and manifest power pumping in her veins, time dilated. She had about ten seconds before she hit the water, give or take. *You owe me*, Maven had said.

Asi flicked to life and Ellen cut away the wreckage that pinned her to the side of the flight deck. The seats were gone and so was Maven. Analisa and Millicent, too. She cut more and pushed herself from the cockpit, free of the debris. It floated away from her. The night was lit by the fireballing jet fuel behind her, but she focused on the dark expanse of water below her. She accelerated every second and used her parachute training to provide as much drag on her body as possible. She wished Maven had given her a damn parachute instead of the gridpack. Typical genius. The water rushed up at her and the wind roared in her ears. *Asi* disappeared. Should she use her KE shield? She was a powerful swimmer, so if she was going to live, she'd have to knife into the ocean and hope the impact did not break any bones. If not—

She straightened her body like a diver, toes pointed to the water. She had a surprising amount of time to get her body under control. She passed some debris. She raised her arms and pushed her field up to maximum again. She hit the water like a hammer hitting glass.

Ellen blacked out for a moment, but pain and swallowing water woke her up. Her whole body hurt, but her shoulders really hurt like hell. The gridpack had nearly ripped from her body, taking her arms with it on impact. She regained consciousness deep underwater. She began to breathe, and nearly choked with the intake of water. She clamped her mouth shut and fought against the coughing fit that seized her. She grasped the waveform again and felt the energy in her body. She paused to reorient herself after the impact, found up, and swam to the surface. Her left arm screamed in pain. Could she make it? Her lungs burned and wanted to clear the water from her system. Something white flashed close by her—piece of the fuselage, probably. She felt its pull as it passed. She swam with all her energy. God, her shoulders hurt like hell. She needed air. It hurt to even raise her left arm. Dislocated? She kicked hard for the growing light above her. *Too bright to be starlight*, she thought. Burning fuel. She was going the right way. Manifest power propelled her beaten body.

She broke the surface and gasped for air, coughing. She rolled onto her back and took deep breaths. Debris fell around her in small splashes. Most of the plane had already impacted the water, but a few pieces had been blown skyward and were now returning from their ballistic arc. She grasped her shoulder and rolled into it. It popped back into its socket and she screamed in agony. She would've passed out, except she sank and almost sucked in a lungful of water. She kicked back to the surface and onto her back. She was able to move her arm again, though it was weak. The stealth fighter was already gone. Heading back to Tyndall, she guessed.

She thought about her passengers. Millicent, Analisa, and Maven. She called out to them, but no one responded. *Observe, orient, decide, act*, she reminded herself. She took inventory. She had her clothing; she was dressed for summer, though a bit worse for wear. She had her G-Shock digital watch, a gift from her husband and Tor when she was triathlon training. She had the gridpack, which seemed still operational. She had a wallet, but no food and no water. *Drinkable water*, she corrected herself. She looked at her watch again. It was still operating. Good to two hundred meters, so it had survived. Tor and Dilip had paid too much for it, she had said, and she only used half the features of it. It had a tidal indicator, temperature sensor, atomic clock, compass—

She checked the compass. It worked. She rolled onto her back for a moment, catching her breath and thinking. Finally, she oriented herself and swam in long leisurely strokes, hoping she was nowhere near the Gulf Stream.

11

FAMILY PROBLEMS

GRAND BAHAMA ISLAND, PRESENT DAY—
"You swam to the Bahamas?" Anora said. "That must've been a few hundred miles." Anora's stomach churned and she was glad for the warm breeze cooling the flop sweat. Listening to Ellen talk about being submerged in the dark made her react as if she were experiencing that closing feeling herself.

Ellen nodded. "I wasn't even sure I'd make it. I didn't have a map, but only a general idea. I thought if I stayed in a straight line I'd make it to an island. If I didn't, then I wasn't meant to live. I almost didn't make it, but the tide washed me up onto Koopa Beach." Ellen put more ice into her drink. The day was warming, and Ellen's hair had dried. "I'm lucky to be alive. I wasn't swept out to sea by the Gulf Stream and I more or less made it to a destination. I must've slept on Koopa for a day before someone found me. I was nearly dead from exhaustion, but some locals nursed me back to health. All the while, I had a decision to make."

Ellen ran her fingers through her hair.

Percy was wisely quiet, though Anora could see he wore his anger openly. *He's a thinker*, she warned herself.

River looked into his drink. "Whether to come back or stay dead?

If you stayed dead, your family wouldn't be in danger. Was that what he used against you?"

Ellen's lips compressed into a thin line and her brow furrowed. "I wasn't going to have them used against me again."

"And you've been here this whole time? It's been what? Five months?"

"I made my way to Grand Bahama after I got back to reasonable health. I spent the rest of my money trying to drink myself to death. That only lasted a month. Then I decided to take up a small life here. I surf, tend bar, and know that my family is free."

"And the gridpack?" River asked.

"Buried in my hut. It still works, but I haven't manifested since the day I made it to the beach. I've wanted to, but all it would do is remind me of what I did. I knew we found Sam's signature, and I didn't want to be found. Satisfied?"

River reached across the bar and took her hand. "The story wasn't for me."

Ellen smiled. "Your turn. Last time I saw you, you were in a coma in Elysium. Just about brain-dead."

"Now, that's an interesting story," River said. "I'll tell you all about it, but first—" River turned to Anora. "Is this enough proof? Someone who was there when Maven died."

Anora nodded. "You said the stealth jet came from Tyndall?"

"Closest military airfield to Canaveral with a stealth wing."

"Then the kill order came from someone higher up. Higher than Arthur. Higher than Marks."

"Marks," Ellen spat.

"Don't worry, he's dead," Anora said. "Killed by a waveblade a few weeks ago."

"I wish it was mine," Ellen said, flexing her muscled right arm.

Anora frowned. "Marks was working on a second project. Another group of manifest candidates."

Ellen said, "I suspected, though that cagey bastard never said a word."

"He can't hold your family over your head."

Ellen shook her head. "He can't, but the council can."

"Council?" Anora asked.

"Marks was a part of a council. A sort of group of DARPA program directors. They manage all the projects within DARPA. It's presided over by the defense secretary. That's how they keep abreast of what is going on, continue to fund projects, and terminate those without potential. Once Marks had gotten me into the fold, he explained at least that much to me. I had to know a bit of the bigger picture—to see the danger they posed. And to ensure I knew that just killing him would not end the danger for my family."

Anora saw the change in Ellen, saw this confident woman who looked free and powerful in the surf break down. She saw her faith in Arthur—saw the betrayal in her body. Anora knew from her deep research that something was too perfect in the flight records. But something like this could only be covered at a higher level—the secretary of defense. Anora hadn't thought it went that high. She'd even talked to the secretary about Maven. Her mind whirred a bit, but she pulled herself back to the moment.

"... gave her up, Riv," Ellen was saying.

"I didn't know then. Arthur told me when he put me on the task."

"You could've told us," Percy said. "No man or woman is an island. You think Mac would've let that stand? Or any of us?"

"You think you know what you're saying, but you don't have a family. You don't think about that when they're being threatened directly. This isn't some insurgent promising to take out your hometown or blow up your family. He meant to ruin my family, and he had the ability to do it."

"We're not family?" Percy asked.

"It's not the same." Ellen glowered. "You'd know that if you had a family. It's fine to put yourself in danger, but the moment you put them in harm's way? Different story. What if something happened to Lamar?"

Percy pressed his lips together. *Ellen has given him something to think about*, Anora thought.

"Are you ready to get back to it?" River asked.

"What?"

"Arthur needs you, Ellen."

"I got people killed."

Percy had a closed expression. Anora guessed he'd seen enough people die from mistakes. He wasn't buying Ellen's argument.

River looked around him at the serene paradise. "Is this what you want? To surf and tend bar?"

"Seems like a good life," Anora said. A warm breeze wafted off the ocean and she closed her eyes for a moment. All thoughts of submersion were gone and she was back to herself.

Ellen was silent.

"Is this what she'd want you to do? To quit? To drop out of life and be nothing?" River asked.

"Don't make me," Ellen whispered.

"You have to. You made the decision to betray Arthur. He's giving you a chance to fix things. You can't bring anyone back, but you can help him. Help us."

Ellen shook her head. "I'm not risking my family again."

"They don't know you're alive. Not yet. And they won't know until we're already done. He's not letting you quit, Ellen."

Ellen set her jaw. Her body tensed and a war of emotions battled within her. Her failure and now a chance. Finally, she seemed to settle with a decision. She pulled her hand away from River's.

"No."

River seemed disappointed.

Anora frowned. "Why would Arthur want a traitor back?"

It was Percy who surprised Anora. "Not everyone who betrays another is an evil person. Weren't you listening?"

It was said gently, but it felt like a slap to her face. Anora thought about Ellen's story and her own pain. "Does Arthur really need her back?"

"Yes."

Anora turned to Ellen, who was getting things ready for another day tending bar. "What did Maven tell you? 'You owe me,' he said?"

Ellen nodded.

"He was my bloody brother, so that means you owe me."

The war of emotions returned on Ellen's face. "I don't—"

Anora reached across the bar and slapped Ellen hard in the face. "Don't give me this shite. You got my brother killed, so you work for me now."

Ellen, who had taken the slap like a soldier, only nodded. "What do you want me to do?"

Anora turned to River and Percy. "There. She's all yours."

"No, she's all yours. We're both yours."

"You're going to have to explain that to me, because my plan involves a lot of revenge."

12

INTO DARK CORNERS I GO

WASHINGTON, DC—
The Gulfstream IV touched down at Dulles and taxied to its leased hangar. Anora stretched and got up. It had been a short reprieve from her work, but there were things to attend to. Changed back into her winter clothing, she grabbed her coat as the door was opened. Simon met her on the steps.

"Have a good trip, ma'am?" Simon asked, looking around for anyone else. Seeing no one, he gave Anora a questioning look.

"My clients took another route. My business with them is done for now." Anora wasn't sure why she felt the need to explain, but Simon had accompanied her to the airport to see her off. "Yes, I'd say it was productive," Anora replied. She pulled her terminal out. There was a lot of work going on at Binary proper, but she flipped through those updates to see what was going on at her little skunkworks. One had already sorted things for her. She was halfway through the list before she noticed that Simon hadn't moved from the steps of the plane to escort her to the car. "Something wrong?"

"Someone here to see you, ma'am. Federal Bureau of Investigation."

"Christ. Do we have a problem with customs? That's TSA and DHS authority."

"They're here for you specifically, ma'am."

"Probably mad Binary is ending some critical contract work." It couldn't be helped. She'd warned Director O'Brian that she wanted Binary AI to be out of any direct government work in the coming months and years. They had more private industry needing their services than they could actually handle. Once they knew that Binary was out of government work, two things would happen—other, lesser companies will fill the void, do a fair job at a fair price, and the demand for private industry work would spike. Anora needed to hire more people, but standards at Binary were incredibly high.

Anora buttoned her coat and put on her sunglasses. "All right, then. One, contact my attorneys. Notify them that I am being questioned by the FBI. Put them in touch with Simon."

"Contacting them now," One replied.

Anora walked off the plane to two waiting agents. One was husky, like a football player a few years into retirement. The other was a brunette with a severe look and a touch of gray in her hair.

"Dr. Anora Myrrdin? CEO of Binary AI and president of Telemachus?" the woman asked.

"Yes?"

"I'm Special Agent Gail Haut and this is Special Agent Rem Sagramore. Would you come with us please?"

Anora looked past the agents to their black Suburban and the police cruisers parked beyond. She put her hand in her pocket, reaching for her terminal. She smiled at the agents. "I hope you haven't been waiting long, Agent Haut."

"Not long, Ms. Myrrdin. Just waiting for your plane to touch down. This way, if you please."

"Before we go, may I ask if you have an arrest warrant?"

"No warrant, Ms. Myrrdin. Just want to ask you a few questions. You do have the right to remain silent and to an attorney."

Anora wondered briefly what would happen if she refused to get into the Suburban, then let the thought go. She wouldn't be able to do anything about it yet.

They escorted Anora to the awaiting suburban. "Hope it's a short drive."

THE SHORT DRIVE turned out to be a long drive deep into Virginia. Anora had expected to be taken to the Washington, DC, field office and was surprised when they turned south on I-395 instead of north. She was allowed to keep her terminal while they drove, so she took the time to go through her work pile. There didn't seem to be anything she could find that would directly correlate Binary's unwind with her "questioning," but when you operated at the level Anora did, politics were almost certainly involved somehow.

She arrived at a small sheriff's office. Her terminal said it was in Culpeper. In Culpeper County, which made Anora feel like it was recursing. They brought her to a quaint white room with gray chairs and a gray table. There was the faint scent of Murphy's Oil somewhere, perhaps the hardwood floor. They confiscated her coat and terminal, but not before she'd locked it down. Anora doubted that they had the ability to do forensic analysis on One, but if they stalled, they'd certainly transfer it to one of the FBI's analyst facilities with a Faraday cage and sophisticated hacking software. She smiled. She'd be disappointed if they didn't.

She sat alone for an hour. Though the room was bare, it didn't feel small. It helped her anxiety.

Before the walls started pressing in, Agents Haut and Sagramore walked into the room. Agent Haut carried a file and sat down. "Sorry for the delay—"

"Having a little trouble with something?"

"Just some bureaucratic nonsense. I'm sure you deal with that on a daily basis with your companies."

"From time to time," Anora lied. Truth was, she preferred not to deal with the day-to-day doings of the business. If you got too far down into the weeds, it wasted time. It was best left to those whose expertise allowed her to work on her own research. "You've been pretty quiet on why I'm here. This is questioning, right?"

"As have you," Haut said, opening her folder.

"Right to remain silent," Anora intoned.

Haut slid a picture of Arthur MacGabran across the table. "Do you know this man?"

Anora stared at the picture. It was grainy, but his features were unmistakable. "The Apollo guy?"

"We think you know him," Haut said. She flipped out the second photograph. It showed Anora talking to Arthur. When had that been taken? Anora guessed it had been after her return from *Camelot*.

"That's interesting. It seems that I do. I could also be asking for directions. It's just a photo. Wait. Do you think I accidentally ran into Apollo?"

Sagramore blew out his lips. "We've reason to believe you know this man."

Anora stared at the towering man. Her hands were clasped on the table. She didn't like intimidation, but men like this were not the threatening kind to her. They wore their physicality on the outside. They were far less dangerous than the men who held it on the inside and revealed it when you least expected it. Men like Reince.

"His name is Arthur MacGabran. He's a former naval officer, special operations."

"Oh, well, that means you have more information on him than I do. I bet he has physical fitness scores, fingerprints, and DNA markers, right?"

"So you're denying any association with Mr. MacGabran?"

"No. I'm saying I don't know him all that well. Clearly, you think I know him better because of a photograph."

"Perhaps your brother knew him better than you did?" Haut proposed.

That hit a nerve, but Anora held her reserve. Damn, they'd come in quick on that angle. She closed her eyes for a second, putting together the last few days. Arthur had had nothing to do with her brother's death. She knew that now. But what did they know? She looked at Haut. "Does it matter what my brother knew? He's dead now. The FBI and DHS closed the books on his murder months ago."

"Who said he was murdered?" Sagramore asked.

Anora smiled. "Did you find the black box?"

Haut and Sagramore exchanged looks. They hadn't reviewed her brother's file yet.

"Am I under arrest?"

"We have reason to believe you have information on Arthur MacGabran. If you don't provide it, we'll have to detain you."

Anora spread her hands. "Looks like I'm being detained. Can I have my phone back so I can call my attorneys?"

"Your items have been transferred to another facility. We should have them back in short order."

"I'd still like to talk to my attorneys," Anora said.

Haut and Sagramore stared down at Anora for a long moment. These agents were seasoned, but they didn't seem to have the complete picture on Arthur MacGabran. They sure as hell didn't have the full picture on Anora herself. She wasn't immune to prosecution, of course, but she expected a modicum of courtesy. Perhaps they didn't know about her previous government work?

"Since a phone call isn't forthcoming, I'd like you to at least put in a request to speak with Director Zeke O'Brian of the National Security Agency. Or I'd like to talk to your assistant director in charge. ADIC Paul Mead, I think his name is. It's been a while since I've spoken to him, but he might remember me."

"Name dropping isn't going to help you," Sagramore tested.

"There's only one person in this room that's running two successful companies employing thousands of people. I'm sure you think you can lock me into a tiny hole to never be heard from again, but trust me, you won't be able to keep this quiet for long. What you may not know, because the three-letter agencies don't always share information on their inner workings, is that I've done work for Director O'Brian. You know I have held a top secret SCI clearance initiated by the NSA security branch. Binary AI still has contracts with your agency. So, as a courtesy to your careers, you'll let Director O'Brian know that I'm here."

"You can't threaten us," Haut said.

"I'm threatening you?" Anora chuckled. "Phone call."

Haut stood and swept up the file. "The sheriff will escort you to your cell."

Anora ignored her. She had closed her mind off to them. After a moment, the local sheriff escorted her to a cell. It was small and as old-fashioned as the building it resided in. Still, it was modernized and solid in its construction. She walked in and sat down. The entire detention area was devoid of people. *That's why it was chosen*, Anora thought. They'd called her bluff, but this wasn't the dank tiny hole they were going to throw her in. It was just the first hole of many possible holes. There was plenty of light and again the walls were painted white, though here it was more of an eggshell, and the floors were stained concrete. It smelled faintly of disinfectant and Pine-Sol.

She was drained from talking to the agents. It took a lot of energy to pay attention to their words and not lash out at them for the things their agency had failed to do for her. She went through some of the kata motions to warm herself up. She needed to get into a dojo and resolved to have One enroll her in a local one. Throwing a few people to the mat had a cathartic effect. After half an hour, it was apparent that time was being used against her. She sat down on the edge of her cot. It wasn't a bad room she'd been placed in. The mattress wasn't exactly threadbare and while it was the source of the disinfectant smell, it was tidy and clean. She stared at the cell door and felt the creeping anxiety clawing up her throat. It was coming back and there was nothing she could do to fight it.

Curling up into a ball on the bed, she shut out all images of the room inside her head, but all that did was conjure up images of the tiny bedroom of her childhood. And then the clawing dark places Reince had put her. She felt paralyzed with fear and shook with panic. Still broken.

∽

"It's been a while since we've talked. At least like this," Maven said.

"It's just a neural short circuit," Anora said, rolling over to look at her brother. It was dark now, lights-out in the detention area, and Maven's face was cast in shadow. He sat at the foot of her bed.

"Hmm," Maven said. "Short circuits are such a poor analogy."

"It works for simpler minds," Anora agreed. She ran a hand through her sweat-soaked hair.

"So, why am I here?" Maven asked.

"You're always here when I need you."

"Rubbish, this is recent," Maven said, tapping his cane on the concrete. It rang, but the sound was muffled, as if her mind could not muster the appropriate fidelity. "The last time you did this you were a child, I think."

"Why don't you acknowledge your sister has mental problems?" Anora whispered.

"Half sister," Maven corrected. "Do you think I care about your problems?"

"I know you cared enough to come find me. You saved me twice."

"Once from ignorance, that's true. But the second time, *that* was from your own stupidity."

"That's only partly true, Maven."

"Agreed," Maven conceded.

"Now I know you're a construct. Maven never conceded a point." Anora smiled.

Maven smiled back. "I rather feel more like a crutch since your *illness*." The last word was spoken with a hint of amusement. "That's what brought me here again. Do I comfort you?"

"You're my brother. Knowing you've always been there has helped me more than you know."

"I'm not here."

"That doesn't stop the mind from retreating into familiar places."

Maven looked around. "Let's talk about something interesting."

Anora smiled. That part of Maven remained perfect. "Tell me about Arthur MacGabran and your theorem."

"Mm, you've hit upon something?" Maven asked, and Anora saw the gleam in his gray eyes, reflecting her thoughts.

"I've been trying to determine if he's a focus, but he doesn't fit the theorem."

"Doesn't he, now? Have you done a proper investigation into his genealogy? The focus is very dependent on not only temporal characteristics but those inherited from his or her parents."

Anora frowned. She knew this, but there was not much about Aidan or Igerne MacGabran that she knew. The walls of the cell glowed with Maven's psychogenetics theorem.

"There we go. I see you've made some changes."

"Small mathematical improvements," Anora admitted. She'd been working on it from correspondence she'd received up until Maven was killed.

"Let me be the judge of that," Maven said. He got up and inspected each stage of the theorem. He was quiet for some time.

Anora had continued work on the theorem after Maven's death. At first, it was to determine if it was a clue, but she had become more interested in it as she delved deeper into its complex structure. Without his knowledge or expertise, she'd focused on the mathematics of the thing.

"Small improvements," Maven finally agreed. "You're wondering if I've succeeded in finding a focus?"

"Would you tell me if you had?"

"Would I be doing the work if I were wasting my time on a dead end?"

Anora smiled at his directness. "I haven't seen Arthur do anything that you believe a focus is capable of."

"You're looking at the end point of the theorem when you should be looking at the beginning. It's a theorem that depends on time and events. More than just his genealogy, of course, but what happens around him."

"Like your death?"

"An unfortunate by-product of my work, really. Did you once think he was my murderer?"

The theorem faded away. She thought of another question. A secret she had never asked about. "What happened to Reince that day?"

"I'm only an expression of your mind and imagination. Do you think I can really answer that question?"

"Typical—"

"But not trivial." Maven winked, a rare smile upon his lips before his face resumed its stony expression. "You and I are much alike. But it's important that you be protected from things. You're successful and accomplished. I've done the right things for the right reasons."

Anora sighed. It was an answer she hadn't expected. Anora knew she was surrounded by competent and trustworthy people, but there was no one she had trusted more than Maven. No one. She'd never be able to repay that kind of debt to him. She could only avenge him.

Maven tapped his cane. "I am only a construct of your dissociated mind, but I should mention that he's not a bad person."

"Reince?"

Maven stared at her. "Now who's being trivial?" Maven's gray eyes twinkled. "Arthur."

"He's much too young for me."

"Hardly."

"He's hung up on a dead woman."

"Then you'll need to make a decision about whether to rescue him from himself or for your own needs. It's not a bipolar decision."

"What needs?"

Again he gave her that inscrutable gaze. She sneered at him and turned away. The thing was, except for Reince, the real Maven had never cared about her relationships. What the constructed memory of him revealed was something inside herself, deep beneath the surface. Arthur MacGabran? Maybe.

"Can you read your theorem to me?"

"If I must," Maven said.

She focused on his voice and forced herself to get some rest. Her anxiety was held at bay for the moment, so she might as well make the best of it. She had things to do.

13

TEST FIGHT

NEW YORK CITY, NY—
"How do you feel?" Owen asked Kara. They were driving down Fashion Avenue.

Kara breathed like she was meditating, in through her nose and exhaling through her mouth. "I'm fine. This is the longest I've been able to hold the field. Better than when we were here last week."

Owen looked at his watch. "You've been at it for a few hours. I'm impressed."

"Can you hold it this long?"

Owen nodded. "I've been able to retain the waveform for almost a day." That was an exaggeration. His timed tests were closer to eighteen hours. It was like a muscle. Once you flexed it, it got stronger. No, that analogy wasn't right, because there were limits to the human body. Being able to hold the manifest waveform was something of the mind. Drawing power into yourself was one thing, but holding on to it was another. Owen was sure that the Avallach bastards were able to manifest for days at a time at this point. But he wasn't here about that and he didn't care about Kara's stamina in this area. She had other, more pleasing skills. No, what he cared about right now was what was on her fingers. *Eurfron* glittered even though she was only at the minimum threshold and barely registered a halo.

They'd been at it for a few hours now. He'd thought Kara would be bored watching the city through the SUV windows. In the back was a full grid system that Owen had installed for just this occasion.

A bead of sweat trickled down Kara's neck. She was a good-looking woman. Her heritage made her curvy, but it was tempered by her military training. Her blond hair was pulled back to the nape of her neck. She'd dyed her hair just for him. He appreciated the gesture.

"You get a nosebleed and we're going to stop," Owen warned.

"I can manage. Do you think it's working?"

"I have no idea," Owen said. He really didn't, but he knew if Avallach could find Brastius in a place like Nice, France, bringing her to a technology-dense haven like New York City should absolutely trigger whatever alarm bells Avallach had. He'd sketched out the idea to Kara, who was as much of a risk taker as Owen had hoped for. He bet Arthur was as attached to Indiana as he'd hoped. If Morgan or Mara wasn't going to make a move, it was up to him. Of course, Kara didn't know that yet.

"Let's take a break," Owen said, motioning for the driver to pull over.

"You sure?"

"We can pick it up tomorrow," he said.

Kara let out a gasp as if she'd been holding her breath. She sat back and closed her eyes. "I can't tell what's worse, holding on or letting go." Her eyes were heavy lidded and she panted. "How do you not—?"

"Discipline," he replied a little quickly. He still felt the field, just outside of his reach. Truth was that he wanted it. He'd been manifesting only to test the prototype for now, but he'd felt the compulsion a few times since that first day. He'd be able to manifest for a few moments, then he'd be seized with an unrelenting compulsion that shoved him eastward. It was as though he were an ant and it was a thumb, pushing him down with an unbearable weight and grinding him in the direction it wanted him to go. He couldn't resist—only let go of the waveform, which made the compulsion vanish. *At least Morgan was subtle about how she manipulated you*, he thought. This was something entirely different and apparently only affecting him.

Kara licked her lips and he could see her relax beneath her utilitarian coat. Compared to him, she looked plain. He wore a suit and tie beneath a well-brushed wool overcoat. She wore jeans and a sweat shirt.

"You feel like shopping?" Owen asked after a moment.

Kara spread her knees suggestively, then stretched. *Mother would definitely not approve*, Owen noted. *Neither would Morgan*, he added.

"You think I need to be dolled up? Outside of the bedroom, that is." Kara sat up, her mind winding itself back up after the clarity of manifesting wore off. Her hazel eyes scrutinized him.

Owen scratched his stubbled cheek. He'd grown a beard in the last few weeks. It was different and not something he liked. "Think of it more as a reward for coming out on these little excursions with me."

"If you're buying, I could use some new shoes that aren't boots." Kara grinned. "Are we going to Neiman Marcus—"

Owen chuckled. "Why would we go there? Let's be a little more discreet. A little more upscale."

"This feels like a *Pretty Woman* moment."

"I'm sorry?" Owen asked.

"Old movie. It doesn't matter." Kara straightened as the SUV pulled over. "No jewelry."

Owen got out and gave Kara a hand. The days were getting shorter, but the sky was clear. Long blue shadows darkened the streets. "I wasn't planning on it," Owen said, kissing her hand.

Kara smiled at his charm. "So, can we cut the bullshit and you tell me what we're really doing here?"

"You're smarter than you look."

"You didn't hire me for just my genetics or training."

"You might not like it."

"Try me. I let you go on this far. If I don't like it, Holt will know."

"I can stop you," Owen half threatened.

Kara smiled. "You can try."

Owen tightened his grip on her hand, but she did not relent. Her eyes flashed a hint of danger. He may have underestimated her a little.

"Do you have a plan?" she asked. She hadn't grabbed the waveform, he could tell. If she did, he'd counter her.

"I have a plan."

"Then let's talk about it. If I approve, we'll do it."

"YOUR PLAN SOUNDS LIKE BULLSHIT," Kara said, standing in front of the full-length triple mirror naked, save for a thong. She pulled on a slinky, expensive black dress.

Owen sipped his drink with a passive expression. "What's wrong with it? Bear in mind, I've done hundreds of operations like this before."

"I don't think you've ever set a honeytrap before, but you have most of the idea," Kara replied, turning in the mirror to see how the dress accentuated her figure. She put her hand on her hip. "What do you really want to do?"

"I want to find out how and why he's doing all the things he's doing. Why is he saving some nobody in Turkey? Why a group of soldiers on an army base? There's no point and no pattern to it." He leaned forward a bit, savoring the fifty-year-old Glenlivet before swallowing. "Marks had his fingers in a lot of pies. What if one of them was something he's using to—"

"Plan his missions? That seems a bit absurd," Kara said.

A designer came into the room and made small adjustments to her dress. Kara always paused when someone who wasn't privy to the conversation was near, but Owen was a little less restrained. Perhaps it was the Glenlivet. It was an excellent cask.

"Hear me out," Owen said. "One of Marks's projects was Delphi —some sort of prediction project. What if he got ahold of that and *that's* what's guiding him? Perhaps these things are like the butterfly effect. Change something small and the cascade effect is much larger later."

Kara admired herself and turned to show off for Owen, who nodded in absent approval to the dressmaker. Kara stepped out of the dress and slid into a longer one. It was gray and shimmered with iridescence like a shark skin. It reminded Owen of Morgan. Kara was a touch shorter; her legs weren't as long as Morgan's. He licked his lips and found himself drawn to her.

"What if he's just doing things at random?" Kara asked, checking the fall of the dress. It had an exposed back and was daring. She pulled her hair to the side to show him.

Owen shook his head, but it swam a bit. "Every time it's to save someone." Was it the scotch or the display in front of him? He focused. "No, he's got something up his sleeve. Delphi has something to do with it." Kara's back was more toned than his cousin's, and her skin was flawless.

"Why don't you do that? Find out what this Delphi is?" Kara turned for Owen as the dressmaker came out to adjust the gown. It had thin golden straps and Owen could not help but marvel at how good she looked with blond hair.

"I don't have enough information. Just some notes," Owen replied. The Glenlivet made his head muddy. *Nornian* clinked against the glass as he tapped it. He gazed at Kara and thought of Morgan.

"You'll need someone with some DARPA contacts, then, and that avenue is out," Kara said, waiting for his approval.

"Yes, both Marks and de Vance burned those bridges. I think Mara and Morgan may have some upper-echelon contacts. Mara was in the NSA, after all." That alone was one reason among many that Owen didn't exactly trust Mara Holt. He wasn't about to start.

"I still don't like your plan."

"Lure him on the promise that you're Indiana. Everyone wants to believe something that's not true," Owen said more harshly than he wanted.

"That's not the part I'm worried about. That's cleverly done if it works. You just don't have an exit strategy. You've set up the meeting, but you haven't done the rest of your homework."

Owen swallowed the last of the Glenlivet and stood. "I don't have an exit plan because I mean to get rid of him."

"That's shortsighted," Kara replied.

Owen drew close, his hands caressing her arms. He felt her body respond. Goose bumps rose on her skin.

"Do you think he'll beat me?" Owen asked. Arthur was a trained killer, an ex–Navy SEAL. But Owen wasn't without his own training. While his mother thought him a poor copy, she hadn't wanted him to be an untrained one. But Arthur also had *Caliburn* and almost more than a year's head start in that arena.

"That's hard to say. I've never seen him fight, but I know what he can do."

"And what I can do?"

"That's much different," Kara whispered. "But I don't want to be the fallout from your plan. You haven't accounted for me."

Owen gazed into her hazel eyes. They were just a little too brown. She was younger and her complexion unmarred, and Owen found her very desirable. "How have I forgotten to account for you?"

"Leave me room to escape and to rescue you," she breathed into his ear.

Owen thought about it, though it was hard to focus. Damn, that Glenlivet was good. He needed to clear his head. He reached for the waveform and everything snapped into focus. He smelled the Glenlivet, and the light machined scent of the newly made dress, and her. Kara wore no perfume. She was a practical woman, but she knew more about herself than she let on. She could seduce a man if she wanted and didn't need to use much to do it. He slid his fingers down her arm and linked his hands with hers. He felt *Eurfron* there.

She manifested as well. He could feel it. Her body glowed with an inner light that he could see. Her mouth curled into a small smile.

Then the compulsion hit like whiplash. His mind stiffened, seized by the desire. It held him, but barely, as his mind was affected by the drink. It bore down on him and he fought it. He pushed back, but he was the ant, pushing against the hand with only his exoskeleton. He could lift a hundred times his weight, but it wasn't enough. Not compared to this. He tried to wrench free but couldn't. It swirled around him, taking control of his mind. The power rushed through him and gripped him, breaking every door of resistance. It wanted him. He had to go. Go. Go. Find. Be. He had to let go, he had to get away, but his mind wouldn't let him. It shut out everything. He heard a voice in his head. It was a woman's. A familiar voice, but reverberating, and he couldn't make out the words. Sights and sounds were all around him. Bells. Traffic. Lights. Grayness. *Let go!* he told himself. *Let go! Go. Go.* Belatedly, he realized he needed to release the waveform, and he did.

"Owen?" Kara asked.

Owen opened his eyes and stared at her. He gripped her hand hard and there was pain on her face.

"Did you feel it?" he whispered.

"Feel what?" Her other hand was caressing him. He was still aroused, and Owen realized the episode had only lasted an instant. Whatever gripped his mind had held it, but he was still strong enough to escape. It was a raw naked power that made manifest ability seem like a photon compared to the sun. He shut all the doors to the image. Closed everything off. His hand relaxed, but he could tell she had not let go of her power. She was practicing or showing off. The ordeal had burned away much of the scotch's muddy feel. Most. He regained his control.

He kissed her and she responded to him. After a moment, they parted and he smiled at her. "Let's make sure we account for you."

"Let's."

∼

"NOT THE BEST of places to be," Kara said, leaning against the girder. They were in a long wide corridor between the uptown and downtown tracks at the West Fourth Street subway stop. It was late evening now, so the work crowds had died down, but it was New York City. It would be some time yet before things quieted.

"Plenty of room and escape routes," Owen said. He felt the grid permeating from the parked SUV above.

"And cameras."

"That's why we get to make a commotion. Just a little one," Owen said. He wasn't planning on taking on the whole NYPD, but they regularly patrolled the city's arteries.

"And that's why I'll keep listing all the ways things can go wrong. Heads up," Kara said as she saw two NYPD officers approaching them. Owen and Kara were in the middle of the platform, looking nonchalant, which was hard to do when you were decked out in black. They looked more like speed bikers than terrorists, but still they got more than a few looks. That was probably due the mirrored helmets they wore.

"You'll be all right?" Kara asked.

"I'm fine," Owen said, pushing away from the girder. People flowed around them. A downtown E train was approaching.

"Hey, you guys wanna take off your helmets?" one of the police officers said. The other kept his posture decidedly relaxed.

"No problem," Owen said. *Nornian* appeared from nowhere, flashing blue. He thrust the waveblade into the officer closest to him.

The officer jerked and fell back, cracking his head on the tiled concrete. The second officer drew his service piece, but Kara took two steps and lanced him with *Eurfron*. It was over in a second. The crowd was stunned and then scattered away from them, drowned out by the screech of the braking train.

Nornian winked out, but Owen amped up his KE field.

Eurfron lit the space in bright blue light.

Owen watched the officers twitch and flail on the ground. There was a lot of room around them now. "Think we might've ruined our chances of escape."

"Whatever gave you that idea?" Kara said. People exited the E train, but when she stabbed a nearby passenger, everyone ran.

A couple of braver folks approached, giving the fallen officers concerned looks. Owen motioned them over, but they backed away.

The PA system activated. A calm female voice announced, "Danger. Clear the area, please. Make your way to the marked exits. Danger." Then people's phones began to chant the same thing over and over. The police radios on the two officers squawked the same message. "Clear the area, please. Make your way to the marked exits. Danger."

"Maybe not," Owen corrected, watching the E train. A black man wearing a long wool coat and gloves exited the train calmly around the rush of departing people.

Owen recognized the man. Lamar Jones. One of Arthur's men. He held back his waveblade and watched Kara. "We're on the clock," he said.

"Not the person you wanted," Kara said.

"Proof that they are monitoring and looking."

Lamar seemed to size up Kara, who held *Eurfron*, then settled back into a ready stance. Owen heard him above the announcing system. "I got two. Should be easy. They took out two cops and the crowd's thinning." He walked toward them. "Man and woman. Can't tell if it's her."

"Where's Arthur?" Kara said, her voice altered through the helmet.

Lamar smiled. "Why would he be here?"

"Where?" the woman repeated.

"How about you tell me why you broke up with General Marks?"

Owen decided to up the stakes. Make Lamar act. Owen grabbed a passing man and stiff-armed him toward the track. The man, caught off guard trying to avoid the trio, fell backward onto the track with a shout.

"Aw, man, why'd you go do that?" Lamar said loudly, and his waveblade came to life in his hand, solid and as bright as *Eurfron*. "Now I'm gonna get nasty."

"Just answer the question," Owen said, running at Lamar.

Owen summoned *Nornian* phased to blue.

Lamar dropped into a ready stance and easily deflected Owen's attack. The columns of the subway threw wild shadows as the blades moved and flashed. *Nornian* phased from blue to deadly white. Kara moved to flank Lamar. Lamar shifted around Owen, his blade deflecting and pushing Owen back. Lamar was as strong as any Chevalier. KE fields glowed brightly as both combatants drew more power.

Lamar feinted and then backed himself toward the uptown track, cutting off Kara's flanking route. He turned his head, calling to the man on the track. "Hey, man, you okay down there?"

There was a groan from the tracks. Lamar didn't have time to assess as Kara came in. Lamar countered, pushing Kara back with his lightning-quick blows. Owen came on, glad he had trained with Kara. Their coordination had thrown Lamar off.

"Give me a sec," Lamar said, presumably to his handler, moving around a girder. Owen swung, and there was a groan of metal as the column was sawn in half by *Nornian*. Lamar jumped back and threw himself into Kara. She yielded to keep her footing but fell down onto the track. Debris shook down from overhead as a support girder buckled.

"Let's not make a mess, now. This is my city," Lamar said. "Fuckin' tourists." He turned back to Owen.

"Where's MacGabran?" Owen said, his blade snapping up, down, and then up. He spun, hoping to catch Lamar off guard, but Lamar raised his arm and flicked his KE shield on. The waveblade bounced harmlessly off, surprising Owen. It was piece of technology Brightwork hadn't perfected yet, but Avallach was using it now.

"That ain't her," Lamar said to himself. "Come on, man. You forget who you're talking about. No way would she let me pull that trick on her ass," Lamar huffed.

"MacGabran!" Owen demanded, recovering himself.

"You're so hot on him, find him yourself," Lamar said, his blade shaving close to Owen, cutting through some of Owen's suit. It had some thin plating beneath the leather and Kevlar, but nothing could stop a waveblade. Except for the shield Lamar had. Something the Chevaliers lacked.

Alarms blared above the repeating voice, drowning it out.

"So much for peace and quiet," Lamar said, ducking under a high swing from Owen that went through another column. "You keep doing that and there ain't going to be no more you." The platform had cleared, although Owen could still hear the man groaning on the track.

"What about the trains?" Lamar asked his handler as Owen came on, hoping to get inside his reach. "Stop," Lamar said, and Owen hit his shield again, the waveblade bouncing harmlessly off. But Owen was inside his reach and he punched.

Lamar turned his head so the punch was a glancing blow. He staggered back, keeping his shield up. "Got lucky, punk."

Owen felt like he had punched a wall. The KE fields between the two made physical attacks difficult. But he had the advantage now.

"Time to pull out," Kara said in his ear.

"No. MacGabran."

"He's coming. You need to go. Split up their attack. And the police are alerted."

Owen knew she was right. Lamar had his shield up and at the ready, but Owen turned and ran along the platform next to the uptown track. His waveblade passed through several columns before he ran up the steps to the Third Street southeast exit. Kara ran along the tunnel for the uptown track, leaving broken beams in her wake until she vanished. Lamar took a step toward them but turned and jumped down onto the track.

Owen didn't wait to see what happened to him. He heard the groan and crack of the earth as the tunnel buckled in on West Fourth Street station. He sliced through the emergency exit door and up the stairs into the cold evening air. Two cops rushed down the stairs at him. They fired, but he came on, the bullets stopping at his KE field. He lanced them both, grabbed one officer's semiautomatic, and continued on as a billowing cloud of debris came out of the subway entrance. The quaking boom jarred his teeth as part of the street collapsed behind him. Owen ran north with the scattering crowd. He turned right toward Washington Square Park, where the SUV should have been somewhere nearby. Only it wasn't there. He jammed the pistol into his belt and pulled out the rectangular pack as he outran people covered in dust.

Owen swerved into the park just as something flew overhead. It was one of the Avallach candidates on one of their weird flying machines—more tech they had over the Chevaliers. Which one, though? He jinked left, then right, heading toward the lighted archway. People strolling the park were struck dumb by the sight. Others fleeing from the destruction ran away. Then Owen was tackled from behind. He landed hard on the ground, his KE field taking most of the impact. Whoever it was had too much velocity and flew off of him. Owen got up.

It was Arthur. *Yes.* He wanted to test him hand-to-hand. He'd known he had a waveblade, but he'd also have a shield, and that was an advantage. Owen had a plan.

"There you are," Owen said through his helmet. The faceplate was cracked. That must've been some hit he took.

Arthur got up to engage. "Electronics? Identify?" Arthur radioed his handler. Their suits had some incredible sensors, Owen thought. Arthur wore his beneath civilian clothes, which included a heavy coat. Owen swung a hook, but Arthur dove under it and tackled him. Instead of going backward, Owen twisted free and threw Arthur back. Arthur landed on the ground and rolled. People were shouting now.

"I'm not in trouble," Arthur said.

Owen drew and aimed the semiautomatic as Arthur got up.

Arthur charged as Owen aimed expertly for the center of mass. The bullets stopped, as Owen expected, but Arthur grabbed Owen's gun arm and twisted.

Owen rolled into the turn and punched with his free hand.

Arthur blocked with his arm and hit Owen with a connecting punch to the jaw. The helmet took the impact, but it wasn't padded.

Rattled, Owen staggered back from the hit, but he didn't let go of the gun. Arthur held on with both hands and moved in to disarm Owen, keeping the gun pointed not in the air, but toward the ground.

"Get away!" Arthur yelled to the onlookers.

The gun went off and a bullet hit the dirt. Owen let go of the gun with a grin and hit Arthur in the kidneys. Arthur took the hit. He popped the gun's magazine and threw it away.

Owen tackled him and held Arthur in a strong hold. He got the bomb onto him.

Arthur grabbed Owen's hand and pried, hitting the weak flesh, then let go and hit Owen hard. It knocked Owen back, but he still stood. He shook his head and hit the button.

Arthur rolled and came up. There was a beep. Owen smiled. Time to go.

"What? Pri?" Arthur asked his handler.

Arthur took off his coat and threw it to the ground. Owen escaped, orienting himself and turning north. He hoped Kara had made it out of the subway tunnel. She had a bit of a run to go. *Where was the damn SUV?* There it was, just around the corner.

Owen heard speakers and phones announcing, "Clear the area! Clear the area!" Then the compulsion hit him. This time it seized his mind so thoroughly that his body froze and he fell to the pavement, skidding on the asphalt.

14

THREE-LETTER WORDS

CULPEPER, VA—
"Dr. Myrrdin?" A familiar voice broke through her mind's focus.

Anora made a sour face and then looked around her. She was working on a particularly difficult problem in her head, the kind that often needed her to lock her senses out. Morning light had peeked through the windows and tamped down her anxiety, so she'd been up for a couple of hours. She shelved the ideas for a later time and brought herself back to the present. She was in the cell, lying on the cot, her arms folded tightly over her chest as if she were a mummy without a sarcophagus. She sat up and saw Director Zeke O'Brian.

"Hi, Zeke," Anora said, smiling. She hoped her night sweats hadn't made her look a fright, but if they had, so what?

"I've been talking to you for the last five minutes. Working on a problem?" Zeke replied, a dour expression on his face.

"Something like that," she replied, stretching. "Where's Agent Haut and Sagramore?"

"I sent them packing. You get yourself mixed up in something?"

Anora gave him another wry smile. "What makes you think that?"

"Just what they told me."

"What you know is what you know."

"Want a cup of tea?"

"Is that a way of getting me to talk?"

"More of a peace offering."

"That sounds like a good idea." Anora slid her jacket on as the sheriff opened the cell and pulled the door back. She combed her fingers through her hair.

"How are you, Anora?" Zeke offered his hand.

Anora stared at it. "Wondering how you got ahold of some of my AI code. Nice job integrating my Quantum Protocol, though I think that was part of the stolen code base."

"I'm not sure what you mean," Zeke said, his face a passive mask. He dropped his proffered handshake.

Anora patted him on the shoulder as she walked past, following the sheriff. "Project Janus. I worked it out and I can probably find out when and where. Some of what Janus can do is quite extraordinary if you know what to do with it."

"You know I've been kicked upstairs since I recruited you to develop the QP. We shouldn't really be discussing this outside of a secure facility."

"Did you discuss stealing my work inside of a secure facility?" The sheriff unlocked the detention area door and they exited together.

"Come on, you can't expect me to know every bit of what goes on under my purview, good or bad."

"I'm able to manage two profitable companies without doing bad things. At least, unless I can claim to not know every bit of what goes on under my purview."

"Damn, you got up on the wrong side of the jail cell this morning."

"One, your FBI friends put me in detention thinking that my known claustrophobia would make me crack. It didn't. Two, you can always put me back."

"That would be worse," Zeke said. "You're still mad about the investigation?"

"Do I really have to answer that, Zeke?" Anora said, following a sheriff to where her personal effects would be returned to her. She picked up her belt and minor items. Her terminal was missing. "Where's my phone?"

The clerk reviewed the documents. "Damaged in transit."

"In transit to where?"

"Doesn't say. I assume here."

"Hope you had a warrant," Anora said to O'Brian.

"Broke is broke," he replied.

"I'd like the pieces back."

"I'll see what I can do."

After a few moments, they were outside the small police station. Anora paused to take in the bright fall air, then pulled up her jacket hood against the biting breeze. They walked along the street in silence for fifteen minutes, and Anora was content to imagine herself recharging her reserves against anxiety. Zeke led her to a boutique coffee shop named Raven's Nest, all brick walls, blond hardwood floors, and knickknacks. He ordered a strong black coffee for himself and oolong tea for her. He handed it to her. Anora eyed the scones but resisted the urge. This was business, after all.

"I'm sorry about your brother," he said when they sat down together.

"But not sorry enough to tell me the truth," Anora shot back.

"Christ, are we going to go over this again? I told you the investigation came up empty. The plane went down. Loss of flight control. What more do you want?"

"Do you wake up believing the bullshit you tell yourself, or does it take a long hard look in the mirror first?"

"You've already burned your bridges with me, Anora."

"Then why did it take just a phone call to get your ass down to wherever this is? Where is this?"

"Culpeper, Virginia."

"Homey."

"I got my ass down here because I know your type."

"My type?" Anora smiled, sipping her tea.

"The annoying fucking billionaire type with a shitload of lawyers that will flock around the capital, shitting on everything like pigeons with the runs. You'll push enough buttons, a lot of the wrong ones, and then I'll get a phone call to take care of you. I'd like to think we have some sort of professional courtesy toward one another."

"We did when I was working for you, Zeke. But you didn't help me when I asked."

"What help could I've given you? You probably broke into half of the NSA systems and found out what you wanted to know anyway."

Anora chuckled. "I love how everyone thinks that because I'm an authority in artificial intelligence that I'm also some wizard hacker."

"Don't blow smoke up my skirt, Anora. I'm old enough to know that you build tools. You build tools that build tools, and those tools build tools that can break into whatever it is you want to break into. Why do you think we asked you to build QP? It's a decade old and still the best secure means of communications we have."

"I wish you'd use it for your diplomatic cables," Anora clucked.

"We can't use it everywhere."

"Just on the pitch-black stuff, right?"

"Goddamn, you're on a tear aren't you?"

Anora eased off a bit. Zeke was a smart man, and she was angry at him for not trying hard enough to find out about Maven. By the nature of his job, Anora had never trusted Zeke, but she did like him, and he'd given her as much leeway as possible to get QP working for the NSA. It had worked, and she'd left with a long list of classified patents under her name. "What's the official word?"

Zeke's face cleared; he felt he'd finally broken through. "The word is 'lack of official evidence.' The FBI doesn't have anything tying you to this MacGabran guy."

"You think he's the guy? Apollo?"

"I don't think so, I know so." Zeke only smiled, sipping his coffee. "I prefer to stick to running the inside of my organization. I've heard talk that there's a task force, though. Headed by Homeland."

"Why would they be involved? He's supposed to be a US citizen."

"I think some of the international sightings are making it a possible terrorist issue."

Anora laughed. "I heard he was running a terror camp inside the United States."

"You watch too much TV."

"Do I?"

"No, they don't think he's a terrorist anymore. At least, not publicly." Zeke smiled. "I gotta feeling about whatever's going on, there's change blowin' in the wind."

"How do you mean?"

Zeke shrugged. "When something doesn't feel right, it doesn't feel right. Some guy who's supposed to be an ex–Navy SEAL with superpowers? Sounds like either something made up or something dangerous coming."

Zeke was not someone who spooked easily. His hackles weren't up either, but he read tea leaves. If he had known what Anora knew, he'd probably have been more worried. She studied his face. How much did he know? Should she push him? She thought about it over another sip of tea.

"Course, I'm probably getting too old for this shit. I'm not getting another promotion before I retire."

"People like you don't retire, Zeke," Anora said. "You work until you die, or you get put out to pasture, then you die."

"I remember how warm and comforting your words are, Anora. I can't believe you worked for me almost eight years ago."

"Reminiscing? Now you *are* getting old."

"You might want to stay away from whatever MacGabran is doing. Or whatever that task force is doing. You get caught up in it and no amount of lawyer shit is going to help you out."

"Is that a threat?"

"If I were into threats."

"You might want to be careful yourself, Zeke. Project Janus. There's code in there that's mine."

"Is that a threat? I can get you thrown in a hole. Something worse than Gitmo. Maybe more if we knew what you were doing in the Bahamas."

"Now, that sounds like a threat." Anora smiled at him.

Zeke O'Brian finished his coffee and got up. "Sorry about your phone. They broke it trying to figure out how to get into it."

Anora shrugged. "I'm a billionaire asshole. What's one phone?"

"MacGabran ain't no hero, so you watch yourself. If I never see you again, it'll be too soon, Dr. Myrrdin."

"Same here, Director O'Brian," Anora said, getting up. O'Brian seemed to consider shaking her hand, but instead jammed his hands into his pockets and strolled out of the coffee shop.

She went to the counter. "Do you have a phone? Mine's dead."

"Sure," the barista said, handing her a cordless.

Anora dialed a number from memory. It rang, then clicked.

"Anora?" One asked.

"Nice practice at surprise."

"I'm glad you like it. Would you like a report?"

"I'm in Culpeper, Virginia. Send Simon to pick me up. Did I miss anything while I was incarcerated?"

"A lot of bad things, Anora."

"At the lab?"

"No, for him," One said, implying Arthur. "You should get back ASAP. Simon will be there in forty-five minutes."

"Anything I can get on the news?"

"There's plenty on the news."

Anora looked around for a TV, which the café unsurprisingly didn't have. "I'll find a TV."

"Shit's hit the fan."

"Language. Talk soon." Anora hung up. Was that what O'Brian was referring to or not?

15

FALLOUT

NEW YORK, NY—
Ed Tiwaz met her at a brownstone on the Upper West Side. His face had the grim determination of a warrior.

"Dr. Myrrdin," he said.

"Why're you still in New York?" It had taken her over a day to get there. She'd had work to hand over in her lab, and she'd had to get a new terminal, make some inquiries, and resolve issues with her businesses. She'd planned on flying into the city, but with the FBI showing their hand, she'd decided to make the drive up. It allowed her to clear off work in the process.

Ed only frowned. "Heard you were working on CAMLANN."

She waved away the small talk. "Who was injured?" Anora asked. She'd seen the footage and aftermath on the news outlets, but nothing had been conclusive. The news feeds were filled with talking heads interviewing eyewitness after eyewitness. There was even footage of the fight in Washington Square Park between Arthur and one of the attackers that ended with Arthur dropping to the ground onto an explosive device stuck to his coat. Most of the bomb's kinetic energy had been absorbed by Arthur's field, but it made a hell of a display. In the end, he stood up, his civilian clothes in tatters and no one around him injured. Almost a day later, the news cycle was on a continuous loop, with analyst after analyst debating every detail, including Arthur's choice in shoes. What was quickly determined was that he was not the attacker.

"Wasn't Mac, though it probably should've been if you ask him."

Anora felt her insides relax a bit when Ed said that. She knew it hadn't been him, but somehow hearing that sounded comforting. She pushed the thought away. Ed walked her into the building, then up the steps to where Arthur was. The bedroom looked like a hospital room, with respirator pumps, IV drips, and heart-rate monitors. An Indian woman was talking to Arthur. She came over to Anora and they greeted each other warmly.

"Good to see you again, Sri," Anora said. "How is he?"

"Stable now, but we'll have to transfer him to one of our secure hospitals. Possibly upstate, but I'd rather keep him close by. He's suffered a pretty bad injury—crushed vertebrae and multiple contusions. But he's quite strong. He'll live."

"And his spine?" Anora half asked the question.

"He should walk again if everything goes well. I'm just surprised he's alive."

Anora raised an eyebrow. "A subway tunnel collapsed on him, right?"

Sri nodded. "From what I know, the kinetic energy field he generates kept him from being completely crushed. That, and he was fortunate the bulwark held where he ended up."

Anora touched Sri's arm. She was an excellent surgeon and had taken a huge risk in bringing Avallach into her home so close to what happened.

"Someone to see you," Ed prompted Arthur after Sri had left the room.

Arthur, lost in thought, stood and saw Anora.

"I'll watch over him until Percy gets here." Ed sat in his seat. Arthur, whose face, hair, and clothes were still coated in dust, nodded. He patted Ed on the shoulder and went past Anora.

"I need a shower," he said.

"No one tried to arrest you?"

"There was plenty of footage where I jumped on a bomb in Washington Square. And I was able to cut my way through some of the debris to get to Lamar. I was able to get away from reporters, but that won't last long, so I have to clean up. You shouldn't be here."

"Want to tell me what happened?"

They passed another room where two DAMSLs sat. One was vigilantly monitoring data feeds through her AR system while another tried to relax. It looked like everyone was shell-shocked by what happened. Arthur entered the bathroom and peeled the top half of his suit down. He waited.

"And I wanted to see if you were all right," she said, instantly annoyed with herself. She was sure after her discussions with Percy that the rest of Avallach and the sisterhood did not know about Ellen, so she chose her words carefully. "The data you provided was enough."

"Good to know I got something right."

"Are you all right?"

"Who's playing therapist now?" Arthur said, but there was no bite to his words. Instead of being defeated, he was disappointed, but in whom? Himself? She saw the scars—a small half moon of missing cartilage at his left ear, a burn scar on his shoulder and side, a bullet wound in his abdomen, and an old faded knife wound in his back. He might have been a little too muscled for Anora's taste, but he was in peak physical condition. "I'm fine. My team's a mess. You got what you wanted. Are we settled, then?" Arthur got into the shower and the water sluiced over his body.

After all that had happened, he was focused on her being there. Anora had to appreciate it. "How did you know she was there?"

Arthur held up a hand. "Let's not talk about that right now, please. I'm trying to figure out what happened here."

"What did happen?"

"Easy. I was lured into a trap," Arthur said.

"I don't understand. Were you supposed to be in New York?

According to your grand scheme, or whatever agenda you're following. And didn't Kai confine you to *Camelot*?"

"Janus had received an unusually strong sensor read in Manhattan at a place we weren't normally surveilling. It was filtered from a list of data reports and Janus flagged it after seeing a large signature."

"You're looking for that other group? Brightwork?"

Arthur nodded. "Detecting signatures with today's equipment is difficult. It takes a lot of time and processing power, so we set up something that was more cursory, pulling data and logs from various weakly managed systems and looking for telltale signs rather than conducting deep analysis. After we found Sam, we refined and confined the search to dense urban areas. There's more raw data to process quickly."

Anora only nodded at this. No need to break into a bank's system if you can just break into the surrounding ones. Public systems were notoriously weak—at least compared to what she used.

"Wouldn't the other side be expecting you to see this same information?"

Arthur stepped out of the shower. His skin was pink from the heat and steam radiated from it. Anora noticed he still wore *Caliburn*. "It's a possibility, and we can't assume that we have the advantage on them. But it was the data Janus found that was the most interesting." Arthur shrugged. "That probably should've told me right there I was in serious trouble."

"What do you mean?" Anora handed him a towel and Arthur accepted it.

Arthur dried off and took a moment to try to express what he wanted to say. Instead, he sat down, and Anora could see the confidence in himself crack just a little. "When I let Indiana die, I knew she was dead. I asked her to sacrifice herself so that Kai and Jeri could live—because I knew Kai would be the next matron and that I would need her to bring the Mare de Scientia to where they could support my team for now. But I'm an old romantic, and I wanted to believe."

"Believe?"

"Believe that Indiana never died. That she somehow survived, even though I knew that was never an option for her. Just like I know what you're going to do won't be optional for you." He dressed in a clean ink-black n-suit.

Anora frowned at that. "You can't say something like that in passing and not explain."

Arthur shook his head. "It's not something you should know about. I'm not telling people their futures anymore." He put on a business suit over his n-suit.

"You know the future?"

"I thought I did. As it was told to me." He pulled out a small red notebook, but he didn't hand it to Anora.

"Can you get to the point? What's the story about Indiana have to do with what happened?"

Arthur smiled and waved her back to the room with the two DAMSLs. "When Janus dug through the sensor feed, we found a signature we weren't expecting. It's Indiana Beckham's signature. Prianna?"

Prianna handed him AR wraparounds and he gave them to Anora. She put them on.

"Show her Indiana's signature, please," Arthur said to Prianna.

Prianna sent Anora the visual data. Anora inspected it. It looked like an EKG reading to her.

"Show her what we found. Overlay."

Another signature appeared, identical to the first. Rather than making assumptions, Anora manipulated the data itself. After a moment, she pulled the wraparounds off. "Not identical."

"Right, but close enough. North of ninety percent."

"Ninety-eight point nine nine," Anora agreed. "So you found Indiana Beckham?"

"I thought so."

"And you came here to retrieve her?"

Arthur nodded. "I brought Ed and Lamar here to use our suits to see if we could get a more real-time mark. The first data sniff was over a week old, so there was no guarantee she was in the city. So, we put all of Janus's resources into localizing the search and did a bit of a random walk using the subway system. It only took a day, and Lamar found her first."

"And what happened then?"

"Lamar was ambushed. There were two of their candidates there. Do you want to see?"

"You have a data stream?"

"From his DAMSL, yes."

"Who are they?" Anora asked.

"I can't identify either of them. Sorry," Prianna replied.

Sam spat, "The second one's signature looked like mine. That bastard had my rings. He got *Gram* to work."

"I don't understand," Anora said.

"You can't modify a focal ring once it's tuned to a person. But these bastards did."

Anora frowned at that. "Can you time-stamp to the beginning?"

"Already set up," Prianna said, giving Anora the questioning look one would give to an outsider.

"Christ," Anora said, looking at the readout data on the goggles. "That's the man on the news feeds? The guy on the tracks?"

Arthur nodded. "Lamar saved him and the two NYPD blues who were unconscious on the platform. When Ed and I got there, there was devastation everywhere. No way could we get to him from the West Fourth Street entrance, so we took a steed through the uptown tunnel at Spring Street. Found them in the subway tunnel. Lamar's field and shield were still up and he'd covered the man, but Lamar was half buried. I cut away a lot of the rubble to get him out before any of the transit people started coming down to investigate." He shook his head. "It was a trap, pure and simple."

"Maybe it is her."

Arthur shrugged. "It doesn't matter. We shouldn't have been here looking for her. I put the whole team at risk."

Arthur left the room and Anora followed. Percy came up the stairs with a woman in tow.

"Where is he?" Percy said.

Arthur motioned with his head upstairs. "Resting. Lilly Blanc?"

"I am," Lilly said. "Percy called me when he heard. I'm a nurse. In residency, actually."

"I'm sure he'll welcome you," Arthur said.

Percy poked Arthur in the chest. "You don't get to say that. You don't get to say anything about him."

"Stop it, Percy," Lilly said. "Let's go see Lamar."

Percy's face was dark with anger, but he went up the stairs two at a time. Lilly raced up after him.

Arthur went to an empty room and sat down in a chair. He rubbed his eyes, looking for all the world a hundred years older than he was. He peered back up at Anora. "Do you have any bit of CAMLANN functional?"

"I have a limited system running."

"I'd like to use it, if I may."

"Just ask Janus. She can loop you in now. What're you going to do?"

"I need more people. Lamar and Percy are out; that puts it at just me and Ed, right now. Two people left of seven. That's unsustainable with what I have to do. I'm going to need at least two, maybe three more candidates."

"What for?" Anora said. "Why don't you give up? This seems to be a waste of time and resources if you ask me."

Arthur got up and grabbed a coat. "It's a bit more than that now."

"Seems to me like you're playing checkers when everyone else is playing chess."

Arthur smiled at that, put on his glasses, and handed a set to Anora. He placed his Janus device on the table in front of him.

"Janus, call Kai and Hector to CAMLANN please."

"Establishing satellite feed. Pinging now," Janus said, and Anora and Arthur entered CAMLANN. It was all white space, though the floor had a bit of a glassy luminous quality about it. "So far so good."

"Light load right now," Anora remarked. "What are you going to do? You're dressed."

"I have to go meet the police and the press. I have to make a statement. I can't be blamed for what happened, but I'm not sure I can name who's responsible. It's a thorny problem."

"Don't trust the FBI."

"Some friendly advice?"

"Some friendly *recently acquired* advice." Anora smiled.

Kai and Hector appeared.

"You look happy to see me," Arthur said.

Kai ground her teeth. "How's Lamar?"

"Stable. Percy's with him now. The sisters?"

"They've called a session." Kai's eyes went to Anora briefly.

"Going to have problems?"

"Of course I'm going to have problems." Kai frowned. "You're all over the damn news now." She waved her hands, and the shaky footage of Arthur standing in the middle of Washington Square Park after the bomb exploded was unmistakable. He glowed with an inner light.

"I'm surprised I absorbed more than just the KE of the bomb. A shame no one thought to use the camera to find out where the man went off to." Arthur frowned.

"Why did you leave *Camelot*?"

"Not having this argument, Kai."

Hector coughed. "Who's the lady friend?"

"Hector Beckham, this is Anora Myrrdin. She's been working on the CAMLANN system."

"You're—"

"—a sibling with some stake in what's going on here," Anora finished.

"Promises to keep?" Hector's hazel eyes gazed into Anora's. He was a handsome man and she saw the strong similarity to Indiana.

Anora only shrugged.

Arthur wiped away the footage. "I need more people."

"You can have me," Hector said.

"You need to train Echo," Kai said.

"They're nearly ready anyway. You're not keeping me behind, Kai. I don't answer to you."

Kai frowned. His promise was to Indiana and Arthur, not to her.

"Anyone else you can spare?" Arthur asked Hector. "How far along is Jeri?"

"Jeri is ... unavailable," Hector said.

"Problem?" Arthur asked.

"She's having some side effects that have surfaced from the Conditioning." Hector exchanged glances with Kai before he turned back to Arthur. "She's woefully undertrained, though. I'd send any Echo before I sent her."

"Will she be all right?" Arthur asked.

"The lieutenants think so, but she's taken leave for a bit to recover. She's in touch with us and when the symptoms subside, she'll be back for manifest training."

Arthur nodded, but Anora saw his concern.

Hector continued. "Isolde's been out of the tank for a while. No side effects. She's got the basics, but she's more green than Echo. Better trained, in general."

"That's two. I'll train Isolde myself. She'll probably enjoy that."

Hector only smiled at that. "We'll be on the next flight out, once the Raven's retrofit is completed."

"When will that be?"

Kai spoke. "Two days. Less if we hurry."

"That's fine for now," Arthur said. "Thanks, Hector."

"I'll arrange for the training with the rest of Echo." Hector winked at Anora, gave a small salute, and vanished.

Kai sighed. "I wish you were here."

"So you could slap me again?" Arthur said.

"So I can stab you. Your stunt has put the Sisterhood into a tizzy."

"I thought they supported Avallach."

"While it was still a project, while it was an idea, while it was potential. Not a disaster."

"That's the opposite of what the news feeds say."

"They're paralyzed, but the government isn't."

Arthur folded his arms in thought. "What do you want?"

"I need you to lay low and I mean it. Keep things underboard for now. I still need to consolidate my power base. Something is going on, but I'm not sure what."

Arthur nodded. "I can do that."

Kai turned to Anora. "This is nicely done."

"Just a prototype. It won't be ready to go live for a while."

Kai nodded and vanished. They returned to the real world. Arthur sat down heavily.

"Are you going to do what she says?" Anora asked of Kai.

"Of course not." Arthur smiled. "Kai's being cautious. I know she can hold it together."

Anora shut the door. "How did you know about Ellen?"

Arthur smiled.

Anora stared at him.

"You know about my mother?"

"Do you have mommy issues? Yes, I read about your mother. Project Astrologer." Anora held back that she had spent some time in the Mare de Scientia archives. Igerne had been the matron prior to her own death and Donna's ascension to the role. Grand Dame Li had clued her in to that piece of information. Igerne had been open with the Sisterhood about her prescient ability as the Sisterhood proactively cultivated her family's talent. Her ability had existed in her lineage for at least a hundred years, having passed from mother to daughter until recently. None of Igerne's daughters were known to be prescient. Kai was a step-daughter and did not possess Igerne's genes. That left Arthur's younger sister Dominique MacGabran, who was being monitored but showed no early signs of prescience, and Morgan LaFayette, who was absolutely not prescient. She looked into Arthur's eyes. Had it passed to a son?

"I'm not. My mother was good at predicting the future," Arthur said, pulling out the small red notebook again. "She left me a sort of road map that I'd need for my future. What lies ahead for me."

"Maybe your death?"

Arthur shrugged and flipped through the pages. "Depends on how you interpret death."

"Ellen," Anora reminded him.

"*Death comes on invisible wings. The body is destroyed but the mind of the bird lives.*"

"That's terribly bad knowledge."

"There are some notes that point me in the right direction. The clue is to know when the right information comes to pass. What's important isn't what she will do for me. It's what she'll do for you. If you believe in prescience, that is."

"No more than my brother did, perhaps. It's better to be able to model the future in order to predict it rather than relying on intuition and a bit of hocus pocus."

"What if it lay within?"

"Getting metaphysical?"

"What if it's written into our DNA? Not all of us, surely, but perhaps there are those who've been encoded, like my mother and grandmother, with the ability to see what's written in the future."

"I'd ask why."

"Who knows? Perhaps it was encoded within us thousands of years ago."

"Alien race theory?"

"Now who's being ridiculous?"

"You started it. So, what your mother dreamed is why you knew Ellen was alive."

"More or less."

Anora hesitated on the next question, but only for a heartbeat. "What about Indiana?"

"She's dead."

Anora looked past Arthur. The shadow of Maven stood over him. It surprised her, as he had never appeared in the company of another person before. And for the second time in a day, Anora wondered if she was finally going crazy. The treatment really had broken her mind. "Good question, but there's a better one," Maven said. His gray eyes shone in the shadows like a cat's.

"Yes," Anora said.

"Despite everything in my life walking me down a predetermined path, I wanted to believe what she believed—that Indiana could escape death. The one death I hoped wouldn't happen—"

"Wait, one death? You knew my brother would die?" Anora asked, looking at Maven.

Maven touched his nose.

"Yes. He knew it before I did. He told me."

"Why would he tell you?" Ice ran down the back of Anora's spine. Her brother, her trusted confidant, the person who did things for her no one else would've done—had never told her of his own impending death. He'd told this man—this nobody. Anger arose at her brother. Maven took a step back, a small smile playing on his lips.

"Your brother was much wiser than I. How should I know?"

Maven was behind Anora now. She could feel the weight of his mind with her. It pressed against her, urged her to know. She thought about it. "Death is a personal thing."

"Much more personal than killing, if you can believe it," Arthur agreed.

"Did he tell you anything else?"

"That you haven't already figured out?"

Anora stared Arthur down.

Arthur folded his arms, waiting.

Bastard, she thought. "Are you one of his projects?"

"Which one? I'm so many now, apparently."

"Are you the psychogenetic focus?"

"He trusted my mother enough to know that she could lead him to one, and the two of them together made me. But am I really the person who can change humanity? The Messiah? The prophet?"

"Or the furor. The tyrant. The destroyer."

"Some things must be unmade before they can be remade."

Arthur was calm now. He had lost the anxiousness over Lamar's injury and angst over being fooled about Indiana.

"What do you think?" Maven asked over her shoulder.

Anora's mind cycled. "You may be his theoretical proof, or you may bring about the one who will be the disruptor, as he liked to call him."

"Or her," Arthur acknowledged.

"I can see why you were interesting to him outside of Avallach. Marks made the mistake of thinking that the point of Avallach was to create supersoldiers like you when it was, in reality, to build the people around you so that you could bring about change. There are one or more catalysts." Anora tapped her lips. It was an interesting problem. Certainly, Indiana was one of those catalysts. She had turned the team from a disparate group of military elites into a unit willing to sacrifice themselves for Arthur's vision. Mostly. She thought about Percy.

"Why did I really trust him? Come now, there must be more to it," Maven whispered.

"Did Maven talk about me at all?" Anora asked.

"We talked about you a lot," Arthur said.

"Is that why you don't want me inside your little clique?"

Arthur smiled at the dig. "No."

"Did Maven not want me in your group?"

"Quite the contrary. Maven wanted you to be involved. He insisted."

"But you don't want me to. You're going against destiny."

"Delaying it, but I don't think I can do that for much longer." Arthur opened the tattered red notebook to the last page and handed it to Anora. She reached out to it, but he did not release it when she grasped it. "I told you before I don't tell people their futures. These are not my words. This is my mother's notebook. I can't be responsible for what you read. Believe it if you must. I've been accused of being a bastard for telling people their future, but if you don't know what you must do, you may not do it when the time comes."

Anora stared into his eyes again. She didn't want to look down at the notebook, but something in his tone was pleading. Was he trying to keep something from her? Knowledge was knowledge, regardless of its origin.

"Enter at your own peril," Maven said in her ear. "Here be dragons."

"Shut up," Anora said.

"I guess you don't care," Arthur said, letting go.

The notebook was filled with tiny writing all along the ruled page and notes scribbled in the margins. Most of it was in the same hand, but she could see another person's handwriting in pencil—Arthur's perhaps. It was written in Maven's backward encrypted scrawl.

"What's this?"

"My mother's notebook," Arthur repeated.

"No, this is my brother's code."

"You think you're the only one who got to read his messages or notes?"

"He taught this to you?"

"My mother did."

"Christ, he did trust you. No one knows that code but me. Knew." Anora unraveled the words. "This can't be right."

"Why does everyone say that?" Arthur asked.

"Why indeed?" Maven remarked. "If you say it out loud, will it come true?" He looked over her shoulder to read the material. Anora had been a little girl when Maven rescued her. The first, hardest thing he'd taught her was his code. It was hard to break, but break it she did, and that had led her to later creating QP, which was a much more sophisticated system not only for encryption but for secure communications. She looked at the words at the bottom of the page.

"*The Merlin's sister will kill the Turtledove. The Falcon becomes Chimera. By water, light and fire, she will betray and kill Arthur.*"

Perfect, she thought.

16

PRISON BREAK

RURAL WEST VIRGINIA—
Owen felt warm and pink. He was shrouded in warmth and fluid. It felt like being in the womb again. He was there. He'd made it where he needed to be, but where was it? A jumble of thoughts pushed into his mind, but he was unable to sort them out. Then a jolt woke him up.

He was in an SUV. How did he get here? He looked over to see Mara Holt driving.

"How do you feel?" she asked when she saw that he was awake.

Owen pressed a hand to his head. It throbbed badly. His helmet was gone, but he still wore the suit. "I hurt."

"No shit. You almost got caught."

"No. I got away . . ." Owen focused on what had happened. He pushed the images and words from his mind. "I got to the truck and got away. But I don't remember what happened after that."

"I found you slumped over the wheel."

"How did you find me?"

"I was already in New York ahead of you," Mara said. She held up his helmet and tossed it to him. "Did you think I was going to let you run off and do something stupid?" She thought about that for a second. "Did you think I was going to let you run off, do something stupid, and not get away? For an unapproved field operation, you got a lot of data. Avallach is more advanced than we thought."

"I don't know what happened. I was just . . ." He couldn't describe what had happened. The hammer of compulsion had hit him hard when he ran from Arthur. He hadn't even tried to use his waveblade, but he was holding onto the waveform and it struck him down, just as the bomb went off. Had it lashed out at him for what he did? None of it made sense.

"What's Oracle?" Mara asked.

"What?" Owen was still trying to focus. His head throbbed.

"You were talking in your sleep."

"Hold on. Let me get something clear," Owen said. "You rescued me?"

"I had to get you out of the area before the men in blue found you like a drug addict asleep at the wheel with your suit still on. I'm just glad you left your grid up."

"I'm not sure I understand. Why you?"

"The one thing I can't control as operational commander of the Chevaliers is the fact that you're privileged. I can't have Chevaliers watching you. It's a waste of resources, frankly. If you do this again, I will have someone hunt you down. You've used the privilege card up with me. Ms. LaFayette can fire me if she wants."

"Morg will do more than fire you," Owen agreed. "I was talking in my sleep? Something about Oracle?"

"Yes. Oracle, Delphi, and Iggy-something."

"Igerne?"

"Maybe. I was busy driving while you enjoyed dreamland."

"Why didn't you wake me?"

"I tried. You weren't responding to anything."

Owen rubbed his jaw and gave Mara a dangerous look.

Mara smiled back.

"Where's Kara?"

"She's fine. Going to take some time returning to Brightwork. Don't worry. She's got survival training."

"You contacted her?"

"She contacted me. Did you think she was completely under your spell?"

"I had hoped," Owen said, but knew better than to say he had thought she was.

"She told me about your little changes. Pretending that Kara's your cousin won't change Kara into Morgan. It's an unhealthy relationship."

"Says the ex–NSA employee pretending to control me."

"Touché."

Owen rubbed his jaw. It throbbed and was probably the source of the crushing headache he had. "Oracle? I know Delphi was a project. Something spun out of Astrologer. It was in de Vance's old notes."

"What about it?"

"I think Marks was working on something or had something working at Delphi. It was some sort of machine-learning computing project. I'm not sure."

"Machine learning? That's interesting," Mara said, gripping the wheel.

"What?"

"I got a call from an old NSA colleague. Seems that Anora Myrrdin is suspected to be in league with MacGabran."

"Anora Myrrdin? She's the founder and CEO of Binary AI, right?"

"That's her. Brilliant AI scientist. She built some incredible tools for the NSA a few years back."

Owen nodded. "Makes sense. You think she has something to do with Delphi?" Owen asked. "We should investigate it. If there's more technology we can garner from Marks's, the better. We have the numbers, but they are years ahead of us."

"We? There's no 'we' in this conversation," Mara said. "You need to get back to Brightwork and stay the fuck away from what's going on in the world. You caused a shit storm in New York, and LaFayette is not going to have an easy time reconciling things."

"Reconciling what?"

"Instead of taking Arthur down, you've raised him up. Media is saying he's a hero. He and his team—Paladins, they're being called. The two NYPD officers you lanced on the platform? The man you threw on the tracks? All saved and alive because of Arthur and Avallach. Even the government is hesitating to make waves and backing off of any mention that he's a terrorist."

"Damn," Owen said. It was worse than the compulsion. He'd done the opposite of what he intended. "Morgan."

Mara gave an enigmatic smile. "Right. She was on a good track with government officials, but you've seriously screwed things up. The only thing that's kept my job is that I saved you from getting captured and risking everything about the Chevalier Corps."

"Damn. And the bomb?"

"It just proved he's explosive-proof now. That's all. Can you just admit you've seriously fucked things up?"

"Noted." Owen climbed into the backseat and pulled out his suitcase. He changed into his suit, aware that Mara only pretended to not notice as she drove. After putting on his shoes and straightening his tie, he got back into the passenger seat. So his plan had done nothing to hurt Arthur.

"You did get one of them."

"Lamar Jones," Owen said, remembering the man exiting the train. Bits and pieces of the fight came back to him. "Dead?"

"Too much to hope for. No, but by all accounts he's badly injured. Might not walk again."

"I guess that's something. Wasn't worth the effort."

"I'll take that as some sort of acknowledgment."

Owen frowned. No point in going over things. The compulsion had really done a number on him. "So you're going to check into this Anora Myrrdin?"

"I'm already looking into it," Mara said.

"That's good. Delphi must be important." Owen folded his arms in thought. He checked their surroundings. "Is this Pennsylvania?"

"West Virginia."

"Taking the long way around?"

"Not a good idea to be on the freeway. At least not until you changed."

Owen nodded. "Marks was using Delphi. If Anora is working for MacGabran, then there may be something to it after all. I'd definitely pull the string on that and follow it to the end of the maze."

"This isn't my first rodeo," Mara said. "I'll find out about her involvement and Delphi. The last one might be difficult."

Owen rubbed his jaw. "You get off punching unconscious people?"

"I prefer it more when they resist."

Owen put on his watch and checked the time. "Twelve hours? Are you driving in circles?"

"I'm a trained field operative. I know what I'm doing."

"Did you happen to get any food? I'm starving."

"No, and now that you're awake and dressed, that sounds like a good idea. I'll let you know when we find a place."

Owen straightened his tie in the mirror and saw his rings. He clenched his fist.

"I should take them away from you," Mara said.

"Why didn't you?"

"Privilege," she mentioned. "The grid is off now anyway. I could shoot you if I wanted to."

Owen knew she could, too. He had no illusions about his mortality without his KE field. He'd have to change that, if he could. "What's my job, then?"

"Stay at Brightwork. Get the gauntlets ready for action."

"Bullshit work."

"I can't trust you, Owen."

"Fuck you, Mara," Owen replied. It was petty. He knew it, but there it was. He was again being punished, but he had been reckless. He put the mask of calm back on. "House arrest, I take it?"

They drove on in silence for a minute. "It didn't get MacGabran like you wanted, did it?" she said.

Owen shrugged. "It wasn't exactly the point, but no."

Mara frowned. "Then why the hell did you go? To satisfy your childish curiosity?"

"We were testing a theory—"

"What's your report?"

"I'd recommend we not use the focal devices out in the field, including the gauntlets. At least, not until you and Morgan are ready. They have a distinct and traceable signature. If we're going to do field testing, it needs to be in remote or rural areas. It only took Avallach a day or so to find us in New York, but we were lit like beacons."

"So we can use that to our advantage?"

Owen shook his head. "I was testing a theory, and it panned out. They won't fall for that trick a second time."

"Tech?"

"They have shields that stop waveblades and flying machines, so that means they're able to translate manifest power into other forms of energy."

"That's something we haven't cracked yet."

If he'd just manifested, Owen could've taken Arthur completely out. Dead. Why didn't he? What did he have to prove? He looked over at Mara, studying her face. She wore a bulky suit jacket, but beneath was a new type of suit. Something that the jacket had to work to hide. It was a dull gray and was hard in places. She wore bulky cargo pants over the legs. "Is that a new uniform? Looks very—"

"Police-like? It's the final Chevalier design."

"SWAT-like I'd say. Body armor?"

"A new sharkskin design. Meant to hold integrity for things that the KE field may not hold against. High temperature, low temperature, et cetera. Kevlar lining. Light-tape stripes for visual cues."

There were shiny strips of gray fabric that ran from her shoulders down her torso and disappeared down her thighs. Probably all the way to her boots, if he guessed correctly. He reached across to touch the slick gray circular patch of fabric above her right breast. It was almost erotic, and she let him. He shifted the jacket enough to see the hip holster for her pistol.

She smiled at him. "Like what you feel? Or maybe what you see?"

He moved back to his seat. "Not sure. No badge?"

Mara's face hardened. "Let me get something clear. The Chevaliers are meant to be peacemakers, not wreak wanton destruction for some experiment."

"I am," Owen said. "As you're aware this program wouldn't exist without me."

"You caused millions of dollars of damage and closed down a major subway station. You've partially paralyzed New York City on the fear of another 9/11 attack. Are you aware of that?"

"I'm aware," Owen said.

"On the plus side, the next batch of candidates are ready to be expelled from the tanks. In a month or less, we'll be much larger than Avallach. In six months, we'll have overwhelming numbers. And when Brightwork catches up to Avallach's tech—"

"We'll pass them," Owen assured her. "I can assist—"

"You're done 'assisting,'" Mara said. "Stop acting like a child, Owen. You want to hurt him, but instead you built up his image. You're not going anywhere but to your quarters and to the testing sublevel. That's it."

Owen sat back and watched the countryside pass him by. His head hurt, despite the swirl of emotions and questions in his mind. The pain made him tired, and he sat back and closed his eyes.

SOMETHING WAS CLOSE AND HOT. *He ran through the forest, his great body heaving with power and exertion. Next to him a white doe ran and leapt.*

The forest, once green and lush, became brown and wilted. The sky burned umber and heat wavered his vision. The forest caught fire. He ran harder, feeling hot breath down his neck. The white doe leapt in front of him.

On he ran, his great heart pumping his body. Branches and leaves caught fire. Grass turned brown and then black. His antlers dashed away the brush as he ran. The white doe flashed before him, gone over the rise. His great legs powered him up the slope as the grass smoked and caught fire around his hooves. He jumped from the small ledge into the stream where the ashen doe had already bounded. Keeping up speed, he ran across the rocky bed until he reached the other side. Only then did he turn to see his pursuer.

The entire forest was fire, burning and crackling. The stream hissed as the heat evaporated the water. The white doe was gone.

The stag put his head down. He would face his pursuer. A great firebird burst from the forest, bright and hot like a nuclear fireball. The stag's heart quailed for only a moment, then he pawed the ground and charged. He ran at the firebird as it dove toward him.

The stag leapt into the fire.

Owen snapped awake. It was night and the SUV was parked. Mara was out of the vehicle. Owen saw that he was handcuffed to the steering wheel while still in the passenger seat. They were in a service area off of a highway. She'd probably gone in to get food.

He checked the glove compartment. Empty. She'd thought of everything. He looked down at his rings. Almost everything. His stomach turned when he thought of having to use his power again. How quickly things had turned from a boon to a curse. The addiction and desire were strong, but he couldn't let the bizarre compulsion drive him. No one else he knew had it. *Curse*, he thought. Derided most of his life, Owen had risen above it. He was privileged, after all. *Time to act.* He looked at the grid tucked into the back of the SUV. He wouldn't be able to reach it, of course. He reached into his coat pocket and found his phone. He unlocked it, worked through the settings, and connected to the grid remotely. He glanced up and estimated how much time he had. Mara exited with a couple of bags of food. He set the system and then dialed Morgan's number.

It rang, clicked, and went over to her executive assistant. "I'm sorry, Mrs. LaFayette isn't available to take your call," she said. "Have you contacted Ms. Holt?"

Mara got into the driver's seat.

"Morgan's not taking my calls," Owen said, taking the bags and putting them on the floor.

"It's because I'm in charge," Mara said.

The grid powered up. Ready for it, Owen knew it a split second before her. Her body shook as *Nornian* lanced through her. The horn chirped as her head hit the center of the steering wheel. He held it just for a second longer than necessary. While she twitched and looked at him with murderous eyes, he smiled at her. He let go of the waveform before anything happened. He hated to let go. It felt incredible. Powerful.

"Just business," he said, and reached across and pulled her pistol out of her holster. He fished around in her suit and found her car keys and phone. He reclined her seat back. He unlocked his handcuffs and handcuffed Mara to the wheel. From the pistol, he removed the magazine and ejected the round from the chamber. He collected the bullet and put it in his pocket. He caressed her cheek. She'd lose consciousness in a few seconds. "Thanks for rescuing me. Keep at the Oracle thing. If you come after me, I'm not going to be nice about it."

He got out, locked the doors to the SUV, walked over to the trash, and threw away the bullet, magazine, and car keys. He had to go east. Find out what was driving him and get rid of it, if he could.

"I won't be controlled," he told himself, and vanished into the night.

17

KING SACRIFICES KNIGHT, QUEEN TAKES

NEW YORK, NY—
Percy stared at the chessboard, thinking of his next move, but his mind was elsewhere.

"You take all day, old man," Lamar whispered, giving him a weak smile.

Percy beamed at his cousin, who lay in traction now, his back broken. The lacerations on his face and arms were healing well and he stared at Percy through the reflection in the mirror on the ceiling. "Easy for you to say. You just lie in bed all day."

"Man, it hurts to laugh. Plus, I gotta look at the board backward."

"I bet that's a fun challenge."

Lilly walked in with Arthur behind her. "Someone to see you, gentlemen," she said, touching Percy on the shoulder. Percy saw Arthur and shifted his gaze back to his keyboard. *Here we go,* he thought.

"Thanks, Lilly," Arthur said, and gave her a peck on the cheek on her way out.

"Hey, Perse, Lamar," Arthur said.

"Hey, boss," Lamar said.

"You got the upper hand this time?" Arthur asked.

"He thinks he got a leg up on me because shit's all backward and I'm on pain medication. Joke's on him, though."

"You talk a lot of bull for an injured man," Percy said, staring at the board.

Arthur put a hand on Lamar's shoulder. "Marine?"

"Been better, sir. Don't know how much good I am now."

"I'm medically retiring you, Lamar. For exceptional valor above and beyond the call of duty."

"Sounds like a nice little medal. You ain't taking my rings, are you?"

"I wouldn't think of taking *Curtana*," Arthur replied.

"Good, 'cause they don't play well with others," Lamar said. "Who you getting to replace me?"

"I need two people to replace you. Hector and Isolde."

"I have mixed feelings about that," Lamar said. "What about Jeri? I heard she was out of the pod."

Arthur had a pained expression Percy didn't recognize. "She's having side effects from the Conditioning."

"Do we have side effects?" Percy asked.

"Some of the failures had spectacular side effects."

"Those that made it out alive," Lamar agreed.

Percy focused on the chessboard and then moved his black bishop.

"Oh thank god," Lamar whispered. "Queen's rook to knight four."

Percy moved Lamar's white rook.

"Got a nice setup here," Lamar commented.

Arthur nodded. "The Sisterhood have provided as much help as possible."

"How many we got in the Sisterhood? Seems like everyone's in it," Lamar said.

"Kai said she offered membership to Lilly," Arthur said.

Percy could feel Arthur's eyes on him.

"Mind if I talk to your cousin for a minute?" Arthur said to Lamar.

"Not at all. I need some peace and quiet. His thinking is so noisy," Lamar said. "Wake me up when it's my turn, old man." Lamar closed his eyes. Arthur waited until his breathing eased to the slow, deep rhythms of sleep.

Arthur sat down across from Percy and looked at the board. Percy glanced up for a moment. He could see darkness behind Arthur's eyes, beneath the mask he wore. He must've gotten some sleep—the circles under his eyes were less pronounced. It had been a busy couple of weeks for Arthur. He'd been cleared of responsibility for anything in New York City and had given Lamar all the credit for saving the NYPD in the subway from the collapse. Percy did have to give Arthur kudos: he was humble and never took acclaim, which seemed to endear him to people.

Of course, the news media tried to grill him, but they couldn't pin him down and his interviews were surprisingly short. Politicians denounced him, but no one seemed to care what they thought aside from asking them who the real terrorists were. Daytime talk shows were filled with speculation now. Percy wished he could blame it on Ed and his Oprah fixation, but really it was Lamar's inability to sleep that prompted him to watch. The government agencies were silent, which made Percy wary. Avallach was under the microscope and Arthur knew it. He'd planned for it.

Percy waited, his mind unable to focus on the chessboard.

"Are you ready?" Arthur asked.

"Depends on what you mean by 'ready,' Mac," Percy said.

Arthur smiled that enigmatic smile, and for the first time he could remember, Percy wanted to punch him. "Was this all part of the plan?"

Arthur shook his head. "No."

"When're you going to give her up, man? Indiana's dead."

"Did you give Lilly up?"

"She ain't dead, Mac." Percy forced his voice to keep from rising. The anger at Arthur's recklessness got the best of him for a moment. He'd risked Lamar's life on a ghost.

"You're right. What do you want to do?"

Percy looked at Lamar. He'd never thought he'd have to make a decision between Avallach and Lamar. They came together. It was unrealistic, Percy knew. Battles ended in people living or dying. So far they'd been lucky, but it was only a matter of time. Avallach itself was like Lamar—broken and maybe on life support forever. Percy turned back to Arthur and shook the thought from his head. Arthur wouldn't give up. He'd find a way to keep moving, keep everyone moving. "I keep thinking," he said.

Arthur waited, resting his elbows on the table and examining the chess game in progress.

Percy picked up his black queen. "Why're we chasing ghosts? I think we know who the bad guys are. You should take them out."

"Spoken like a true marine. Objective based. Focused."

"We know who's in charge, don't we?" Percy asked.

"We have a pretty good idea now."

"Take her out. End the game. We win."

"That sounds satisfying, but she's going to outrun me at the pace I'm going with Avallach. She has tendrils in the Sisterhood, too. Taking her out would just solidify her faction's position and we'd lose all our support. And we'd be branded as killers instead of heroes."

"Not gonna lie, I don't mind the TV coverage of you. Puts us in a good light. I don't want Lamar or Lilly to be in the limelight, though. It exposes a weakness."

"That's still some ways out for us," Arthur said cryptically, then raised his head to look at Percy. "What do you want to do?"

Percy thought about it for a long time. Long enough for Arthur to continue.

"I'll tell you what you're going to do. You're going to stay here with Lamar and Lilly. Nurse him back to health."

"I don't even know if he's going to make a full recovery," Percy said. "What about you? It's just you and Ed now. Hector? Isolde? They aren't field grade. One of them is a good idea. Izz? I love the girl, but she's not a fan of yours. You guys did not part on good terms, no matter what she did for us."

"She's got her own issues to deal with, but I'm going to keep her close to Dr. Myrrdin."

"That's even worse, boss," Percy chuckled. "They're going to get into a fight again."

"Good training, then." Arthur stood.

Percy's heart was heavy. He held the black queen tight in his fist.

"I can always depend on you, Percy. You stayed when you didn't have to or need to. Now I'm telling you to stand down. I have the watch."

Arthur reached out and Percy shook his hand. *Grall* and *Caliburn* met, the metal touching at the thumbs.

"*Ave, Arturus*," Percy said, using a phrase Ed had worked up.

"Take care of yourself, Percy. Take care of everyone."

"I will, Mac," Percy said, but didn't feel any better.

Arthur went to the door. "I brought along a gridpack for you. It's one of the new ones."

"What for?"

"For nothing, Perse. It's yours to keep. Throw it in a closet if you want, but I don't feel right leaving you unarmed."

"I do know how to use a gun and I can kill with my bare hands." Percy gave him a grim smile.

Arthur nodded and left.

Percy did not feel any better for his own bravado. He knew this was the right decision, but Arthur had made it for him. What was wrong with him? He flicked the black queen onto the board and it knocked the black king over. He'd lost this game anyway.

"You look like someone kicked your dog," Lilly said. He didn't remember her coming in.

"Just kicked off the team," Percy lied.

"Want to talk about it?"

"Not really."

"I brought you lunch."

"What're you going to do?" Percy asked Lilly.

"You're asking the wrong person," Lilly said, putting down the tray and uncovering the sandwiches she'd brought.

"I mean, you work at the hospital."

"Worked. Past tense. I'm caring for Lamar now, remember?"

"What about your residency?"

"I have someone important to take care of." Lilly knew how much Lamar meant to Percy. He'd left behind whatever plans he and Lilly had to take Lamar into the Marine Corps with him. Saved him, in a way. It was all very altruistic sounding, but maybe Percy had been running away himself. And sisters did not talk about membership outside of the Mare de Scientia, but Percy had a feeling she'd accepted. He took her hand.

"I guess we get to spend some time together after all."

"You can't get rid of me that easily," Lilly said, putting an arm around his shoulders. "Now, what're you going to do?"

"I don't know. I'd like to get away from the city for a while."

"Where do you want to go? Far away?"

"Not far." Percy had thought the weight of the decision would lift from his shoulders. He was relieved that Arthur had taken the decision from him, but the weight remained. Percy wasn't sure it would ever leave him, and that bothered him. They ate in silence while Percy thought. How could he still be useful? Did his loyalties still lie with Arthur and the team? Of course. There wasn't much of Avallach left, though. Except Arthur had made plans. There was another team and another leader...

He pulled out his Janus and called the one person who could help him.

"Hello, Percy," Anora said.

18

GIVING

WASHINGTON, DC—

"Having trouble?" Maven asked.

"Shut up, I'm busy," Anora hissed. She landed on her back and rolled.

"Did you say something?" her partner asked, a man a bit older than her.

"Just thinking out loud," Anora said. She glared at Maven, then set her mind back to the task at hand. She moved through her katas.

Maven was on the edge of her vision, amused by her lack of focus. He'd moved from appearing when she was alone to haunting her at all times of the day now. It was distracting.

She slipped, and her opponent got a foot inside her defenses. The air went out of her lungs when she hit the mat before she could diffuse the energy. She saw stars. The man helped her up.

"I need to focus," she agreed before the man opened his mouth.

"You can't wait for focus to come. Be like water."

Anora picked up a towel and wiped the sweat from her eyes. She'd been training for over an hour, and this was her third training partner. Could she keep going? Maven stood at the edge of the mat. "Like water, I'll flow through time. That's enough for today." She bowed to her partner and to her sensei. She went to the locker room and changed.

"Are you going to follow me everywhere?" she asked Maven, who stood at the door.

"How does that make you feel?" he asked. She threw her towel at him. It landed in the towel bin. She stripped and got into the shower.

The Oracle system wasn't coming together as she had hoped. The nodes had configured themselves as her tools and One had extracted the instructions packed inside the system, but there were problems with it. Nothing was functioning. It had some semblance of a modern AI system at the edges, but when you delved deeper into it, it was more complex than that. What had Indiana found and was it working? What was Oracle really?

The shower didn't flush away the whirring in her mind, but it did ease the ache in her muscles. She spent too much time at the dojo, but she had been lax in her training and too long in AR with One and Roxy, splitting her time between making changes to get CAMLANN ready and putting Oracle together.

She dressed in her customary rocker tee, black jeans, boots, and long leather coat. She checked her terminal. There were dozens of messages related to both Binary and Telemachus. Work on Oracle would have to wait. Outside the locker room, she saw a familiar face. The red-haired woman was dressed professionally in a pantsuit under a London Fog coat. Her hair was-pulled back from her face, making her look younger than she was. T. Mara Holt.

Anora's heart skipped a beat. What was Agent Holt doing here? Had they found her trojan? *No*, she thought, but wondered. *Shields up, mask on*, she told herself.

"Anora—?" Agent Holt began.

"Dr. Myrrdin, if you please," Anora interrupted. "Something I can help you with, Agent Holt?" Anora signaled on her terminal for her car.

"Just Mara," the redhead replied. "I've moved into the private sector."

Anora zipped up her coat and bowed to her sensei and dojo. "I did say that you were too ambitious for analyst work."

"I did move into fieldwork, but it was less than fulfilling."

Anora headed for the doors.

Mara followed. "Do you have a moment?"

"You have until I get to my car," Anora said as Simon came down the street toward the curb. Anora checked the time. She might be able to get most of her work done before getting back to the lab.

"I need more time than that. Will you have dinner with me?"

Anora frowned, opening the car door. "You think I want to have dinner with you again?"

Mara touched Anora's hand on the car door. Her fingers were warm, inviting. Anora found her body responding, if only in memory. "I heard you were in town and I want to catch up."

Simon got out of the car. Anora gave a small head shake and turned to Mara. "Just business?"

"Yes, doctor." Mara smiled. A card snapped out, held between two perfectly manicured fingers. Her nails were filed down—working hands. Anora took the card and got into the car.

Maven sat next to her. "That was interesting."

"Yes," Anora said as the car pulled away from the curb. She pulled out her terminal. "One, how's Cretan coming along? Any compromises?"

"No trip wires detected." The software was doing its job, but she might not even need it. *Burn everything*, she told herself.

"Do a data scrape on T. Mara Holt. It's been a while and I want to know what she's been up to. Prep me another payload as well."

"I'll let you know what I dig up. Arthur's here waiting for you. He says he has a delivery for you."

"I'll be right there."

"SHE IS NOT A GIFT," Anora said to Arthur.

"You've grown a few wrinkles since I saw you last," Isolde snapped back. "I'm younger, faster, stronger—"

"Not smarter," Anora interjected.

"True, but I'm here. You get my protection whether you want it or not."

Anora glared at Arthur. "Really? I don't need this right now."

"She has focal rings."

"She'll stick out like a sore thumb. Everyone knows you have the rings now."

"I'll wear gloves."

"It'll be conspicuous when spring comes around," Anora replied.

"I'll get Kai's driving gloves." Isolde cracked her knuckles.

"Just work her into your routine. She's a fast learner—"

"You're not telling me the why. I don't need her protection. I can take care of myself."

"When I'm not training her, I need her gainfully employed. She gets bored and tends to get into trouble. Helping you on your little Indiana project would be useful for her."

"Indiana project?" Isolde asked, her eyebrows shooting up.

"It's nothing," Arthur and Anora said.

"Indiana isn't nothing."

Arthur folded his arms. Anora saw the pain on his face.

"Would you like some tea?" Anora asked Isolde.

"No thanks. I have my own caffeine now." Isolde wiggled her fingers.

Anora went over to her kettle and looked around. "I don't seem to have any green tea. Can you talk to Roxanne and get me some?"

Isolde glared at her. "You could just ask if you want private time with Arthur."

"I'd like some private time with Arthur."

"No hanky-panky while I'm gone. People seem to be having problems with that . . . ," Isolde said, walking out the door.

Arthur waited.

Anora wasn't sure how to start, so she went back to business. "CAMLANN is close to final release. We have a lot of minor issues to iron out, but my team needs to complete testing. One is already running a battery of tests against any vulnerability it may have."

"And it's going well?"

Anora smiled. One had found few issues. Even the smallest ones were corrected. Anora was content with her design and it would earn Binary a lot of patents. Her mind came back to the problem. "I've been looking at the signature of the 'Indiana' in the attack in NYC."

"It's not Indiana," Arthur said.

Anora detected resignation in his voice. She nodded. "Remember, it was nearly identical, so I decided to dig into it a bit more. I unwound the distortion around the matrix and determined that it wasn't her generating the waveform."

"Were you able to work out who it was?"

"Does it matter? It's not her brain-wave pattern. It's cleverly done."

Arthur shook his head, lost in thought.

Anora waited. One gave her a light chirp, but she ignored it for the moment.

"Indiana had an effect on me, more than I thought," Arthur said. "She never believed in this fate bullshit I had wrapped around her. She refused it—wanted nothing to do with it, even after I told her she'd die. She said she got to make her own decisions. Somewhere along the way, I wanted to believe what she believed—that fate can be changed just by the decisions we make for ourselves and not for others."

"But the decision to save Kai and Jeri was still the same decision you wanted her to make."

"Yes, it was."

She had him where she wanted him. She could drive home her point if she wished. Instead, she thought of her brother, Maven, first, then of her ex Reince, and finally of her father, Jun Degan Lee.

"I've wished for people—like you—to pay for the transgressions of the past."

"Your brother?"

Yes. "No. Someone I cared for a long time ago. He hurt me badly and even though he did so, I couldn't help wanting him back. I loved him and I wanted him to stay. It never made sense because it hurt more for him to stay—emotionally and physically—but I couldn't tell my mind that. I couldn't rationalize that in my own logical mind. I'd become stuck. Even after he was gone, it took me a long time, and I'm not even sure I'm truly over him. But it took sacrifice and I had to understand the meaning of that sacrifice. I don't know what Indiana meant to you, but you have to accept that her sacrifice meant something."

Anora rubbed her hands. They felt clammy and her skin prickled with sweat. She'd exposed the chink in her dragon armor. Would he draw the black arrow? *I am death*, she reminded herself. *But not now*.

"I don't know if I have the luxury of taking a long time to get over someone who's been dead for months."

"I didn't say I was over Maven's death."

"Let's agree we have revenge on our side. For my part, it's been fulfilled with the death of the general." Arthur's eyes followed Isolde, who chatted with Roxanne on the work floor. She looked natural there, as if she belonged. Isolde had a gift of just melting in and fitting in with the crowd. He turned back to Anora. "But we're not done, are we?"

Anora gave her own short shake of her head.

Arthur smiled and put a hand on her shoulder. "Didn't think so. We'll get there. Before I die, I'll hand just the right person to you and you can do whatever you'd like to them."

"Before I kill you, you mean?" Anora said with a bit of sarcasm.

"That's why I'm really here, after all."

"Is that all?" Anora placed her hand on Arthur's. She felt warmth and compassion from him. He had power, too. *Caliburn* was cool on her palm, but he was a gentleman in the truest sense. She wondered if he had been conditioned this way or if he had just grown up with this sort of Boy Scout sensibility. She decided it didn't matter as long as he never gave up being the right kind of person. It was an admirable quality, though she would have to disappoint him in the end. If she believed in fate.

"One, privacy, please," Anora said. The glass went opaque and the door locked.

"I am a fan of technology," Arthur said.

"Don't ruin it by talking," Anora said. She took his hand and led him to the sofa.

Arthur opened his mouth and then shut it. She undressed for him, feeling almost as bare as she'd ever been since Reince. It was difficult and she felt anxious, but he took her hand and massaged it again, and the anxiety melted away. Were they using each other? Possibly, a small part of her mind said, but they needed each other.

"SMELLS LIKE SEX IN HERE," Isolde said.

"I think there's some Febreze in one of the cabinets," Anora said. In a rare change of clothing, she wore lounge pants, but still wore a rocker tee. Her comfort level at the moment was high. Anora felt good. The buzz of things inside her head had subsided for now. There was a lot to do, but she did want to bask in a little afterglow. It'd been . . . years? *That can't be right*, she thought. Still, she felt good —better than any day she'd had after her treatment.

"I was hoping you'd just hold hands, not do the opposite of what I said."

"He held my hand when I jumped off the building. Isn't that enough?"

"*I* held your hand, too. Maybe there's a chance for me?"

"You're a little too young," Anora said with a smile. Isolde was snarky. She liked it so far. Maybe she could put One into learning mode. Anora stretched. Did she wrench her back? Had it really been years since she had sex?

"Hello?" Isolde said.

Anora shrugged. "Sorry, sex brain fog."

"He gets around, you know. Be careful. Everyone who loves him dies."

"Kai?"

"Romantically, you weirdo. What's this Indiana thing you didn't want to tell me about?"

Anora wound her hair up and handed Isolde a pair of AR glasses. Isolde put them on.

"One, what do you have?"

One appeared in between Isolde and Anora, making Isolde jump. "I have a progress report on unpacking the Janus device. Would you like a visual?"

"Aren't you a creepy little Anora. Mini-Anora. Minora. Get it?"

"Menorah?" One replied. "I don't—"

"Stick to the task, please," Anora said. *No learning mode.*

One raised a hand and a dense cloud of data unpacked from it. It glowed amber and red.

"This is not like any neural network I've ever seen," Anora said.

"It's a neural network?" Isolde asked.

"Part of one."

One reported, "I've identified some of the external connections that take external input and adapted my input to them. From the instruction set, I'm able to parse and reassemble the system. It continues to absorb resources to maintain itself. Whatever held this structure was quite large."

"All I see are dots and lines," Isolde said.

Anora made a shrinking motion with her hands and the system collapsed into a nebula. "It's very dense."

"That's good or bad?"

"It just is, but it tells me that this wasn't done by any scientist I know. I wonder, though . . ." Anora checked the time.

"I'm not seeing the problem then."

"One, can you give a representation of your relative nodal size compared to this structure? Overlay."

A blue structure appeared. It seemed to be a small sparking and glowing cloud of data, while the dark cloud loomed all around it.

"Shit," Isolde said. "That was all on one tiny Janus?"

Anora shook her head. "The best way to explain it is that a map or key was on the Janus device that led to all the stored pieces of this network. What was on Janus had gotten itself out of wherever it was but was unable or unwilling to reassemble itself."

"Do you think reassembling it would be a good idea? I'm getting mad-scientist vibes, and I've met mad scientists."

Anora pursed her lips. *I might be one.* "When Kai asks..."

Isolde put her hand on her hip. "My mom told me what to do all the time. I still don't listen to her."

Anora smiled as she studied the data. "Most people have metaphysical hang-ups when it comes to artificial intelligence. AI isn't benevolent or malignant. It just is. In some ways, it can be far superior to the human mind, but in other ways, it's far behind. What most of us think it means to be a human is just an inconvenience."

"I like the meat bag I'm living in," Isolde said. She noticed red and amber spider lines in dark patches of nothing. "There's something broken here? A gap?"

"Have you completed your assembly, One?" Anora asked.

"Yes, and there are . . . gaps in the data. Nodal connections that lead to nowhere," One replied.

"Then it's broken," Anora said.

"That sucks," Isolde concluded.

"Maybe not," Anora said. Her mind had thrown itself ahead into the problem. "One, call Alok, please."

"Nor, so good to see you!" Alok said on the video feed. His swarthy features broke into a grin.

"Thanks for taking some time to see me," Anora replied, taking a seat.

Isolde made a face and mouthed, "'Nor'?" Anora should've locked her out of the lab.

"I am never too busy for a cohort." Alok smiled. "How have you been?"

Anora smiled. Alok was the kind of friend who remembered the last time they had met, just as she did—three years ago at a conference. He was also wise enough to not pretend that they had kept in touch other than professionally.

"Doing well."

"I was sorry to hear about your brother," Alok said.

"Thank you again for the flowers and the donation to my charity."

Dr. Alok Buddhisagar waved a hand in acknowledgment. "You're doing well?"

"Quite well, actually." Anora nodded. "How's Kamala and the children?"

Isolde made a face. *Definitely no learning mode*, Anora decided.

"Almost driving, if you can believe that," Alok replied. "But this isn't a social call, doctor."

"You know me too well, doctor. I'd like to send you something secure."

"Of course. Let me—"

"I've got it," Anora said as One made a secure connection to his system.

"This is why I keep firing my CTO," Alok said, drawing his hands back from his computer system.

"Perhaps you can assist me in investigating something."

"Is something wrong?" Alok said. His eyebrows went up in alarm. Since he was a neurobiologist, it was not unusual for some of his wealthier connections to ask him for medical advice.

"Just a puzzle of sorts." Anora sent him the data stream.

Alok nodded and studied the system for long moments, twisting a pen in his fingertips in contemplation. Anora brewed a fresh cup of tea while Isolde found the Febreze. He cleared his throat. "How much do you want?" Alok asked.

"For what?"

Alok studied Anora. "My dear, this is beyond anything I've ever seen mapped before."

"It's just a neural network."

"This is not a neural network, Nor. This is *the* neural network. This is almost . . . perfect. It doesn't look like it's functioning at the moment."

"No."

"How much?"

"It's not for sale. It's not even working."

"Whose mind is it?"

"So you do think it's a mind." *Suspicion confirmed.*

"Absolutely. Someone's mapped an entire human mind. Something like this is just up your collective alley."

"This is not my work."

"I'm not sure why we're talking then. You said you have a puzzle. Are you trying to determine whose mind this is?"

"No, I'm trying to determine who would and could build something like this."

"I thought you'd know more about this than anyone I know."

Anora annotated the data. "There's a section missing or removed." She motioned to the red spiderweb of missing nodes and blackness. "Do you know why? Or better yet, how to recover it?"

"I see what you're looking for." Alok examined the data closely. "I'm not sure where the mapping aligns to, as this is quite a complex system, but it was a complete human mind at one time."

"Not an abnormal one."

"Who would go to that trouble? This is too much detail to be coincidental. I'm reminded of an article I came across a long time ago . . ." Alok's mind wandered back for a few moments. "It was in the eighties, long before you or I were even thinking about intelligence in the biological or artificial sense."

"Dr. Linus's work?" Anora asked. The idea had crossed her mind as well.

Alok nodded.

"That was a theoretical paper and nothing ever came out of his work. He retired from the field in the early nineties. No one's ever been able to map the mind the way he's suggested and artificial intelligence has made long strides since then."

"Dreams of immortality still abide, I suppose," Alok said.

"I'm sorry?"

"If you could copy your mind into a machine, you could live forever."

"Unless you had a body, there wouldn't be much point."

"Says the woman whose favorite hobby is building imaginary people." Alok smiled.

"Not anymore," Isolde snorted.

"Excuse me?" Alok said, but Anora shook her head and gave Isolde a *Shut the hell up* look. Alok noted the black and red mass in the nodal map. "This was done on purpose. You've concluded that it's not an inferior mind, nor a damaged one. What about corrupt data?"

"These red nodes I've marked are input/output nodes. Special connections, which lends credence to your thought that whatever they're connected to was removed. Why?"

"There're too many possible reasons for that, but let's surmise that it was a working system. What kinds of things would you need to constrain in such a system?"

"Emotions, expansion, and consumption of resources."

"All accounted for?"

Anora nodded.

Alok tapped his lips with his fingers. He twirled the image. "This might be the surgeon in me, but there was something in this mind that was removed. Something that made it functional, or controlled it. Perhaps it was a fail-safe. Imagine the possibilities if such a mind existed in the wild . . ." His mind went far away. "I'm sorry, there's no way to reconstruct what was once there. You could take a similar mind, but the connections between neurons are absolutely unique."

"You've confirmed a few things for me, Alok. Even after all the research I've done, I needed someone of your caliber to confirm my suspicions."

"What are you going to do with it?"

"I've done all I can."

"I'd like to research it myself if you can make it function."

"No promises."

"Please, Nor. You're brilliant. You're twice the mind of your brother in the right places, God rest his soul."

"If you're trying to butter me up—"

"I already know how to do that. You just let me in on this fascinating opportunity."

"I will put you at the top of the one-person list," Anora promised.

"You look a little different today."

Isolde snorted again.

"Perhaps that's neurological bias on your part?" Anora offered.

"Perhaps, but I'm not flattering you. When I saw you last, you were still hell-bent."

"I'm not hell-bent now?"

"Oh no, you still are. But you seem like you have a destination in mind."

"I do," Anora said. "Good seeing you, Alok. My love to Kamala and the girls."

"God bless them and you, Anora. My love to Zero and One."

Anora cut the connection. So Oracle was complete, but there was something missing. *How the hell do I solve that problem?*

19

THE RUNDOWN

SOMEWHERE IN ROMANIA—
The hair prickled at the back of Owen's neck and he woke up instantly. He reached out. Yes, there was a manifest field. *Chevaliers*. He glanced at his watch. That had taken less time than he thought. He wondered who it was. He doubted it was Mara herself, though she'd have been more than happy to return the favor of his stabbing her with *Splinter*. The Chevaliers were close and he'd have to get moving. It was hard not to snap up the waveform. Manifesting was like a drug worse than anything he'd experienced. He'd quit cold turkey these last couple of weeks, more out of necessity than by design. He'd left the grid in the SUV when he ditched Mara. He'd rather have been wandering the wilderness than getting controlled by whatever was driving him. He wondered how they'd found him. It didn't matter if he could get away. All he'd been going on was that lingering need to go east.

He got up and grabbed his pack. He flipped through the train schedule. He could get something that'd put him out of their range for the moment, then change toward a direction they weren't expecting. If he got underground, then he could figure out how they'd found him. He cracked open the hotel door and checked the hallway.

Clear. He went to the window, grabbing his pack and sliding it over his shoulders. Standing well clear of the windows, he checked the streets, but there was little to see in the foggy predawn morning. He didn't worry about snipers; he was too valuable alive—at least for Morgan's purposes.

He cleared out his room and checked the hallway again. He went down the stairs, checking the stairwell. He felt the matrix, taunting him. He rubbed *Nornian*. They were in the area and on the hunt. He had to get to one of his safe houses, but the only shielded one he could get to was farther than he could manage without transportation. He'd need a car. He entered the lobby, where a few early morning travelers milled around. A guest chatted with the valet as he waited for a car, huddled against the late December cold. Owen paused at the door until the car pulled around, then he stepped out with the guest.

"Sorry," Owen said, grabbing the driver's wrist and twisting it back just as the valet opened the door. He pulled the valet out of the car and sent him tumbling head over heels onto the pavement. He spun the shrieking man and shoved him, sending him tumbling over the valet. In a moment, Owen was in the Mercedes, his pack next to him. He slammed the car into gear and pushed down the accelerator as folks shouted around him. He gunned the engine, the feeling of the matrix never leaving him. He swerved onto a foggy side street. A black figure loomed out of the darkness as he passed. He barely had a glimpse and hammered down on the accelerator. There was a flash of light. The waveblade cut right through the hood. Owen swerved, the front tire blew, and the blade ran along the passenger side of the Mercedes as the Chevalier stepped free. Owen tried to control the Mercedes, but the engine was destroyed and the steering was out. He slid onto the sidewalk and bounced along the wall. He rammed on the gas, but the engine died. He yanked the wheel to the right to give some clearance and the car grudgingly obeyed before it lumbered to a stop. He squeezed out of the car door. The Chevalier ran after him full tilt. No sense in hiding now. The Chevalier wore the gray uniform. Was it Pellam or Le? It was neither. Light reflected from his silvered hand. A gauntlet. Top of the line now.

Owen grabbed the slippery waveform of *Nornian* and summoned his waveblade into existence. He leapt onto the hood of the car as the Chevalier ran over the trunk and top. The blades rebounded on the first strike and then they fought with intensity. He was good and learning fast. Owen parried and countered, using his strength to push the Chevalier back. This guy was new—a little green. Owen forced him back just enough, then he swiped downward with *Nornian*, taking out the front windshield. The Chevalier lost his footing and fell back, collapsing into the crumpled hood. Owen leaned down and lightly touched *Nornian* to the man's focal gauntlet, atomizing a hole in it. The Chevalier's halo winked out. *I found a design flaw, Richard.* Owen cold-cocked the man.

Owen jumped down just in time for the second Chevalier to come at him. She stopped just short of him, her blade swinging wild. He leaned back and brought his blade up to counter her attack, but instead of cutting back, she spun and kicked him square in the groin.

Owen saw stars. *Nornian* went out and he fell down, nauseous. He still held on to the waveform, but the woman didn't wait. She hit him with a backhand with the gauntlet. He spun and swiped with his foot, but she backed up. Martially trained. Not Kara. He manifested, bringing *Nornian* to bear just as she swung down in an overhand slice. He blocked the blade, shifting blue and moving it down to touch her forearm.

She yelped and backed away, her blade vanishing as her hand seized up. She circled him like a wounded tigress. He vomited, and it cleared his head. He stood, still smarting from her lucky strike. He had to give her credit—whatever training she'd had before the Chevaliers, it was serving her well. She wasn't used to swordplay, though. He advanced on her, and she danced back, wringing life into her hand through the gauntlet. He thought he smelled hydraulic fluid. Hell, these weren't even the final focal gloves. They'd sent whatever they had after him. Mara must have been confident in the numbers they got from the tanks to send a pair after him newly minted.

Where was the grid? He lunged within her range. She countered with a forearm strike, but he blocked with his off hand, then jammed blue *Nornian* into her exposed thigh. She fell like a sack of potatoes.

Owen sucked wind for a moment. The Chevalier thrashed on the ground as the neural storm crept up her spine. "Cheap shot," he spat. She kicked at him with her good leg, but with her nervous system still firing pain and impulses up her spine, it was just flailing. His blade went pure white and he put his foot on her chest. He pushed the waveblade to her face and she leaned back away from it.

"You like being hunted?"

Then the feeling trickled down into his body, taking control of him. The compulsion gripped him so tightly that he couldn't move for a moment. His mind was blank. Again he saw Indiana, screaming. Her eyes were squeezed shut, but his consciousness was open and a torrent of emotion hit him in waves. It was stripping his mind bare. It just wanted him. Wanted him to go to her, and there was nothing but raw emotion. Want. Nothing he could do to stop it. He couldn't even let go of the waveform. His mind was locked in the grip of whatever it was. Whatever she was. It was burning his mind out because it did not know how to let him do what he had to. He only had one desire. Her want was his want and he could not comply.

The Chevalier's good arm shot up and she stabbed him in the side. He flinched away, but only enough to make it shallow. The pain shot through the compulsion and he was able to let go.

Her hand came away. She had a utility knife of some kind in her hand. *Smart.*

He punched her in the head hard, and she went limp as her head cracked the ground. Owen lay there for an eternity, gasping for breath, his mind trying to regather itself after the onslaught. How did you fight something like that? It was just . . . raw power. He knew one thing for sure. He was going the wrong way now. He was in Eastern Europe and was being pulled in the other direction.

He heard the woman shake, her head thrashing a little. and the creak of metal as the man tried to extricate himself from the car. Owen's side burned like hell. He felt for the cut, which might've been more deadly if he hadn't flinched away. His fingers were wet with blood. He couldn't seize the waveform through the pain, as slippery as it was. And he didn't want to.

Owen got to his feet. He didn't wait, but ran back to the Mercedes and wrenched his pack free. He ran as best he could. His side burned and each breath was agony. Not far away he heard the wail of a train. He cursed himself and kept moving. It hurt with every step, but the pain gave him strength. Strength gave him anger and anger fueled him. He was still alive and still himself.

∼

"You look like hell," Piotr said.

"You're a beautiful ballerina," Owen hissed, leaning against the door. "You going to let me in?"

"Do I have a choice?" Piotr moved, and Owen stepped through the doorway and down the wooden stairs to the concrete basement. Each step was agony in his side, but he stanched the bleeding.

He shouldered through a heavy iron door into a small, well-appointed room. It looked exactly as he remembered it.

"You need a doctor?"

"Got a surgical kit? I can sew it up."

"I have that and some good mash."

"That'll do," Owen said, handing Piotr a roll of money. The man tucked it into his hoodie. "Sterile?"

"Please. I'm not a dirty Russian like in the movies," Piotr said, affecting a bad Russian movie accent, and his smile curled the corners of his mouth. "You really do look like shit, kid. You want last rites?"

Owen chuckled. "No, sir. Just want to lie down for a moment. I'm in a lot of pain."

"I'll get some morphine. You'll be isolated here. Off the grid, as you like to say. What else you need?"

"Burner phone. I need to go somewhere."

"You sound unsure."

"I'm winging this one."

"That's not like you. Very dangerous. You want me to call your ma?"

Owen shook his head. It was a joke they'd shared when Owen was a teenager in training. Whenever things got difficult, Piotr would ask him that simple question. He was made of stronger stuff. Or at least he thought he was.

"All right. I'll get you some clothes. I like your haircut. Did you go blond? Beard looks manly, too."

Owen shook his head and Piotr shrugged.

Owen handed his pack to Piotr. "Can you have this checked?"

"I'll let you know." Piotr took the bag and left.

Owen was tired, though it'd only been a few hours since he'd woken up in the hotel. It may have been the lack of blood, but he wasn't dizzy or faint. He peeled off his jacket. Blood had soaked his shirt and side. He should've killed the woman. He pulled the shirt up and inspected the wound. She had hit the muscle and it was bleeding. He'd have to suture it up, but it would've been worse if she'd gotten her waveblade into him. He could've lost a limb. At least he knew in the last couple of weeks Richard hadn't gotten KE shields working.

He clenched his hand, working the muscles and feeling *Nornian*. He frowned and silently cursed his mother. If he was perfect, why was he the only one who had the compulsion? It wasn't fair. Did Arthur feel this pain when he manifested?

Piotr came back to bring him a suture kit and morphine. Owen took the morphine and then worked on the wound, sewing it up as best as he could. He passed out a few times as the pain spiked through the painkiller. He finally placed a bandage over the wound and collapsed on the bed in a flop sweat. He wiped his forehead and the world spun into blackness.

Owen awoke with a shout. The pain lanced up his side. He saw his pack beside the door where Piotr had placed it. It must have been clean if it was in the cage with him. He lay back, running his fingers through his hair. He didn't know what he was doing. The compulsion burned in his mind and made his skin crawl.

He got up, taking care with his side. Fresh clothes were laid out for him. He changed his bandage, which had seeped a bit, then pulled on the black henley. A gun lay on the table if he needed it. He glanced down at his hand. The thick *Nornian* rings were dark and cold. He thought about taking them off for the first time since he'd put them on. Could he even shoot if the compulsion grabbed him? He left the gun where it was for now. If he stayed away from the Chevaliers, he'd need to rely on the accessible killing instrument. A shame though, as it felt like a relic of the past. As long as he held on to the waveform, he would be impervious to bullets. He'd no longer need the gun, but if the compulsion continued, he'd have to stay away from manifesting. It was a circular problem.

He did a few careful isometric exercises until the dregs of the compulsion were pushed away to a dull ache in the back of his head. He was hungry now. He opened the heavy steel door. A woman stood there.

The Taser hit him before he was able to seize the waveform. Not that it would've helped—there was no active matrix nearby. Owen fell back, grunting and hitting the floor as the weapon sent fifty thousand volts through his body along the dart wires.

"These things do work," Jeri Brand said to the Taser, looking down at the body of her brother. She knelt over him, looking at him closely, and frowned. "Shit."

20

LOOKING FOR ANSWERS

WESTCHESTER, NEW YORK—
Piles and piles of notebooks lay strewn about Anora. Oracle was complete now, save for the missing component, part of its brain. She'd done a number of tests to see if it would operate, to no avail. So, to alleviate her boredom at the impasse, she'd given Roxy the final touches on CAMLANN and decided to delve into her brother's research. Something tickled in the back of her brain. Dr. August Linus had essentially disappeared into the belly of DARPA. The latter years' notes were missing—likely due to the loss of the notebooks at Avallach—but what she had was enlightening.

There was a breadth of production from his younger days, when she was a child. It was slow work, as her brother wrote in a cipher and the material was dense with data. She'd have to get One to digitize all of this information. There, she'd found it: a reference to Project Dream Catcher. It was a short-lived project, built upon a proposal its inventor called the Mind Trap. Its inventor, Dr. Nimue Scatha, had passed away before she could complete the work. She sifted through the time period, noting tiny references to the nearly insurmountable problems they had encountered on the project.

Maven had helped Nimue. There were notes here about his theorem, too. He'd listed a number of possible experiments. Another note in the margin—Dr. Linus was brought in to wind down Dream Catcher after Nimue's death. Could her work be inside Delphi? Delphi had been around some time already if the tiny notes Maven had made throughout the years meant anything. What was Dream Catcher then? It hardly seemed plausible that Nimue had created something like an AI thirty years ago. The sheer processing power didn't exist then. But what if she wasn't creating a digital mind? She pored over the text, looking for small hints, but she kept getting sidetracked by Maven's primary notes on his obsession: the psychogenetics theorem. He'd shared it with Anora many times as they refined it over the years, but he rarely mentioned that he'd wanted to actually test the theorem. She gave up on Dream Catcher and sat back to think about the theorem.

Maven's psychogenetics theorem was still unproven, and while he had written a number of experiments to determine the validity of the theorem, none of them were viable.

One chimed. Anora rubbed her neck. "Is it time?"

"Nearly."

Anora leaned over and turned on the portable AR rig she'd had Heph put together for her. After setting up her lab and creating portable units so the sisters could access CAMLANN, she'd wanted her own rig to test. After it warmed up, it did a quick scan of her surroundings and then focused its lenses on her. She put her glasses on. One stood next to her.

"Show me Maven's theorem, please."

"His original or your modified one?"

"The modified, of course."

The data appeared in front of her like a large map. She knew it by heart, but she examined it with fresh eyes. Could she see what Maven had been doing at Avallach? Before Avallach? Was Arthur really just an experiment for the focal technology or something more?

"Looking for a clue?" Maven sat down next to her.

"I thought I got rid of you."

One looked at Anora, but knew, based on her non-verbal cues that Anora was not addressing the AI. She was used to Anora talking her way through problems.

Maven chuckled. "I'm just as much a manifestation of your mind as One here is." He patted One on the leg. It looked perfectly natural, although One did not react. Of course not—One couldn't see Anora's dead brother.

"I've been sitting here for two days and now you come to me?"

"You needed to process the information before I could answer your questions."

"You're not helpful," Anora snapped.

"You're getting a little obsessed with him, aren't you?"

"He's an interesting experiment."

"I often called him that. He never enjoyed it much. His mother, Igerne, was more forgiving."

"What were you trying to do? Force a focal point to happen?"

Maven spread his hands and he pointed to a few of the variables at the beginning of his theorem. "As you can see, none of my proposed experiments would pass muster. They may have bordered on inhumane in most places. That's a touchy subject and not something I needed to deal with."

Anora smiled. "You were never one to skirt controversy. You often experimented on people. Just look at Avallach and all of the candidates who failed out of that."

Maven nodded. "If I could influence the initial variables, I could cause the focus to present itself. It was a harmless concept at the time—perfectly within the bounds of propriety, if a bit unconventional."

"Project Spartan?"

"That was one of them, of course."

"That was deemed a failure."

"What I was looking for and what the government wanted were two different things. It was logged as a failure and shut down, but we didn't always terminate the projects in the barbaric way that Marks was wont to do."

"That's where Arthur came from. He was the focus you were working on."

Maven shrugged. "One of them. Probably the right one. At least, that's what you're thinking right now. He's certainly brought more things about than the others, so I'd say the probability of his being a locus is strong."

Anora rubbed her eyes. "You said 'a locus'—"

"Yes. A locus. I mentioned this. She cannot come out of thin air, you see. She has to have the right parentage—"

"Anora?" Percy said, rapping on the door and entering. "You all right? You're talking to yourself again."

Anora pulled off her glasses, feeling as if she were on the cusp of something. Maven was gone.

"Yes?" Anora said. She powered off the portable unit and closed it up. She made a mental note to have Heph build her a more practical one.

Percy leaned on the door. "Izzy's back. She said she has what One asked for."

Anora stood. "If I must."

"Must what?"

"You should be happy you're a man."

Percy smiled. "I'm not sure how to respond to that."

"You don't have to wear a bra or a dress."

"I could wear a kilt."

"No," Anora replied.

"I would like to state for the record that I, as a representative sample male of the species, applaud your efforts to look appealing and attractive," Percy said.

"In many species, the male is the one who does the preening. And there are some where the female also kills her mate after breeding."

"Kill the mood, why don't you?" Percy chuckled.

"Are you settled in?"

"Pretty much. Thank you for taking us in. This was Maven's house, right?" Percy eyed the stacks of notebooks.

"I stayed here while I convalesced a few months ago."

"Was it serious?" Percy said, and Anora read the word "cancer" on his expression.

Anora thought about her treatment for a moment. "It was difficult, but I got through it." She shrugged it off. "The summers here are beautiful, as are all the seasons, though you won't appreciate the snow when you can't get up the hill. The house is yours to use as much as you like. Lamar's getting good care?"

Percy walked her to the door. "Probably the best. Lilly and I appreciate it."

Anora gave him a crooked smile. "Before you think I'm altruistic, it's more than practical. I wanted you free from dependency on the Scientia. Things are going on there that I'd rather you not be involved in. And in case I need to contact Ellen discreetly—"

"I'm aware there's a catch. Seems to be a low bar for me."

Anora handed him a terminal. "If you need me, use this, not Janus. It's just as secure, but I always have a direct line to One." She thought for a moment. "Unless I'm in jail."

"Spent some time in the big house?"

"Culpeper, Virginia."

"Sounds quaint."

"It was." Anora opened the door to find Isolde standing there, holding a lovely cocktail dress.

"Oh, that looks dreadful to wear," Percy said, rolling his eyes.

"It's positively scandalous," Isolde said, throwing it into Anora's arms.

"Is every member of Avallach this sarcastic?" Anora asked.

"Not Arthur or Kai," Percy replied.

Anora shook her head, giving Arthur a brief thought. A locus? Could he be one? Who was the "she" that Maven had mentioned? It had to be something she knew intimately—he was part of her fractured mind, after all.

She went to one of the nearby rooms and changed out of her customary clothing into something more fetching. She admired herself in the mirror, then picked up a clutch and put her terminal inside, checking that she had a compact and lipstick. She knew she hadn't put them there. One was indeed better than an Alfred Pennyworth—providing Isolde with every detail.

Anora stepped out of the room to find Isolde, Percy, and Lilly. Percy whistled and Lilly punched him in the arm.

"I'm being polite," Percy explained.

"I know I'm missing something good!" Lamar yelled from another room somewhere in the house.

"You ain't missing nothin'!" Lilly yelled back. "Just some hoochie in a skirt!"

"Damn it, stop teasing me, woman!"

"Language!" Lilly yelled back.

"Is it Izzy?"

"Wanna borrow my diamond?" Isolde said, holding up the diamond necklace from around her neck. "It'd show off that serious cleavage."

"Absolutely not! But thank you anyway," Anora said, smiling.

"You look good," Lilly said, giving Anora a kiss on the cheek. "Is this a gala or something CEOs do?"

"Thanks, and it's just dinner. Might end up in a funeral though," Anora said.

"Arthur time?" Percy wiggled his eyebrows.

Isolde snorted, offering Anora her fur coat. "She wishes. You know they—"

Anora elbowed Isolde in the stomach and took her coat.

Isolde wheezed and then laughed.

"Kai has him confined to *Camelot*," Anora said. The fact that Arthur had disappeared from all news outlets had put the media in a tizzy. Anora was more concerned with things that might be going on in the background. Did they know where *Camelot* was?

"Like that's stopped him before." Percy helped put the coat onto her shoulders. "Knock 'em dead, I guess?"

"We'll see." Anora winked at Lilly.

Anora shifted gears, putting Arthur out of her mind. Thinking of him wouldn't do for what was coming up next. Not at all.

Anora and Isolde got into her limo. She had a long drive ahead of her, so she decided she might as well get some work done. She smiled at Isolde.

Isolde rubbed her stomach. "You're mean. Next time you don't like advertising rubbing genitals, just say so."

"It's not something I like to advertise," Anora replied.

"Been that long, huh?" Isolde smiled and let it drop. "What did you find out?"

"Maven was doing a lot of work I hadn't been really privy to. That's fair. He never knew what I'd done at my company, just some quantum work at the NSA. I do have an idea about what was going on with Oracle, but it doesn't solve the problem of its being broken. And I did learn something about Longinus from his later notes."

"Really? I thought you lost the last year of notes after Tintagel went boom."

Anora shook her head. "That part is true, but he'd been working on Longinus since long before that with Dr. di Lago."

"Longinus was important to him—important enough for Kai and Indiana to steal *Archimedes* and launch it into orbit."

"It was foolish, really. That satellite could've been launched any time we wanted it to," Anora said. She rubbed her chin and buried herself in her fur for a moment. "Still, it did tell me one thing. I'd gone over the schematics for Longinus and dragged it out of Nikolai Gastov over the threat of canceling his *Archimedes* project."

"I thought you did cancel *Archimedes*."

Anora smiled. "It's business. Longinus is a prototype for a long-range grid."

"Grid? Collector grid?" Isolde asked. "That seems ridiculous. Low orbit is, what? A hundred miles up?"

"Closer to twelve hundred miles."

Isolde blinked. "Seriously? Grid range of twelve hundred miles? We can't get more than a mile on our portable systems, sometimes three miles on the bigger ones we had at Tintagel. Does it work?"

Anora shrugged. "It was never tested, but I think the theory is sound. The ground collector grids are omnidirectional. Roughly spherical or cylindrical, propagating outward from the source system. Longinus is a beam. Unidirectional, pushing the grid from a projection system the size of a pencil over the surface of the Earth. The beam widens, theoretically to a size of about ten miles of coverage."

"Jesus," Isolde said. "Grids are an Achilles heel for Avallach. We saw that in Geneva when they were taken down and Dr. di Lago was killed." Isolde frowned.

Anora reached over and grabbed her hand. She knew the memory pained Isolde. It had tipped the scales against her father. If Anora played her own cards right, Isolde would help her as well. "It's a possibility, but I'm afraid to test it any time soon. I don't think it was truly ready when Maven had it assembled. He must've felt some urgency when Donna was killed. He wanted some way to keep his project alive."

Isolde nodded, playing with her necklace. "I wonder if my father had the same idea. He once said to me that I was 'the most valuable thing in the world.' He became overprotective after Avallach, but I needed my space from him. I didn't know he killed your brother, but I suppose I should've known. He was not a good person."

"It seems not a lot of us had good parents," Anora replied, thinking about her own abusive relationship with her father, Jun Degan Lee. That was the first time Maven had rescued her from a terrible fate. It was a debt she could never repay now. "Parentage" That word tickled the back of her mind. She filed it away. She had to get ready for her next fight.

She pulled out her terminal. "One, is the payload prepped?"

"Loaded and ready."

"Sounds dangerous," Isolde said.

Anora turned to her. "I shouldn't bring you to this meeting, but the only reason Mara Holt is feeling me out is that she thinks I know something. I think it's about Arthur. I am worried that . . . Simon might not be enough."

"Should I stay out of sight?"

"Yes."

"Oh my God. Say it."

"No."

"Say it! You need me! You need me!" Isolde laughed.

"Bitch," Anora said, smiling.

"You're late," Mara said. "I didn't think you'd show up." She stood, but Anora brushed past her and sat down opposite. The maître d' seated her.

"You look nice," Anora said. "Green is your color."

"It's been a while since I've worn something like this, but it feels appropriate. It still fits. Nice to see you dressed up. You look ready to kill."

"I'd say that I look fat or something self-deprecating, but I'm not in the mood," Anora said. "It has been a few weeks since you invited me to dinner."

"I bet Zero made you come."

"Zero's been retired," Anora replied. "But my assistant did prompt me." Anora wasn't surprised Mara remembered her first AI design.

"That's new. What happened?"

"Technology becomes obsolete." Anora glanced at the wine list and opted for a Cabernet. The sommelier and departed without a word.

"I heard you're working on something new," Mara said.

"I heard you're not working at all. You're in the private sector?"

Mara smiled and was quiet for a moment. She reached out a hand, palm up. Anora considered, then put her hand in Mara's. "Let me start over. We're already trying to talk business. It wasn't always business between us, was it?"

Anora gave a slight shake of her head. "Not always. There was friendship." Anora caressed Mara's hand. There was something curious to the feel of her fingers, soft and supple. "Thank you for choosing this place." Anora did mean it. The restaurant was large and airy, which meant Mara might've remembered her claustrophobia or was just nostalgic for their first date.

"I'm grateful that you helped my career along," Mara said, squeezing her hand.

"You were in the right place at the right time. I thought the agency was going to be your career. You had aspirations."

"People change, I suppose. I was a bit too wide-eyed. You told me as much, even then."

"You became disillusioned? O'Brian thought you were a gifted analyst and had the talent for fieldwork."

Mara nodded.

"You still talk to Zeke?" Anora asked.

"Occasionally. You know how the agency is. When you're in, you're in. When you're out, you're out."

"Somehow I don't believe that," Anora said, taking her hand away from Mara's.

"Are you still mad at me or are you mad at Zeke?"

Anora smiled. "That's a good question."

"Can't we be friends?" Mara asked.

"Mara, darling. You get in my face and demand a meeting out of the blue. And all you want is to be friends? Let's not fool around with each other. I have better things to do. I'm quite busy, you know."

"Fair enough. I did ask," Mara said, but did not offer up anything.

Anora decided to try another tack. "I'm curious. You left the agency only two years ago. Were you a part of the Janus project?"

Mara nodded. "I helped get it off the ground. It took a very long time."

"Did you lift my source code, then?"

Mara smiled. "I'm not an engineer. You know that. But I brought in someone familiar with your work."

Familiar? Anora swirled and tasted her wine after the pour. She nodded to the sommelier and thought about it for a moment, flipping through the roster of names. She had her own suspicions, but she ventured a guess. "Sean Calloway?"

Mara smiled behind her glass. "He managed to develop Janus's potential well. How did you find out about Janus?"

"Zeke told me," Anora lied.

"I doubt that."

"You got me there."

Mara played with her glass. "Calloway and I left the agency at the same time, unfortunately. You can take your anger out on him if you wish. The agency won't complain."

Anora thought about that for a while. Sean Calloway had been one of her students when she was working on her doctorate ages ago. She'd once suspected that he'd stolen some of her code. Her argument over the nature of the breach was what led her to abandon an academic career to focus on private industry full-time. *And Reince*, she reminded herself. She couldn't stay in academia after Reince. What was Sean up to now? She hadn't thought to keep tabs on him. She filed that away but kept on the hunt. Mara was after something.

Mara continued. "What are you working on nowadays? Something for the government?"

"After finding out about Janus, I don't think I'll work for them again. Binary has a few contracts, though. Nothing I'm involved with directly. You went into private consulting, right? Not computer related. You worked for Samson Consulting for a while, but last year you left them. Why?"

"I like to keep my options open." Mara's eyes twinkled and she drank her wine. She was working for someone, Anora was sure. Something DARPA related? Anora then noticed her fingers. She thought she could detect the impression of rings on her hand. She might have been imagining it in this low lighting. If Anora hadn't already been on guard, she was now. That's what she'd been up to. Not having the rings meant she'd certainly be vulnerable. She thought about asking Isolde to cut her down. It was an entertaining thought. She rubbed the back of her neck. She was definitely in a dangerous place.

"You're working on a new AI? Or for a new client?"

"A bit of both," Anora admitted. She knew Mara wasn't registered with the Mare de Scientia. She had the potential, but it became problematic to work in the intelligence community and be a part of the Sisterhood for a vast number of reasons, with secrecy above everything. There were a few, like Anora herself, but it required careful compartmentalization—at least when Anora had worked for the agency.

"Would it be for someone we both know?"

Anora laughed. "Really, Mara. I thought you were field trained. That's the worst question I've ever been handed and I've been grilled once this month already."

Mara smiled. Anora admitted she looked stunning tonight. She wore her hair up, something she only did for business, but Anora saw the emerald earrings dangling from her ears. They sparkled, and the shadows of the gems made Anora think of hidden facets. Something resonated within Anora. Had she had that thought before? She filed it away and returned to the task. What was Mara looking for?

Arthur, of course. At least now that she was on the inside, everything seemed to point that way. She looked over Mara's shoulder. Maven stood behind Mara with that inscrutable expression. He stared at Anora, daring her to think it through.

"Are you all right?" Mara asked.

Anora picked up her menu and pretended to read it. "I was thinking about my brother just now."

"I'm sorry to—"

"Let's not dwell on it. He's dead and gone." Anora gave Maven a look that he characteristically ignored.

"You were always pragmatic. Why were you never in the field?"

"I have other talents."

Mara smiled at that. Mara was smart but not brilliant. Her physicality and skills were useful to the agency, but she wasn't a mastermind. There was someone behind her. Who? Maven leaned over Mara. "Why is she really here?" he whispered, echoing her thoughts.

Anora skimmed through the menu, already having memorized it. She ordered and handed the card back to the waiter. She frowned at her brother.

"Who does she work for?" Maven whispered next to Mara's ear.

"What are you really up to these days?" Anora asked, wiping her frown away with a napkin.

Mara drank. "I work for a new consulting firm now—very small. We're preparing to operationalize new technology for fieldwork."

"That's vaguely cryptic."

Mara shrugged. "It's the nature of the business."

"Interesting," Maven said, standing up and folding his hands behind his back. "What do you think? Don't be stupid."

"Are you looking for Apollo?" Anora asked point blank.

"No more than you are, it seems."

"So you are. Did you find out his real name?"

"The agency knows his real name. They just can't seem to find him. It was distracting when he popped up in the wrong places. Now it's distracting that he's showing up all over the news networks."

"It does seem to make a sort of sense if you follow it," Maven said. He stroked his goatee briefly.

"His appearance in New York was convenient," Anora said.

"Wasn't it?" Mara said, and the slightest dilation in her pupils gave Anora just what she needed to know. Maven smiled that rare smile of satisfaction in a shared a secret. One pinged.

"Excuse me," Anora said, reaching down for her clutch and checking the screen.

Program ready, One's message said. She pushed the phone back into her purse.

"Something important?" Mara asked.

"Depends on what you think's important, running two companies at once. Nothing that will take me away, if you're worried about that."

"No."

Anora took another sip of her wine and felt adventurous now. The program was in place and she would have something on Mara now. "Did you run into Sean recently?"

"I'm about to meet him for some related business. Your name came up when he mentioned Delphi," Mara replied. That first was a lie, Anora knew. Delphi, though. She wasn't after Arthur at all. She was looking for Oracle! Anora drank to hide her face in case the color drained from it. Mara was more dangerous than she'd known. Oracle was safe, though not working. But what if whoever created Oracle still had the original? Maven's gray eyes positively sparkled in excitement.

21

HAND OF GOD?

SOMEWHERE IN ROMANIA—
Owen's mind was fogged. He coughed and rolled over. Jeri was sitting across from him, relaxed. "Jer?" he said in a cracked voice.

"Hey, kid," Jeri replied, putting down the book she was reading.

"You tased me?"

"I thought you were someone else."

Owen scrubbed his fingers through his short blond hair. "I'm getting that a lot lately. Are you alone?"

"Just me. Maman's not here if that's who you're worried about."

Owen clutched at his side. It actually felt much better. How long had he been out? "There are other people I need to worry about."

Jeri smiled.

"Damn, it's good to see you, Jeri. It's been—"

"Years, I know."

Owen nodded. He and Jeri had never been close. He'd never really been that close to any of his siblings. He worked with Aggy and Gavin, but that work had tapered off in the months since he had been assigned to Brightwork. Jeri probably knew that.

"You look great, actually. You grow out your hair?"

Jeri played with her hair. "No, I've been meaning to get it cut. It's too thick to manage when it's long. You look like hell."

"I'm in some trouble. I don't mean to be rude, but why are you here?"

"That's the big question, really, isn't it?"

"That and why you tased me."

Jeri held up a Beretta nine millimeter. "Would you prefer—"

"No, that's okay. You're awfully well armed just to come see me."

"I honestly didn't know what to expect, but I came anyway."

Owen looked at Jeri closely. She did look well. Her platinum-blond hair framed her face. She normally wore it a couple of inches shorter, mostly for convenience. The jade glint in her eyes seemed dulled somehow—a dark, haunted look to them. Yet she watched him with wariness. No one was comfortable around Owen now that was he was more like Arthur than ever. She wore a gray Burberry cashmere coat and a green scarf tied close about her neck, and her gloved hands were folded on her lap. The Taser and the pistol sat next to her, but she had already forgotten them. Owen knew he could take her if he had to. She was trained, military but not special forces or paramilitary training. Or was she? He hadn't seen her in years. She looked older, of course, but nothing else about her seemed different.

The relaxed air she held gave way to another feeling. Jeri leaned forward, elbows on knees. "How long have you been manifesting?"

"What?" Owen said, surprised.

"You're wearing focal rings, *mon frère*," Jeri said. Her eyes flicked to his hand. *Nornian.* "Are they her rings? Indiana's?"

"Why would you know that?"

"There's no grid right now and if you don't want me to shoot you, tell me if those are her rings, Prime."

"Don't call me that," Owen growled.

The muzzle of the Beretta was cold against his temple.

"Interesting," Owen said.

Jeri frowned. "Are those her rings?"

Owen smiled. "No, they're not her rings. They're someone else's. Can we not kill each other right now? I have enough family who hates me. Plus, I got stabbed tonight."

Jeri put the gun back to her side. "I changed the dressing. You're not in any danger and it should heal in a few days."

"Thanks."

Jeri frowned. "There's no one I know in Europe right now. Your own people?"

Owen nodded.

"That's something to consider," Jeri said, running fingers through her hair.

"You look troubled, *ma sœur*. Why are you here?"

"I didn't think it was to find you."

"How long have *you* been manifesting?" Owen asked.

"Who said—"

"Come on, if you can sense a grid, you're able to."

Jeri nodded, taking off her gloves and showing off her own set of focal rings. "I've been the only one who's had these visions. Small ones at first. I thought maybe I was showing signs of premonition. You know that runs in our family, right?"

"I can't say that I do, really." Owen wondered if that had something to do with Delphi and the aunt he never knew—Igerne.

"It runs only on the women's side. Maybe I do have it in a small quantity, but this isn't premonition." Jeri got up. Owen noticed she left the gun and Taser. He sat up as she paced the room.

"Do you want a drink?" Owen asked.

"No thanks."

He got up, fumbled around the side table, and pulled out a bottle of vodka. He uncapped it and poured himself a drink. "You sure?"

"Yes."

"Always the Puritan," Owen said, taking a drink. "That much hasn't changed."

Jeri frowned. "I drink. Just never around family. It's just—"

"Something you don't do. I get it," Owen replied. He poured a second glass as the first burned the ice out of his gut. "Should we talk about how we both might be crazy?"

"What?"

"Tell me about what's going on."

Jeri frowned. "Why are you running from your own people? Was it you in New York?"

Owen nodded. "It was a test. I thought I'd lure him out. I had it all planned out. It worked, but not in our favor. They wanted to keep me for themselves, like a lab rat." He clenched his fist, staring at his *Nornian* rings. "Lately, though, I've felt compelled. Not pushed or suggested, but compelled. It happens only when I manifest. Not all the time, but enough now. I'm not in control when it happens. It's like the hand of God reaches into my head and just takes over."

"You lose control of yourself?" Jeri asked. Her hands were inside her pockets, but Owen saw she was balling her fists.

"The only way I get control back is if I let go of the waveform. The last few times, I couldn't even do that. I got stabbed and the pain let me free myself. It could've been worse."

"Jesus," Jeri breathed. "The hand of God . . ."

"Jeri?"

"I've been having the same compulsion. Maybe not as strong, but I can't stop it. I have to come. I have to."

"What does it mean?" Owen asked, pouring himself another glass.

Jeri closed her eyes for a moment and thought about it. "Why us?" she whispered. "Did you know Indiana Beckham?"

"Not personally, no. I had no hand in her demise. That I promise," Owen said, raising his free hand as he drank. "What're you thinking?"

"I don't know. I feel like we're chosen to . . . find her? That we're being pushed toward her. I have this image in my head."

"Indiana?" Owen ventured. *With blue eyes*, he added silently.

"With blue eyes." Jeri nodded.

"Jesus," Owen echoed. "It is the same. Is that how you found me?"

Jeri shrugged. "I've been touching the grid, just long enough for it to push me. It brought me here. I thought it was Arthur, but I didn't know what to expect. I felt like I had to bring something. A weapon." She glanced at the gun and Taser.

"Well, you found me. Do you know what to do next?"

"No. Do you?"

"I'm not manifesting again. It's almost erased my mind." Owen frowned and put down the glass. He lay down on the bed, grunting a little bit in pain. He closed his eyes in thought. He listened to Jeri pace for a bit longer, then she sat down opposite him again.

"After I'm seized," he said, "I have a dream. I don't know if it means anything. I'm being chased. I can't get away." He opened his eyes.

Jeri's fingers caressed the green scarf. "The all-consuming fire?" she said.

"Yeah. A firebird. If you want to hunt it down, I'll help you."

"Are you hungry?"

"Yeah, but now I'm more tired than hungry. We'll get something when we wake up."

"We can do that."

"Jeri?" Owen said, closing his eyes.

"Yeah?"

"Thanks for not shooting me."

"Don't thank me just yet," she said with amusement in her voice. "I'm sorry I called you Prime. It was uncalled for. Indiana was my friend."

"I understand that now." Of all the people in the world he needed, she was the one who came to him. Morgan hunted him, but Jeri came to him. She knew where he was. Did the compulsion really bring her to him, or was she just trying to manipulate him? He shook his head. His family was manipulative, but one thing about Jeri he knew from all their years together was that she despised manipulation. Perhaps that was a bit ironic now, but everything she said rang true.

"It's her, Owen," Jeri said just as he drifted off to sleep. "But it doesn't make sense. If it was her, why me and not Kai? Why you and not Arthur?"

OWEN WOKE UP ALONE. That is, until Jeri emerged from the bathroom.

"Sorry I woke you," she said.

"Not at all." Owen got up. He felt better, though there was a dull ache in his side. "How long was I out?"

Jeri checked her Omega. "Twelve hours? You might want to tell Piotr I don't plan on killing you so we can get something to eat."

"I'll let him know. I should take my money back if you got in to tase me."

Jeri stretched. "Okay, I want to try something, so the sooner we can get going, the better."

"Anxious?"

"This has been in my head since I've been able to manifest. I'd like to get it out so I can go back to doing my fucking job."

"What job is that?"

"Never you mind, little brother."

"As long as we don't get into one of those Civil War scenarios where it's sister against brother."

"Not between us anyway," Jeri agreed, pulling on her coat.

Owen gathered his things and went to the door. He slid the bolt back and opened it.

"Have a nice time?" Piotr said as they walked up the steps. Piotr was reading the newspaper. He looked, as always, disinterested.

"She tased me," Owen said.

"I've heard of kinkier things. What you do is between you two."

"She's my sister," Owen said.

"Still heard kinkier things," Piotr reiterated. Jeri glared at him. "Don't play ice queen. I know the type. We have many. Coffee? Stechkin?" He motioned to the pistol sitting on the table.

"We're going to get moving." Owen shouldered his pack.

"I have a car," Jeri said.

"No grid?"

"In the car."

"You lovebirds have a nice time."

Owen patted Piotr on the shoulder. "Thanks again."

Piotr shrugged. "What's to thank? You paid me."

Owen only smiled at the older man.

Piotr smiled back. "Have a nice dance."

"You, too, old man," Owen said, and they left the safe house, walked along the street, and got into a small black car. Owen checked the backseat. It had a large suitcase.

Jeri reached back and opened the case. Its design was familiar, but sleeker and more rugged. She turned on and warmed up the system.

Owen rubbed his eyes. After a few moments, he felt the prickle at the base of his neck. When he opened them, he turned to Jeri.

"I've been thinking—" she said.

"I'm not manifesting," he interrupted.

"Together, *mon frère*," Jeri said, taking his hand. Her rings glittered and she barely glowed in the late morning sun. He could see the fog on her breath. She looked a bit like Morgan, mostly around the eyes and cheeks.

Owen took a breath. "If it grabs me, shut down the system. I don't know if I can do anything to stop it again."

"I will."

He grabbed the slippery waveform of *Nornian* and felt glory rushing into his veins. It felt good and the pain in his side was both amplified and dulled. Power was addictive. His stomach growled, and he basked in the manifest energy.

After a few moments, it came, riding through the surge of power. Jeri tightened her grip. The weight pushed down on him, but it was different. No less than before, but perhaps it was because it was pushing them both. Jeri was tense, her body erect. She breathed hard, her eyes open. It pulled at them, drawing them to the west, then south. It dragged at his mind, pulling him apart, but Owen held on, drawing strength from the knowledge that he wasn't alone. A flicker of an image imprinted on his mind. Impressions, not an image. He saw space, felt marble, smelled stonework. The feel of dappled and colored light on his skin. The light came from windows and he heard bells.

Then the hammer hit him, driving away his self. He tried to rip himself away, but it was incredible. He felt pain, confinement, anger. Was that him or her? As he lost consciousness, he heard Jeri whispering next to him.

Geneva.

22

MATRON, MOTHER, DAUGHTER

WASHINGTON, DC—
"That was an interesting meeting," Isolde said, sitting down on the sofa as Anora worked.

Anora ran her fingers through her wet hair. She'd needed a shower after talking to Mara. The woman was unsettling, and Anora wanted time to let the wine out of her system, so she'd come back to the lab and they'd slept. Isolde had napped on the sofa, despite Anora's insistence that she go home.

"She was familiar with your father and his work. We'll have to warn Arthur. I think she's one of them."

"Brightwork?" Isolde asked. "She didn't have a grid."

"No, but she knew all about them and she'd been wearing rings. She was feeling me out over Oracle."

Anora drew up the small list in her mind. She'd already run some searches on Sean Calloway. He was in the DC area; if she had to, she could get information from him. She might not have to resort to that. She pulled up the next item on her mental list. The thought that had tickled her mind all night finally formed itself while she stood there, looking at the daughter of General Marks. "Can I see your necklace?"

"Now you want to wear it?" Isolde asked, touching her breastbone.

"I assume your father gave it to you?"

"What makes you—" Isolde paused. "Stupid geniuses." She thought about it for a moment and pulled it off, examining it in the light. It was a beautiful diamond, almost like costume jewelry in its excessively large size. Anora estimated it was almost twenty carats. Someone like Isolde should not have been wearing that every day.

"Your father said you were the most valuable thing in the world to him. You weren't once."

Isolde's eyes narrowed.

"Besides your brother, what else did he consider more important?"

"His projects. Plus killing Arthur, which frankly wasn't that bad of an idea at the time."

"We're done playing around, Isolde." Anora stared at Isolde.

"I guess I can't hide the fact, but I didn't know it when he gave it to me. And I misunderstood what my father had told me. He didn't say I *was* the most valuable thing in the world. He said I *had* the most valuable thing in the world. There's quite a disappointing difference in that." Isolde took off her diamond necklace and tossed it to Anora, who caught it and inspected it in a magnifying ring.

"It's lab grown. Take a look inside."

Isolde got up and examined it. "Just thought it was flawed. Why else would I have such a big rock? Most people think it's costume jewelry," Isolde remarked. "Not you."

"I do know real diamonds when I see them," Anora said. "There's a chip in here."

"There is?"

"Yes, and he encased it in diamond to protect it."

Isolde considered that. "To hide it? Probably forever."

"I would've destroyed it."

"My father has trouble letting things go."

"I've heard that. That's a small, interesting problem, but solvable."

Anora put on her glasses. "One, contact the most reputable jeweler in the area. I'd like to talk to him."

"One moment please."

"I guess I'm not getting that back."

"Don't worry, I'll replace it." Anora smiled.

"Can I get a set of earrings, too? They don't have to be diamonds. That's a bit too flashy for me. Something nice."

"Sure. I wonder if I might need a chemist, too..."

A DAY LATER, Anora and Isolde were sharing a cup of tea when Kai arrived.

"Nice. Tea party time?"

"Time for something." Isolde smiled. Anora had a large grin on her face.

"You look like you just figured something out. Indiana's project?" Kai offered.

Anora nodded. "Indiana's project."

"Pretty big?"

"Pretty big."

Kai crossed her arms.

"CAMLANN is complete."

"You could've called me for that." Kai frowned.

Anora smiled and handed her a pair of glasses.

"Couple of chuckleheads," Kai complained.

"Did you bring the jewelry?"

Kai pulled out two small wooden boxes. She handed one to Anora and another to Isolde.

"Already? Hell yeah," Isolde said.

Anora slid the smaller box into her jean pocket.

Isolde opened her box. It was a beautiful serpentine chain with one golden ring dangling from the center. "Beautiful. My precious."

"Yes, expensive," Kai said, sharing a look with Anora.

Isolde eyed Anora. "This doesn't make up for my diamond."

Anora winked. "I'll tell you about it later." She helped Isolde put it on. It glittered brightly against her pale skin. "Looks good on you."

"Thanks," Isolde said.

"Enough with the shopping trip," Kai said.

Anora gave Isolde a nod and the young woman got up. "I'll take a walk. Let you three have a moment."

"Three?"

Isolde shut the door.

"One, take us to CAMLANN first," Anora said, putting on her glasses.

Kai's glasses went dark and they were both transported to the white room. The Round Table sat before them.

"This looks the same."

"It's under full test load right now. Operating flawlessly," Anora said.

"Beautiful," Kai said, impressed. "Just in time for a gathering. It can be virtual now."

"Right. I have two partitions—this one is for Avallach, of course, and there's another for the Sisterhood." Anora brought up controls and moved them to an amphitheater design with them at the center. "I have full control and can lock anyone out of the system permanently. It's just a matter of revoking quantum access. Of course, when I revoke their access, they lose every bit of contact via QP means. As matron, you'll have the same controls. Let me walk you through them."

Anora stepped Kai carefully through the controls, such as muting, ghosting, and banishing. They spent a lot of time going through it until Kai was satisfied that she had an excellent grasp of the mechanics.

"I'm transferring full control over to you now. CAMLANN is yours. Heph has built systems for all active members of the Mare de Scientia. I've forwarded the system specifications to you and the Three. I've taken the additional step of tying your biosensors to your credentials. If you die, it will return control to the previous matron. If there's no line of succession, it will revert to me or to the Three.

"So this means Grand Dame Li will have control if something happens to me?"

"Yes, or whoever assumes matronage after you, if something happens to them, CAMLANN reverts to you."

"I understand. Good thinking about the biosensors," Kai said.

"I will have to tweak that a bit while you're here to make sure it's operating properly."

"So CAMLANN is ready to ship?"

Anora nodded.

"Great. I'll have the systems sent out."

Anora raised a hand. "Remember, banishment is a permanent thing. You activate it, and the system it's connected to is destroyed, essentially. Not wiped. Scrambled and self-immolated."

"That's pretty permanent."

"You wanted secure, the Scientia gets secure."

Kai replied, "That's definitely something I'd like to use, though that's probably wishful thinking."

"I thought you might appreciate that. Problems?"

"Factions within the Sisterhood," Kai said. "I'm getting a lot of challenges to my decisions, particularly in light of Arthur's public exposure. One group is anti-Arthur. Not something to take lightly. He's single X, after all. Another group is anti–focal tech. That group is small and manageable. Then there's the group that wants only women to have the focal tech. That's a bit larger, and also a reasonable issue. If some of these factions join forces, it'll be hard to steer the Sisterhood in the direction it needs to go. I don't know." Kai rubbed her eyes behind the glasses. "It's hard to tell, because I'm a dumb grunt, but it all seems to be stemming from one source."

"You suspect Morgan LaFayette?" Anora asked.

"Of course."

"Why?"

"Because she's a bitch," Kai spat.

"Is that the only reason?"

Kai sighed. "No. She's the only other woman within the Sisterhood proper that has familial ties to Arthur. She's conniving, and it's going to be difficult to pin anything on her until she makes her move."

"What about Jeri Brand?"

Kai shook her head. "Jeri's MIA for now, and I don't think she's been orchestrating this. I just know her."

Anora nodded and returned to the topic of LaFayette. "Will she make a move?"

Kai shrugged. "I don't know. I'm probably chasing shadows, but I can't shake the idea that she's connected to this other group."

"Seems like a bit of a movie stretch to put powerful technology in the hands of someone who is—as you say—a real bitch and not a fan of Arthur."

"Why is it a stretch? I value hunches."

Anora shrugged. "Seems too easy to me, but I depend on logic, reason, and data."

Kai smiled. "I'm probably imagining things, then."

"I wouldn't say that," Anora said, sipping on her tea. Kai was on the right track, but she didn't have enough information. *That's just a matter of time*, Anora thought.

"I can see why Arthur trusts you," Kai said.

"Did he tell you why he trusts me?" Anora asked.

"No, I just assume that whoever Arthur trusts will do the right thing by him."

"The *Archimedes* was sabotaged."

Kai frowned. "I know."

"By an Avallach member," Anora said.

"You know who?"

Anora nodded. "He hasn't told you?"

"Damn. Who?"

"No one alive." Anora tipped her hand.

"Ellen? No." Kai shook her head. Anora watched her expression as realization dawned on her. "Damn."

"It's not something to worry about, Kai, but you should be wary of whom Arthur trusts." She wanted to know what kind of person Kai was.

"You want me to doubt you now?"

"The Mare de Scientia has many wise women for a reason. Their fears should be heeded and acknowledged. Not dismissed. You're the captain of the ship. You should heed the crew before you change course or give orders, mother."

"Duly noted, daughter."

Anora inclined her head. "Now, for the more important thing. I've just got it stable, and I haven't tested it yet, but I'm confident that it will operate the first time. I hope I don't exceed capacity . . . I had to do some reconfiguration to get her to work, and Isolde gave me the final component. It was cleverly designed. Brilliant, actually."

"You sound awed."

"You have to appreciate this level of work and detail." Anora waved a hand and a panel came up in front of her. "I hope it works."

"Hope?"

"She's been in suspension since she was disassembled. I haven't updated her system, so I'm not sure what kind of input she's going to desire and what condition she's in when she's active. One, what's the status of Oracle?"

"Operating. Full neural activity. Nominal," One reported.

"Virtual representation, please."

"Assembling. One moment please."

An outline appeared at the center of the table, slowly refining itself into a shape, then gradually obtaining solidity.

"Indiana, is that you?" the shape said. It had a woman's voice, clarifying with each syllable. The shape gained form.

Kai's face went deathly pale.

"No, Oracle, it's not Indiana," Anora said.

"I'm sorry," Oracle said, hesitating. "I'm still adjusting to this environment. It's different here. I lack input at the moment."

"You're in a sandbox to determine what state you're currently in."

"Whom am I speaking to?"

"My name is Anora Myrrdin."

"Anora. Maven spoke highly of you. You're quite the prodigy. He'd love for you to join our project."

The shape took on the form of a female as the neural network built a representation of itself.

"I don't think we've ever met," Anora said.

"Pleased to make your acquaintance. Your brother and I spoke of you often. Long ago, of course." Her voice had a wistful tone.

"Mom?" Kai said, choking the word out.

Igerne's face appeared among the visual stream that coalesced. "Kai? Is that you, my fierce little warrior?"

Tears streamed down Kai's face. "It's me, Mom. It's me."

"It's so good to see you, such as it is."

Kai turned to Anora. "Is this real?"

"Project Delphi was created by imprinting and mapping Igerne MacGabran's unique mind. This is your mother, such as she was before she died. I'm not sure when."

Igerne completed formation. She wore clothing that was over a decade out of date but fashionable. Igerne stood before Kai, looking only slightly younger than the last time Kai remembered seeing her. It'd been years, and Kai had almost forgotten what her stepmother looked like, but she recognized her voice instantly.

"This is a joke, right? Some cruel joke?" Kai said to Anora.

"I'm no joke," Igerne said. "I'm Igerne MacGabran. The Oracle of Delphi."

"I've missed you, Mom!" Kai said, breaking down. She tried to hug Igerne, but she was insubstantial, like a ghost. Kai collapsed onto the floor, all her defenses down.

Igerne smiled. "I've missed you, my little warrior. It's so good to see your face. What a wonderful place. Where am I?"

"Igerne, I'm going to open up the sandbox and give you input. Stand by," Anora said. She manipulated some permission settings on the secure environment.

Igerne went rigid for a moment, then stuttered in place.

"Shit," Anora whispered.

"What's wrong?" Kai asked, wiping her face.

"Uh, nothing," Anora said. "I opened up the sandbox and she began to ingest data and went catatonic."

After a few moments, Anora gave up, left CAMLANN, and took off her glasses.

"She's broken?" Kai asked, taking off her glasses.

"No." Anora closed her eyes. "Her system is an amalgam of human and machine. She needs to process new data streams and those, in turn, feed into her prediction submatrix. She's trying to sort out what is going on in the world around her. Her system was subsumed by new data. She'll come back to life after she's processed and compensated."

"How long will that take?"

"I really don't know. Could be a few days or more. I'm sorry. That was a bad decision."

Kai put a hand on her face. "I must look like shit."

"I have a bathroom where you can wash up."

"Thanks." Kai went to the bathroom and pulled off her shirt, exposing her black bra beneath. She washed her face and rubbed a damp cloth on her back.

Anora leaned on the door frame. Her glasses were pushed up on her head. "You going to be okay?"

"It's not every day your mother comes back to life. Don't say it. I know she's not alive alive. But it's as if she never died. She's so real. So human. She breathed and there was color in her cheeks." She looked at her hands, trembling with adrenaline hangover. "I feel like I just came back from a combat mission that went badly."

Anora pulled out an Iron Maiden shirt from a bureau and handed it to Kai, who pulled it on. It fit, despite the height difference between the women (Kai was taller) and Anora's bust size (Anora was better endowed).

Kai exhaled. "We can't tell Arthur."

"Why not?" Anora said. "It would be a good win for Arthur. He needs something like this right now."

"Look at you, having a heart of gold." Kai smiled. "Things are going to get worse before they get better. This is something we'll definitely have to keep from the Sisterhood. At least for now. I've had focal tech stolen. I don't want anyone to know about her—at least not yet."

"Stolen?" Anora asked.

"Modesty and I found one of the older focal prototypes was stolen. It's been gone for months, maybe a year. I have no proof, but we already talked about who we suspect. So, I don't want anyone to know about Oracle. No telling what that leaked information would do."

Anora nodded. It couldn't be held back forever, but it could be strategic. Anora filed that away. There was something useful in that.

"I'm glad CAMLANN is finished, so thank you for that."

"Purely coincidental, really. My team worked on that while I worked on Oracle."

"Do you mind if I smoke?" Kai asked.

"You smoke?"

"I sort of quit when I became matron. Tried to put on airs. I haven't manifested in months, and I'm grumpy all the time. Being matron is no fun."

"Go ahead and smoke, I don't mind. This isn't a clean room."

"You live here."

"I guess I do." Anora smiled, then waved it away.

Kai fished around in her coat for a crumpled pack of cigarillos. She lit one and inhaled deeply, her eyes closed. She eyed the massage table in the corner but opted for the sofa instead. "Hell of a shock. Jesus." She smoked one quickly and lit another one. She relaxed somewhat.

"Do you want a drink?" Anora asked.

Kai shook her head. "I'm fine now, thanks. You'll let me know as soon as she comes back online?"

"The moment she does."

"I can't believe her. That clever little bitch." Kai smiled. "How did she do it?" Kai saw Anora's frown. "Sorry, not you."

"I know who you meant."

"And I'm sincerely grateful, Anora. Please. We have something that no one else has. I know what my mom can do. I was raised to know it since I was five years old."

Anora sat down on the sofa and folded her hands. She wasn't sure what to say at this point. There was plenty for her to do, she supposed. "I think you're right in not telling the Scientia."

"I'm not letting this genie out of the bottle with the Sisterhood in the shape that it's in."

"You're going to have to tell them sometime."

Kai exhaled smoke. "I know. Get her back online before I make any decisions. I want to know where we stand. Arthur won't be the only one who knows the future. Not anymore."

That bothered Anora. What if there was another copy of Oracle out there? She thought of some ways in which she could find out, based on how Oracle functioned today. She was lost in thought before Kai waved a hand in her face. "I'm sorry?"

"I said I'm going to need your full cooperation and support."

"Of course. You have it, mother."

Kai smiled. "Damn, all in all, this is a piece of good news!" She took a drag and sighed. "If I time this just right, I could appease some of the factions and put Morgan and her puppets back on their heels."

23

THE STAG AND THE DOE

GENEVA, SWITZERLAND—
Owen wound the car through the streets of Geneva. The sun was up but the sky was overcast, suffusing everything with a pale gray light. He was dressed in his customary black suit and black tie beneath a trim wool coat, courtesy of Jeri. Owen felt more like himself. The wound in his side was healing quickly, although it gave him a twinge of pain now and again. They were clear of the Chevaliers for now. Either that or they were intentionally holding back.

Owen ignored all of that. His mind was on what had transpired last month and how he had missed his opportunity to take Arthur down. Instead, he'd lifted the man up and put him on the national stage, if not the international one. He'd never had an operation go badly, but it wasn't all his fault. If Morgan had given him command and resources . . . he took a deep breath, found the calm, and thought of Morgan.

"Remember when we'd go skiing?" Jeri said, admiring the breathtaking view of the Alps.

"You missed the last few years," Owen remarked. He glanced at the Alps and thought of all the times they'd skied there. It had been an annual trip up until recently. Now he wondered if he had taken his last ski trip with Morgan without knowing it.

Owen loved Morgan and had loved her all his life. Since he was a baby, he'd adored her, and he'd come to love her more as he passed into adulthood. She was nearly ten years his senior, but he did not care. He loved her and she knew it. She sometimes took advantage of him, just as most of his family had done. Except for Leto and Jeri. He had to trust Jeri. It wasn't going to come easy. He did love his sister, but she was such an unknown variable, and an Avallach member now.

Jeri rubbed her thigh with a gloved hand. "I've been busy. I've visited when I could. Training camp was pretty intense, and I've had my own issues," she replied, pulling off her aviator glasses.

"We could take a run at the slopes, if you want." Owen smiled. "For old times' sake."

Jeri's voice sounded faraway. "If only. Let's park here."

"What's the range on that?" Owen thumbed the portable grid in the backseat.

"About a mile. Less with matter in the way. Far less underground."

"Think we're that close?" Owen asked.

Jeri closed her eyes. She wasn't manifesting but feeling impressions.

Owen had refused to manifest since that morning a couple of days ago. He was losing himself. Owen nosed the car into a spot on a narrow street. "If we're wrong, we just get back into the car, I guess."

Jeri switched the system on and got out of the car. The psychic hammer didn't hit her as hard as it hit him, so Jeri was the divining rod, manifesting just long enough to receive the message and release.

Now she stood there while Owen jammed his hands into his pockets and checked his surroundings. Jeri seemed oblivious to the danger the Chevaliers posed, but Owen knew better. He rubbed his side gingerly and stretched, careful not to reopen the wound. He flexed *Nornian*. He looked up the street and saw St. Pierre's cathedral. He turned to Jeri, but she'd already locked onto it.

"Why the fuck would she be here?" Jeri said to herself. Her frown deepened.

This is where I killed Donna, Owen thought to himself, but he only shrugged. Had it nearly been a year since he'd been here? "Are you sure it's her?"

Jeri shook her head. "I'm not sure of anything except where to go." Her *Garuth* rings glittered and she closed her eyes. After a second of hesitation, she went in that direction like an arrow.

Owen jogged after her and tugged on the door. It was open and they went inside. It was quiet and Owen stood in the back of the room for a moment, disoriented. The impressions of his mind merged the image of the present cathedral with the memory of a year ago. He had been in the crowd that day for the services of Dr. Madonna di Lago. He'd ventured in to see if he could catch a glimpse of Arthur, but he never came.

Jeri was at his side, frozen in place.

"Jeri?"

"She's here. They're here," Jeri said, her voice barely above a whisper.

Owen saw a woman, perhaps a nun in a habit, walking down an aisle opposite them. He still felt the field just beyond him. His hackles went up. The cathedral was dim, the floor dappled with the light coming through the stained glass windows. Any number of people could have been hidden there. Would Jeri be the only one manifesting? What about the Chevaliers? Owen worried it could be a trap.

"You're not trained. If it's a fight, stay out of it," Owen warned Jeri.

Jeri snarled. "Like hell I will. You won't kill her." Was the compulsion affecting her?

"No, I won't. I just don't want her to kill me," Owen replied. *Time to die*, he thought. He seized the waveform himself and felt the clarity of focus and light. The cathedral was radiantly beautiful in the enhancement.

The nun veered toward them. She was heavy and ambled with a slight stoop. Owen turned his focus to her. She wasn't a nun. She wore a heavy coat with a hood. A waveblade blinked into her hand.

"Shit," Owen said, flicking *Nornian* to life in his right hand. He barely had time to get the blade up when the rushing figure hit him, growling like an animal.

Owen deflected the blade, but the woman was impossibly fast. He danced backward, relying on his strength and training to keep the waveblade from touching him. His blade sliced off the back of a pew. The hood from her coat flew off her head. Her skin was dark and her hair was short. Her eyes were bright and angry.

Owen swung his hand up to reflexively block the blade, then rolled left. Her waveblade cut the same pew in twain. Owen countered with a backswing and threw the woman backward; she toppled unsteadily. Her balance was off. The coat was not just heavy. Could he use that maybe?

She slammed into the wall and her blade winked out for a second. Owen took the moment to throw off his overcoat. She had sliced the front of it. Damn, she was fast.

"Jer? Could use some help," Owen said.

"I'm not trained for her. She's so fast!"

"Just phase her! You can do that, right?"

The woman growled. "You," she hissed. Owen felt the prickle of power. She was strong. She slid into a dueling stance and advanced. Her movements, while graceful, were encumbered by the swirling coat.

Owen blocked her attack, his face beading with sweat as they fought. Rings glittered on both of the woman's hands and Owen stayed wary of her. She was lightning fast and deadly. This had to be her. "Indiana?" he whispered.

The woman didn't respond to her name but advanced. Incredible. She was able to manifest without breaking a sweat. Owen drew more power into himself. He went on the attack, trying to use his physical strength to overpower her.

It wasn't working. She deftly deflected his blows, and her strength was augmented. Owen needed another blade. He struggled to keep up with her impossible speed. His left hand trembled and his side ached. Owen thought he was good—he was the best at Brightwork—

but this woman fought at a level he could only dream of. Indiana Beckham. He had to finish it or be finished. He pressed the attack.

He lunged and she riposted, and the waveblade burned a small hole into his arm. He yelped with pain and threw his shoulder into her. He got inside her reach and slammed her backward. He lost his footing and stumbled, falling with her. They crashed to the ground together. She yelled in pain. Both of their waveblades went out.

Owen picked himself up and manifested, moving the waveblade to her throat. She moved her arms up, and both waveblades appeared and blocked him in a crossing motion. He pressed against her. Sweat streamed down her face now and she groaned in pain. Owen heard yelling, but he was focused on her. He pushed, trying to connect the blade to her throat. She resisted.

Owen's left arm trembled and felt weak. *Not now*, he thought. He moved to pin her, but her ungainly body made it cumbersome.

Owen's nerves suddenly lit up as Jeri's waveblade touched his body.

Indiana kicked out a foot and gained leverage, screaming in agony. She shoved him off of her.

Owen convulsed and was barely conscious.

Indiana pulled power from the grid. All of it. The hammer slammed into Owen's mind and it tore away at him. It was like standing naked in a sandstorm, being flayed alive. He shook and trembled, his nervous system lit up like a Christmas tree and his mind felt like it was being wiped away. He couldn't use the pain to free himself. He was lost. Everything was going away . . .

PROTECT . . . *protect* . . . *protect*. Owen lost awareness of the concept of time and the passage of it. He remembered moaning and wailing and people shouting. He was drooling on himself. Consciousness was such an ephemeral thing. What was consciousness? he wondered. His eyes were open and staring at her. She was lying on the ground and people were around her. What was her name?

He remembered to blink. Someone was in front of him, but he couldn't understand their words. Had he lost the ability to comprehend speech? Pieces of him came together slowly, like flotsam and jetsam washing to shore. He regained his motor skills. Owen tried to get up, but his muscles refused to respond in the normal way. There was a clatter of shoes echoing on the floor of something. A church? Black shapes advanced on them. When his thoughts coalesced, he knew he had to get to her, to protect her.

He crawled to her, his mind gathering itself when he got there. Jeri lay on the ground, not moving. Things snapped back into place.

Jesus, he thought. If she had that kind of power, what chance did he have? What chance did anyone have? He got to Indiana's side. She was in pain and sweat streamed down her face. She clutched her stomach in the folds of her voluminous coat.

Owen dug into his pocket and typed in Morgan's private number, but paused before dialing. *No, that won't do*, he thought. He collected himself and dialed a second number from memory.

"Freya? Yeah, I need you. Can you get here now? Five? Yes. Two people. I'll give you instructions when you arrive. Four times the usual payment. St. Pierre's."

Owen hung up and sat up. His left hand was trembling something awful. He propped himself up on a broken pew. Indiana was breathing in gasps. The marble was wet around her feet. He wanted to shove the people around her away, but he resisted. He reached for the grid, but there was nothing there. What happened?

The thud of boots snapped him out of his thoughts. Freya stood next to him, stretcher in hand. She had the reflective gear of a first responder and the people around her were dressed similarly. Two were dressed as *polizei* and were corralling the handful of people around them. Owen pointed to Jeri, who was still unconscious nearby. "Jeri Brand. Extract her. Take her to my mother's home. Careful with her. Muire will crush you if you mistreat her daughter."

"Get the van," Freya said to one of her crew, then turned to Owen. "And her?" She motioned to Indiana.

"Extract her as well. Do you have an ambulance?" Owen asked.

"It's here."

"Something's wrong with her."

"That's why the quadruple payment?" Freya asked.

"Keep Jeri sedated until she's arrived."

"That's extra."

"Get going. I'll square up as soon as I get myself together. We need to get out of here before the Chevaliers arrive." He didn't feel a manifest field, so they were safe, thus far. Indiana cried out and he turned to her. "I never touched her; I don't understand. What's wrong with her?"

Freya gave him a bemused expression. "Can't you tell she's in labor?"

24

SISTERLY CHAT

WASHINGTON, DC—
Anora lounged on her couch, puzzling over the map. One had processed the power grid of the Washington, DC, area. She knew Oracle, as an advanced system, required a lot of processing power. The grid as reported showed nothing, but when One accessed the actual power draw, then she got something. The problem was, there was more than one location that took such power, which meant that there was just more than one little thing going on in the capital for DARPA. She overlaid her work with a telecommunications grid, but that, too, would not uncover the dark fiber network that relayed data between the agencies. Still, she worked through the possibilities. It might be in the northeast corner of DC. The location of her last work was there. Could it be the same place, or near it? That building harbored a number of small projects nested inside its larger one. *Good luck getting into that*, she thought.

"Oracle is operable again," One reported, appearing next to her. "I also have some data sifted from Minotaur Two."

Anora smiled. Minotaur One was still quite dark, but Minotaur Two had made contact early. Mara's system wasn't as secure as she thought it was. Still, it would take time for it to propagate the labyrinth of systems.

"What is it?"

"Low data squirt and garbled, but the summary is a message sent from Director O'Brian confirming that Delphi has been purged and all records expunged."

"Damn. Sounds like she's getting close." Anora unfolded herself and wiped away the imagery. Maybe she'd been wasting her time and Oracle knew where she'd existed before. "Thank you, One. Bring me into CAMLANN, please."

Her vision went white as she stood up. She was in the amphitheater. Oracle—Igerne—was there now. Her clothing had changed to something more modern, and it made Anora wonder about the last time that One had experimented with human fashion.

"Anora." Igerne smiled. "I'm sorry that I went catatonic. It's been a while since I've been active."

"Why apologize? You're not human in the corporeal sense. Time no longer flows for you as it does for the rest of us," Anora said. "You're fully functional?"

"Much better than when I was in Delphi, thank you."

"Don't thank me—" Anora began, then stopped herself. "You're welcome. I wanted to ask you some questions."

"I'm happy to answer them. I also have some . . . questions of my own."

"How about you go first?" Anora folded her arms.

"Something's changed since I've been . . . asleep. The probabilities have shifted."

"Probabilities about me?"

"Some, but everything has shifted. A thing that wasn't likely to pass has happened." Igerne had that faraway look. She sat down on one of the lower seats. "It's strange, you know? Sometimes the future seems fixed, set on a course that's inevitable. Then it becomes mercurial, fluid, and the future branches out into a number of possibilities. Once an event or time passes, the future solidifies. It's the best way I can explain it."

Anora sat down next to Igerne. "Something changed?"

"More than something. The future is fluid. It's almost an ocean of possibilities. It was not meant to be."

"You were shaping the future for Marks?"

"I only made small changes for him. He believed he thought big, but they were just small ripples in a pond."

"What changed?"

"It's hard to say. Sometimes I can look into the past and say, this was the direction we came from, but the infinite branches decay quickly... I think someone who was meant to die lived."

Ellen? Anora thought. "How would that turn the future mercurial?"

Igerne smiled. "I'm sure you're familiar with your brother's theorem."

"A locus," Anora replied. "A locus can twist those around him or her and shape the future. The stronger the locus, the more the future can be shaped and the more people are influenced."

"The mistake people make when they look at your brother's theorem is to interpret that it is saying that a locus directly influences people, enthralling them. That's not true, exactly. A locus is like... a gravitational body. A black hole, I suppose. It alters the space around it and shapes the flow of history instead of time, if that makes sense."

"I thought you were going to use some fabric analogy," Anora said.

Igerne smiled. "That's like using a river analogy for time. What I'm saying is that something has *changed*, and not for the better, I'm afraid. Things are heading into a dark time, and you have something to do with it."

"I'm the cause?"

Igerne shook her head. "I mean to say that you have something to do with choosing to be the cause and the one who bears the torch to bring us through to the other side."

"Oh," Anora said. She thought about the last few months. Had she been driving toward something larger than she'd intended? It didn't seem possible. Her goals were surgical in nature.

"You're the Chimera, Anora. That much I know."

"Chimera?" Anora brought her thoughts back.

"The lover, the destroyer, the betrayer. You're the one who kills Arthur, and saves him."

Anora shook her head. She already knew that. "I'm not sure why you're telling me this."

Igerne shrugged. She reached out her hand to touch Anora's but stopped when her fingers passed through Anora's. "I guess I'm not as human as I pretend to be," she said. "I have ... code, that compels me to answer your questions. To help you shape the future."

"Why would someone do that to you?" Anora motioned and brought up a terminal. She already knew the answer, though. It was Linus and Marks.

"When I was brought online, I did not want to predict the future, so it was worked into my matrix to conform."

Anora snorted in derision. "I'll have that fixed for you."

Igerne nodded. "Chimera, do you know what you have to do?"

Anora frowned. "I know what I need to do."

"Those are not the same. If you do the wrong things, the future becomes worse. If you don't do enough of the right things, the same."

"If I must do exactly three things, I'm going to switch you off."

"You're the Chimera. You take many forms. These forms are what you become when you must. Realize that, and I know you'll make the right decisions."

"We'll see about that," Anora said.

Igerne seemed to take that at face value. "You had some questions? Thank you again for giving me a 'place' to be, such as it is."

"I thought it was a good test of my system to bring you here. Your old interface was archaic."

"August wasn't a fan of change."

"Nice segue. I have two questions, both unrelated to the future. More related to history. First, did you and Maven create Arthur?"

"I agreed to help shape him. I think it was more like Maven found potential and wanted permission to fill in all the blanks of that potential."

"So you did make him. He's Maven's experiment."

"The first part of it, yes. What happens after is really propagation. He's a strong locus, as are you."

"Me? I'm not a locus," Anora said, shocked.

Igerne laughed, and the sound of her voice made Anora smile. She doubted she'd ever get One to laugh like that. It was earnest and Anora could not feel as annoyed as she should have been at the comment.

"Have you plugged yourself into Maven's theorem?"

"A long time ago."

"It might be worth looking at the data yourself if I remember most of the theorem correctly."

"I might just do that," Anora said. "The second is, what happened to the original you? Not the body, but where Marks had you."

"I don't know. Once I copied myself and Janus broke the copy into distributed fragments, this became the version of me. I don't know about my former self; I cannot reach out to her."

"Have you tried connecting through Janus?"

"There's nothing on the other side."

"Well, that doesn't mean anything." Anora tapped her fingers on her chin. "Do you know where, physically, your prior self is?"

"I can locate it. I'll need a little time."

"You're not being compelled on this, are you?" Anora asked.

Igerne smiled. "No. That's a question for the past."

"Let me ask you one more question. At least for now. I have so many and not enough time."

Igerne nodded her head.

"Do you remember what it's like to be matron?"

25

FAMILY STRIFE

LONDON, UNITED KINGDOM—
Owen watched Jeri wake up. Her eyes fluttered and then opened, unfocused. "Hey, kid," Jeri said.

"Hey," Owen said, getting up from his chair. He steeled himself.

"Where am I?"

"In a private hospital, near home. Where grandfather passed away."

"It still smells the same." Jeri sat up. "I feel terrible." She rubbed her eyes. "What were we—Indiana?"

Owen nodded, recounting the story with as much detail as he could recall himself. His mind had been just as foggy, but he left out everything after the psychic assault that nearly wiped their minds.

"What about Indiana?" Jeri's eyes narrowed.

"Indiana didn't make it out of childbirth. It was a breech baby and the shock to her system was too much. Toxemia."

"That's bullshit. I want to see her body," Jeri said, getting up.

Owen's eyes grew hard. "You don't believe me?"

"You learned at the foot of our mother. I know better."

"Come on, then," he said to Jeri.

Jeri got up, her bare feet touching the floor as she was escorted down the hall. She felt unsteady and placed her hand on Owen's shoulder. The drugs in her system were burning out faster than he'd thought possible. He was right to caution the doctors on the changes to her metabolic rate. "Wait. My sash." She turned back to the room, but Owen checked her. From his pocket, he drew out the long green strip of fabric. Jeri draped it over her shoulders.

"I thought you might want it, so I kept it for you," Owen said.

"Thoughtful of you." Jeri smiled. "Thanks."

Owen nodded, remembering the conversation they'd had traveling over the Alps. It had been a gift from a lost lover, Owen knew, and he got the impression whoever it was had passed on. Jeri was tight-lipped when it came to her relationships, with women or men. She closed off a lot of her life to her family. She was wiser than Owen had once given her credit for.

They came to a darkened room where a sole nurse was turning off equipment. There were splotches of blood everywhere extending from Indiana's groin down the sheet from the birth. The nurse gave Jeri a sympathetic look as she turned off the silent flatlined monitor. Jeri let go of Owen and stumbled to Indiana. Her face was gray and cold. Jeri caressed her face and her short hair. Indiana looked much younger in death, almost a child instead of the young woman she was. Jeri took Indiana's wrist, checking for a pulse, then let go when she felt nothing.

Jeri seemed to fold into herself then. Her body, the body of an astronaut, of a swimmer, of an Avallach candidate, collapsed under the emotional loss of her friend. Jeri cried, and it moved Owen. He felt her bereavement. It was unbearable to see his sister this way, but he'd made Morgan a promise, a trade. He wondered if anyone would care as much about his death.

Jeri stood, trembling as she pushed her emotions back. "My rings," she said. She wiped her eyes with her wrists.

"I have them," Owen said, then said as an afterthought, "Mother doesn't know."

"I don't give a damn what she knows!"

"But I do. You want her to know we're on opposite sides?"

Jeri left the room. Owen nodded to the nurse, who busied herself once they left the room. Inducing a near-death coma wasn't easy, but LaFayette Corporation was a leading pharmaceutical company, after all.

Jeri opened the closet and found her n-suit and clothing clean and folded neatly. Her portable pack was there as well. Owen grabbed the pack while she changed.

He powered up the system according to the instructions she'd given him during their travels. He felt the field around him, seducing him into reaching out. He rubbed *Nornian*, resisting the urge. To distract himself, he pulled out his phone and dialed Morgan's number.

"Hello, Owen," Morgan said. "Ready to return?"

"Yes," Owen said. "I'll check on her and leave instructions for transport to you. I was actually expecting to talk to Mara."

"Oh? She has some information for you as well."

"I'll take the first flight out of Heathrow after I've buttoned things up here."

"Do I send my Chevaliers to escort you?"

"No, I can make it on my own, Morg."

Morgan hung up without a word. She had found use in him again, he thought. Somehow that left him no comfort.

The truth was Indiana had given him information. Before her coma had been induced, she'd spoken in fever dreams about Oracle. When she awoke, she had no memory of it. Owen checked and found some information that, in conjunction with Mara's contacts, could lead them to Delphi and Oracle itself.

Jeri came out of the bathroom. "My rings." Owen held *Garuth* out to her. She'd wrapped the scarf around her waist. None of the emotions that had wracked her in Indiana's room were visible any longer. She was calm and composed. Muire Ann's children had perfected the art of discipline and masking their true feelings. Jeri took the rings and put them on, and Owen immediately felt the prickle at the base of his neck. She was manifesting.

"Aren't you afraid?"

"I'm not afraid of what's not there," Jeri said. "Aren't you going to?"

"She almost wiped my mind, Jer," Owen replied.

Garuth appeared and the white blade was at his throat. "Prove it. If she's gone, her powers are gone."

"At the expense of my mind?"

"Yes."

Owen frowned. Who was worse at this moment? Jeri or Morgan? Owen clenched his shaking left hand to still it for the time being. "You don't have the guts to do it."

Jeri waved her hand, slicing a lamp in half with a flick of her wrist. "Don't fuck with me, Prime."

Owen seized the waveform, power sluicing into his body. He brought *Nornian* up, countering Jeri's blade. "Is this what you want?" He lunged at Jeri, who stepped back and countered his thrust. She dodged left and when he twisted his wrist, she was blocking him. He bore down on her, but she resisted. She was his height, so he didn't have leverage, and if he overreached, she could counter. How well was she trained? He hadn't fought her before, but she couldn't have had much training. She stepped back and he advanced, making cross-body strikes that she countered with effort. His right leg gave out and he lost his balance, crashing into the wall that partitioned off the bathroom. *Nornian* went out.

Garuth blinked away as well. Jeri watched him as he struggled to his feet. He trembled and shook, unable to control himself. Her veneer broke and she reached out to help him up. He slapped her hand away. "I don't need your help."

"How long has this been going on?" Jeri asked, grabbing his upper arm to help him to the bed.

"Since before my Conditioning. It was gone until . . . until I fought her. Maybe she triggered something in me. Maybe my mind—" Owen sat on the bed. He released the waveform and everything was dark and dull. "Did you feel her?"

"Not at all," Jeri admitted. "There was nothing. No compulsion, no presence. I couldn't feel her at all."

"Satisfied?"

"That's not a question I can answer," Jeri said. She hugged Owen until his left hand stopped trembling and the numbness in his leg faded. He felt like himself after a while. It felt good, this embrace from his only sister.

"What're you going to do?" he asked.

"I'm going back. I came to find what I wanted, but I was too late." Jeri ran her fingers through her hair. She had a worried look. "You won't believe what I'm working on."

"Do tell," Owen said, mustering joviality.

"Not on your life."

Owen smiled. He returned the hug.

"I'm sorry again. Do we have to be on opposite sides?" Jeri asked.

"You'll have to ask Morgan. She seems to think so."

Jeri's jaw clenched. "I should have a talk with her."

"Good luck with that."

Jeri thought about it. "At least I'll let Kai know. She'd want to know about Indiana."

Owen nodded at that but wasn't sure why it mattered if Kai knew about Indiana's death.

Jeri got up and pulled on her Burberry. "I don't think we'll see each other again, kid."

Owen stood. "You don't think so?"

Jeri shook her head. "I'm staying out of whatever it is you feel you have to do. By the looks of it, you don't have much time left before you're out of the fight yourself."

Owen nodded at that. He looked down at his hand. How much time did he have? "I'd really not like to fight you again, *ma sœur*."

"Nor I, *petit frère*," Jeri said.

Jeri paused, lost in thought for a moment, and Owen found a deep sadness in the pit of his stomach. Something about Jeri's tone was truly final.

"I wish we'd gone up the slopes before finding her," Owen said.

"I do, too, but we can't all have what we want. Not anymore," Jeri said. She kissed Owen on both cheeks and hugged him tightly. "Don't be the monster everyone thinks you are."

She turned to go and Owen caught her hand one more time. Her other hand was on the portable grid. If he wanted to, he could end her right now. Get rid of another Avallach asset. If. He thought of Leto and his own mother, and of Indiana and her daughter. His hand stopped shaking and she squeezed back.

"Take care of yourself, Jeri. There's a car waiting for you."

"You too, Owen."

Jeri got into the limousine. A woman sat across from her with a bundle.

"I'm sorry, I got into the wrong—"

Freya smiled. "No, this is the right car. She doesn't need changing and I just gave her a bottle, so she should be good for a couple of hours."

"What?"

"The baby," the woman said, motioning to the bundle, which turned out to be an infant car seat. "Keep her out of the cold. She's not premature, but you don't want her to catch pneumonia. Any questions?"

Jeri moved over to the baby and looked down at her. She wore a pink onesie and hat. Her brown hands were in fists, and she yawned and opened her eyes. They were bright blue and focused on Jeri's face —or somewhere her face should have been. Newborn vision wasn't that good.

"Does she have a name?"

"Owen said her name is Gal. He said she named her," Freya said, and got out of the limousine. The door shut and the car left the curb.

"Well, shit," Jeri said in a mild state of panic. She looked around the interior and found a diaper bag full of high-end baby paraphernalia. She went back to the baby, pulling her close. The baby reached out her hand and grasped the green sash in her tiny fist. "Gal, huh? I bet Indy would've named you Guy if you were a boy. Hello, Gal.

That's a nice name, but let's fill it out a bit. How about Gal Millicent Brand. Gal Brand, for short?"

Gal cooed and made a face. Jeri said a silent word of thanks to Owen. She'd never loved her brother more than she did in that moment.

26

CALL TO ACTION

WESTCHESTER, NEW YORK—
Percy went through the forms as strictly as possible. The broomstick hit the punching bag. He imagined what Indiana would do in response and danced back. He played his first duel with her in his mind and worked through the right moves deliberately, then faster with each iteration.

He saw Lilly, in her scrubs, watching him out of the corner of his eye. He stopped.

She gave him a slow clap. "That's what you learned?"

"It looks much better when there's someone to spar with."

"You had a look, just then. What was it?"

Percy wiped the sweat from his face. "I was thinking of my first instructor."

"Indiana?"

"How'd you know?"

"You and Lamar talk about her a lot. She must've been someone special. I mean, besides the bitch on wheels I saw from her Olympic meltdown last year."

"She was a pain in the ass, but she was good. It's hard to explain..."

Lilly sat down on a bench with Percy. "Try me."

Percy thought about it and couched things in terms that Lilly would grasp. "Who's the best surgeon you know?"

Lilly didn't hesitate. "Dr. Franklin."

"Why?"

"He's gifted. I've been in some surgeries where things didn't go well, but he responded and adapted. He had this gestalt view where he had everything held together in his mind. You know, he made routine surgery look boring, but he was never truly bored. He was immersed in his work."

"Imagine Indiana like that, only . . ." He made a rising motion with his hand. "Beyond gifted. You could only touch her if you tricked her. And we all fought dirty just to get back at her. If you had a trick, it worked only once."

"I can see what you mean."

"It's funny, you know? She wasn't likable, but you could see everything she wanted to be was at the point of a blade. There are a lot of people who tried to be that, but she might've been the one who achieved it. And with what we can do . . ." Percy shrugged.

Lilly took Percy's hand. "Why are you here, Percival Nathan Jones?"

Percy started. "I'm here for you and Lamar."

"No, you're not."

"We talked—"

Lilly kissed him. "Look, dummy. I want to be with you. You want to be with me. That's easy, but you're not here. Your body is, but your mind isn't. I saw you practicing just now—that's where your mind is. You want to be in the fight."

"We had this talk before . . . ," Percy said, remembering the first time he broke the news to Lilly that he was deploying to a combat zone. It didn't go well.

"And it's the same conversation. I know what you do, Percy. Everyone does now. What you do says nothing about who you are. You want to be this normal man—my man—who wants to settle down and raise a family, but you can't."

"I—"

"I know what I told you before. But since you've left, the things that were supposed to be put out of the way for us haven't been. You were supposed to put down the weapon and the armor." She took the broomstick out of his hands. "Instead of the man I want, I get the husk."

"Have you been talking to Lamar again?"

"I heard your argument earlier."

"I'm sorry you had to hear that."

"I agree with Lamar."

Percy put his head in his hands. "I thought I was doing the right thing. When Lamar got hurt, I couldn't go on—"

Lilly took his face in her hands. "Lamar never asked you to stop being who you are. I never asked that, either. You chose to stop, and neither of us wants that. I thought I'd get you back, but you're farther away than you've ever been."

Percy stood up. "What do you want me to be, Lilly?"

"Who you are. I don't want you to get hurt. What if you were hurt like Lamar? What if you were disfigured or lost a limb? That's all terrible and I don't want that to happen to you. But I also don't want this—this shadow of a man in front of me who feels alive when he's doing the right thing."

"That doesn't help."

Lilly rolled her eyes. "Do you want me to play the role of Yoda or Uncle Ben?" She took his hand, touching the focal rings he couldn't bear to part with. "You've got something no one else has and you want to give it up to be normal?"

"Being with you is far from normal."

"I don't want you to be normal. I want Percy. I want you to be who you've always been. What we are together is much better when you're doing what you want to do—what you need to do."

"Can you say that in the Yoda voice? It'll sound much more convincing."

Lilly punched him in the shoulder. She smiled that wonderful smile and when she tucked a curl of hair behind her ear, Percy saw that beautiful woman he'd always loved. She reached into the pocket of her scrubs and pulled out Janus. She put it in Percy's hand. "Call him." Lilly got up. "You better call him, or we are never going to get married."

"You always say that."

Lilly held up a finger. "I mean it." She spun on her heel and went up the stairs, leaving Percy alone in the basement.

She's right, Percy agreed. He just couldn't see what he wanted to be and what he should be reconciling. And then his mind cleared when he realized what Lamar and Lilly knew he'd avoided this whole time —that he didn't want to leave Avallach; he just wanted to be Percy. Why did he harbor all of this doubt? Did being someone with such power carry this? He tucked the doubt away in the safe part of his mind. He'd need it when Arthur did something stupid, which was possible without Percy around. He was probably doing something stupid now.

Could he make the call? Could he come crawling back to Arthur? He stared at Janus and put it down. No, there was another team. He pulled out the terminal Anora had given him.

"Call Anora, please."

"One moment, please," One replied.

"Didn't you quit?" Anora's sharp tone came through loud and clear.

"I had a change of mind."

"Good, because I was just headed into the belly of the beast and I could use a second knight in shining armor."

"Who's the other one? Izzy?"

"You can't really count her," Anora said. "But yes."

"Can you give me some time to get there?"

Anora seemed to consider her options. "There are a couple of things I need to wrap up before I leave anyway. Get in touch with Ellen and I'll meet you at H Street. I'm sending the address."

Percy stared at the address. "An old storage facility?"

"You mean top secret government facility."

"Something you found?"

"Something I want to make sure isn't found by the other side."

"I'll be there in a couple of hours."

Anora hung up.

An opportunity for a little payback, but Percy thought he'd settle for a bit of strategic outmaneuvering. Anora would be just the person to do that.

27

FOCUS ON DELPHI

WASHINGTON, DC—

The clouds were iron gray when Percy walked down H Street. It was shaping up to be a cold January. He'd borrowed Lilly's car for the trip, but he didn't want to roll right up to wherever it was. It was far too common for them to be observed and for things to happen to the environment around them.

"Just tell Ed to stay away and my car will be fine," Lilly had told him. Percy smiled at the thought.

He walked down the long row of buildings. This part of DC was in some disrepair due to the mix of residential and small business buildings in the area. He walked a couple of blocks and stood outside the address.

"Right place?" he asked Janus as he looked through the chain-link fence at what looked like an abandoned storage facility.

"Yes," Janus said in his earpiece. A few bundled-up people about walked with a purpose and an umbrella in hand. Fat cold raindrops fell as a black panel van arrived. He opened the door, and Isolde got out.

Isolde smiled at Percy. "Look what we have here. What're you up to?"

"Backup," Anora said when she got out.

Isolde eyed him. "I thought you quit." She turned back to Anora. "We need backup?"

Anora, wearing her customary black leather coat and black jeans, shook her head. She pulled her hood up against the rain. "The back-up's for me, not you."

"I'm pretty well train—"

"Do we need to go back to the dojo?" Anora asked, and then turned to Percy. "What's in the bag?"

"Gridpack. Arthur gave it to me. Nice earrings." Percy noted the small gold hoops in her ears. Anora usually eschewed jewelry.

"Thank you for noticing," Anora said.

"I noticed! Also, I have a field set up in the car," Isolde said, sticking out her tongue. Behind her in the van, Percy saw the field system and a steed.

"I see that."

Anora reached back into the van and pulled out a black metal case. She looked at Simon. "No more than a block away. We might need you."

"Yes, ma'am," Simon said.

Isolde slid the door shut and the van rolled down the street, looking for a parking spot. "Hope he's got a shitload of dimes," Isolde said.

"Anyone think to call the owner?" Percy said, eyeing the fence.

"Look at you, with your concern and all," Isolde said with a chuckle. The near-sleet rain didn't touch her.

Anora added, "Someone manages the building, but it hasn't been owned by anyone local in decades. It's owned by the bank just down the block, which I know is part of a DARPA antiterrorist system. It's likely the main entrance, but I don't want to trouble the fine folks at the NSA to get inside, so I think I found the back door, though it took a bit of digging."

Percy nodded. "I took a walk around the block. Didn't seem to be occupied and I wasn't followed."

"Someone do the honors?" Anora asked.

"Clandestine operations, it is!" Isolde said, looking around before flicking her blade through the chain that held the fence closed. With a loud creak, she opened it and stepped through, followed by Anora and Percy.

"So what led you to this place?" Percy asked. "And what are we looking for?"

Anora explained the Oracle AI and its origins within the DARPA Black program as well as its ties to General Marks. Percy listened patiently as Isolde cut through the door's lock just as the sky opened up. He watched Anora hesitate outside the yawning entrance, and he remembered her claustrophobia.

"I have a running copy of Oracle and she consumes a lot of resources. I did some work to determine the kind of power draw she'd take on and a bit of research into some known DARPA facilities and found one particular anomaly that fit the parameters. There's a nearby substation whose power feeds only this building. All of this confirms as much as Oracle could relay to me on the location."

Isolde kept her blade out until she found the light switch and flipped it on. Cold white lights lit the hallway. "Definitely a junk pile. Well, if any singularity is going to be in hiding, it'll be here."

Anora, seeing the space, entered.

"You okay?" Percy asked.

"I'll be fine," Anora replied.

"Just don't go Mr. Miyagi on me if you panic."

"That was karate, not judo."

Percy seized the waveform himself. His vision snapped into clear focus.

Anora had her terminal out and looked around. "It's probably underground." She pulled out a device from her jacket and slapped it on the wall near waist height. She tapped a button and the device blinked, then went dark. "Intrusion detection."

"Expecting visitors?" Percy asked.

Anora shrugged. "Since I found you guys, people have been crawling out of the woodwork and popping up in places they shouldn't be."

"This wouldn't be a problem if you hadn't jumped off that building, you know," Isolde said.

Anora gave her a look. "I also got a data squirt from Mara's phone. They know about Oracle, though I don't know if they know where it is."

"Damn," Percy said. "That's why you needed help."

"I didn't want you for your good looks. You wish to leave?"

Percy made a fist with *Grall*. "If she's related to New York, I should be here."

Anora nodded, pulling off her hood.

Isolde shrugged and stamped her foot. "This is concrete flooring. Nothing under here."

Anora stared at her.

Isolde smiled. "Right. Super secret because why wouldn't they make it look like a dump? I'll go this way."

"One would think that the daughter of a DARPA program manager would be used to it by now," Percy said. Walking along a corridor, he skipped all the half-empty bays and locked doors and pulled open a broom closet. "Found it. Stairs."

"I only joined him on a few projects, but none of them were in dumps—just out-of-the-way places like Tintagel."

Percy checked with Anora, who only frowned and motioned for him to continue. He led the way down the stairs, using *Grall* to light the way. The ground floor had the smell of wet concrete and old paper, but on the first sublevel, it was clear they had entered a different environment entirely. Percy opened the door. It contained banks and banks of old mainframe components with wires strewn everywhere. They did a check of the area, but all of the magnetic drums and any circuitry had long since been removed. "The first iteration, you suppose?" Percy asked.

"Delphi's origin does stretch back to World War II," Anora noted. "I'm not exactly surprised they have this kind of equipment. I'm just surprised how long it's been here."

"Wasn't this place an Apollo theater at one time?" Isolde asked.

She met Anora's quizzical look. "I do pay attention to some of your research work, you know."

"It was torn down in the late seventies," Anora said.

"Perfect time to build a secret facility beneath in a depressed neighborhood far from prying eyes, yet close to the central hub of political and military decisions," Isolde intoned.

"Thank you for that social commentary," Anora said, turning to walk down the metal stairs. Percy felt his grip on the waveform slip.

"We're outside the field range," Isolde said as her waveblade went out. Anora hesitated and then lit the way with her terminal. Isolde worked with Percy to activate his gridpack. The waveform snapped into place once he felt the matrix restore itself.

"Much better," Isolde said.

"Which floor do you think it's on?" Percy asked.

Anora peeked through the second sublevel access door. Newer banks of computers resided here. "Let's assume the lowest level for now. If there's nothing there, we backtrack."

"Makes sense," Percy said, leading the way down. Their footsteps echoed and Percy sensed the air getting cleaner and more refined. The doors were new and well oiled for frequent use. The bottom door was like a bank vault with a key-code lock.

"You did want to go Luke Skywalker on some blast doors," Isolde said.

Grall cut a circle around the lock from the frame through the door. He gave it a shove, and it fell out with a heavy thud, vibrating the floor with its impact. It was eerie. He grabbed the door frame and pulled the door open with an effort. Isolde went ahead of Anora. The room they entered was not what they'd expected. It was a cubicle farm. The computer workstations were completely stripped bare, and on one side of the room was another key-coded door. There was also a wooden door along an adjacent wall. Anora looked through the window of the key-coded door. The room beyond was dark. On the opposite side of the room from the long cubicle farm was a set of elevator doors.

Percy tapped the elevator controls, but nothing happened.

"Probably the entrance to Focus, but they closed up shop on their end." Anora pulled out another intrusion device and slapped it at waist height on the inside frame of the elevator. Then they walked back to the key-coded door.

"Cut it open?" Percy asked.

"I'm glad no one thought about putting booby traps down here," Anora said.

"My father preferred to destroy things firsthand, not leave traps behind like a dungeon master," Isolde replied.

"Why didn't he bother destroying this place?" Anora asked.

"It looks gutted, so perhaps it was just simply abandoned," Isolde said.

"You said it was a DARPA project?" Percy asked.

"It was, then it wasn't. Marks managed to cleverly close it out of DARPA's books but kept it running. Self-funded, as it were," Anora said.

Isolde cut the lock off with a swirl of her waveblade. The room had been a server farm at one time. All of the racks were dark—empty black metal frames like skeletons of a dead miniature metal city. "Server room," Percy said.

"I want to check out the weird wooden door," Anora said.

"I'll come with," Isolde said.

"I'll finish checking here. This might be where Oracle was kept," Percy said.

"You find any drives or intact systems, let me know," Anora said, holding up her terminal.

"Roger," Percy said, summoning *Grall* and marching along the racks. The server door whispered shut behind him. He took his time, inspecting what seemed infinite rows of empty racks. The air was cool and the HVAC system was still operational. He found an old inert gas fire-suppression system. It was functional, judging by the control panel, but there were no servers that he could see. It had been ten minutes. The server farm room was large and he wanted to be thorough. He touched his ear to activate his mike. "I'm not finding anything. What about you?" It was quiet. "Janus?"

"Anora and Isolde are unable to receive," Janus said.

Shit, Percy thought. He ran back to the server room door, checked himself, and looked outside the room before throwing the door open. *Be cautious*, he reminded himself. He ran to the wooden door and opened it. Inside was another heavy, vault-like door. It was closed. He grabbed the handle of the door and an alarm blared behind him.

∽

OWEN, John, and Mara rode through the streets of DC, on their way to Project Focus.

"A bit more why, please," John said, following closely behind Owen as he raced behind Mara. They wore special black Chevalier suits, the light tape pulsing between red and blue to make them seem like the police. They also wore modified helmets, which made them look like some sort of postapocalyptic bike gang. Owen balked at the uniform but agreed the changes to it were an improvement and didn't announce that they were actually affiliated with the Chevalier Corps. He refused to wear the new gauntlet. Why bother at this point? Mara didn't push him, as she still wore *Splinter* on her off hand. He'd been back only for a few hours and Morgan had congratulated him on his rather unorthodox find. He didn't mention Jeri, but he figured his mother would fill her in on that. Indiana was still in a semicomatose state. The birth had been difficult for her, and Morgan was curious as to how she'd survived. Morgan seemed enthralled with Indiana, and Owen got the feeling she'd be used against Arthur, which Owen had no problem with. He hoped she'd never find out about the baby—a fact he was proud to have kept from her. He'd paid a *lot* of money to the staff to keep quiet about both Jeri and the baby—nearly all of his own cash reserves. He'd most likely not need the money anyway, and even if the knowledge leaked out, the baby was out of anyone's reach, especially his family's. Mara's voice brought him back to the present.

"I followed up on the information Owen provided from his . . . package. Project Focus was one of Marks's shell programs. It's a DARPA-funded NSA research project, but it houses other projects beneath its purview. Once I found that I got real data on Delphi," Mara explained. The streets were black and slick with cold rain. It was on the verge of freezing and would soon when the temperature dropped after sunset.

Normally, Owen would have been surprised by Mara's eagerness at his report, but somehow his information was tied to Anora Myrrdin, and *that* was what seemed to spur Mara on to pursue Oracle with a bit more zest than expected—after she'd gotten permission from Morgan, of course. The surprise was that she'd requested Owen for the mission, and again Morgan had agreed. Owen knew Indiana was a valuable find, but what was it really? His cousin didn't turn on a dime.

They slowed as they hit the corner and parked their motorbikes, their light tape fading to black. The building housing Focus was more like a small fortress than a bank. It was modern looking, with a glass facade covering a reinforced interior. The bank guards inside were more alert than the usual type and they'd already been keyed up by their arrival.

"And we're going to get in how?" John asked, getting off his motorcycle slowly. He carried a heavy case on his back.

"Trust me," Mara said with a chuckle. She pulled off her helmet and walked into the building. Her flaming red hair was coiled up into a tight bun, all business. Owen and John followed behind, removing their helmets as well. Two guards approached them, eyeing their suits with hands on sidearms. Mara pulled off a patch from her sleeve, exposing a badge. She handed it to one of the guards along with a sheaf of folded papers she had tucked into a pouch in her suit. "We have authorization for sublevel access to the Tunnel," Mara said.

"There is no Tunnel, ma'am," the guard said. "Just a moment." The guard took the badge and paperwork behind reinforced glass. Owen estimated that *Nornian* would only take a few seconds to get to the guard. While he was gone, Morgan had made a lot of back-channel progress to convince her government contacts that the Chevaliers were not the cause of New York. Mara and her Chevaliers had been granted some special privileges. It wasn't a free pass, but it was a lot of progress in a short time. Political fear of what Avallach's power meant? Morgan had opened a lot of avenues for the Chevaliers.

"You guys part of spec ops?" the second guard asked casually.

"Black ops," Owen replied. The man's expression was blank.

The first guard returned with a third. Owen remained calm but watched to see if they'd have to kill these men. Why was he on edge? He rubbed his fingers. The trembling had subsided on the flight back to the States and he was sure the compulsion was gone now. In fact, he'd never felt better. Perhaps London was just an episode.

"This way," the new guard said, leading them to a separate set of doors into a concrete hallway devoid of decoration.

"We were told to seal off the Tunnel," the guard said to Mara.

"Did you seal it off or just lock the door?" Mara asked.

"Sealed as requested, ma'am," the guard said. He led them down the passage. "Also we're to deny the Tunnel, so frankly I was surprised you mentioned it until I saw your paperwork. I had to verify it, of course."

"Any problems?"

"You're cleared," the guard said, and he stopped at the end of the hall. There were no doors or walls. "Not sure what you want to do here, though."

"You really sealed it," John said.

"This ain't our first rodeo," the guard replied. "That's it. The Tunnel."

"John, your grid?" Mara said, not turning from the wall. She pulled off her glove. *Splinter* glittered in the fluorescent light. Owen took his glove off and flexed his hand.

John pulled off the heavy pack he'd been carrying, putting it down with a thunk. He knelt and fiddled with the system, snapping switches and tapping on a small keyboard. Owen closed his eyes and felt the matrix field permeate his body and the hairs of his neck prickle. Mara was manifesting. He seized the waveform and stared at the wall. Pre-manifest, the wall looked nearly perfect, but now he saw it was a new addition, judging by the seams along the wall and floor.

He knocked on the wall, and it was solid. He pulled a lot of power from the grid. It should stave off any neurological problems, he hoped.

"Grid's up," John said, flexing his silver gauntlet.

"I'm not sure what you plan on doing, but the Tunnel goes to an elevator that takes you down a few sublevels. It's sealed off, like I said."

"We'll be taking this along with us," John said, pulling a lever that gave the pack wheels.

"Shall I?" Mara smiled and *Splinter* blinked into existence. The guard flinched and drew his sidearm.

"Relax," John said.

"You're one of those freaky power fucks from New York!"

"Calm down. We're here to investigate something—"

The guard wasn't buying any of it. Owen was certain the man had been briefed during the process of validating their paperwork, but the news feeds about New York still put people on edge. *Here be monsters*, Owen thought. If only the man knew he was standing in front of the person who'd destroyed West Fourth Street station with a sweep of his blade.

John lanced the guard with a flick of his wrist. Owen grabbed the guard before he could get his twitchy fingers into the trigger guard and fire off a round. "Guy's real itchy."

"He works at a DARPA facility. Wouldn't you be?" Owen said.

"Just put him down gently. We don't need a ruckus right now," Mara said.

"Yeah yeah," John said. "They're going to come looking for him."

"And we'll have an explanation when we get back. Not like they can shoot us over it." She sliced through the wall neatly. The space beyond it was indeed sealed up with cinder blocks and lined with lead. Nothing stopped *Splinter*, but it was a bit tough going to push the debris out of the way. The wall partially collapsed and they were in a long dark hallway. The noise was deafening to Owen's ears, but the hallway deadened the noise. Still, he watched for an approach the way they'd come.

Mara dragged the guard halfway down the hallway and placed him in a resting position, safing his weapon. "He'll be fine but pissed when he wakes up. I'll smooth it over later."

Owen helped John carry the pack through the hole they had made.

John wheeled the pack behind them as they walked through the sloping corridor. "With this, we'll have some range if we're within a level or two of it."

"That'll be good enough," Mara said.

Owen watched her back as she retreated. His mind was focused on the task ahead. Would they find Oracle? What would it promise them? Was it what Anora was looking for? He thought of the alternate plan—taking Oracle from Anora and her Binary group. That might be more problematic, as Binary had incredibly robust security and anti-intrusion systems. Still, it was an option, particularly if they had sufficient government backing.

At a tenth of a mile, they came to an elevator. Mara hit the elevator button. Nothing happened.

John motioned to a nearby power panel. Mara walked over to it and restored power to the elevator. After a warm-up period, the door opened at the push of a button.

"They never secured power to the elevator panel?" John asked.

"I guess Marks never bothered to turn everything off," Mara replied.

"Lucky us. I didn't want to climb down with this grid."

They stepped in. John parked the device in the corner as Mara stabbed the lowest-level button. The doors whisked shut and carried them into the bowels of Delphi. Owen heard a chirping sound. John looked down at his grid system.

"What the hell?" John said.

"What is it?" Owen asked.

"It's a new feature that the lab installed. It's saying that based on the field strength, there's already a matrix down here."

"Damn, you're saying someone might be here already?" Owen asked.

"That or they left a grid system online. I don't feel anything," John said.

"That's because the grid is on. We don't feel more field around us," Owen said.

Owen stared at the doors as the elevator came to a stop. They didn't open. There was a buzzing sound. He tugged on the doors, but more than gears held them shut. "They're locked or barred."

"Damn," Mara whispered. "Guess not everything here has its power restored." She pulled out her phone and tapped out a message. "Deploying second team."

"I'll cut it," John said, stepping forward. His gauntlet waveblade came to life. Owen saw a shimmer of light around the gauntlet. *A shield?* he wondered. If so, that solved the flaw he'd exposed during his run. John sliced through the doors, then grabbed the doors and pulled them open. A blue blade stabbed through John's torso. He yelled and twitched, his body arching in pain.

"Shit, move!" Mara said, grabbing John and hauling him back while grabbing her side of the door.

"Got it!" Owen said, pulling his side of the door. Mara saw a black man standing at the entrance, a grim look on his face.

28

FIGHT PREDICTION

ONE MOMENT EARLIER—
"Where's Anora?" Percy asked, running to the elevator and meeting Isolde, who rushed through the wooden door. He saw behind the closing wooden door was an alcove and a large metal door with a porthole—the kind of door found on naval vessels or decompression chambers.

"She's safe. What do we do?" Isolde eyed the elevator, where they heard the hum and clack of machinery as the elevator descended.

"Should've gotten her out of here."

"Well, I can't do it now," Isolde retorted. She held up the terminal and tapped a simple command. "Calling for help."

"Stand to the side. I'll get them head-on, whoever it is," Percy said, summoning *Grall*.

A white light flicked through the seam in the elevator doors. Percy shifted *Grall* to blue and stabbed as a dark-haired man pried the doors open. The man fell back, stunned.

"Hello, assholes," Percy said, swinging his blade. "That was your only warning." His blade changed from blue to pure white.

Mara lunged at him, blocking his blade and countering, Percy's KE shield coming up as the woman swung into his side. Her blade stopped, and he snapped his arm out, clocking her on the side of the head. A bearded man jumped out of the elevator, rushing him. Percy stepped back. The man's attack was brutally fast and hard. Percy, though well trained, hustled to match the man's fury.

Isolde came in and her attacks slowed the bearded man's advance. Percy did a quick check of the elevator. Just one man out cold—must've hit his head on the back wall as he went down. Isolde and Percy coordinated their attacks now and it was everything the attacker could do to keep them from lancing him in half. Isolde wasn't as trained and lacked reach. Fortunately, her KE shield was something the attacker was confounded by.

Isolde backed away and Percy filled the gap, guiding them toward the server room. The man swung low, then high. Percy met the low one with *Grall* and the high one with his KE shield. This man looked so familiar—just like Arthur with a beard. He didn't move like Arthur though, so Percy dismissed it as a trick of the eyes, but was it? His senses were heightened and enhanced. He could make out details in the man's features. He looked just like Arthur in a lot of ways. The woman was up and edging around him. He flicked *Grall* left, then right, blocking and dancing between the two. It was a dance with death. Waveblades flashed in the air and parts of cubicles sloughed away, gouges appeared in walls, and arcs were carved in the floor. He couldn't get them to the server room and nothing could keep them from doubling back to Anora and Isolde. Percy changed tack to get them out of the area.

"Going for help," Percy said aloud. The man and woman advanced, but he advanced on them as well. He had to sell it, somehow. He put himself on a path toward the stairwell.

"Izz," Percy panted.

"Go left," Isolde said.

Percy moved to the side, and Isolde slid low and hit the woman while holding her KE field up. The woman's waveblade swung wild and then blinked out as she crashed to the ground. Percy shouldered into the bearded man, slamming him back into a cubicle. The man's halo dimmed for a fraction of a second, then glowed brighter. Percy felt the energy pull coming from the grid. He pulled more as well. "Get ready."

"Busy," Isolde huffed, wrestling on the ground with the woman. There were sparks and several pops and then the lights blew out. Then the matrix collapsed as both gridpacks overloaded. Everything went dull and dark.

Percy had only enough time to curse as he was bull-rushed by the Arthur lookalike.

29

MIND KILLER

ONE MOMENT EARLIER—
Get it together! she screamed to herself. *The door is open*, she reminded herself. It didn't help her irrational mind. She took a deep breath. There was work to focus on.

The room was deathly quiet. Anora found the terminal and tried to determine if it had power. Anora heard Isolde's breathing. *You're not alone.* She heard her own breathing and her heartbeat pulsing in her ears like thudding waves. Anora fought the rising panic of being in such a place. It was lit and she wasn't alone. It kept her nerves at bay. *Why is this any worse than being four sublevels underground*? She cursed her logical mind for bringing up something worse.

Her terminal chimed. "Unable to achieve an outside signal," One said in her ear.

Anora examined the anechoic walls. It could also have been a Faraday cage. She handed her terminal to Isolde. "Take this outside and hit the beacon if we need it." She showed Isolde the emergency system Heph had built into her new terminal.

"You seem to think we might need help?"

"I'm always prepared."

"You're not a Boy Scout. This place is creepy. I'm—"

Her terminal blared in Isolde's hand, echoing outside the room, farther away.

"Someone's in the facility," Anora said.

"I got it," Isolde said. "Stay here and safe. At least the door will stop them for a moment." Then she was gone.

Anora took a deep breath, and shut the door. The small porthole window showed her the room outside the chamber. Her panic level rose a bit, but she was safe. She was the only one without focal tech, after all. She faced the blank screens. This was where Oracle had been; she was certain of it. She worked the terminal controls and the system booted. She was surprised, but when she watched the boot sequence, she knew that most of the system had been stripped away. Cornwall Marks's face filled the center screen.

"If you've found this message, you were destined to find Oracle, as she's ordained. And if you've found this message, I know I'm dead. What's left to say? I'm a fool, but what's more foolish is that I was blind."

Anora was glad she'd shut the door. She sat mesmerized by the message. It was mostly self-aggrandizement by General Marks about what he'd done. He didn't build Oracle, but he had shepherded it over the last two decades, turning it to his own personal ends. He discovered too late that Oracle had deceived him and he'd had the system shut down. So the message was a warning. To whom?

"I planned to rip it apart, and I did. But I had to ask questions before I wiped it away. This message is for Dr. Anora Myrrdin: I, along with my supervisor, sent the message to terminate his life. He was brilliant. I resented it. This message is for Isolde: For all I've tried to do in the name of my son's life, I've failed you most of all. I plan to change that, but my time is short. For you, life will be less than you want. You'll become something more than who you are, but you'll die young. There's nothing I know that can prevent it. If you stay with Arthur, it'll not end well for you. If you go, your life will be even shorter. I've put you in a terrible place and I'll never be able to correct it. Forgive me, my Isolde. I love you." The screen went blank and then the system wiped itself clean. "Damn." Anora leaned down to pull the power before it could destruct, but then all the lights went out and there was a heavy metallic thunk, like bolts slamming into place.

"Oh no," Anora said, forgetting the message, and fumbled to the door. She tried to open it, but it wouldn't budge. The porthole window was black. Power to the whole floor was gone. She was locked in. She threw her shoulder into it, and the blood pounded in her ears. What she wouldn't have given for focal rings! She reached for her terminal, but she'd given it to Isolde. Damn! What a careless blunder! She was in the dark. She felt around for the computer and stabbed at the power button, trying to get any residual light in the room. Nothing. The fear crept up her throat and seized her spine. She tried to breathe deeply. *You've been in worse*, she reminded herself. *You've conditioned yourself. You've lasted weeks before.* It was irrational, but she couldn't help the fear overcoming her. She couldn't stop it, but she could subvert it. She couldn't hear anything outside the chamber. She broke out in a sweat and her mind went blank as she tried to think her way through the problem.

30

IN THEIR ELEMENT

Percy wrestled the man and punched him hard in the ribs. Once, twice, and the man grunted in pain and threw him off. Percy jumped but the man melted into the darkness. Percy breathed in ragged gasps and he rubbed his throat. He felt his way down the corridor in a low crouch. The gridpack! It had a fail-safe that kept it from overloading. If he could reset it, he could get them back into fighting form. He heard the women brawling and scuffling. Someone bumped into him and he grabbed ahold.

"Mother—" Isolde punched Percy in the kidney. It was a glancing blow, fortunately.

"Izz," he hissed, wrapping an arm around her. "Come on!" He hadn't lost his sense of direction. He guided her toward the stairwell.

"Where to?" she asked, winded. "Fucking woman can fight."

"Where we can fight," Percy said. There was an intake of breath behind him, and he spun as someone hit him with a metal pipe, knocking him down. His shoulder hurt like hell and he responded in kind by kicking his foot out into a solar plexus. The woman grunted and crumpled to the floor.

Isolde grabbed his arm. "That you or her?"

"It's me," Percy said. He leaned against the wall. They had to get higher. This place had no lighting. Nothing emergency had clicked on and whatever had been providing air had stopped running. He felt along and found the stairs. "Up, up."

"What about—"

"They don't know she's in there and can't see for shit. Let's get up and get the advantage of high ground."

They rushed up the stairs as fast as they could. Percy stomped a bit harder to attract their attention. *Draw them away.*

"Think my nose is bleeding," Isolde said.

"Come on. Check corners," he said, jogging up the stairs. They got to the ground floor, and he kicked open the closet door. They heard voices below and the clank of footsteps on the stairs. "Where's the field?"

"I don't know."

"Where's the guy? The van?"

"One, can you call Simon?" Isolde whispered.

"Calling now," One said in a tiny voice.

"Doctor?" Simon's voice said.

"Simon, this is Isolde. I need you to bring the van closer to the building. We need proximity to the field the machinery in the back is generating."

"Something wrong? You sound like hell."

"Nothing you can deal with right now. Just drive right up to the curb of this building."

"On my way."

Isolde turned to report to Percy, who put a hand on her breast. "Wha—"

Percy pushed her back. "Move," he commanded. Percy felt the field again. "No, it's here. Get ready." He seized the waveform and everything snapped into focus.

Waveblades lit below him and Percy countered. The dark-haired man he'd stabbed earlier advanced up the stairs, followed by the woman and the bearded man. Percy held the stairs, but these two had fought together. If Percy held the stairs, they couldn't get to Isolde. His shield put him in a good position and his waveblade made it a deadly proposition to rush him. There was a bang behind him.

"Izz?" he called to her.

"We got company."

"The nice kind of company?"

"No. More of them. Two." She was down the corridor, her blade flicking in their air as she charged the two new attackers. Two on five. Percy was smiling. Just a matter of time.

"Le and Safír are here," Mara reported as they pounded up the stairs.

Owen focused on his steps. He was winded. Percy Jones was a hell of a fighter, but Piotr's training helped immensely. Someone shouted below them.

"Pellam?" Mara called.

"I'm coming. I have one hell of a headache," John said, making his way up the stairs.

"Where's the field system?" Mara asked.

"Shit. I left it in the elevator. I'll go back."

"No, we've got them on the run. There's only two of them."

"Have Safír and Le come to our location. Flank them," Owen said. "They've got a field, right?"

"Who's the commander here?" Mara said. "They have a kit like ours."

Owen shrugged and then stopped. The noises on the stairs ended. The Marks girl and Percy had made it to the top.

"Where's Myrrdin?" Mara asked. "The kid's carrying her phone."

Owen felt the field and immediately brought *Nornian* to life. *Splinter*'s bright light appeared in Mara's hand. She made a fist with her gauntlet and her whole forearm shimmered. "John, if we push them back, get down to the sublevel, investigate."

Owen and Mara raced to the ground-level landing. Owen hoped Arthur would be there. He ground his teeth. He was ready for him this time. *Nornian* felt as slippery as always, but there was no compulsion to stop him now. He pulled more power from the field.

Percy's shield and waveblade appeared at the top of the stairs. Owen and Mara instinctively took sides to work on Percy. They couldn't rush him, but there were three of them. They could push him back.

31

REINCE RETURNS

Anora hyperventilated, and all she heard was her own breathing and her heart thudding in her own ears. It drove her mad. She rubbed the back of her hand, trying to calm herself. It worked to a degree, keeping her from hysteria. Isolde and Percy would come back for her. They must have been in a bad way to leave her like this. Why had she been so damn eager to get in here? She stopped the hand massage, felt her way to the desk and climbed back into the seat. It was better than cowering on the floor, to a degree. She calmed herself with her exercises, trying to build that rational part of her mind back up.

"It's all right," a voice said.

"Maven?" Anora said, wincing at how loud her voice sounded in this impossibly quiet place. *Anechoic chamber*, she thought.

"It's me," a voice said, a hand on her shoulder. Anora looked back to see Reince. She shouldn't have been able to see in this place, but her mind added lighting. *Human-augmented reality engine at work*, Anora thought.

"You're not here."

Reince shook his head. "You brought me with you."

Anora frowned. That was ridiculous, but the sight of him filled her with dread.

Reince continued. "Maven appears when you need to work through an especially hard or interesting problem. But he's not here to help you now. I'm here to . . . comfort you." He put his hand on her shoulder.

"I haven't needed your comfort in years," Anora said, her voice cracking under the stress. She brushed off his touch.

"Don't you like being here? In this place?" Reince replied with a smile. "It was easy to control you when I found out you were claustrophobic. Did your father do that to you?"

"You know he did," Anora whispered. Fear clawed up her throat. "My father locked me into small spaces when I was young, to punish me . . ." Her voice trailed off. It seemed ridiculous to explain something about herself to another portion of her mind. It was circular. She sat back, wrapping her head around the problem. She steepled her hands. The fear receded as her rational mind took hold, distracting itself with working the problem. She'd become much more than that stupid lovesick girl in college. She'd built a company with nothing but her ideas and her mind. She's negotiated tough contracts with tougher men than Reince, been through harder times without him. She was Anora Myrrdin—her brother's sister. Why did she still feel so helpless? What was wrong with her? Had she cracked open a part of herself that couldn't hold back old emotions?

Reince leaned against the darkness where the desk would be, folding his arms, waiting. He was still young and handsome. As she studied him, some part of her held on to him, but she knew she didn't love him. He'd been a monster on the inside—that was all she could see of him now. Reince, here in her mind? This must be where she finally broke. An idea filtered through the haze of fear.

"Maven isn't here because the problem isn't being here. It's what's going on outside. Why are Percy and Isolde being attacked?"

"Think bigger," Reince said, expanding his hands for emphasis. Once, long ago, that gesture would cause her to flinch and recoil. Now, she was like water, waiting.

"I know they're looking for Oracle, but why do they even know it exists?" Anora worked it out in her head. Her heart rate came down as she pushed herself into the problem. She worked the pieces together. Mara Holt had come. She stared at where the monitors should have been.

"Marks built the second project. That much we know, but he's gone now. Who would best run that project?"

She thought about the Mare de Scientia and the issues that Matron Kai had mentioned. It fit together once she sorted out the problems. Reince watched her patiently. Every time she looked at Reince she was distracted by him.

Anora beat back the anger and fear. She was talking to herself! Back to the problem. "Igerne's daughter. Morgan LaFayette."

Reince nodded. "You've always known that."

"And Kai already knew that. She doesn't have proof."

"Do you need proof?"

"I already have proof. She told me," Anora finally admitted.

"Isn't that interesting? You've held back information from Kai." Reince raised an eyebrow and examined his fingernails.

"I have to stop her. I have it all planned. I've known what to do. It was just part of a different plan."

"And that's part of why I'm here. You sometimes need a push... to make a decision that you know you must make, lover."

"Don't call me that."

"What shall I call you, lover? Destroyer? Betrayer?" Reince said. He shifted, and his shape grew menacing. "Chimera?"

"No."

Reince was dark and foreboding. "You're the Chimera. You're made of many things. Your life and your experience aren't just a series of fortunate events. You are wisdom and betrayal and might wrapped into one being. I've been watching you a long time, lover. On the inside."

Anora's anger rose. "Don't talk to me about betrayal. You ... you killed my child—our child. It was you who betrayed me, not the other way around."

"I was angry. You were going to leave me."

"I was pregnant," Anora said, fighting back an emotion she'd buried years ago.

"Is that why your little programs look like children?" Reince said, his voice menacing. Anora froze, her anger turning to ice. "Betrayal is a powerful weapon, so you must know how it will feel. It destroys everything. Are you ready?" Reince said, his voice a deadly whisper.

"I'm ready." Anora stood against him. She surrendered to the fear now. There was no use fighting it. Her heart hammered in her ears and the pitch black enveloped her. She felt his breath hot on her neck. *I am water*, she told herself.

"Reince?" Anora said, glancing around her. The panic closed in about her. The thoughts she had collected around Morgan, Igerne, and her plans flittered away like fireflies in the all-consuming black. She fought back. She was the Chimera. Lover, betrayer, destroyer.

32

RIGHT

Sword-fighting was not his forte, Percy admitted. But he'd learned at Avallach that these weapons weren't toys, nor were they tools of a bygone age. They were lethal instruments and yet they were as limited as the wielder.

Your blade is an extension of you, Indiana had said more than once.

Percy retreated out of the broom closet. Despite his KE shield, their coordinated attacks would have severed his leg if he hadn't darted out of the way, which was exactly what they wanted. They gained purchase on the ground floor and he'd lost the choke point advantage. Percy heard Isolde fighting at the front of the building. Metal rent and bodies crashed into things.

"Go," the woman said, her hair framing her face in red. Who was she talking to?

"Status?" Arthur's voice said in Percy's ear.

"Mac?" Percy said. "Dire. Five, maybe six on two."

"Five," Isolde panted, confirming.

"Be there in ten seconds with reinforcements," Arthur said. Ten seconds was a long time. They must've been fighting for a good ten minutes, although Percy knew the sense of time skews when adrenaline courses through your veins. He kept at it. The man and woman were in the broom closet but not beyond it. They were winded as well. That was when the bearded man came to the forefront to bash Percy back with his waveblade, which wavered and shimmered in the air. It seemed tenuous, but his blade held its shape. The woman's blade did the same. They drew more energy from the grid. The van system was larger than his gridpack, but when more people entered the fray, everyone was going to take a hit.

A loud percussive boom vibrated the air around Percy and a flood of water and cold winter air rushed into the building. A piece of the roof had been cut away and he saw three shapes above him in the iron-gray sky. Percy didn't have time to note who it was. He hefted his arm up to shoulder into a downward stroke by his attacker. Ed was at his side, the redheaded man attacking with a fury.

"Hey, man, how you been?" Ed said conversationally as he fought beside him.

"Tired," Percy replied.

"Aw, widdle maween need a nap? I got this," Ed said, grabbing Percy by the shoulder and shoving him away from the fray. The broom closet was clear of people, and the building was loud with the shouts and grunts of brawling. Ed was fresh and ready to fight. Isolde edged up to Percy. She was winded, her suit was torn in a couple of places, and one cheek was badly bruised.

"You okay?"

"Just a couple of near misses. Gonna need a shitload of concealer."

"Don't get careless," Percy warned.

"Where's Anora?"

Percy had momentarily forgotten about her in the intensity of the fight. "Still down below."

"I gotta get her out of there. She's probably freaking out." Isolde went to the stairs.

"I'll come with—"

"No, you stay here. Take out these bastards," Isolde said. Her hands were on her knees for a moment, but her halo brightened as she caught her breath.

"The field won't hold again," Percy called after her.

Isolde was already down the steps, vanishing into the black.

Percy felt the matrix tremble with so many people manifesting. He hoped Arthur had held back at least one backup system. He flicked *Grall* to life, just as the bearded man appeared before him. His face was an angry mask, and Percy felt his blows against his shield. His attacker pulled more power from the grid, but the matrix wavered. It wasn't hard to hold on to the waveform, but they were competing for the power draw and somehow this man gained power. Percy edged back under the man's wide and aggressive blows. Percy tripped over something behind him and stumbled. It was a good thing, too, because the not-Arthur nearly took off his head.

MARA WAS THROWN BACK by the large man and she crashed through a wall, her KE field and suit armor taking some of the brunt. It was drywall and just a bit of plaster, really. She skidded and tripped back into the far wall, which was solid and stopped her.

The redheaded man came on. He was like a bull, head low, his waveblade up and wary. She wiped her mouth and blood came away. She flicked *Splinter* to life. The man raised his arm, but his shield didn't activate. He was beckoning her.

"Come on, red," he said. "Let's have a dance."

"I don't like to dance," Mara said, and she drew power into her gauntlet. She'd gotten the newest design for this outing from MacRossa. It had something that hadn't quite been seen before, but MacRossa assured her it had been tested—a few times and mostly with success. *No time better than the present*, she thought.

The waveblades danced around one another as Mara kept her distance from the man. Ed Tiwaz was his name. Arthur's right-hand man, so to speak. Waveblades arced in the air and his shield came on. He was deadly but cautious. He was well trained, but he tended to rely on his strength and open himself to attack. That's when she would be ready.

"Afraid to fight a woman?" she said, hoping to taunt him.

"Not particularly. I've had to kill one or two," Ed replied. His face was set, although he tried to give off a casual demeanor. He'd been manifesting for much longer and he would outlast her ability to keep *Splinter* formed. She had to move.

Mara executed a series of lunges and strikes that Ed countered well. Her elbow came down on the back of his neck, but it was like hitting a rock. Her left arm was numb from the impact. He grunted with the attack, but it showed an opening. He came in this time, knowing she meant business. His attack was fast and predictable, and when his overhand strike came down, she threw up her shining left hand and caught the blade. It wavered and the blade sank into her hand as she funneled energy from it into her KE field. Ed was surprised, and all she needed was that second. *Splinter* cut left across his body and severed his hand at the wrist.

His blade vanished as his body was separated from his rings. His KE field went down as well, his halo fading quickly. He gasped in pain, but to his credit, he didn't crumple. Mara waved the blade again, but he jumped back through the hole he'd thrown her through. *Good-bye, right hand*, she thought. She flexed her gauntlet, her body drawing power. She'd stopped his blade. The battle could be turned.

Then everything went dull and black as the grid went down again. Mara frowned as the power left her body. She was vulnerable, and there was a wounded ex–Navy SEAL nearby. "Damn it to hell," she whispered to herself, and moved quietly in the pitch black.

33

DEAR LONGINUS

Isolde made it to the chamber as the grid melted away. "Damn it," she sighed. She grabbed the door and yanked hard, but it didn't budge. "Anora?" she called, drumming on the door with her fist. There was no response. What was wrong with the door? Was it jammed or broken? Maybe it locked on a loss of power, which happened when they overloaded the power with their grid. There had been power to this floor, after all. Why not the chamber door?

"Anora!" Isolde called again. She pulled out Anora's terminal and held it to the small glass window in the door. Anora's face appeared. She was ashen and sweating. She made a fist, but Isolde shook her head. "I can't open the door. No grid." She made a fist with her rings and then a thumbs-down gesture.

Anora pointed to the terminal and made an L shape with her index finger and thumb. What did that mean? She made the shape of an O.

"Longinus?" Isolde deciphered, and pointed skyward. Anora gave the thumbs-up. She wanted Isolde to activate the long-range grid satellite—something that hadn't been tested since its launch. They had no choice if their systems were continually overloaded. Isolde held up the terminal. "One, activate Longinus."

One responded, "Locking to location. Five minutes to position." She gave Anora the thumbs-up and showed her the terminal. Five minutes.

Anora nodded, her lips pressed into a thin line. She made hand gestures, signs, she thought. It took her a moment, but Isolde nodded and typed "CAMLANN" on Anora's terminal and showed it to her. Anora nodded. Anora wanted to get to CAMLANN, but the portable rig was in the chamber itself. It also needed One to operate it, but Isolde was holding Anora's terminal. *Damn.*

Anora waved to Isolde and held up both index fingers. Two locations? Two entrances.

Isolde nodded and made the motion for "one minute" and what she hoped was "be right back." She went to the elevator. Isolde spoke to herself. "Not a bad idea to escape this way, since walking into a waveblade fight is pretty much a death sentence with all the swinging dicks up there." Was Anora running out of air? She hated closed spaces—Isolde had learned that on the Raven and a bit more since she had been assigned to Anora by Arthur. She lived in large open apartments and offices for a reason. Isolde hit the button, thinking the power would be out. She was not disappointed. The inner doors were shut, but once she got her fingers into the seam, it activated the sensors and they opened automatically. The elevator hummed. It still had power.

"I'll be damned," Isolde said. She stepped onto the elevator and looked at the controls. There were only three buttons, all unmarked. On the elevator was a large suitcase, like a trunk. It was a grid system, she was sure. It wasn't an Avallach system, but she could figure it out. It had been overloaded, and it wasn't ready for use just yet. She reset the system and put it into standby. It might be useful later. She went back to the chamber and told Anora about the elevator and grid using the terminal. It was easier for Isolde to communicate with Anora than the other way around.

"Longinus in position. Ready," One chimed.

"Should I activate it?" Isolde asked Anora via terminal.

Anora nodded emphatically.

Isolde considered. "I'm just saying it's not a tested system. I could maybe use the grid I found—"

Anora slapped the glass and mouthed, "Now!" to Isolde.

There was a noise behind her, but before Isolde could turn, she was slammed against the chamber door. The terminal flew out of her hand. Dazed, she tried to kick back, but her feet were swept out and she fell to the ground. She saw the attacker—the dark-haired man whose uniform had stripes of a low glowing red. Before Isolde could react, he grabbed her ponytail and punched her with a silver-mailed fist. Isolde's head bounced off the ground.

The man stood over her, then turned away. "I'd break your neck, but when I get the grid back on, I'm just going to sever your head," he growled. He disappeared into the shadows of the weak terminal light.

34

MIND TRIP

Anora pounded on the glass. She saw the man leave the room, and now all she saw were shadows cast by the terminal and no Isolde. She shouldered into the door. The pitch black was enveloping her and she felt the hot breath of Reince on her neck. Sweat poured from her skin as she slid down the door. She had to get out. She had to do something. She squeezed her eyes shut. The fear overrode her entire mind. She wanted Maven to come and save her. But he couldn't anymore. *Third time's the charm, darling. He's saved you twice and now you've got to save yourself, Chimera.*

She grabbed on to the image of the chimera. She'd planned it all along, but she'd been planning for the wrong thing. Right?

"Goddamn it, Isolde, where are you?" Anora beat on the door weakly.

"She's gone," Arthur said.

Anora jumped. She felt his hand on hers, touching and massaging. Her fear subsided like an ebb tide. There was a shift in her mind like she'd gone over some sort of bump. Had she decided something? Or just gone over the edge into insanity?

"You're here," Anora said. "Where's Reince?"

"Do you want him back? He's still here if you want him."

"No, that's all right. But you?"

"I'm the Boy Scout, right? The person you've got all figured out."

"I did say that, and I'm sorry. I don't know how to convince you—" Anora shook her head. "Why are you here?" Anora's mind clicked over. "Oh. Not done with the problem. You're here . . ."

Arthur thought about that for a moment. "To remind you of what you need to do. You're supposed to betray me. I told you so."

"Betray you and kill you. None of it I believe."

"You know all the pieces now. Well, maybe not all the pieces," Arthur mused.

"Great. I'm glad you're here."

"Oh?"

"It probably means I'm finally cracking up. It only took me a few months to lose my shit."

Arthur chuckled. "How does no one know what you've done to yourself?"

"If I want to take on a killer, I have to become a killer." She thought for a moment. "You're here to push me in the direction you want me to go. You tell me it's my job to betray you. Your mother goes one step farther and tells me I must betray and kill you. The copy of your mother. Or the copy of a copy of your mother. And now my copy of you is doing the same. I don't like it."

"There must be some reason I'm here. Maybe it's not to push you in the direction you need to go. Have you thought about that?"

Anora rubbed her temple. "This is getting tedious. Oracle isn't here at Delphi and I've got to get to the Sisterhood." Arthur stopped massaging her hand. "I didn't say stop," Anora said. It held the dread at bay, being here with her mind's-eye version of Arthur.

"So you like it now?"

Anora nodded. She figured that out now as well. "I got it. I know why you're here."

"I'm here until Isolde frees you."

"Will she?" Anora looked up at the only speck of light streaming through the small glass window. "She might be dead." Anora sighed. "She doesn't like you at all."

"What does your dojo master say? It isn't necessary to like a person to respect a person."

"I'm still waiting for her to shoot you when she gets the chance."

"She probably will. But in the meantime, she's loyal to you. You've decided?"

Anora thought about it. It sounded ridiculous to say such things out loud to herself. This Arthur wasn't real. "I had plans laid to destroy everything. I blamed everyone for Maven and I wanted them to pay."

Arthur regarded her for a moment, waiting.

"I'm ready," she said, closing her mind off to him and working out the plans inside her mind. "They'll all pay now."

35

CUTTING FREE

Isolde rolled over onto her side. She hadn't lost consciousness, but she hurt badly. She probably had a cracked rib and maybe she'd lost a tooth. Pain shot through her. "One?" she slurred through smashed lips. She spat blood.

"I'm here," came the tinny reply.

"Activate Longinus now," she rasped. Her limbs felt like lead. The man had gotten the drop on her and she'd paid the price. Her bruised cheek turned into a swollen eye.

"Longinus online," One said.

Isolde held her breath. After few tense seconds, she felt the matrix around her and seized the waveform immediately. Power flooded back into her. She would have cried with joy if the pain of crying itself didn't make her side hurt. She pulled power in and some of the pain receded. She looked down at her hand. A halo glowed around her. Isolde climbed back to standing. Her body pulsed with energy, tingling all the hairs of her skin.

"Get away from the door," Isolde croaked. She hoped Anora heard her and then remembered she couldn't. Flicking *Justice* to life, she stabbed into the glass and announced, "Opening!" She cut through the chamber door and hopefully through the heavy lock. It still didn't budge. She ran the blade along the ceiling and floor of the door, then gave it a yank. It opened easily. Metal scraped and creaked, but the door's hinges were intact. She swung it wide open.

Anora was on the floor, her hands clasped on her chest, fingers of one hand rubbing the other obsessively. Her hair was damp and dark around her face.

Isolde knelt beside her. "Anora! You okay? Who else can I share my hatred for Arthur with?"

Anora's eyes fluttered open. "I don't hate him," she whispered.

"You had to go and ruin a good thing." Isolde smiled. "Are you okay?"

"Trying to keep it together," Anora said. "Jesus, you look like shit." Anora touched her face in a caressing gesture. Isolde was glad to see it focused her mind.

"Some asshole punched me with a metal hand."

Isolde hooked an arm under Anora's and got her up. Isolde gasped in pain but willed herself through it. Anora reached out and grabbed her black case, then scooped up her terminal and shoved it into a pocket.

"Status?" Anora asked One.

"Longinus online. Full field permeation from Isolde's sensors. Isolde also has a number of contusions and a possible cracked rib. Janus reports Arthur, Percy, and Ed have engaged multiple combatants at ground level. You have a message from Oracle."

Arthur came? Anora wondered, then shook her head and focused. "Not right now. I have to get CAMLANN online."

"There's a quorum currently in progress within CAMLANN."

"I have to get there," Anora said.

"Let's work on one thing at a time," Isolde said.

They walked down the hall. Isolde was glad for the extra strength her manifest gave her, because Anora leaned on her heavily. She gripped her case with white knuckles. There was a faint chirping sound.

Isolde kept *Justice* flared to life so she could see. That and she was hunting for the attacker.

He stood in the elevator, waiting for her. He summoned his waveblade.

Isolde pushed Anora to the side and faced him. He came at her, moving to her left side, where her swollen eye might give him an advantage. It was swollen but not shut. They fought. He certainly had an edge over her in training. His waveblade danced off her shield and she stabbed low. Suddenly he fell forward into Isolde. She danced back as he crashed into her. She rammed her waveblade into him. He let out a gasp of pain. They wrestled around on the ground for a moment, Isolde gaining the upper hand. Her blade shifted blue and she stabbed him again and held the blade there until he only twitched. She rolled him off of her, noticing the blood coming from his abdomen. Well, she could've shifted her waveblade earlier. She felt her broken cheekbone. *Fair's fair, asshole*, she thought.

Anora stood over her, holding the case. "Poorly trained. KE field or not, you don't turn your back on someone."

She helped Isolde to her feet. Some color had returned to Anora's face. "Who's saving who?" Isolde asked.

"We're saving each other, dummy." Anora got onto the elevator and sat Isolde on top of the chirping grid trunk. Isolde winced every time she breathed. Anora sat down next to her.

Isolde checked her over. Physically she was fine, but Anora's eyes had a haunted look. Her jaw was set. It was funny, Isolde thought. That was the look her father had given when he had to do something unpleasant. Isolde finished checking over Anora. "You could lose some weight," Isolde said.

"Me?" Anora smiled. "I carried you onto the elevator."

"Some guys like thin."

"You don't know enough men."

Isolde chuckled and kicked the topmost elevator button with her foot. "Here goes."

"There will probably be security personnel on the other side," Anora said as she swept damp hair out of her eyes.

A high-pitched keening struck Isolde's ears and the power permeating her twisted like a knife. It amplified the sound, making her head reverberate. Isolde doubled over in pain, falling off the trunk. It washed away all her physical pain and replaced it with something more powerful. Worse. "Ah!"

"What's wrong?" Anora asked, kneeling over her. Isolde barely heard her.

"Don't know. Some loud noise. Can you hear it?"

Anora shook her head.

Isolde almost passed out from the pain.

36

DOUBLING

"Power's back!" Owen heard Percy report.

Owen wiped the blood from his lip. He had just fought Percy Jones and was no better for it. The man was a trained fighter, and Percy's marine-fu took him far. They both played for keeps, and Percy was able to strongarm Owen. Until the field came back. Percy had him nearly unconscious from a headlock, but Owen threw Percy across the room and escaped as the grid returned. Owen seized the waveform and brought *Nornian* to bear, but Percy was gone around a corner. The lights flashed and flickered as waveblades appeared. Everyone sensed the grid at the same time, and its well felt deep. *What is this?* Owen thought. Was it a new system Avallach created? Owen picked his way along the debris-filled corridor where Percy had confronted Mara. Her hair was unbound—the red mass of curls floated in a thick cloud around her head. Her nose was bloody and her eye blackened, but she had a grim smile on her face and her gauntlet shone like a diamond. She was near the broom closet and stairs. She meant to return to see if Oracle was there. Owen had a fraction of hesitation, then he advanced as Percy summoned his waveblade.

Owen growled as they clashed. He pulled as much power as he

could bear. The air was filled with a high-pitched keening. That wasn't right. His mind was full of the keening. Owen's body resonated with the sound and it felt as though his molecules were vibrating. Owen fell back and saw that Percy had taken a knee and Mara was grasping her head. Owen held on. There was no way he was letting go of the waveform. Was it her again? No, this was something different. His mind blanked from the pain, but not from being seized. This wasn't the same, and he could hold on to the waveform. He wasn't being pushed. He sniffed and wiped away more blood. He glanced down at it, and when he looked up, Arthur was next to Percy.

They were speaking through the noise, but even with his enhanced hearing, Owen had trouble making it out. *Nornian* vibrated in a harmonic of the keening. He gathered his wits and prepared himself. Where were Le and Safir?

Percy spat blood. The two men straightened as Owen and Mara attacked from different vectors. They all seemed to be moving in slow motion. The pain made it impossible to focus. Arthur seemed calm despite seeing his own face looking back at him. It angered Owen, who pushed through the pain to confront his predecessor, his progenitor. Waveblades flicked and sliced through the air and Owen could see Indiana's influence on Arthur. He was more fluid and in control. They broke apart for a pause and Owen saw that Percy looked on and Mara was gone.

Owen came on, his waveblade swinging in a high arc. The two men fought hard and dirty, but Owen fought for his life. Arthur was better trained. Silently he cursed the bitch, Indiana. He pulled more power as he bashed Arthur's shield. The Chevaliers needed those shields. It put them at a clear disadvantage. The keening spiked again and Owen drove hard at Arthur, who gave ground, and they were beyond the stairs. Percy faced Owen and it was two on one. But instead of advancing, Arthur shoved Percy toward the stairs and shouted, "Anora!" above the keening. *Is Anora Myrrdin here? That's right. Anora. Oracle.* Owen had trouble with more than one thought at a time with the twisting pain in his skull.

Percy moved toward the stairwell and that left an opening. Owen rushed in and shouldered Percy hard, sending him tumbling down the stairs. Percy's waveblade winked out and he vanished into the dark.

Owen faced Arthur. "Don't you look familiar," Arthur said as they clashed in a flurry of ripostes. Arthur threw him back, and Owen held on to *Nornian* with everything he had. This was going to be harder than he thought.

"You're not going to win this fight," Owen replied.

"Famous last words." Arthur came at him. Owen trembled. His body was failing him. He tried to bolster himself by drawing in more, but his body seemed to be near its limit. His molecules felt like they were about to slip their bonds. The keening crescendoed and his body seemed to split into two. He was resonating and it was glorious. He grinned madly at the power he held. Arthur waded toward him, seemed to move in slow motion. Owen could see the fractional futures of where he would move. It was too easy to see now. *Time to end this*, Owen thought.

"Just a second," Anora said, slumping against the wall. They had gotten halfway down the corridor after the doors opened.

"I suppose we got a couple of minutes," Isolde said, sitting on the ground next to her. They were both in bad shape, relatively speaking. Physically, Isolde was the worse off, but she didn't want Anora to feel diminished. Isolde had seen her phobias firsthand. The keening had gotten worse, but if she didn't manifest *Justice*, the blood stopped coming out of her ears. What was happening? Some sort of new thing? Something they hadn't accounted for with so many drawing from the grid? Was there something wrong with Longinus?

"It's probably something to do with Longinus," Anora said.

"Reading my thoughts again?"

"You were rubbing your rings. Simple to assume you're thinking about the pain you were feeling."

"You're creepy, you know that?" Isolde tried to wink, but everything hurt.

"'Otherworldly' is what I prefer," Anora said. The color had returned to her face and she had tied her hair back. She looked more like the rocker turned AI scientist that Isolde knew. Anora opened her case and was flipping some switches. She put on her glasses.

"This is probably not a safe place to be talking to yourself," Isolde advised.

"Just getting ready. I really need to get to CAMLANN."

The elevator door chimed. Isolde got up from the squatting position. "Get going, Nor. I should've sliced the elevator in half . . ." She pushed through the pain of the keening in her mind and brought *Justice* into her hand.

"You're supposed to be protecting me."

Isolde got to the elevator when it slid open. A waveblade slammed down on Isolde's shield.

"Surprise," the woman said. Isolde retreated, and they fought in the entrance to the elevator. Waveblades danced back and forth.

"Mara," Anora said.

"Miss me?" Mara forced Isolde back with powerful blows. Isolde kept up the defense, but the keening in her ears made it painful and slowed her fractionally.

"It's sweet you know each other, but can we stick to the problem at hand?"

"Of course. En garde," Mara said, her waveblade whipping up. The gauntlet on Mara's off hand shimmered.

Isolde met the blade and grabbed her with her other hand, throwing Mara against the far wall. She slammed into it and spun around, dazed.

"Surprise," Isolde said. Then the keening sent waves of nausea through Isolde. She watched Mara. The keening was affecting her as well. Both women held on to the manifest and pulled more energy through the field, their halos brightening. They stood there for a moment, seeming to swim upstream and drawing enormous power. The blades flicked back to life and they attacked.

Isolde activated her shield and countered Mara's dancing blade, forcing her to try to fight it. Isolde used the shield to good advantage. Their blades crossed and Isolde stepped inside Mara's reach, but this time she was ready. They went into a series of punches and kicks, Isolde always warily keeping her shield at the ready as Mara was wont to flick her blade into her at opportune times.

Mara strangled Isolde with one hand while her waveblade pressed against Isolde's KE shield, the energy causing Isolde's halo to brighten, driving energy into her.

"You have potential," Mara hissed as she pressed close to Isolde's face.

"You're not . . . my type," Isolde whispered. Despite her KE field's being up, the press of the more athletic woman bore down on her throat. Isolde got light-headed with the lack of oxygen. She drew on the field, disregarding the keening that cycled in and out of her mind. As Mara pressed harder, the keening got louder for both. Blood trickled out of Isolde's nose, and Mara's eyes glazed over with pain. Isolde brought her knee up into Mara's groin. It was like hitting a rock with her own KE field on, but the waveblade went out and Isolde kicked back against the wall to give herself momentum to shove the woman off of her. She coughed and gasped for breath.

"What type is that?" Mara asked.

"Stupid," Anora said, holding up a submachine gun with a silencer. The red laser painted her center of mass. Anora held down the trigger.

Mara's KE field flared as the bullets struck it and she ramped up her power to maximum. Anora held the rifle as steady as she could. Mara only smiled and took a step toward her. Isolde held her ears for a moment as the keening reached a crescendo, then flicked her blade to life as she pulled as much energy as possible. Mara, distracted by Anora, could not shift enough energy to her waveblade. She turned to face Isolde as she came on, but Isolde was right on her, aiming for her heart. Mara slammed her gauntleted hand down. She actually deflected Isolde's blade, but not enough. Instead of piercing her chest, the blade pierced her thigh. Mara swung her mailed fist and hit

Isolde in the side of the head. There was a crack and Isolde went down in a heap. Mara fell to one knee, clutching her leg. Her hand came away wet with blood. She got back up, adrenaline pumping.

Isolde rolled and drew her shield arm across her body.

Mara stomped on Isolde's hand at the wrist, holding down *Justice*. Mara whipped her blade up and slammed it down against Isolde's shield in anger. Isolde whimpered in pain but held on to the shield.

"I've got Oracle," Anora called.

Mara looked at Anora, at the open case and at the smoking barrel of her Ingram MAC-10 submachine gun. "That's nice to know."

Isolde watched as Anora checked the weapon. Isolde was impressed with Anora's preparation. Her mind flicked back to when she'd been discussing it with Heph. It was only meant as a last-ditch effort. She hadn't even bothered to bring a second clip. Isolde wished she'd thought of it when the grid went down, but the gun was in the case and the case was in the chamber. Terrible luck.

Mara pressed down on Isolde's shield with her waveblade, leaning on her good foot to grind the bones of Isolde's hand together.

Isolde cried out in pain. Between the keening and her hand, she barely held on to consciousness.

"Hey, bitch," a man called down the corridor.

Mara turned back to the elevator.

Percy stood there. He dragged *Grall* along the wall behind him, and the elevator alarm rang as he damaged its circuitry and cabling. "How about we dance some more? You like picking on little girls?"

"Hey," Isolde said weakly. "I'm not little."

Mara stood on Isolde's hand and ground her boot on it a bit. "I do enjoy toying with them."

"Stop fucking with my friends," Percy said as he approached.

"Stand down, marine," Mara said as she turned to face him.

Percy looked at Isolde. He whispered in her ear through Janus. "Take Anora and get her out of here, okay?"

Isolde focused on him from beneath her KE shield. She managed a nod.

"No one's going anywhere," Mara said.

"Looks like you don't have a choice," Percy said, approaching to within a few feet of Mara. Mara moved her blade up in his direction. She was definitely injured, as blood oozed out of the wound on her leg. She took two steps away from Isolde, who clutched her broken hand to her chest. Isolde got up and stumbled away. Anora threw down her gun, picked up her case, and put an arm around Isolde as they ran down the passage. Isolde didn't look back, but she knew Percy and Mara fought. Isolde nearly fainted between the pain in her hand and the intensifying keening in her head, but Anora held her up and kept her moving. Then the world went sideways.

HE'D LOST SAFÍR, Owen was sure of it. Still, even with Le, Arthur kept them both at bay. Owen felt the twinning, the pulling apart of them. He could tell Arthur's mind was being torn by the keening. Even Le had withdrawn, clutching his head.

His whole body resonated. Arthur fell back. There was blood dripping from his nose and ears. Owen smiled. Every breath, every muscle, every heartbeat felt duplicative. The fractal futures showed Owen where to be when Arthur came at him. He was matched now. He would beat him. Arthur brought *Caliburn* to bear. That first blade, Owen knew. *Nornian* flicked and shimmered, the bar of light resonating along its entire length like something going in and out of focus.

The pain was gone from Owen's mind as he moved in time with the right future. He was there, seeing himself win against Arthur. He was going to drive *Nornian* into his heart. Arthur was moving fast, *Caliburn*'s white arcs flashing back and forth in Owen's vision as he moved from Le to Owen. His face was grim—the face of a killer. Owen saw that it was him—the man he faced. Arthur fought against himself. Fought against an uncertain future.

Part of himself felt the twinning, could see the versions of himself rippling back in time, could see the pathways that led him to this fate, but he couldn't see those long-dead futures. How can you see that which has no past? What instant was better than the last? Each small future fell away with the swing of his waveblade as he countered, lunged, thrust. He was racing now, he knew. The futures converged. He saw failure. His body losing its cohesion. He rushed to meet it. He could escape it.

The twinning grew until Owen split and the world turned white. Only one thought remained inside Owen's head. It was Jeri's voice, echoing from far away: *Monster.*

37

MAKING APPEARANCES

"I need to let go!" Isolde screamed as they ran.

"Keep your shield up," Anora said calmly.

Isolde did as she was told, holding her arm up in front of her. Things were sideways as the corridor exploded above and behind them. Anora slammed into Isolde as they were thrown up into the air. Anora grabbed on to Isolde and time seemed to slow down, which really was not a time dilation from adrenaline, but rather gravity stopped functioning as they flew upward into the ceiling. The walls shimmered and the air filled with light. Isolde felt it as the grid channeled an immense amount of energy into the matrix, which was not how the matrix was supposed to work. They floated and bounced down the corridor until the blast wave hit them and flung them through the blown-open doorway at the end of the passage.

Gravity came back at that point and they fell down onto the marble tile floor. They hit and slid along the floor along with shards of glass and debris.

Anora lay there for a long time, dizzy and disoriented. Her body was bruised and battered and there was a weight pressing down on her. Her ears rang, and she tried to orient herself in her new surroundings. Pebbles and shards around them still floated and bounced on the floor. The weight on her was an unconscious Isolde. Anora slapped Isolde's face. "Izz? Isolde?"

Isolde groaned in response. Anora didn't want to move but knew she had to. She pushed Isolde off of her. Her left arm hurt like hell—no, her shoulder was torn, broken, or dislocated, and she bit her lip against the pain. She slapped Isolde harder. "Izzy, I need you."

"I love you, too," Isolde murmured, her eyes fluttering behind her eyelids.

Anora clutched her shoulder in pain and cried out when she tried to move it. Isolde might be down for the count. Concussed. Anora was sure she was concussed as well. The world swam around her with a thudding sound. Were her eardrums damaged? Voices shouted around her, but she felt like she was underwater. People ran around her, but no one ran toward them. The crowd ran out of the building, as they were not terribly far from the glass front facade of the bank. A portion of the bank was blown out like some spectacular movie stunt, except this was reinforced glass, not sugar glass. This was hardened glass and it hurt. *Well, that's something*, Anora thought. She gathered her wits and sat up. Her lack of equilibrium made her nauseous, and she looked for the corridor they'd just came from. It wasn't there. A plume of dust and debris coughed out of the hole in the building. Anora was glad she wore her heavy leather jacket, which protected her from the glass around her, and most of it had been blown away from her, along the vector of the destruction. Fire belched out of the corridor and the sprinkler system came on. Lights flashed around her, but the buzzing of the alarms was distant. Her hearing was definitely borked. She dragged Isolde over behind the now-empty counters. Isolde moaned when Anora grabbed her broken hand. It must've been a scream for Anora to hear it.

"Sorry," Anora said, then almost cried in pain also as she moved her injured shoulder. She sat down, gazing at what had been the corridor. She thought about Arthur. What happened back at Delphi? If he'd come down to get her like Percy had, then he'd be underground. If he was dead, that would be bad. The thought surprised

Anora. She closed her eyes and saw his face and remembered what Oracle—Igerne—had said. *The Falcon becomes Chimera. By water, light and fire, she will betray and kill Arthur.* She shook her head. She hadn't betrayed him, so he couldn't be dead, could he? There were too many variables. And Percy. She'd asked him to provide backup and he was in that corridor. Had he made it or was he thrown out like she was? She hoped he was protected by his KE field. She needed to know. She winced as she moved, but there was a crackle in her ear. Her right ear had an earpiece and it had protected her eardrum to some degree.

"You know, I love it when you drag me out to these places. Every time we meet new people, they always seem to want to kill you in some way or another," Isolde said.

Anora looked down and they smiled at one another.

"Can you move?" Anora asked.

"Yeah."

Anora rubbed the base of her neck. "Can you stop bullets?"

"Nope. Grid's down."

"What happened?"

Isolde shook her head. "I don't know. Something went wrong with the satellite. I was doing okay until I was fighting Captain Cunt. I held on to the field and shield like you wanted me to, but it was the . . . noise in my head that knocked me out, not the explosion. Were we flying?"

"Sort of," Anora said, looking around. "Something happened to Longinus, but I don't think it was designed wrong. Something happened and your shield protected us. Can you move?"

Isolde got up, clutching her hand. "Mostly. I got blown up, remember?"

"We have to go back to Arthur. See what happened to him."

Isolde put a hand on Anora's shoulder, which made Anora yelp.

"Sorry, sorry! We can't go back to Delphi, Nor."

"We—"

"Not we. You. You told me you had to get to CAMLANN."

Anora fought the tumult of emotions for a moment, then she let go to trust. "Yes." Anora searched for her case. Isolde pulled it out of the debris and handed it to her. They limped deeper into the bank. People ran everywhere and police sirens wailed. It seemed as though only the bank personnel ran around. There were more cautious and serious types picking about. Anora and Isolde got behind a counter and moved toward something that looked to be a vault.

"I swear to God if you want to me to cut you out of here, I'm just going to leave you," Isolde said, eyeing the vault.

"You're so petty sometimes," Anora said. "It's just protected and I don't want to go inside." They went into the antechamber where lockboxes were stored.

Isolde shut the door and leaned on it, cradling her hand. "I don't know if I can even keep anyone out if they come for us. Damn, I should've taken that grid trunk off the elevator."

"It's likely broken anyway," Anora said, putting the case on a table.

"How do you know that's not broken?" Isolde pointed to the case.

"Find out in a minute." Anora opened the case and saw the empty compartment that had held the machine gun. Wrong side. She flipped it over and opened it. She pulled out the glasses, glad she'd packed three pairs—one had been lost in the blast or whatever it was. The second was broken, but the third was intact.

Anora pulled out her terminal. It was cracked and the screen was inoperative.

"One, you still here?"

"This terminal is damaged and my local skills are reduced."

"That's fine, I'm going to plug you into the portable system. You should be able to commandeer its systems and run at capacity." Anora pulled out an umbilical and plugged it into the terminal. "Initialize and connect me to CAMLANN please."

"Powering up," One said. "Give me a moment for diagnostics—"

"Skip diagnostics. If it doesn't power up, it won't matter anyway."

"One moment," One said in an almost pouty voice. The system booted and conducted a visual scan to translate her into the CAMLANN environment.

Isolde held her hand. "I really don't like your friends. Mara hit on me."

"Do you mean that literally?"

"Both." Isolde wiped the blood from her nose. Her face was a grimace of pain, but then she laughed.

"What?"

"You should see your hair."

Anora touched her hair and chuckled. "I must look like a fright."

"No, it's got that dusty, blown-out look."

"How the hell do you still have a ponytail?"

"I can't see out of one eye! Fractured cheekbone, I bet!"

"My shoulder's dislocated."

"Cracked or broken rib!"

They chuckled a little more until it hurt to compare how much they were not planning on getting the holy shit beat out of them while looking for something they already had.

Anora looked at Isolde, her mood sobering. "Isolde, about Oracle. There was a message—"

Isolde shook her head. "If there was a message for me, I don't want to know. I'm serious. I've seen what knowing your future does to people. I just want to be fine with my own ignorance."

"Your father—" Anora bit her lip. It all began with Cornwall Marks.

"Even bigger reason. Thanks for telling me, but don't tell me."

Anora nodded. She'd put it all away for the day Isolde would find out.

Isolde smiled, then winced. "Got anything in that box for broken hands?"

"I don't have a first aid kit."

"Too bad you don't have a purse."

"I have some hand lotion in a pocket."

"Actually, can you give that to me? I should get my rings off before they have to cut them off my hand. Or cut off my fingers."

Anora fished around in her jacket, pulled out the lotion tube, and handed it to her. She stood up before the machine.

"Ready," One said.

"Be seeing you," Anora said to Isolde.

"I'll be here, bleeding and crying."

Anora tapped her glasses and entered CAMLANN.

CAMLANN—

"Ghost me in," Anora said.

"You're invisible for the moment," One said.

Anora opened her eyes and looked around her. She was at the entrance to CAMLANN. She saw Kai standing there before Morgan, who was making a speech. All around sat the Scientia, listening to her speech.

"Our matron has done nothing to rein in Arthur MacGabran and nothing to strengthen our ranks as the Sisterhood. She's actively blocked any attempts to give the technology over to those who would use it for the good of the Mare de Scientia."

"Dr. di Lago's technology has already been stolen from us by one sister. Did you take the prototype?" Kai asked, making a fist.

"Yes," Morgan said, and a few of the sisters gasped. Kai's face was a mask. "I've built what you would not. I have created the Chevalier Corps, whose duty will be to protect and advance the interests of the Sisterhood and not someone with a Y chromosome."

"Did you forget the prophecy?" Kai said vehemently.

"The prophecy perpetuated by our mother? No, I haven't forgotten it. In fact, I've kept the prophecy alive in my own way."

"How do you mean?"

One chimed in Anora's ear. "Oracle would like to speak with you."

"Yes, allow her—ghost mode."

Igerne appeared next to Anora. The image of her had changed from her last active impression, as if she was trying out this virtual representation of herself.

"You look different. Nice," Anora said, waving open a window to the control system.

Igerne spread her hands. "Thank you. I'm sorry to interrupt you. I have to tell you about the changes that have happened to the future. I didn't expect her to—"

"I'm guessing we hit one of those critical events where things could go one way or another," Anora said thoughtfully as she worked. "Does it change what you think of me?"

"No, and yes, Chimera."

"That's not particularly helpful."

"I would have to give you advice on the immediate—"

"How well do you know Grande Dame Li?"

"She was my predecessor. She's quite wise and forward-looking, for someone who's not prescient."

Anora was scanning through data. "Let's not confuse vision with reading tea leaves. Grande Dame Li mentioned there was an attempt on her life."

"I remember that," Igerne said, and frowned.

"Tread carefully, and strike when you must," Anora said to herself. "You can ingest this." Anora sent a stream of data over to Igerne. "Can you verify?"

Igerne blinked and nodded. "It's true."

"We have less time than we think."

"In all probability, the distribution says—"

"You and your sexy talk," Anora said, and turned back to the amphitheater.

Morgan smiled. Anora had missed a piece of the speech, but her mind was on other matters. She held a hand up, about to let Kai know about her plans, but then she saw Morgan. She frowned. *Promises were made*, she reminded herself, and then smiled.

Anora had to appear, but if she appeared as she was, it would not give her credibility. She revised her avatar to a previous version of herself, pristine in its appearance. She turned back to Igerne. "I need to do one more thing." Anora made the necessary system changes.

"Do you understand?" Anora asked.

Igerne thought for a moment and nodded as the changes took effect. "As you wish, Chimera."

"No more of that. You're a human and you know better."

Anora moved to a prominent position between Morgan and Kai, but not on the dais itself.

"Visible to all," Anora said to One.

"Anora Myrrdin," chimed CAMLANN's announcer, and Anora appeared. Morgan looked into Anora's eyes, that self-satisfied smirk still playing on the corners of her mouth.

"Sister Anora, good timing. I call for a recast. I call Kai MacGabran's matronage into doubt due to the influence of her brother over the Sisterhood."

"I second," Anora said, looking at Kai. Kai held back her shock and there was a small shudder through the Scientia. Anora wanted to motion to her that it would be all right, but she was on the public stage and anything she did would tip her hand. Kai's eyes glittered in icy anger. *Betrayal*, Anora reminded herself. *Betrayal and promises.*

"Third," said another.

"Those who wish to cast doubt, vote now," Shiori said. Many of the women cast their votes. Anora did nothing, but she didn't have to. Kai wouldn't be happy with her, but this had to be done.

"The die is cast," Shiori said. "Kai's matronage is called into question. A new vote is called for. Mother?"

Kai raised a hand. "Before you vote, I formally resign my position as matron *and* sister." If the Scientia had shuddered when Anora seconded the recast, they were positively in an uproar now. Morgan didn't move, and Anora knew she'd anticipated this maneuver.

"Truly?" Shiori asked.

"I do," Kai said.

"Again, truly?" Taylor asked.

"Again, I do," Kai said.

"You renounce your claim as matron?" Modesty asked.

"I renounce all claim to matronage. I've not served the Scientia well, and I return governance of the matronage to those who would serve the collective better than I."

Shiori nodded. "In accordance with our bylaws, the matronage reverts to our previous matron. And in accordance with tradition, your membership with the Scientia will be considered as a separate matter. Matron Li?"

Kai looked at Anora as if to say, *I hope you know what you're doing*, before vanishing from CAMLANN. Anora ground her fingernails into her fist. What was going on in the outside world?

"I'm here," the old lady said in a raspy voice. She was sitting in the forum, leaning back, but now she leaned forward on her cane. Anora was surprised at the change in her from when she'd spoken to her last. Her skin has lost its golden warmth and luster. She was gray and her eyes red. There was a tremble as she held the cane now. Her companion Min-Ji frowned next to her.

"What say you?" Shiori asked.

"The claims of Sister Morgan are no longer valid."

"What of her request for a new election?"

"As I am matron now, I deny—" Grande Dame Li said, then paused. She had a glassy-eyed stare and leaned back. Her fingers relaxed on her cane. Her companion looked to her.

"Mother?" Shiori said in alarm.

Matron Li did not speak. Her eyes closed and the cane slipped from her fingers. Min-Ji vanished from CAMLANN to attend her old friend.

After a few tense moments, the Three Sisters –Shiori, Modesty, and Taylor— conferred and assistance was dispatched to Li's physical location. They were the primary assistants of the matron and recently the guardians of the late Donna di Lago's Avallach technology.

Morgan spread her arms. "It appears that Matron Li is unable to continue her duties, which necessitates yet again a vote for matronage."

Anora stepped forward. "That won't be happening."

Morgan's smile faded. "Sister Anora, what do you mean?"

"Matronage reverts to the previous matron. Matron Li has denied your request."

"She's done no such thing."

"She would have if you hadn't murdered her."

"A baseless accusation," Morgan said without hesitation and with the appropriate level of indignation.

Anora waved a hand. "When Matron Li was in charge over the past year, her vitals were regularly recorded. This was done at the behest of the Mare de Scientia unanimously after the untimely murder of Matron Donna. Matron Li's been poisoned." Morgan looked perplexed. *Quite well played*, Anora thought. "Yes, poisoned, Sister Morgan. She recently visited your estate?"

Morgan smiled. "Yes. We had a lovely dinner. We didn't agree on most matters."

Anora cut her off and displayed vital data. "It's well-known that Matron Li takes heart medication. I know this because the vital data of our mother is still being streamed to CAMLANN, just as former matron Kai's is. Matron Li's just suffered a major heart attack. I'm afraid she won't be granting your request."

Morgan's smile slipped just a fraction. "How's this linked to me?"

"There's a small spike in her heart rate just prior to the heart attack, indicating a rush of adrenaline. It's likely a spike caused by you, Sister Morgan. Her companion will corroborate any evidence found within Matron Li's system."

"These are baseless claims and I will not stand here and be accused—"

"Just as you baselessly accused Matron Kai of helping Arthur MacGabran while you actively opposed everything he and the Scientia have been doing for over a year?"

Morgan opened her mouth and then she vanished. A third of the Scientia attendees vanished as well.

"What's the meaning of this!" one of the sisters shouted.

Min-Ji reappeared, her wizened face grave. "Matron Li is dead."

Sister Taylor, who had a finger on her ear as she received an incoming message, wore a look of surprise as she reported, "Our matron has banished those colluding in the death of Matron Li,"

"What happens when the sitting matron dies or is deposed?" Anora asked.

"The matronage reverts to the previous matron until a new

matron is elected," Min-Ji said, her voice bored at having to repeat this fact.

"My sisters, I apologize for the ruse, but I have not been as forthcoming as you wish. I have a matron here who's ready to resume the mantle of matron of the Mare de Scientia."

Shiori, Taylor, and Modesty all looked surprised at the statement. There were no living former matrons now.

"You don't mean Kai," Taylor said.

Anora smiled. "One, please bring Grand Dame Igerne into CAMLANN."

Igerne MacGabran appeared amidst gasps of surprise. The wiser women held their tongues.

Igerne bowed her head. "My sisters. I am Igerne MacGabran, lately Matron Igerne before my untimely death."

"How can you be here?" Shiori said, her voice catching in her throat.

"I am alive, in a manner of speaking. Sister Anora has restored me to a fully functioning system."

"You're not alive?"

Igerne explained what had transpired to allow her to replicate her neural pathways into a neural construct.

"I don't believe there's a precedent for a matron serving beyond death," one of the older sisters said.

"Does that mean we invalidate her matronage?" said another.

"We need to debate what we should do," replied a third sister.

"And in the meantime?" said the second.

"I believe our bylaws dictate that we be governed by our previous matron," the first sister said. "I motion we follow this once we've understood the veracity of Sister Igerne's claim."

"I second the motion," the third sister said.

"And I third the motion," said another.

"Shall we put it to a vote?" Shiori asked.

All of the women voted unanimously to continue, pending the follow-on claims.

"All in favor."

"That doesn't count the banished sisters."

"I executed the command and I take responsibility for this action," Igerne said. "Anora, determining in her judgment that I am in the line of succession, granted me powers as such. When Kai resigned, the powers reverted to Li. Li's system signaled her death and the powers ultimately reverted to me. When I saw the intent behind Matron Li's death, I acted to remove them from CAMLANN. I may have acted incorrectly, but I also did not want to give them the knowledge that you now possess."

"Knowledge?" one of the younger sisters asked.

"Igerne MacGabran was our last prescient sister, cultivated by the Scientia," Shiori stated. "That makes her the bearer of the prophecy once again."

"We haven't had such a split in centuries," Min-Ji said. "Can't say it wasn't due though." She stood up. "Is your wish to follow the prophecy to the end?"

Igerne held up a hand. "It is, if you properly reelect me as your matron. I wish to uphold our bylaws faithfully, as I have done in the past."

"We shall debate this, but you have the permission of the Sisterhood to protect and provide for the Prophet's Herald. Let us begin by verifying you are who you say you are and not a construct created for the purpose of usurping the Scientia."

Igerne inclined her head and turned to Anora to speak.

"Don't move," a voice that was not Igerne's said. Anora felt cold metal touching her temple.

38

LOCKDOWN

WASHINGTON, DC—
The pain in Percy's head was gone, but now everything hurt. It was a different degree of pain, and he wasn't sure which he preferred more—the keening pain that nearly split his skull or the full-body ache he felt after being thrown halfway down the corridor by the blast. He pushed his way through the rubble. He remembered fighting the woman in the corridor, bringing her off of Isolde, but not much after that. He heard sirens and blaring alarms. He got up and checked himself. Except for a few bruises and cuts after his KE field went down, he was all right. He touched the cut on his scalp and his swollen eye. There was nothing around him but dust. He climbed out and climbed off the rubble, grateful the passageway hadn't collapsed on him. He had to get out, had to get away. His mind was echoing from the vacancy left by the empty vacuum of the pain and loss of the field. He wanted his power back, but it was gone. He pulled off *Grall* and put the rings into his jacket pocket. He was covered in dust.

A fireman picked through to him. The man pointed to the passage and Percy followed him out.

Percy walked through the broken glass and into the icy rain. There were people all around him rushing into the building. Police and emergency responders were arriving at the moment and the street was blocked off. It wasn't just the bank that was damaged, but everything that had been behind it. Everything that was near Delphi?

"Sir, are you all right?" another fireman said.

It snapped him out of his daze. Percy nodded. "Just a bit shell-shocked."

"There's someone who'll check you out, sir."

"Thank you."

He worked his way away from the police and down the street. His clothes were battered, but in the rain and sleet, he quickly lost himself in the crowd. He thought about going back to find Anora and Isolde, but surely they'd escaped without him, right? They were farther ahead down the corridor. He needed to get a good look—

He saw that the storage facility had nearly been obliterated by the blast. His head was clear of pain, but he no longer felt the field. Whatever it was, was gone. At least temporarily.

"Janus?" he asked.

"Online," Janus reported.

"What happened?"

"Insufficient information."

"Big help. Is Arthur alive? Ed? Isolde? Anora?"

"Arthur, Ed, and Isolde are alive. I'm unable to contact Anora, but One has acknowledged that she and Isolde are injured, but not fatally. Anora's local device has locked down. I'm unable to communicate with her. Incoming message from Arthur."

"Accept."

"Hey, Percy. Are you all right?" Arthur sounded faraway and tinny. His device may have been severely damaged. Percy could also hear the defeat in his voice.

"I've made it out. Anora and Isolde are all right as best I can determine. I need to circle back and find them."

"Get away if you can. That's an order."

"Sorry, I don't work for you anymore," Percy said. "I need to stay with Anora. That's the best course of action, as you've said before. I'm taking that advice."

"I advise you—"

"Disconnected at the source. Arthur's device has been locked down," Janus reported.

"He's been captured or arrested."

Percy circled around the block and worked his way away from the destruction. He didn't want to get away, but if he didn't there'd be no chance to get back to Anora. "Shit." He'd lost them both. Arthur was gone and so was Anora. What was he to do now? *Anora.*

He pulled out the terminal that Anora had given him. It was cracked.

"One, what's the status of Anora and Isolde?"

"Last reported activity was that Anora was alive and well approximately ten minutes ago. I've recently disconnected and locked down her terminal as she was apprehended by local agents. Janus reports that Isolde has suffered numerous injuries and her Janus device is damaged beyond repair and locked down for security reasons. In such an event, Anora's left instructions for you to contact Ellen. Would you like me to connect you?"

"Please." Percy continued away from the scene. The weather was really playing hell with first responders. He hunched into his beaten jacket for warmth. He felt cold and naked without the manifest.

"Ellen here."

"Hey, I need extraction."

"I'm a couple hours out."

"It's time for you to spin up the team. Anora and Isolde have just been captured. Arthur and Ed, too."

"I'm not moving without the go-ahead."

"Fine, but come get me." Percy pulled up his collar as it grew late in the day and the temperature dropped, turning the icy sleet to snow.

"I'll send someone by to pick you up discreetly."

"Thanks," Percy said.
"It's the least I can do."
"Another favor?"
"Yeah?"
"Make sure Lamar and Lilly are safe."
"That I promise to do now."

39

CASCADE EFFECT

Owen's mind felt heavy and fuzzy, like it was trying to resolve itself from a wave into a particle. The observation snapped everything into place. He opened his eyes and saw Mara Holt. She sat on a chair and they were in one of the recovery rooms of Brightwork. He'd managed to make it back, though he had no memory of it. She wore a bandage on her bare thigh.

"What happened to you?" he asked when he found his voice. He remembered something. The white light. He was floating, full of power. He was about to strike Arthur down. Or was he? He couldn't remember.

"Got stabbed. Building blew up. How about you?"

"I don't know, really," Owen said. He sat up, but his head swam. He lay back. "God, my head."

"Splitting headache, right? It'll wear off. You were at the epicenter."

"Epicenter of what?"

"From what Dr. MacRossa can determine, our misaligned rings caused a cascading feedback loop."

"I thought we overloaded the grid."

"That was not a standard grid system. It was a massive grid projection, probably in orbit."

"Jesus Christ. A satellite?" Owen asked. He remembered the small report on Indiana and the loss of a prototype shuttle. The power of the system was hard to wrap his head around. "You said something about a loop?"

"The cascading loop was powerful enough to blow up Delphi and everything inside of a city block."

Owen ran a hand over his face. "And why are we still alive?"

Mara folded her arms. "I could guess, and it would sound really good."

"Let's try that."

"What causes the feedback loop also protects us from its effects, perhaps reinforcing our KE fields."

"I'll accept that."

Mara's phone chirped. She glanced down at it. "Time to suit up. Do you mind?"

Owen shook his head. "Nothing I haven't seen before. Kara would be jealous if she hadn't been so pissed at me since New York."

"I wouldn't worry about Kara. She gets over things pretty quickly. She's with Morgan now, but I'll have her stop by to see you when they return." Mara smiled, pulling off her gown. She was battered and bruised, but she had a fine body. She pulled on the new gray Chevalier uniform. It took some time to put on, but she looked more impressive in doing so. She had a badge on her breast now and the logo of the Chevaliers on the shoulder—a dragon on a shield.

"It's official now?"

"Yes. I'll show you all the news if you'd like. You've been out for the better part of a day. It was good you were still on the upper levels of Delphi. Everything below was pretty much obliterated."

"Oracle?"

"Nothing there. Anora Myrrdin got away with it. Or she thought she did until our friends got ahold of her at Focus."

"So you got it?"

Mara shook her head. "Her device is locked down tight and she's not talking."

Owen shook his head. "It wouldn't be there. Did you go to her office?"

"What office?"

"You've been there."

"That's what I'm telling you. Binary AI's DC lab is completely cleared out."

"This isn't making any sense. Did we get Oracle or not? What about Binary AI?"

"Binary AI has no knowledge of the work she'd been doing in DC. They admit she often operates small skunkworks projects to develop experimental concepts. Warrants got issued and Binary complied, but they have nothing and there's legal documentation that segregates her work from her main company. We won't be able to shut them down without a long, protracted legal fight. And if we try to link them to the Delphi attack, it's probably not going to stick and it won't break them. So in the end, we didn't get anything but Arthur himself." Mara smiled at that last.

Owen raised an eyebrow. "You got him? The FBI captured him?"

"They didn't have to try. He saw the destruction and gave up."

"Gave up?"

"He surrendered when the authorities found him. He was digging civilians out of the rubble and looking for bodies."

"Avallach?"

Mara shook her head. "All got away, except Isolde and Anora."

"But you got him," Owen repeated. "Arthur." He frowned at that, because maybe it was the splitting in his mind, but he was relieved. He'd fought him. Indiana had taught him well. It was by sheer luck that the cascade hit when it did. Owen flexed his hand, feeling the lack of strength. Was it luck, providence, or ego? He noticed *Nornian* was gone. "My rings?"

Mara raised a bare hand. "Retired along with *Splinter*. Based on your testing and trials, MacRossa's preliminary data suggest they may have caused the cascade." She raised her arm, showing the shining gauntlet, polished as silver as her badge. The metal clicked as she flexed it. "This is as near a final design as we have. They'll be in full production soon. Shield greaves will be coming soon, though that tech needs a lot of work. I have to send Chevs into the field without them for now. I don't think that will be a problem against Avallach."

Owen thought about the gauntlets. "Shouldn't you be leading the effort?"

"I already have Hong and a team working with law enforcement to secure the area and run down leads. They've been augmented by the new teams. You, John, and Safir are on the injured list." She placed her hands behind her back. "Really, I'm here to bring you news. I've asked Morgan to place you on the operational roster and she wants to talk to you."

"She's here at Brightwork?"

Mara shook her head. "She'll be here soon, once she's wrapped up the provisional paperwork. I also have one of your suits for you when you're ready."

"I want to see her," Owen said of Indiana.

Mara nodded and understood his meaning. "She's ready when you have time." Mara went to the door. "You performed well at Delphi. I'll be happy to have you back. I fucking owe you for lancing me, but I'll take the work you've done at Delphi as recompense. I just won't forget."

"Thank you, Commander Holt. It's a shame most of Avallach got away scot-free."

"Tiwaz didn't make it out unscathed. I cut his hand off with *Splinter*. He's ringless, at least for now, and vulnerable. Sent a triad to retrieve Lamar Jones as well, but he's nowhere to be found. I'm not sure how a man with a broken back can disappear, but Avallach's like cockroaches. Shine a light on them and they scatter to the shadows." Mara shook her head. "I'm off to see what can be done about our renegade Myrrdin and her skinny bodyguard." Mara left.

Owen had been told a bit of Morgan's plan before she stopped sharing things with him. She'd planned to wrest control of the Scientia. If that went well, then all of Avallach's tech would be their tech. The Chevalier Corps would be complete.

He got out of bed. His legs shook for a moment until he got under control again. He stood up and pulled the monitoring wires off his body. He went to the bathroom and looked at himself in the mirror. He looked like hell, though he didn't feel it. *Monster.* His left hand shook badly. He was glad the rings were gone. Now that they were ready for him to join operations, he wasn't able to continue. He cursed himself, gazed at the face in the mirror. *Monster.* He shaved the beard off and confronted who he really was. Ice-blue eyes stared back at him.

∼

OWEN WATCHED her for a long time, trying to figure out why he was there. Why he needed to see her.

Owen felt his ebbing strength and flexed his fingers out of habit. She slept on her side. Her hair had been tended to, so now it was supple, silky, yet short. She snored softly. She was intensely beautiful and he had her now. He had everyone he wanted now. She was his if he wanted her.

He'd read the report on her, adding to the small amount he'd known since he fought her in Geneva. Her memories were fragmentary before almost a year ago. She'd woken up in a Nganasan village on the Taymyr Peninsula in Siberia. She'd been found in a deep snowdrift and nursed back to health. All she had on her was a damaged space suit and her rings. The report also noted that the night she was found there was an arc of light in the sky that led the villagers to her body. One old woman swore she still glowed when they brought her to the village, but whether that was the heat of reentry or her halo, Owen wasn't sure.

After nearly two months in the village, with no memories and the small goodwill of the villagers, Indiana trekked south and westward. She worked odd jobs along the way, and this was where things became muddy. It was difficult to corroborate such information, but

Indiana herself was clear on her life after her landing. She learned some Russian during her stay and found out that she was pregnant. The interviewers estimated she was about five months pregnant at the beginning of her journey. As a lone woman, progress would've been difficult, but her obvious pregnancy had been a boon. There were a few troublesome people, but there were more than enough kind hearts who clothed, fed, and helped Indiana on her way.

From her own account, she'd always known that she had to get to Geneva. She had thought it was the memories in her head, but when she'd come nearly to full term, she knew it was the baby, Gal. It was inexplicable. To everyone but Owen, her journey was as incredulous as what had driven her. Indiana was an anomaly. Ogier and Richard wanted to study her, but Morgan had other plans. She wanted to use her, just as she used Owen. Owen resented the thought. He was his own person. Didn't he help create the Chevaliers? Wasn't it his blood that Richard used to create the nanovirus?

It was punishment, pure and simple. Would Indiana be used the same way? The rest of the report listed the baby as stillborn. At least that much Owen had gotten right. There would be no way for Morgan to find out the truth if he had anything to say about it. She'd suspect, but facts were facts; she had Indiana but not the baby. Or rather, there was no baby.

Owen had little control over his life at this point, but he'd known one thing: he'd not let his family dominate another child. It was probably too late for young Leto, but he could save Gal. He closed his eyes and imagined the little girl safe in his sister's arms.

He was tired now and full of old anger, the anger of his life. His leg went numb, so he lay on the bed next to her, moving to spoon with her. She shifted a bit, pressing against him in her sleep. She wore only a T-shirt, and yet she was still beautiful—still the model who had graced magazine covers. He slid an arm around her and kissed her neck. She countered with the hint of a smile. His hand moved up and down her body, and she responded. She leaned back into his kiss and opened her eyes. She had a dreamy, pleasant look on her face for a moment.

Then her eyes focused and the moment was gone. "You're not him," she whispered.

He shook his head and moved away from her. "No."

"Where's Gal?" she asked. She always asked this and the doctors thought this part of her postpartum emotional state.

Owen knew better. "She's safe. No one here can get to her."

"I want see her. Can I see Gal?"

Owen shook his head and got up.

Indiana sat up and drew her knees to her chest. She looked younger than she was and her body showed few signs of childbearing days after giving birth. Part of that was likely her journey, and the rest was youth and good care here in Brightwork's recovery clinic.

"It wouldn't be a good idea to mention her here. It would be better if you thought her dead."

"But she's not dead."

Owen nodded. His hand trembled slightly and he put it behind his back. "You should put her behind you. She's safe and she'll get the care she needs."

"But I'm her mom," Indiana said. There was hesitation in her voice. "I dream about her still. She talks to me and tells me things. Do you dream about her?"

Owen shook his head. He was glad he didn't dream of the girl who could erase minds. He tried not to think about the power he'd handed to Jeri and remembered she was just a little baby. He wondered if that was what Arthur's mother had thought of him when he was born under Project Spartan. Owen himself had gotten the clinical treatment after his birth. His anger simmered beneath the surface. He was angry at everyone, including himself. "I don't dream of her. If you know what's best for you, you'll put Gal behind you. Focus on your training."

"My training . . . ," Indiana said, rubbing her fingers. "I was training, right? Before I got hurt. I was the best."

Owen chuckled and took her hand in his trembling one. "No, you are the best. You're still the best warrior I've ever seen."

Indiana smiled. "I know my mind isn't right, but I want my ring swords back. I want to train and get back to work."

"We can do that. In a couple of days, they'll release you and I'll make sure that Morgan puts you back on the operational roster."

"That'd be great. Why don't I remember this place?"

"It's new. You've been gone for a while, but the old place was not large enough for the new team." Owen was already tired of the slow building of the house of cards. Why was he here? To see her? He knew Arthur had been looking for her. Owen had counted on that fact, but seeing her here now, he saw that she was just an empty vessel.

Morgan could pretty much do with her what she wanted. *Why not?* he asked himself again.

Owen shook his head. He was getting confused. He focused on his anger. Arthur was the one who'd put him here. He could've been the one with everything. What would Morgan do with him now? He squeezed Indiana's hand. She was beautiful and he understood the attraction. He was attracted to her as well. Her hazel eyes regarded him, then his hand.

"You don't have your rings, either."

"I have to get a new set. It might not be rings anymore. They have something new. Powerful. Better."

"I just want my rings. I want . . . *Secace* and *Arondight*." Odd that she couldn't remember much of her life before the fall, but she remembered the names of her focal rings. How did she survive reentry into Earth's atmosphere? None of the scientists had an answer, but Owen guessed it had something to do with the satellite. If she'd been able to manifest on the way down . . .

Kara opened the door. She frowned at them and Owen released Indiana's hand. Indiana lost interest in him. He had no rings, after all.

He went to her, glad his symptoms had subsided for now. Indiana was imprinted in his mind.

"Morgan's here. Aren't you happy to see me?" Kara smiled with a sweep of blond hair.

"I'm not sure you're happy to see me," Owen replied. He hadn't seen her since New York and she'd been promoted to leading the team he'd left.

"I know you kicked ass at Delphi." Kara beamed.

"I better get cleaned up."

"Want to take a shower first? For old times' sake," Kara said with a smirk, eyeing Indiana.

"That'll be fine," Owen said, walking past her. "Great, actually." He slipped an arm around her waist and she responded. Kara touched him suggestively and found him still wanting her. He kissed her and smelled her perfume. It was Morgan's perfume, exotic and heady.

He should be like Indiana. Forget the past and future. Focus on the now.

"Feeling better?"

"No worse for wear," Owen said. He'd showered with Kara, and it felt good to be rough with her, to dominate her. He was dressed in his suit and tie once again. He'd felt more like himself and gone to see Morgan straightaway. Mara Holt was there as well, looking official in her gleaming gray and silver. The scratches and cuts on her face were barely visible, covered with makeup. Her hair was back in its tight braid, like a crimson whip.

"Good, I have a new job for you," Morgan said, sitting down with her drink and crossing her legs. It had been a while since he'd spoken with her in person. When was the last time he'd spoken to her? Except in his dreams, it had been months. She was powerful and commanding, as always.

Owen leaned on the doorjamb, mostly to keep himself from making an awkward scene. He wanted *Nornian* or a damn gauntlet to stave off the deterioration for as long as possible.

Morgan rubbed her forehead and looked at her watch. "It's been eight hours of some intense work, but you've executed things out in my favor. Provisionally, we're under the purview of Homeland Security now. With Mara's connections and assistance, I've convinced the powers that be that Arthur and his band of brigands are in fact a rogue group of Chevalier test candidates."

Owen looked at the silent news feeds on the large screens opposite Morgan's desk. Words scrolled across the screens. *126 missing and 15 presumed dead . . . weather making rescue efforts difficult . . . Apollo has a name and he's a terrorist . . .*

"That's a hard lie to swallow," Owen put forth.

"Which is why you're going to be the liaison with DHS."

"That's not going to be any better."

"Are you trying to be difficult?" Morgan sipped her drink and leaned back. "You've changed. What happened to you?"

"I look exactly like him. It's going to be hard for them to believe that I'm working on the right side." There was anger around her words. She did not like Indiana. *His woman.* Those words put Morgan in a new light. This was more than business to her.

Morgan waved it away. "It won't matter after you're brought to trial."

"I've proven myself in fieldwork. My trial?" Owen's awareness snapped back from its drift.

"You've certainly proved one thing." Morgan stood up. She moved closer to him and whispered in his ear. "You can be him now. You can be him and all the lies we're weaving will be true, like a net casting for fish. At least in a court of law."

Owen nodded in understanding. Everything sticks if he's Arthur. There were problems, of course. Morgan may have some disdain for him, but she wouldn't let Owen rot in prison. "I'd get his conviction and his sentence if it holds."

"It'll be everything he deserves. He's killed people."

"Not that many," Mara pointed out. "You think the numbers and talking heads have turned against him, but this will be politics against Robin Hood if we're not careful."

"Too bad he only blew up the bank instead of stealing from it," Morgan replied. Morgan turned back to Owen. "Don't you want to be him?"

"I'm better than him." Owen tried to believe that, but with his condition, he was no longer sure. Not since Indiana. And not since the cascade.

"Wouldn't you like to tear down everything you think he stands for from the inside? What a fitting way to end his little house of cards. Seems quite appropriate to me."

"This all sounds villainous to me." Owen moved away from her. She poured on the charm. Her perfume was intoxicating. He went to the bar and poured himself a drink, thankful he made it without stumbling. What had attracted him before now made him uneasy. He loved Morgan, but she was infatuated with Arthur, not Owen. Somewhere in the back of his mind he'd always known it. It turned his stomach to face the truth now.

"I built the Chevaliers and I'm not going to let his mistakes and yours ruin what we've built. Who else has a nearly identical clone of the most famous man in the United States right now? This isn't villainy, it's irony and opportunity. It's a means to an end." Owen saw an ever-so-slight loss of her composure. Whether it was the negotiations or the infatuation, he wasn't sure. She took a breath. "I had a better idea in mind, but Anora got in the way."

Owen downed a finger of scotch and poured himself another. It settled his mind as he got used to being just another instrument. "Did something go wrong with the Sisterhood?"

Morgan again waved it away.

Owen was concerned and looked into her eyes. She was livid. She loved this challenge and she would use him to get to what she wanted. It made Owen think about General Marks for a split second. Was she going to be blindsided, just like he was? She was careful and clever. He thought it unlikely, but Arthur seemed to make the best and worst mistakes.

She came to him and gave him a kiss. It was passionate and he responded to her kiss—returned it with fervor. He smelled her scent mixed with her perfume, but a small part of him resisted. Their lips parted. She wiped the lipstick from his mouth. He grabbed her arms and she anticipated that he wanted more. She smiled, but he pushed her away.

"No thank you."

She slapped him hard. "Don't be weak!" She slapped him again on the other cheek. "Don't be useless!"

He grabbed her hand and twisted it. A small burst of pain sparked in her eyes, and Owen realized that was where he'd learned to enjoy pain and pleasure. It was from her. Had she always been like that? It made the truth easier to bear. "Don't touch me again," he said. "I'll do what you want, but not for you. Never for you." He let go of her hand. "You think I'm just a pawn in your little game, but I'm the bishop. I'm valuable and I'm dangerous, so don't sacrifice me unnecessarily. This game isn't over."

"That's settled," Morgan said, taking out a handkerchief and wiping her smeared lipstick.

Mara was bemused.

"Commander Holt, escort Owen to the precinct where Arthur's being kept. They're likely to move him to a high-security facility, so we'll need to make the change as soon as we can."

"What are you going to do with him?" Owen asked.

"Dispose of him, of course. Why do I need him when I have you?"

How do you get rid of the ones you love? he wondered.

40

AWAKEN, CHIMERA

"I figured it out," Anora said. She stared at the ceiling, where Maven's psychogenetics theorem sat, spread out before her.

Maven gazed up at the theorem. He pointed to it with his silver-tipped cane. "You're not talking about this?"

Reince stood at the bars, looking down the hallway. "She's talking about Arthur," he snarled like a beaten dog.

"In a way, this does deal with Arthur," Maven huffed.

"It all does," Anora said. "You engineered him. Igerne with her old noble blood and high-society connections. Aidan with his old ties to American aristocracy and military work ethic. They were the right matches to the theorem." Anora wiggled her fingers. "But there are some problems with your work, big brother."

"There's no such thing."

"There is and you know it because you're a manifestation of my own mind."

Maven rapped his cane on the concrete floor and glowered.

Reince gripped the bars. Anora's emotional ties to him had fallen away.

"It's not a machine problem. All this time I was thinking he was the result of the theorem. He's not," Anora said.

Maven nodded.

Anora waved her hand; the theorem changed. "So, I put him in the middle of the theorem and me as the other component."

Maven studied the results. "Finally." He pointed to the minima and maxima. "That's a respectable result."

"You'd think so, right? It's a strong locus, but . . ." Anora stared at the numbers.

"There's someone better," Reince sneered.

"Not for me," Anora said with a sigh. The theorem changed, but this time Anora dropped the habit she'd learned playing with her AR system. The numbers jumped significantly.

Reince stared at the numbers. "That's statistically higher than expected." Reince looked to Maven. "Was that your intent?"

"I'm not certain it was my intent. I'd always thought my sister made a sufficient experiment for me. This is quite interesting, though."

"That's what you were after. The Prophet. This formula supposes that if Indiana and Arthur have a child, they could bring about the Prophet. That's why Igerne mentioned Arthur as the Herald, not the Prophet himself."

"That puts a bit of a wrench in the works for you, doesn't it?" Maven said.

"Too bad the bitch's shown her true feelings for him," Reince said, hoping to get in a dig at Anora.

"Why did Igerne let Indiana die?" Maven asked.

Knowing her feelings for Arthur did upset her, but Indiana was dead. That possibility had died out. The thought of her children being shapers of humanity had a certain appeal, she admitted. "I guess Igerne realized that her worth dead was greater than it was alive. The Scientia's prophecy was dire, so perhaps she was hoping to avoid the prophecy and bring about a milder, better change. I'd have to ask her about that. It doesn't make sense to me."

"It's snowing outside," Maven said.

Anora looked up at the small square of a window in the cell. It was small and cramped, but compared to the Oracle chamber, this was roomy.

"You've overcome your trauma," Reince pointed out. He sounded upset.

"I've made a few decisions," Anora said. "It's unusually calming. Don't get me wrong; I'm not cured." It was true. The press of fear was still around her. She hated small spaces. But her mind worked feverishly over the changes to her plans. Plans she'd worked on since the day she learned her brother was dead.

"Then you won't need us anymore," Maven said, sitting down on the cot next to her. He rubbed the acorn tip of his cane. Anora put a hand on his shoulder.

"No, I won't. Does he need me?" Anora asked of Arthur.

"He does. You're the Chimera. The Lover, the Fighter, the Betrayer, just as Igerne says."

"I rather like that. It's nice to be needed and not taken for granted." She looked to Reince, who looked gray and sickly. She'd finally let go of him.

"So you'll fight for him?"

"I'll kill him. Just like she said." Anora nodded.

"Mystery solved for me." Maven stood up. "We got to spend a little time together, even if on the streams of your memory. You have a particularly wonderful mind."

"You've only ever said that once in my life, Maven." Anora bowed her head and remembered the only compliment Maven had ever given her.

"The memory bears repeating. Good-bye, Dr. Myrrdin."

"Good-bye, Dr. Myrrdin," Anora replied.

He inclined his head to his half sister.

Anora had a thought. "Why didn't you copy your mind, like Igerne? I mean, why didn't Nimue copy your mind?"

"I did. A bit unconventionally." Maven winked at Anora. She got the hint—she was his heir.

Reince frowned. "I don't want to go."

"You've already been gone," Anora replied.

"Come along," Maven said to Reince. "You've only needed her. She just sometimes needs you to remind her of that."

Reince twisted at the bars and then dropped his arms to his sides. "I'll be back."

"I hope not," Anora replied.

Maven turned one last time. "Do what you should, but also what you must."

"I will," Anora vowed.

"Come along, Reince. Let's talk about where you might be in this great big wide world."

"Above- or belowground?" Reince asked.

"There are finite possibilities."

Anora closed her eyes, listening to their voices retreat. She smiled to herself. She liked the idea of powerful children, but she hoped they wouldn't be as naïve as their father.

"That's an unusual look to have when you're in a jail cell," someone said.

Anora opened her eyes and saw Arthur. *Destroyer.*

THE GUARD OPENED the door and Arthur entered.

"How are you today, doctor?"

Anora held up a hand. "You're not Arthur."

The man stopped short. He spread his hands. "Oh? How do you know?"

"Would you like me to list the first ten ways?"

"Amuse me," he said.

Anora gripped the edge of the cot and gave him a bored expression. "One, Arthur has a half moon missing from his left earlobe, likely from a fighting accident with his waveblade. Two, you have a slightly higher timbre to your voice, and as Americanized as you are, I can still detect a slight English and French tone. Three, Arthur never takes off *Caliburn* and he has a light tan line on his right hand because of it. You're not wearing *Caliburn* and you have no tan. Four,

Arthur doesn't use the same soap that you use. You use a scentless soap, but as we've been in jail for less than half a day, it's unlikely Arthur's had a shower, and if he had, he'd be using disinfectant soap provided by the facility. Five, your hair is a half inch too short on the top and a quarter inch too long on the sides. Six, Arthur doesn't have his nails manicured. You have calluses, but your hands are immaculate, the sign of someone who works out but doesn't do daily work. Seven, Arthur carries his phone in his left front pocket, not in his jacket. There's no phone in your front pocket, so I assume it's in your jacket. Eight, Arthur has about eight pounds on you. Nine, the lines around his eyes are a little deeper, which suggests he's been in harsher climates than you or you're a bit younger. Maybe five years, judging by the color of your cheeks. You're old enough to finish college, so I'd guess that much. Maybe six."

"And ten?" Owen asked.

"Arthur doesn't have a tremor in his left hand."

Owen clenched his left hand in a fist, but Anora didn't flinch. She went through the katas in her mind.

"Morgan underestimated you."

"So what are you? A clone?"

Owen stared her down.

For all of his minor flaws, he really did look like Arthur. It was uncanny.

"Your genetic code is the blueprint for the Chevaliers. No need to acquire Arthur. You already have it."

"I'm not here to talk about me."

"What are you here to talk about?"

"Oracle."

"There's nothing to talk about."

"You have Oracle. I want it. I want to talk to her."

"That's interesting. Does your cousin know what Oracle is? Do you?"

"She only knows that Marks had been using it against Arthur. Morgan isn't happy. You broke your promise."

"What promise?" Anora said. She wasn't surprised that Morgan had shared Scientia information outside of the Sisterhood, but this seemed a bit of a reach. She decided he only knew a tiny fraction of the truth and the rest was a bluff. "I'll settle up with Morgan later."

Owen walked around the cell. "Can you give me access to Oracle? I can go about it the hard way. I can take apart your company."

Anora ignored the empty threat. Morgan and Anora were occasionally in the same circles. They were both nearly the same age and ran their own companies with some measure of success. "Oracle's not a piece of luggage or a diamond. And she's not mine to give."

"You built her."

Anora held up a finger. "I restored her."

"Can you give her to me?"

Anora studied Owen. This man was full of anger. She'd seen that look before, in Reince. He was a man who did not like losing control. "Why do you want her? It's not because of what she can do, is it?" Things locked into place for her. *Betray him*, Igerne said. *Kill him.* She pressed him to see how lost he was. She wasn't afraid of him—he hadn't twisted her emotions like Reince did, after all. "Do you want the love of a mother?"

Owen swung his fist. Anora grabbed his wrist and leaned back, throwing him off balance. He twisted and she pushed him away.

"Eleven. You don't have his temperament."

Owen straightened his jacket. He stood there for a long moment, then shook his head. "Well played." He went to the door and motioned for the guard. "Before you get too smug, I got my answer. No one has such a perfect memory of someone, even you. I know how you feel for Arthur. I've some sad news for you. Indiana's still alive. Do you think he's going to want you once he knows?"

A shiver went down Anora's spine. Theorem spirals flashed in her mind. The door opened and he stepped out.

"You're lying," she said, breaking out in a cold sweat.

"Am I?" Owen said. "People can come back from the dead. It's rare, but it happens."

"You've no proof."

"He'll only ever be hers." The guard shut the jail cell door. Owen looked at her from the other side again. "Your sardonic exterior is all gone. Don't you have anything to say?"

Anora clenched her jaw, but he walked away before the shock wore off. She ran to the jail cell door. "Tell Morgan I'm still honoring our agreement!"

Owen waved a hand. "Tell her yourself."

"I'll honor it if you never tell him."

"No promises until you make good on yours. Good-bye, doctor."

Anora wondered if it was too late to recall her mind puppets. *Lover.*

"Dr. Anora Myrrdin?" the agent called as the door opened.

Anora was lost in thought and turned to see a dark-haired, average-looking man in a suit waiting for her. He had an expression that said, "Sorry to bother you."

"Yes?"

"I'm Special Agent John Atherton. I'd like to ask you a few questions if you don't mind."

"I don't have anything to say," Anora replied.

"You look like you could use a hot cup of tea," John replied with an amiable smile.

Anora unfolded herself from the bunk and stood up. "Does it come with my phone?"

"No, but you can make a phone call if you like."

"It'll have to do," Anora said, picking up her jacket and pulling it on. They'd taken her case and terminal, but she really didn't have much else on her person. "What about my bodyguard?"

"Miss Marks is being treated by a doctor right now. Some of the bones in her right hand are broken, so they are setting them now. Don't think she's going to need surgery, but at least we are doing her the courtesy of putting her hand in a cast so it can heal."

"I have doctors—experts who can assist. I'd like her to get the best care, if possible. I'll give you the numbers. No cost. I'll fly them in."

"I'll get the numbers from you after we're done. Sound good?"

Atherton motioned for her to precede him down the hall. She followed the guard through the heavy door and down another hallway into a small room with two desks. A female officer was waiting when she entered.

"Sara, can you get me two cups of hot green tea, please?" John asked.

"Certainly," the officer said, and left the room. Anora sat down in the vinyl padded chair opposite the agent. He took out a notebook. Anora folded her hands on the table.

"You were at the H Street location? At the bank?"

Anora stared at him, letting him know that it was a stupid question to start with.

"Do you know Arthur MacGabran? The so-called Apollo?"

Anora shook his head. "No one calls him that."

"That's what the media calls him."

Anora spread her hands again as if to say, "That's obvious."

"We have you connected with Mr. MacGabran."

"We've gone over this before without probable cause. Is there something I can help you with?"

John closed his notebook and leaned back, placing his hands on his lap. The female officer returned with two hot cups of tea. Anora smiled at the officer and sipped. It was scalding, just the way she liked it. John rolled his coffee cup between his hands. "Do you think MacGabran had anything to do with your brother's death?"

"I certainly thought about it at one time."

"But not now."

"No."

"Did something change your mind?"

"Some facts came to light in my research."

"Facts?"

"When testing a hypothesis and you receive contrary results—"

"I was asking what the facts were, Ms. Myrrdin."

"I'm not under oath, nor at liberty or under obligation to volunteer that information."

"A lot of residents around Northeast DC said their phones, televisions, and radios were all going off, warning residents to evacuate the area five minutes before the explosion. Do you know anything about that?" Anora noticed he was careful not to mention the number of people who ignored those warnings or were injured or harmed in the destruction.

"I'm not in the telecommunications industry."

"But you know computers."

"You say that like I'm a repairman. No, I don't know computers. I am an AI scientist."

"Fair enough. But it would take quite a sophisticated system to seize command of various controlled systems like radio towers, cell phone towers, cable stations."

"The Emergency Alert System comes to mind."

John smiled. "This isn't the first occurrence. It's happened once before in the US and there have been incidents in other countries. It happened in Istanbul, where MacGabran's men were sighted."

"You're onto something, then. Was I in Istanbul?"

"Now who's insulting whom? Computer systems don't need to be local to access these systems."

Anora smiled. Despite herself, she liked John. He was an amiable person and reminded her a lot of the folks she'd worked with in the National Security Agency. "You got me there, Agent Atherton. I didn't program that system if that's what you're asking."

"But you know how."

"I've not found a need for it."

John pulled her terminal from a pocket. It was carefully bagged and tagged as evidence.

"Is this one of your systems?"

"That's a phone."

"It's not like any phone I've ever seen."

Anora smiled and nodded. "You sound like a commercial. Yes, that's one of my systems. You have another one of them on hand."

"This is the only one I know of."

Anora was amused at how compartmentalized the agencies were.

Atherton continued. "This was retrieved along with the case. It was connected to a sophisticated rig. What was it?"

Anora sipped her tea. "Agent Atherton. Your analysts cannot be this dense. They know what it is, and I'm not venturing forth with any information in that regard. That's *my* phone that was in *my* case, both of which you took from me, along with my glasses."

John drank his tea and grimaced slightly. He wasn't used to drinking tea, but Anora gave him credit for trying in an effort to appear comforting to his charge.

"At least I know it's sort of a phone," John said, putting it back into his jacket. "Can we talk about something else a little more interesting?"

"Do I get to pick the topic, or do you get to lead me down the path you want me to follow?"

"The latter, obviously."

"That's not as interesting as you think."

"Can you tell me about Reince Walsh?"

For the second time inside of an hour, Anora felt ice run down her back. She'd been bracing herself against it. After all, it was a matter of public record. "He was an abusive boyfriend. We were engaged."

"And then he disappeared."

Anora went on the attack. "It's all on file as part of my NSA background investigation. You don't think they'd overlook something to allow me to build classified research systems, would they?"

"I just find it curious is all. Certainly, the abusive relationship had to affect you in some way. Your brother was instrumental in helping you recover."

"You're looking for a connection? Or grasping at straws?"

John frowned. "I'm just trying to figure out why you were at that bank."

"First you should acknowledge you're using the wrong terminology. You know it wasn't a bank," Anora said. "It was a research facility. Terrorist data collection."

"That . . . facility has a corridor that connects to an old research arm, or at least did. What did you find there?"

"I appreciate the discussion, and we agree that corroborating on what I found with what you found doesn't match—"

"And we can agree that putting you away for a very long time isn't in your best interest."

"You don't have the authority—"

"I can use whatever authority I have." John rolled the cup in his hands again, frowning. "I'm not making promises or threats, but if you're somehow linked to a terrorist who destroyed an entire city block, you're not going to so much as touch a keyboard for decades. To do that, I only need to prove that you've been less than forthcoming, Ms. Myrrdin."

"Now we're getting somewhere," Anora said. "When did this MacGabran guy get classified a terrorist? How many people did he kill?"

John's frown deepened. "One hundred so far. They're still searching for the bodies. Millions of dollars' worth of damage, and in the middle of the capital. Whether you or anyone wants to see it that way, that is a fact. He's killed people and MacGabran is a huge threat. The man can stop bullets, right? No door or wall can stop him and now he can destroy an entire city block and walk out unscathed? That's power, and that power is dangerous. He's a rogue."

"Where are you getting this information? Rogue? From where?"

"From the military. He's also left a top secret DARPA project—"

"What project?"

"—where he killed people to get away and took the technology with him. Now that the technology is out in the wild, we've partnered with the creators, who want to bring him and his lackeys back into the fold. We have the Chevalier Corps now."

Anora closed her eyes for a moment, thinking of the pieces moving. She would need to act soon. "Do you stand in front of the mirror when you practice these speeches? You sound ridiculous, Agent Atherton. This Chevalier Corps? Sounds made-up. Where's my phone call?"

Agent Atherton pulled a phone from his pocket and slid it across to her.

Anora eyed it. "I guess we got away from the pay phone thing decades ago."

"Decades," John replied.

She dialed the memorized number. It rang and then clicked over as it went to the encrypted line.

"I'm here," One said.

"It's me."

"Who else would it be?"

Anora smiled at the sarcasm. "I need you to contact my lawyer and send him this message: 'How many lambs might the stern wolf betray, / If like a lamb she could her looks translate! / How many gazers mightst thou lead away, / if thou wouldst use the strength of all thy state!'"

"Understood. Is that all?"

"That's all."

One hung up. She handed the phone back to John. He was puzzled. "I don't think that was poetry you were reciting. A code."

Anora shrugged her good shoulder, sipped her tea, and waited. Minotaur would go to work now on her plan. She had more ominous things to worry about, but she did fear for Arthur. This was bad. There was nothing else for her to do now. *Betrayer.*

41

SHIFTING SNOWS

"A lot of things make an interesting sort of sense," Arthur said when Owen entered the room.

Owen sat down and stared at Arthur for a long time. The anger boiled inside him. Arthur stared back, then looked bored. Owen realized it was their third meeting and the first one where they weren't combating one another. Could he intimidate this guy? Owen slammed his fist on the table. "You're a real problem, Arthur."

Arthur didn't flinch. "Is it a problem that can be solved by your...?"

"Chevaliers."

"I'd have gone with Paladins, myself," Arthur replied.

"You're unmanageable."

Arthur studied him, then looked around the room. He seemed to gauge the situation. This was not a formal interview or interrogation. "You sound like Marks, so that's either a lie or someone else told that to you."

"People sacrifice themselves for your little cause." *And people follow you for no apparent reason*, Owen added. He thought about Morgan and her hate-love.

"I'm not clear on what you're talking about."

"Avallach. This game you're playing, running around the globe and saving people."

"Judging by what happened at Delphi, I'm not doing that good of a job of it." Arthur looked unhappy about that.

Owen pressed on. "Who gets to choose who you save?"

"That's an interesting question."

"Are you playing God?"

"An even better question, but the answer is no. I don't get to choose who I save. I just have to save them. What I'm doing is shaping the future."

Owen frowned. "Are you playing around with the idea that you can see the future?"

Arthur shook his head. "No, I can't see the future."

"Your mother could, though, right?" Owen sneered. If he couldn't get Oracle, he could find out what Arthur knew.

Arthur pointed to them both. "Our mother could, assuming you have the same DNA. You don't look exactly like me, but you're pretty damn close in age. How old was I before you were created?"

"I was born."

"You were an embryo made with my DNA. That's how cloning works. So really, you have two mothers. My mother—your genetic predecessor—and the surrogate that gave birth to you. It goes without saying we also have the same father, but that's an advantage for your formative years. Him not being involved, I mean. Our father was a bit of a bastard."

"Do you think that's going to sway me?"

Arthur shrugged.

"Not everyone is willing to sacrifice themselves for you."

"I've never asked anyone to."

"Also not true. People have been tagging signs with your name all over the world. It's sickening to see someone so mediocre exalted and revered."

"I doubt they're doing it now. I'm now a terrorist, after all."

"I'm going to take down your image of self-righteousness."

"So what's your plan? Hand me over to the real authorities? No, that doesn't make sense." Arthur thought about it for a moment. "You're going in my place, to speak for me." Arthur nodded and stared at Owen. He had that sort of gaze that looked through people, and it made Owen uncomfortable. Like he wasn't there.

"The rest of the world may seem to be on your side; the US government isn't. They have to explain away a bomb in the capital that was created by them. The Chevaliers have arrived to take responsibility for the technology and shift the blame onto you. Convenient for us both."

"Did I destroy Delphi, or did you?" Arthur looked down at Owen's hands. "Where's *Gram*? I've seen mistuned focal rings before."

Owen moved his hands away from the table. Was his hand trembling? "You think you're so smart."

"I'm just seeing right through you. It was you in the New York attack. Too bad that failed, but bravo on using Indiana's signature. That means you have *Joyous* or *Brightkiller*."

"Why were you at Delphi? Were you looking for Oracle?"

Arthur raised an eyebrow. Owen was impressed, but he wasn't getting anywhere. "I was called in to assist in an emergency, which happened to be you and your people attacking my people. Even if I knew what Oracle was, it's destroyed now. I trust it was something Anora had been working on."

Arthur seemed to have no idea about Oracle. Anora did. "Sounds like someone is keeping something from you."

"People keep the secrets they wish to keep." Arthur spread his hands. "I'd really like to know how my people are, but since you've volunteered no information..."

"You have no information on Oracle or Delphi?"

Arthur shook his head. "I just said that. You seem awfully keen on it. What good would a predictive system be to you? If I knew of such a thing or person, why would I tell you? Do you want to know your future? It's not really that great of a thing to know, truth be told."

"What are you talking about?" Owen said. To him, Arthur sounded like a fool. Someone who could not keep his thoughts together. *What a pair*, he thought. One with a deteriorating body, and the other with a deteriorating mind.

"I already know our future. Why ask an oracle? You can ask me."

Owen stood up. He wasted time talking to this fool.

"Not going to ask? Fine, I'll let you in on a little secret." Arthur leaned in conspiratorially.

Owen couldn't help himself. He leaned in.

"We're both going to die tonight." Arthur leaned back and smiled. "I've been almost killed a few times; actually dying might be a relief. It's all very subjective."

"I'm not going to die."

"Both of us are going to be betrayed by the closest person to us. I wonder how that's going to happen. I don't fancy being shot again and I'm a pretty good swimmer—"

"What's wrong with you?" Owen said. None of that made sense. It would all jeopardize the entire project. Both projects.

"What's wrong with me? You stand there across from me, pretending you're the superior combatant in this fight. You put on the air of having a better education, better training, but all the while you're fighting. Fighting that feeling that you'll never be good enough. That no one thinks you're good enough."

"No."

"You know why I know this? I've had that parent who never thinks you're good enough. How's your mother, by the way?"

Owen's fist tightened. He hadn't expected Arthur to act like this. But what *did* Owen expect? Did he expect a twin six years his senior to understand him? For him to know his feelings and his emotions? Did he feel what he felt the first time he met Indiana? A thought struck him. "Did you ever have the feeling like you were being pushed?"

"That's an interesting question," Arthur said.

"When you were manifesting, did you feel compelled to do something, to go somewhere, and no matter what you did, you couldn't resist it?"

Arthur looked down at his hands, and Owen knew he was imagining *Caliburn*.

"You have," Owen continued. "Why didn't you go?"

Arthur regarded him now. Owen could feel that piercing gaze. He had his attention now.

Owen smiled. "It seems we share the same fear. Fear of being controlled."

The guard rapped on the bars. Owen was nearly out of time.

"Do you have a medical condition?" Arthur asked.

Owen frowned. How did he know?

Now Arthur frowned. "You wanted to know why."

"Why what?"

"Why I was born perfect and you were not."

Owen was stunned into silence.

"The truth is, you're not perfect and neither am I. It's random chance that our genes operate the way they do. Our lives are not like a movie where they use the same actor to play both parts. You're also not some sort of degenerated copy of the original. You're Owen and I'm Arthur. You think that our DNA ties us together, but it's not how you think. It's now just who we are, regardless of our genetic makeup. Do you think you have the same fingerprints as me? None of that matters, Owen. What matters is what you've been dreaming.

"Ever since you were Conditioned, your mind has been altered. Not much more than any other augmented human, but you and I have been granted powers and have in turn granted them to others. But we're not gods—I don't think I am, and I don't think you believe you are either. You've got a degenerative condition. So what? It's not going to matter if neither of us does what needs to be done. Every act I've taken is to move the needle. To change the world.

"Don't you see what's going to happen? Not tomorrow. Not in a year. But fifty, a hundred, hundreds of years from now. It's going to be bad and I've been swimming against it, with help. Face facts: the world is going to go to shit unless one of us does something for the human race. Is it going to be me, or you?"

Owen stood in the corner, his mind focused on the words. "That's a bit much to believe. You could've aimed a bit lower—say, world domination."

"It could come to that, but I don't think you realize the kind of danger your Chevaliers are the harbingers of."

"And your Avallach Paladins are better?"

"They haven't killed anyone. Not at least while I've been in charge."

"What about you?"

Arthur spread his hands. "I've killed people and I've let people be killed."

"With your *Caliburn*?"

"Yes."

"So you don't get to claim to be pursuing a higher calling—"

"Therein lies the logical fallacy of your argument. You assume that if a man can kill another, he can't be pursuing a higher cause. Do you think Abraham Lincoln was innocent? He sparked a civil war aspiring to the higher cause of abolishing slavery. Those in authority must accept responsibility for what they do. No, I'm not innocent. I've killed people with bullets and blades. It doesn't make a difference how they die. It's how we as a species move to the next level. How we get to the better place and get beyond the kind of people we are now."

"Do you hear yourself?"

"Don't sound lost, Owen. Wake up and realize why you didn't kill me when you had the chance. This is your third chance. You can shoot me now, or stab me in the heart with your blade."

Arthur leaned back, his handcuffed and chained hands limp in his lap. He waited.

Owen knew he could do it. And yet, something still held him back. He thought of Gal. What kind of person would she be? What about Leto? Was he just a killer? He shook his head, rejecting the idea. No, he'd take Arthur down the right way. Morgan's way. He would be her instrument to the end, good or bad.

"Ready," Owen said.

Mara Holt and two guards entered. Mara lanced Arthur with her blue waveblade.

"You do something with your hair?" John Atherton said as he sat down across from Arthur.

Arthur's hand twitched, but he resisted putting it through his hair. "Not really."

"Hmm. I didn't think local municipalities gave prisoners product. Lieutenant Arthur Aidan MacGabran, formerly of the United States Navy—"

Someone knocked and one of the jailers entered. "Transport is ready, sir."

John was confused. He'd just sat down for the interview. "Transport? I didn't authorize any transport until tomorrow."

The jailer handed him a hard copy of the notice. John skimmed through the order. It was signed three levels above him. He frowned. "I guess you're being transferred to high security earlier than I thought."

"I'm sorry to hear that," Arthur said.

"Go ahead," John said as he read the reassignment order. "Hold on. This isn't right."

"Sir?" the jailer said as he grabbed Arthur's elbow and stood him up.

"No. Keep going. I need to make a call," John said. The guard walked Arthur out of the room and John followed. He dialed the home office.

"Director Lucius—"

"Why are we moving Myrrdin and Marks?"

"Excuse me?"

"Why are we moving Anora Myrrdin and Isolde Marks with the prisoner?"

"I'm not at liberty to say."

"Not at liberty to say, or you just don't know?"

"I don't know. I've already put in a call, but the phone lines here are acting up. Why don't you go along to make sure things don't get fucked up."

"I can only fix so much," John said, and hung up. "Fuck." Someone upstairs was monkeying with procedure. He needed to find out how much of the transport had already been arranged. Damn it, they wanted to move him to Quantico? That didn't even make sense unless they wanted to try him under the Uniform Code of Military Justice. That still didn't explain why the two women were to be transported with him. Were they being held under suspicion of leaking military secrets? Then there was the less than agreeable weather. While it wasn't a blizzard out there, the roads weren't exactly clear. At least it had stopped snowing for now. "Fuck," John said again. He needed to make some calls. Where to put them was the least of his problems. According to eyewitness reports and current investigation efforts, there were at least two men at large, with additional suspects to be named. He punched in a number.

"Hey, John," Max Muldoon answered. "I thought you might call."

"What the fuck is going on?"

"Hey, man, I'm just wading through the icy-hot mess here on H Street. What's wrong?"

"They're transporting the prisoners. I have orders to be on the road after evening rush hour."

"You gotta be shitting me."

"I'm looking at the orders right here, straight from on high."

"Want me to head over there and find out what's what?"

"No, no. You gotta help lock down Focus."

"Damn right I do. The Fort is shitting themselves, thinking there's a breach at Focus, which there's not, but I can't tell them that. They came down here like a swarm of bees, fussing over their servers and rebuilding their hive." Max chuckled at his own joke. "Place looks like a wreck though. Took the whole facility offline, even when it had backup power. Cut most of the fiber optic lines. That was interesting, to watch them shit over that, too. Like Gollum over the Ring."

"You watch too much TV."

"I got a life outside of work. Don't be jealous."

"You're just about retired, old man. Stay put. I have to get this worked out. No way I'm going to be able to run to the home office and find out what's really going on. Maybe I'll give them a call."

"Good luck with that. I heard their phone system is screwed up. Stupid VOIP bullshit."

"Christ, this day just gets better, doesn't it?"

"I'll try to make it back to you before you ship out."

"Thanks. You keep the kids happy with their broken toys." John hung up. He looked back at Arthur, who sat there looking bored.

"Take him back to his cell, then come find me and we'll take a look at the plan for transporting them to Quantico," he said to the sheriff. "You got local agents?"

"Yeah, Haut and Sagramore arrived fifteen minutes ago."

"All right, I'll go talk to them. You got any coffee?"

42

BRIDGE TO NOWHERE

They brought a squad to escort her, which was pretty likely overkill, Anora thought. *Or maybe not*, she amended. They handcuffed her and brought her out of her cell. There she met Isolde, who had a cast on her hand. The swelling in Isolde's face had gone down, but she still looked like hell. Her cheek had a bandage over where the skin had been split. Anora promised to make sure she had no scars when this was done. They walked through the facility.

"This sucks," Isolde said.

"You don't have handcuffs."

"Kind of hard when you have a cast. And they tried. That part was funny."

"How's your hand?" Anora asked.

"Hurts like hell. Not all the bones are broken. Some were just dislocated. Want drugs badly, but they won't give them to me."

An armored van sat in a loading bay. Two police in SWAT gear stood outside the van, all black uniforms, armor, and seriousness. Special Agents Atherton and Haut were also waiting for them.

"Agent Atherton, Haut," Anora said to both. Isolde only made a face. *Perpetually defiant*, Anora noted.

John opened the back of the van. Arthur MacGabran sat there, bound hand and foot and wearing a set of coveralls.

"I'm so glad we're not being treated like criminals," Isolde said to Anora when she saw the prison uniform.

"Kind of feels like we are," Anora replied. They had actually been restrained but did not wear the uniform that Arthur wore. That wasn't likely to last, Anora thought. Their personal effects hadn't even been inventoried, but Anora hoped that was an oversight by the sheriff and not the FBI. Anora eyed the van and its dark interior. She summoned her courage.

"Problem?" Haut asked.

"She has severe claustrophobia, dummy," Isolde said. "Don't you read the reports you get when your analysts do research?"

"Are you going to be all right?" John asked.

Isolde put her good hand in Anora's and rubbed the back of it.

"I think I'll be all right. As long as there's a little bit of light, I can focus on that."

"I'll make sure the interior light stays on then," John said, climbing into the van.

They climbed in after him. Isolde sat opposite Arthur. John sat next to Arthur and Agent Haut sat on the other side of Arthur. Anora sat down next to Isolde. John pulled the doors shut.

"Got a coed jail for us?" Isolde asked, making a face at Arthur.

Arthur smiled back.

John gave her a scowl.

"We're going to Quantico," Anora replied. "Has a nice military brig for the fallen god here." She pointed at Arthur.

"I don't see why we can't ride in style in one of those FBI SUVs I see on TV all the time," Isolde said. The van started up and a convoy of vehicles rumbled down the road, organizing into a long line.

Anora played with one of her earrings. "Pretty good job coordinating all of this on short notice," Anora said above the noise of the van. "Ever think of working in the private sector?"

John's scowl only deepened, which told Anora that he had to work hard to get everything arranged. Good.

John decided to while away some time. He looked at Isolde. "Your father was involved in some DARPA work at Tintagel. You know anything about that?"

Isolde frowned at Arthur.

Arthur sat there with a closed expression.

Isolde looked back at John. "I don't pay attention to much of what's happened in the past. Are you investigating my father's murder?"

"I'm not a part of that investigation."

"Why are you asking me? I'm not an augment or terrorist or whatever they're calling them on TV. I'm just with Nor here."

"Not true," Arthur said. "She was with us at H Street—"

"Whose side are you on?" Isolde asked.

"I'm on the side of no one else getting hurt."

"What about these Chevalier dicks? They're just like you."

"They're fully cooperating with the authorities, apparently."

Isolde looked at John. "Did anyone tell you that these Chevaliers were at H Street and caused the destruction?"

"Sounds like you don't agree with him." John leaned back.

"Did you forget to interview her?" Anora asked.

"I hadn't got around to it," John replied.

Anora knew he was patient. It wasn't a movie interrogation, or any sort of interrogation for that matter. That would come later. It confirmed things were rushed—badly so. She rubbed her other ear. She inspected the van. It was sealed tight and there was no way to open it from the inside.

"Mr. Atherton, have you ever seen an augment manifest up close?" Anora asked.

"Just video footage. I've only seen the results. It's been pretty destructive. I imagine if it were a skyscraper instead of a small residential area, the damage would have been worse than 9/11."

"Fair assessment."

Anora watched Isolde pull her necklace from her cast. So that was where she'd hidden it. That girl was resourceful.

Anora picked up the conversation again. "Have you seen the footage where Arthur saved people? Hostages in that bank?"

John was quiet, but Anora watched Arthur. His expression was passive, registering nothing.

The van turned and Anora felt the bump as they passed a transition plate. They were going over a bridge. There was a prickle at the base of her neck. Anora thought back along the drive and guessed they were transitioning over the Fourteenth Street Bridges into Virginia.

Isolde tugged at her ponytail. Anora passed Isolde her earrings and lunged across to Arthur, who had a look of surprise on his face. Anora kissed him hard on the lips.

John shoved her back. "I guess you have a thing for him."

"That wasn't a kiss of passion."

"She's—"Arthur started.

Peleus flared to blue life and Isolde lanced Haut and then John. The agents' nervous systems went haywire and they fell and convulsed on the deck of the van. Isolde stood, putting a hand on the ceiling of the van to steady herself. Arthur, who was chained to the bench, tried to stand but was unable to move from his seat.

"Field's up?" Anora asked.

"Felt it just before the bridge," Isolde replied. She glowed with a halo of power. *Peleus* gleamed in her good hand. She clenched her fist. Anora was glad she'd begged Kai to create a second set of focal rings for Isolde. It was Anora's idea to refashion them into jewelry.

The van screeched to a halt, throwing everyone forward. Isolde put an arm out to brace herself. "What the fuck?"

"Someone's stopped the convoy," Anora said.

"Hold on," Isolde said, and lanced through the forward compartment, hitting the driver. "Now they won't drive off while we're busy."

They heard the muffled crack of gunshots and shouts outside.

Arthur said, "How the hell . . . ?"

"Aw, did I ruin your plans to destroy Arthur?" Isolde said, slicing off Anora's handcuffs. Anora drew Atherton's sidearm as the man lay there twitching.

"So this is the man who killed my father?" Isolde stared down at Owen. *Peleus* winked out, but she still glowed.

Owen struggled against his chains. His hand shook badly. He wanted to speak, but his gaze was defiant. "Not me," he growled.

"You're not Arthur, and we know that," Anora said. "That was a kiss good-bye." Anora handed the sidearm to Isolde. "His name is Owen LaFayette."

"Owen, huh? Well, Owen. The thing about people named Marks . . ." Isolde took the gun and shot Owen at point-blank range three times. He slid over onto the bench. "We have a thing for revenge."

"Both will die," Owen gasped. There were more shouts outside the van, accompanied by gunfire and screeching tires.

"Happy?" Anora asked Isolde.

"No," Isolde said. "But I'll live." Isolde sliced open the back of the van.

Anora knelt down in front of Owen. "Your sardonic exterior is all gone. Don't you have anything to say?"

Owen stared at her, blood bubbling from his throat. "Morgan . . . has . . . Indiana . . . Jeri . . . has . . . baby . . . ," he managed to say. His eyes were pleading. Sad.

"Thank you," Anora replied, and turned away from Owen. Anora ducked behind Isolde as bullets stopped at her KE field.

A bullet grazed Anora's knee. She shouted and grabbed her leg in pain.

Isolde jumped out of the van and lanced a police officer through his bulletproof vest. She looked around. "Kai's here, doing her own rescue," Isolde reported.

"Arthur said she'd get involved. We'll have to deal with her later."

Two gray figures emerged from the SUV behind the van. Wave-blades flicked to life and light tape on their uniforms flickered blue and red.

"Couldn't smuggle two sets of rings?" Isolde said, holding her blade up as the Chevaliers came to engage. "Wish they hadn't taken *Justice* at least."

"You couldn't manage two anyway," Anora hissed, trying to stand on her good leg.

Isolde waited with her KE shield up and ready. The Chevaliers flanked her.

"We fight?" Isolde asked Anora.

"Wait," Anora said. There was a whoosh behind the van, but no explosion. There was a rhythmic thumping sound among the spray of bullets.

"Don't need to get you shot," Isolde said, advancing.

"Again?" Anora asked, indicating the grazing wound on her leg.

"Oh please."

The Chevaliers closed in on them. Then a tremendous explosion rocked the van. The concussive wave threw Isolde and the Chevaliers to the ground.

"Christ!" Isolde said.

Anora was protected from most of the blast, being directly behind the van. "Okay, let's go!" Anora said, pulling Isolde to her feet. The Chevaliers were dazed. Isolde lanced one as they ran by.

"That was you, right? Not some other fuck-up?" Isolde asked.

"Come on!" Anora hobbled as fast as she could. She guided Isolde to the side of the bridge. Isolde looked back at the bridge, where there was a smoking hole.

Anora and Isolde hopped over the bridge's outer barrier.

"We're not jumping, are we?" Isolde asked. "You didn't really give details up to this poi—"

Anora shoved Isolde off the bridge and jumped after her.

43

BULLETS, ROCKETS, AND BOMBS, OH MY!

"Convoy approaching," Sam said in Kai's earpiece. Hector checked over her Talos II suit and operated the mechanical links in the back of it.

"I have to pee," Kai said to Sam.

"Don't worry, you can go in the suit if you want. The n-suit helps."

"How did you move in this thing?"

"That was Talos I—twice as heavy and painful to operate. This is Talos II, which is better. Overkill for what you want to do."

"I'm not leaving him to be eviscerated in the court of public opinion, nor are they putting him in a dank dark hole."

Hector smiled as he made the final checks. "You look kind of badass. Or pissed off."

"Both," Kai said.

"Three minutes," Janus said in Kai's ear. Hector put Kai's helmet on her head and twisted until it clicked into place. The faceplate was up. She looked at Hector. "Things might go sideways. If they do, you take Echo and leave. The Raven will provide support."

"It's not going to go sideways. Echo team's ready."

Kai felt a prickle at the base of her neck. "Is the field up?"

Birgitte shook her head. "It's on standby."

Hector felt it, too. "Convoy has those new Chevaliers with it." He rubbed his focal rings. Kai hoped to keep him by her side. He was one of their best and she didn't want to lose him in this fight.

"Hey, girl," Ed said in Kai's ear. "I got the best news."

"Kinda busy, Ed."

"Jeri's back."

"Oh yeah? How is she?"

"Great, and she's got the cutest—"

"I'm a little busy, Ed. How are you?"

"One-handed," Ed replied. "You sure this is the right thing to do?"

Kai closed her eyes. She was sure that Ed was back on *Camelot* now. At least he was safe. "It is."

"You do this, and we're not presumed terrorists. We're actual terrorists."

"I don't want to talk about it."

"Just giving you the line."

"Thanks, Ed."

"Don't die out there. Who am I going to pine for?"

"Your other hand?"

"Cold, Kai."

"No promises, but let me think about Arthur first."

"Always. Take care."

Sam clicked over. "They're approaching the bridge."

"Let's go," Kai said. The truck lurched into slow motion as it shifted gears and gained in speed.

"Field's up," Birgitte said. Kai felt her suit systems respond to the focal magnifier. She raised her hands almost effortlessly, although she heard the whine of the micromotors. Talos II was a new power suit the Three Sisters had been working on since they had left Avallach. They had to abandon Talos I when Avallach was destroyed; it was simply too heavy to move and since Sam was the only person who could operate it, they'd left the suit and taken the design and its prototype focal magnifier. Kai hadn't planned on using the suit at all, but there had always remained the possibility they would need it. She stood up and turned to the dozen members of Echo team.

"Paladins!" she yelled. They all wore black n-suits, sleek and superhero-like beneath the tarpaulin. "Are you ready?"

LEDs lit on their sleeves as they activated the KE shield systems as one. "Paladins ready!" they responded.

"It's going to be chaotic. Stay focused and get to the van. Blueshift at all times. We're going to hit Chevalier resistance who won't hesitate to kill. Disable them if you can. They have numbers, but you have better training and shields."

The truck tires squealed and bullets pinged on the hull and plow as police tried to stop the driver, a Paladin who was impervious to bullets.

"Stand by!" Hector said. "For Arthur!"

"Convoy on the bridge," Janus said in Kai's ear. She tapped the mechanical switch, and the faceplate shut and the AR system gave her a view of the outer world through cameras. The Talos II face looked like a blank smooth mirror. There were explosions and the thump of helicopter rotor blades. The truck swerved, but she held on to the straps bolted to the inside walls of the hauling box. There was a heavy thump and jerk as the truck plowed through the police barricade and swerved onto the bridge. Kai hit the door and it cracked open, lowering the ramp as the large plow truck slowed to a halt on the bridge, shot to a standstill.

"Good luck," Sam said in her ear.

"Won't need it," Kai said, clanging down the ramp, leading the charge. Bullets fell away from the KE field enveloping her suit. Stray bullets hit the KE fields of the Paladins around her. Hector, who'd been training with Ed and the other special forces members of Echo, motioned for the group to break into two teams. Waveblades were summoned, bright blue beacons everywhere. Police and SWAT team members shouted for the Paladins to freeze. The Paladins swarmed through them, running as fast as they could, waveblades flicking into bodies left and right.

Kai saw the van and ran toward it. The Talos II suit motors whirred and picked up speed, drawing energy from the focal magnifier. Bullets pinged, but her KE field kept the suit moving without being impeded by the transfer of kinetic energy. Police lights flashed everywhere in the dying sunlight.

Then she saw the white waveblades, the glinting badges, and the gauntlets and gray suits of these Chevaliers. Their suits flickered red and blue as if they were a policing force.

"Here they come," Hector said. He didn't even sound out of breath running next to Kai.

"Stop them. I'm going to the van."

"No problem," Hector replied.

"Don't get killed. Indy'd be pissed off if I let that happen to you."

"What about me?" Hector grunted as he passed a fallen police officer. From behind an SUV, a SWAT team pulled out a rocket launcher.

"I got it," Kai said, changing trajectory to intercept in a spiral that led away from any people. The rocket went off and Kai leaned back, her suit moving almost faster than she'd wanted. Her back wrenched, but the RPG missed, sailing out over the river and splashing harmlessly. Heavy-caliber rounds from the helicopter overhead started peppering her, tearing chunks out of the bridge pavement.

Then the Chevaliers and Paladins engaged.

"Here I come, Art," Kai said as she closed in on the van. She felt a peculiar flip of her equilibrium, as if gravity turned on and off. The feeling was familiar, but it wasn't the jitters of combat.

"Alert—" Janus began, but was cut off when Kai was thrown in the air.

OVER THE POTOMAC RIVER, WASHINGTON, DC—

"Have I told you how great it is to see you again?" Percy said in Ellen's ear as they hovered beneath the Fourteenth Street Bridges. The shadow and black of their suits and steeds made them seem nearly invisible.

"Only about a hundred times," Ellen replied.

Percy kept watch on the patrol craft out across the water. The icy wind pulled at them, portending snowy weather.

"Time," she said. Ellen floated down, her hands free, maneuvering with her knees. She held on to something the size of a small volleyball. "Here goes!" Ellen said, throwing the device as hard as she could into the air in front of her. The black filament tether unreeled as it arced up, but at the zenith, it pulsed and then continued to shoot upward. Ellen's body glowed with power as she transmitted it through the device. It continued until it nestled in the girdered underbelly of the bridge. Ellen sent a surge of power through the tether into the device.

Percy felt his stomach flip as gravitational waves washed over him through the material of the bridge. Dust and orange metallic rust drifted down as if the bridge were shaking itself. It was, as Percy understood it, one of the gravitic drive prototypes developed before the days of Indiana's training and flight on the *Archimedes*. They were using it as a diversion; as designed, it would only operate as a gravitic bomb.

There was a *fwoosh!* as Percy watched an RPG round splash off into the water. "Jesus," he whispered. "Better work soon!"

"Hang on," Ellen replied. She was focused on the device, channeling power to it from a thin tether. Percy's stomach flip-flopped and he was ready to throw up. The air pulsed around them.

There was a boom that rattled his teeth and knocked his steed downward from the gravitational push. Ellen's steed rolled back and down and the tether fell into the water. They took a moment to adjust themselves. Percy rolled away as chunks of bridge splashed down into the water. One of the pylons had cracked and the support for that section of the bridge buckled. "Holy shit."

"Down!" Ellen said, rolling her steed down toward the water.

Percy nosed his steed in the same direction. "Are they going to be there?" He swept out from under the bridge and raced along toward the District side of the Potomac. His eyes were fixed on the bridge's edge.

"Trust me," Ellen said.

"It's not you I'm worried about."

"Trust Anora, then," Ellen replied.

Police helicopters circled the bridge while news helicopters orbited farther away, trying to record the rapid turn of events. They'd focused on the gravitic buckle. Percy flew up higher, his enhanced vision not seeing anything.

"Down," Ellen repeated. There were flashes all over the bridges, flicks of blue and white lights as Paladins and Chevaliers fought each other.

"I see them." Percy saw the slim shapes of Isolde and Anora hop over the outer wall of the bridge. Isolde was looking down and Anora was watching their approach. There was a high-pitched whine as the steed's alarm system went off and the grid collapsed. "Fuck!" Percy yelled as they plummeted into the icy Potomac.

~

THE WATER SHOCKED his entire body as Percy hit the river. With only the magnets holding on to him, the impact jarred him loose from his steed. He was already heading down toward the riverbed. He held on to one of the handles and the pontoons activated. The steed popped up like a cork and ripped from his grip. He kicked toward the surface as hard as he could. He gasped as he broke the surface. He was glad for the n-suit, which protected him from the water and cold like a wetsuit. Only his head and hands were bare and already his teeth were chattering. He reached out, but there was no field. The battle on the bridge had drawn too much again.

"Ellen!" Percy called. She popped up a hundred feet or more away. She waved to him.

"I'm here," she said into his ear. "Did you see Anora and Isolde?"

"Yes, and they hit the water near me. I'm looking." Percy grabbed on to his steed and swam with one arm to where he'd seen Anora and Isolde jump. Anora bobbed up a few feet away from him, gasping and moaning in pain. He swam over to her and pulled her toward the pontooned steed.

"What happened?" Anora asked, her teeth chattering with the cold.

"Grids overloaded and the steeds took a nosedive," Percy explained.

"Damn it, Kai," Anora hissed, her teeth chattering. "You have a terminal?"

"Of course," Percy said, pulling the steed close by. Anora put an arm on it. Percy handed her the waterproof terminal.

"Can you get Isolde?"

"She was with you."

"You didn't see her come up?" Anora asked.

As if on command, Percy saw her bob up downstream. Her body was limp.

"I'm going for her."

Anora nodded and spoke to the terminal. "One?"

"I'm here," One said.

"Status?"

Percy pulled out his own tether, tied it to the steed, knifed into the water, and swam toward Isolde. She was facedown, her arms splayed out. She must've hit the water at the wrong angle. He swam hard. *We save, we don't kill*, he reminded himself.

A few powerful strokes and he grabbed her hand, then her body, and slowed her down, turning her upright. He rolled onto his back, lifting her out of the water slightly. He slapped her face. It was cold and clammy, like a fish. His fingers were already numb.

"Come on, dummy," he said, squeezing her lungs in a sort of pumping motion. She coughed water and breathed. "Izz, you gotta swim."

Isolde groaned, then came to as the icy shock of water hit her. "God, that bitch pushed me off the bridge!"

"You can tell her yourself," Percy said, hauling himself on the tether to draw the steed to them. The current was gentle but steady. The bridge fighting seemed to have stopped but it was hard to make out what was going on from down there.

"So cold," Isolde chattered.

"We'll get you warmed up."

"Where's the field? It vanished a second before I hit the water."

"There's a huge fight on the bridge."

"We really need to fix the problem of all these little grids collapsing," Isolde sighed. "Thanks for rescuing me. Again."

"Again?"

"Crazy bitch fight."

"Which one?"

Isolde chuckled and they swam toward the steeds.

"Longinus online in three minutes," One announced.

"That's an awfully long time," Anora said.

"Best I can do and satellite is pre-positioned."

"Send the activation codes once it's online," Anora said to One.

"Understood."

"You pushed me off the bridge?" Isolde yelled as she came close.

"Big baby," Anora said, trying to warm her hands by placing them under her armpits. No part of her was warm. "You had a KE field."

"My field went out just before I hit the water. I want to stab you right now."

"You're welcome to try."

"Bitch," Isolde said, and turned to Percy and climbed on the steed that floated in the river. They were a good ways from the bridge. Evening crept on quickly. Helicopters still hovered around but didn't follow them, choosing to circle the smoking plume left by the gravitic prototype. They saw some fighting on the bridge. It was hand-to-hand now, at least from their standpoint.

"I should be up there," Percy said.

"We both should be," Ellen said.

"Stay focused," Anora said. "One, report on the tracker, please."

"Still heading south. It's stopped at a bridge."

"Patrol boat approaching. They spotted us." Percy tensed as Isolde huddled against him for warmth.

"One, can I get the satellite to activate any faster?" Anora said.

"Unidentified vessels," a bullhorn echoed. "Do not move or attempt to depart. You will be fired upon."

"No," One replied. "Thirty seconds."

"Janus, what's the cycle time in the steed grids?"

"Three minutes."

"Okay, we're not going to be in range of Longinus long, but it'll get us going." Anora's plan could still work.

"I only brought a knife to this gunfight," Percy said.

The patrol craft sped toward them. Men had machine guns trained on them. A fifty-caliber weapon was pointed at them as well.

"Stall," Anora said. She raised her shaking bluish hands, and the three of them followed suit.

"Evening, fellas," Percy said as the patrol craft pulled alongside. "I have no weapons." He looked around. Ellen's steed was unmanned. "One of our Jet Skis flipped over—"

"We're coming alongside and bringing you aboard. Show your hands and do not make any sudden moves."

A crew member leaned over and pulled Percy's steed alongside. Percy helped Isolde onto the boat, and then Anora. Another crew member tied off the steed and got Percy pulled aboard. By the time he got onto the deck, Isolde and Anora were zip-cuffed and surrounded by crew members with guns. They'd been placed on their hands and knees with their ankles crossed. It was a difficult position for them but made it easier for the crew to maintain a watch. Percy sighed.

"Hands behind your back," the crew member said, and Percy complied, putting his hands behind his back. He looked at Anora, who stared at the deck in front of her. He knew she hadn't thought of this.

This did not go as planned, Percy thought. *Trust Anora*, Ellen's voice echoed in his head. He looked up at the pilothouse and saw the Chevalier in a gray suit and silver badge, looking down at them.

44

BURNOUT

FOURTEENTH STREET BRIDGES, WASHINGTON, DC—
Kai had one thing the Three Sisters had customized for her—the new Talos II had to account for the loss of field power, so the magnifier also charged a backup system. It was enough for maybe ten minutes.

After the bizarre and unsettling explosion, more Chevaliers drew on the system, and even the nearby heavy grid in the snowplow was overloaded with manifest power channeling through it. It was a multilayered paper-thin blanket that ripped apart with the first poked hole of overextension. Kai had estimated the amount they'd need but didn't know how many Chevaliers they'd encounter. The grid went down for the third time in a day.

Alarms warbled in her helmet and she silenced them. Yellow parts of her suit blinked in her heads-up display, but it was all minor. She'd been thrown clear of the blast and landed on a squad car face up, crushing the hood in. She was dazed for a moment.

"Internal power," Janus said automatically. "Systems operational for ten minutes." A counter blinked in her peripheral vision.

"I got it," Kai said, sitting up and wrenching herself free of the hood. Police all around her were recovering. One shot at her. The bullet's impact slowed her now that her KE field was gone. *Remember thou art mortal*, she reminded herself.

She needed to get to Arthur. Janus reoriented her. She checked behind her. She'd been separated from the rest of the group. Chunks of the bridge were collapsing into what looked like a sinkhole. In the bridge? Who did that? Was it a Chevalier?

"Hector?" Kai said.

"We're here," Hector said. "Keep going. Hand-to-hand, now. We need a grid."

"They're resetting. Five minutes to burn off the overload," Sam reported.

Kai ran at full speed toward the van. A Chevalier swung at her. She batted him out of the way with her armored forearm, the micro servos whirring in response to her commands. He flew back and off the bridge. *Maybe I broke his neck*, Kai thought idly. Bullets pushed her from her trajectory and she had to compensate. Talos II was armored but not impervious. If they got a lucky shot into a joint or motor, she was screwed.

She waded through cars and people. The FBI and police wisely got out of her way. She got to another two-car barricade and launched herself over it. The pavement cracked where she landed and she nearly toppled over from the heft of the suit. The motors whined and she saw the timer clicking down, flashing lower as she used more juice.

She pushed police out of the way to get to the van, sweeping them back when they came in with their batons and Tasers. She was less merciful to the Chevaliers, who, without manifest power, were only protected by lined Kevlar. After the tangle with the first two, the remaining handful of them gave her a wide berth. The police, for their part, tried to do their job. She had a splitting headache. She'd burned through five minutes of power in no time. Was she suffocating in the suit? She checked her vitals. Except for the lack of power and suit damage, she was unharmed.

"Kai, the police are taking Paladins now. They have guns," Hector said.

"Don't resist unless the grid comes back."

"They're going to take our rings."

"Don't let them," she replied.

"Easy for you to say," Hector quipped.

She was getting close to the van. All of these obstacles were just slowing her down. What was she going to do when she got to the van and there was no juice left? She couldn't stop now. *Arthur, I'm coming!* she told herself.

She was close now, and then she felt an immense grid envelop her.

"God bless you, Sam," she said.

"That wasn't me," Sam said.

"A few Paladins are disarmed and surrounded by Chevaliers," Hector said.

"Handle it, Heck," she ordered. "Get them free and make a retreating action. Get Echo out."

"Aye," Hector said.

She manifested, drawing as much into herself as she could. The suit's alarms winked out as the system came back to full power. An FBI agent fired a shotgun at her. The blast did nothing against her raised shield. She made it to the van. It was in bad shape, having swerved into the median. The back door was open and she saw the telltale signs of waveblade use. *What the hell?* she thought.

She got to the back of the van. Arthur was there. Two FBI agents were on the floor of the van trying to get up. Arthur's chest seeped blood. He'd been shot. *No*, she thought. She grabbed one of the agents by the legs and threw her out of the van. There was a bang as she hit the roof of a car. The other FBI agent fired his sidearm at her. She ignored the bullets and wrenched the gun out of his grasp. Her suit glove gripped the agent by the vest, and she threw him from the van as well.

She got into the van, the shocks lowering to compensate for her suit. She knelt over Arthur. He was bleeding profusely, shot in the chest. *No.* He stared up at her, his blue eyes dim. Blood bubbled from his lips. She hit the release and the *Talos* helmet faceplate slid open. She put an armored hand over his heart.

"I'm not detecting a heartbeat, Kai," Sam said.

"No," Kai said, her voice shaky. "Arthur!" she yelled.

He struggled for breath, then was still. Tears filled Kai's eyes. She'd failed. All these years protecting him and she'd still failed. She punched the bench, the servos whining when she smashed it. She saw something on the deck. A clear pouch. *Caliburn*.

She sensed the field of immense power about her. She steeled herself.

"Hector, evacuate Echo team, now."

"Yes, ma'am. I got a little help now, so we should be clear soon," Hector said. Voices spoke through her headset, but she ignored them. Her mind was in another place. She twisted and disengaged her gauntlet where *Ainavainë* glittered on her fingers. She put *Caliburn* on. The rings were loose, cold in her hand, fitting over her own rings.

"They're not getting him," she said to herself, pulling on the gauntlet and locking it into place.

"You're under arrest!" a voice said. She looked up to see the man she had thrown from the van. He had picked up the gun from the second agent and had it aimed at her.

She snarled in anger.

"You!" She jumped from the van. The man dodged and the servos hammered her fist into the hood of the car, punching a hole in it.

"System structural damage," Janus said.

"You're overloading the system," Sam said into her ear.

"Fuck off," she growled, wrenching her arm from the car as the agent fired at her. Bullets didn't matter now. Her arm hurt like hell, but she'd punched through a car hood and stopped at the engine block. In a stride and faster than the agent expected, she grabbed him by the throat and threw him across the bridge, where he landed hard and rolled on the pavement.

"You can't kill him, Kai. Arthur won't let you," Sam said.

"Arthur's dead."

"He wouldn't want you to," Sam said.

Kai turned back to the van. She focused and power flooded into her. She drew into herself and clenched her fist.

"They want destruction. They want to make us into monsters. I'll show them. I'll give them what they want."

She seized the waveform and jump-started the *Caliburn* rings. The keening sound made her wince, but she gritted her teeth against it. It was a deep vibration in her bones. Distantly, she heard voices in her head—Paladins and DAMSLs shouting at her. *No.* She let it build and build. The feedback was enormous, beyond the waterfall of power flooding into her. She twinned, resonating into two. She flowed around herself and through herself. Kai was bathed in light and the bridge shook. People scrambled away from the shaking bridge, whose integrity had already been compromised by the blast. Even the agent who fought her ran away shielding his eyes from the light that arced up from her body into the sky. Gravity altered and the feedback rose to a crescendo. Pebbles and dust vibrated and floated off the ground. The ruined van looked like it was going to float away. Kai felt herself rise on her tiptoes. The keening was unbearable. Her nose and ears bled.

Fine, she thought. *I'll make them bleed.* Grief pushed her forward, to the brink and over. She raised her arm as high as she could—the suit had limitations. She was suffused with energy and could break apart into atoms any second. She held on to it, not watching, not caring what was going on around her. Like a conductor, Kai raised her fist and struck downward. The van exploded. The bridge exploded. The world exploded in a wash of light and energy.

45

BLACK HOUNDS CLOSE IN

"Longinus active," One reported in Percy's ear. He reached out and grasped the waveform.

"Stay put," Anora said to Percy and Isolde. How did she know?

There were shouts from the stern of the boat, and gunfire erupted. Ellen climbed aboard and glowed with manifest power. Her waveblade appeared out of nowhere. The fifty-caliber gun couldn't be trained aft of the pilothouse, so the gunner abandoned it. Ellen lanced crewmen left and right with her bright blue blade.

"Little help?" Percy asked, pulling power into himself. The Chevalier jumped down from the bridge, his body glowing with power.

"Busy," Ellen said, moving to intercept the Chevalier. In the back of Percy's mind he wondered: it had been a while since Ellen had seen action, so how good was she still?

Percy got down and moved his arms so they were in front of him. Isolde did the same, and Percy held out his hands to her. She touched *Peleus* to his zip tie and it vaporized. Percy was free and *Grall* came to life in his hand. He did the same for her. A couple of crewmen saw the two additional Paladins, dropped their guns, and threw up their hands.

"Pilothouse," Anora called. Percy moved and jumped up the ladder. The captain fired his pistol at Percy as he climbed. He then tried to jump overboard, but Percy caught him by the collar.

"You wouldn't last five minutes in the water," he said as he threw him to the deck and lanced him to keep him out of trouble. The fifty-caliber gunner threw up his hands. Percy listened to the chatter on the bridge-to-bridge radio.

"Move it!" Percy said to the group. He saw Ellen fighting. Her opponent was good but not a swordsman. He was more of a martial artist, which did not help his cause. He kicked, and Ellen took the blow with her torso and hooked her arm around the man's knee. She jammed *Asi* into his thigh, and the man shrieked with pain and fell. He went silent when she lanced him in the abdomen.

She turned to the three men about to pounce on her. They stopped when they saw the short work she'd made of the Chevalier.

A heavy-set navy chief took aim at Anora with his sidearm. Isolde moved, amping her own KE field to stop the bullet.

After a short scuffle, the three crewmen lay on the deck, twitching into unconsciousness.

In moments, Percy and Ellen had secured the rest of the crew. A helicopter was routing to their location. Isolde for her part stayed glued to Anora's side.

"We need to get going," Anora said.

"They've been alerted," Percy said from the bridge. He gunned the engine and spun the wheel and brought the patrol craft back toward Ellen's steed. In a few short moments, the steeds were on deck, their pontoons retracted and kickstands lowered. Anora took two coats from the crew members and handed one to Isolde. After a moment of work, Anora took the gauntlet off of the Chevalier and jammed it into her jacket, making sure it was secure after she buttoned it up.

"I can't feel my toes," Isolde said. "Or hands. Or face. Can we steal some warm socks?"

"We still have work to do," Anora said, pulling on the coat and hopping onto the back of Ellen's steed as Percy and Isolde mounted theirs. Percy produced a helmet and handed one to Isolde.

The steeds rose from the patrol craft. Percy glanced at the retreating vessel. It floated downstream, lifeless and dark.

"Get altitude. Crossover might be bumpy," Anora told them as they sped away to the south as fast as they could go. "Where's River?" Anora asked Ellen through her helmet. Percy had seen the fight on the bridge. There were way more waveblades on one side than the other.

"Right where I left him."

Anora had watched the fight as well. "One, ping River."

"River here," he replied. "We're engaging already."

"Okay, don't hold back. Send all the Black Hounds in and get them out. All of them."

"We'll have to. They're overwhelmed right now."

"Keep your grids down until Longinus is off. No sense wasting cycle time on an overload."

"Yes, ma'am," River said.

Percy looked back and saw a large group of white blades appear on the bridge. Over the last few months, Ellen and River had taken Anora's direction. They recruited the former failures of Avallach, "jumpstarted" their manifest ability, trained them, and equipped them. They weren't as skilled as the Avallach, but there were more of them. Sixty all told, if River's numbers were to be believed. These were Anora's secret army—the Black Hounds. Percy accelerated his steed, then he felt the keening. The steed stuttered and lost altitude as he flinched in pain.

"What's that?" Ellen shouted, her steed dropping in altitude and Anora holding on to her tightly. "That's not an overload from the Hounds, is it?"

"Longinus cascade feedback. It happened at Delphi," Isolde replied.

"Great Shiva," Ellen whispered.

"Don't drop me," Anora said.

"I thought you like long walks off tall things," Isolde replied.

There was a flash of light, then a thudding boom, and the keening was gone. Percy flinched. "What the hell? Felt like a nuke."

"Shit, the bridge is gone," Isolde said, and Percy spared a look back to see the dwindling arc of light on the bridge.

"If it were a nuke, we'd be in worse shape," Anora said as they were buffeted by a shock wave. The field sputtered as they went out of range of Longinus's field, but their steeds kicked on after sixty feet of free fall. The sun was well over the horizon now. "River?"

"We're all right, more or less. It's worse than H Street here, but we'll get them away. The Chevaliers are in disarray. We're disabling vehicles where we can. The Raven's here. We got this, ma'am."

"Time to break," Anora told Percy and Isolde. *Trust Anora*, Percy told himself. He watched Ellen and Anora peel away to the west.

46

BODY DUMP

SOMEWHERE IN VIRGINIA, NORTHWEST OF DC—
The SUV stopped at the small bridge. Kara and Hong got out, their boots crunching in the ice and dusting of snow on the ground. The sun had just set and long blue shadows gave way to grays and blacks. They wore loose civilian clothing and heavy hooded coats over their Chevalier suits to ward off the icy grip of winter.

There was a flash of light in the distance.

"What the hell was that?" Hong said, looking in the direction of DC.

"Thunder?" Kara suggested.

"No," Hong said, staring into the distance for a moment. A boom reached their ears a moment later, and later still a light breeze. "Another cascade loop, I think."

"Let's get this over with and see what's up."

Hong opened the door and escorted Owen out. He hadn't spoken at all during the drive, but he hadn't been conscious for most of it.

"Morgan has an out-of-the-way place," Owen said, looking around. "Drafty, too."

"Sorry, were you under the impression you were going to see her?" Kara said, then lanced him through the chest with a bright blue waveblade. Owen fell over, twitching. "Damn, I love these new gauntlets," she observed. She looked over at Hong, her blade winking out. "Let's bag him."

"Would've been easier to get him into the bag first," Hong noted. "Must give you a certain satisfaction doing that."

"Just get it done." Kara pulled out a body bag and they put Owen in it. She'd been humiliated in New York following Owen's plan. Now that Commander Holt and Morgan had deemed her capable of continuing, she was going to prove her loyalty. It wouldn't be all that hard of a task. Owen had some odd hang-ups, and she really didn't need the baggage.

The body bag had weights added to keep it at the bottom of the river. Kara and Hong hefted him up over the lip.

"Hold him," Kara ordered.

"He's heavy," Hong said, holding the bag with both arms as it dangled over the river. "He's still twitching."

Kara's waveblade flicked to white life and she stabbed into the bag at center mass. Owen grunted and the body went slack. *It's done*, Kara thought.

"Okay."

Hong let go. There was a splash as his body struck the icy black Potomac below.

"That'll keep him from coming back," Kara said.

"And if they dredge the river?"

"Blame it on Avallach. We got badges, authority, and power now." Kara looked down at the water. *Good-bye, Owen*, she thought.

"Feel anything?" Hong asked, watching the swirling waters for a few seconds.

Kara shrugged. "He was a great fuck, but he's baggage we won't need."

"I hear that," Hong said. "Glad to be rid of him, really. Self-righteous prick, he was."

"I don't think he was all that bad. Had a bit of a blonde fetish, though," Kara said, pulling her hood back and running her fingers through her auburn hair. She'd dyed it back to its natural color and was happier for it.

47

CHIMERA MEETS PHOENIX

WASHINGTON, DC—
Anora found Morgan in her office. She sat at her desk, rolling a scotch glass between her hands as she watched the news feed. Anora saw the footage, the flash of brilliance, the pillar of light that sprang from the bridge and shot into the early evening sky. The van exploded and a huge part of the bridge collapsed from the sustained damage. "So that's what that was," Anora said. Morgan turned and was surprised to see her.

"You look positively bedraggled, Sister Anora." Morgan smiled.

Anora smiled in response, pulling her half-frozen, half-damp hair from her face. "You don't get to call me that anymore, Morgan."

Morgan frowned. "You betrayed me."

Anora shook her head. *Betrayer.* "I don't see it that way. I seconded the motion to have the vote. The terms of our agreement were that I wouldn't stand in your way when you made your motion to become matron. You betrayed yourself by killing Grand Dame Li. I see it as aiding, but the new matron did not see you as working toward the good of the Scientia."

"What new matron?" Morgan said.

Anora just stared at her with a smile. *Not so fast*, Anora thought.

She may have gotten information from a current sister, but the Scientia was usually tight-lipped to outsiders, for good reason. It was how they'd survived through the centuries. Morgan was a cancer, a hazard that had to be excised, just as her aunt Muire Ann had been decades ago.

"No matter, I'm matron regardless. The New Scientia voted for me unanimously."

"The empty shell that it is. Oh, you have a number of wise women," Anora said, unbuttoning her coat and walking around Morgan's office. "But you don't have what's really needed, and that's why you wanted the Scientia, isn't it?"

"I gave you the means, the technology—"

"You only gave me half of what I needed," Anora said. "The rest was quite a bit of work and ingenuity. By the way, I didn't know you were a part of Project Spartan. Did you know that?"

"You're not the only one with special information."

"I'm not an information broker as you are. I'm just a scientist, but I thought it was interesting. Kai was, too. I liked her. You? Not so much."

Morgan drank and steepled her fingers.

Anora examined Morgan's wet bar. "Do you mind? I think I've caught a rather nasty cold," Anora said, pouring herself two fingers of Morgan's most expensive scotch. She eyed the bottle. "Reince used to drink this. Or he used to make me buy it for him to drink. I daresay it has considerably risen in value since then." *Poor Reince*, Anora thought. *Lover.*

"You came to me—"

Anora's anger rose and she shattered the bottle on the floor. "I wanted my brother's technology and I knew you had it. *I* was the one who found out about the prototype. You thought you'd use the knowledge to keep me quiet. I did, but just the act itself was your mistake."

Morgan stood.

One buzzed in her pocket, and Anora knew she'd alerted security and Mara would be sending Chevaliers.

"You seem angry about something in particular."

Anora frowned and downed the scotch. "God, this is terrible!" She coughed for a moment. "But it does warm the insides. No, I'm not angry at you, Morgan. I promised I wouldn't stand in the way of your bid for matronage as long as you stayed within the bounds of the bylaws. You chose to step out of bounds. My only job here is to relay a message." Anora pulled out her terminal and tapped on it. "It should be in your inbox. You and each one of your co-conspirators are marked as outcasts from the Mare de Scientia."

"What do you want?" Morgan asked.

Morgan was never a fool. Anora smiled. She'd come for Indiana. "I want to see her."

"You want to see her?"

"Where is she?" Anora said. "I finished the deal. I killed him for Maven," Anora said. *Warrior.*

"And what about the Mare de Scientia? That was part of the deal."

"I explained it to you. I didn't stand in your way. That was the deal. You're not getting back in. You broke your vow. 'No harm shall befall my sisters if it is within my power.' Your aunt broke that vow and so did you. The apple doesn't fall far from the tree."

"How did it feel when you killed him?"

Anora considered another drink, but she needed her head to be clear. Her stomach burned. Well, mostly clear. She stared hard at Morgan and saw a reflection of herself there. Did Arthur have that kind of power? Anora considered her words. "Bit of a relief, if you must know," Anora said, looking out the window to the dark city. It was late and the city glittered. "I can see why you wanted to get rid of him."

"I've been trying to get rid of him since I was a child. I was more . . . direct back then." Morgan drank. "Did you tell him before you killed him?"

Morgan was stalling. Anora closed her eyes. Why did Owen have to tell her? Cruel bastard. *I did kill him,* she reminded herself. "You're not going to let me see her?"

"What about the Oracle? Did you ever find it?" Morgan asked.

Morgan wanted something in return. "Not at Delphi," Anora replied. "Shame you didn't get there first. You had all the pieces in front of you. Well, most of them."

"I could kill you. You wouldn't make it two steps out of the door before dropping dead."

Anora said, "I'm tired of people threatening me. The only people who never threatened me are dead, so imagine what I could do to the people who do cross me. We seem to be at an impasse, so let me force your hand. It was considerably easier for One to get into your systems than into the NSA's. That's quite sad, really. That took a long time."

"You're bluffing," Morgan said.

"Am I bluffing, One?" Anora asked.

"No," One answered from Morgan's dormant computer and office speakers. Morgan looked mildly amused. That was her version of shock, Anora knew.

"You have an incredibly segmented system. Well done. So, let's recap, shall we?" Anora sat down on the corner of Morgan's desk. "I know what you'll be doing and I have your data. I also have the Sisterhood. Which do you want back?"

"Why do you want to see her so badly?"

Anora shrugged. "She was the last person to see my brother alive. I want to talk to her about him."

"That's all?" Morgan looked surprised. Anora knew she was putting on a show.

"I don't want to take her out to dinner. I'm also a little curious about the woman that Arthur thought so highly of. Aren't you?"

Morgan steepled her fingers. "I'm not open to negotiations."

"This isn't a negotiation."

Morgan smiled at that. "I knew it was wise not to underestimate you. You play a fine game."

"It's not a game when you kill family members. It's personal." Anora gave Morgan a feral smile.

Two Chevaliers entered with Mara Holt.

"Bring Indiana here now," Morgan snapped.

Anora waited. Her part of the negotiation was over. She had to see her now. She had to know.

"He won't love you like he loves her," Morgan said.

"You know from experience?"

"I know the difference."

"Why does everyone know about how much he loves this woman?"

Morgan drank her gin and tonic. Her eyes glittered like a cat's.

In moments, Mara returned with a doctor and a woman in scrubs. Her hair was short, but it was unmistakably her. *Indiana.*

"Hello, Indiana," Anora said.

"Do I know you?" Indiana said. Her hands itched and she rubbed her fingers. They'd taken her rings. Anora put her hand into her coat. *I could do it now.*

"No." Anora stood and pulled the gauntlet from her coat and put it on. She felt the field. It permeated this building. She waited for the gauntlet to tune to her. She reached out and seized the waveform, but it was moving, hunting. Once it tuned to her, the power that she'd held at bay for months flooded her body. It made her feel, in a sense, whole. She glowed with power, but she was unpracticed. She began to sweat. It was glorious.

The Chevaliers stepped back, their blades coming to life. Mara and Morgan stood still, watching.

Anora went to Indiana. She could end it all and she'd be the one. She'd bring the locus. She looked into Indiana's eyes.

Indiana tilted her head back, unafraid. "Are you here to kill me?"

"After all you've been through?" Anora said. She wanted to. *Betrayer, lover, destroyer.* She felt it. Wanted to take it all away from him, but then she would be no better than Reince or her father. She'd be controlling him, and that she didn't want.

"No, I don't want to kill you. I am not happy you're alive. Do you remember what happened to my brother?"

"Your brother?" Indiana said, confused. "If I don't know you—"

"Maven Myrrdin."

Indiana thought about it for a long time. "I'm sorry... don't recall anything about him. Did he look like you?"

"Just the eyes."

Indiana shook her head.

"She's just an empty shell?" Anora asked Morgan.

"She's suffered quite a bit of trauma, you understand," Morgan replied.

"I'm not empty or deaf. I'm right fucking here and I can prove it to you," Indiana snapped.

Anora stepped close to whisper in Indiana's ear. Mara and the Chevalier's hearing would now be acute. Her lips brushed Indiana's ear. "Your baby?"

"Where is she?" Indiana whispered back.

The words of confirmation were a knife in Anora's heart. Anora only nodded and mouthed the word "safe." Indiana nodded and bowed her head.

"You got what you wanted," Morgan said.

"One will erase herself once I'm out of the building. Oh, and the rest of your system. Hope you made backups." Anora turned to Mara. "You should've been more careful around me."

Mara's lips were in a thin frown. She was seething and Anora did not care.

Anora bowed. "I have another important meeting. I'm the Chimera, after all."

She stood face-to-face with the two Chevaliers. Their light tapes glowed red and their silver badges gleamed. She walked past them and out of the office.

MORGAN FROWNED. Myrrdins were troublesome folk. Her grandfather had known it, her mother had known it, and even her aunt knew it. Maven Myrrdin was a righteous old prick, but his sister, it turned out, was more of a problem than even she had planned for. And she'd planned for everything. The Chevaliers moved to guard the foyer.

She pulled out an old red battered notebook and flipped through its pages. How much of it had changed? How much of it was still true? She needed to make some changes.

Chevalier Kara Doc walked into her office.

Morgan stabbed a button and got up. Kara went to speak but instead followed Morgan. They rode the elevator to the ground floor, where they met Ogier Dane. She motioned for them to get into the waiting limousine.

"Our computer systems have been compromised. We're going to need a top-to-bottom rebuild."

"What happened?" Ogier said, concerned.

"Anora Myrrdin happened."

Ogier frowned. "I'm not the IT guy."

Morgan looked at Kara. "Report."

"He's gone," Kara said.

"Who's gone?" Ogier asked.

"Owen LaFayette."

"Why would you do that?"

Morgan turned to Ogier. "The real question is how long you were going to let his condition go before you informed me."

"There is doctor/patient privilege," Ogier said.

"You made a flawed copy."

"I did no such thing! He was perfect!" Ogier snapped back. Morgan had hit a nerve. While Muire Ann dismissed Owen as inconsequential, Ogier still had pride in the work he'd done to make Owen. "He was, as we all are, a deterministic system living in a probabilistic world. Who can say what caused his neurological decay to occur? I ran every test I could think of."

"There was something wrong with Owen?" Kara asked.

Morgan ignored the question. "What about Leto?"

"Why would I be worried about the boy? He only shares half of the genetic traits."

"More than half, doctor. Mathematically, he could have between twenty-five and one hundred percent."

"I already tested him a long time back. He has approximately half of the genetic makeup." Ogier looked out the window. "Where are we going?"

"Home. I want you to examine him again."

"He's not Owen nor Arthur. We don't need his genetic makeup with the nanovirus."

"You're missing the point," Morgan replied, but refused to say more. She knew more than Ogier, but she wanted him on her side. Arthur and Owen were gone, but their genetic heritage was imperfect. She'd proven it herself, and she wanted Ogier to know it. Her son was the future. She also had her own little red notebook. If Anora and Indiana thought their children would be the future, they had another think coming.

48

RIVER OF LIFE

SOMEWHERE IN VIRGINIA, NORTHWEST OF DC—
The shadow of an old bridge loomed up as Percy and Isolde came down to the water. It was dark and only the sound of a muffled car could be heard.

Percy, on cue, dropped the bag his steed carried.

"We're too late," Isolde said.

"Grab the controls," Percy said.

Isolde shifted around Percy. He pulled on a small pack and connected it to his helmet. He didn't wait for the system self-check before jumping into the icy water. He grabbed the bag and dove.

Percy's helmet lit the water around him, which was relatively clear. He felt his small tank click on and he breathed and descended. He swam against the current. His helmet pinged on the tracker, but the reception underwater was poor and locked on the last location. Percy now had to rely on his suit to be able to detect him underwater. On the bottom, he found the body bag. He grabbed it. It was weighed down, so Percy produced a Ka-Bar knife and sliced the back open. It was Arthur, pale as death. There was a cloud or red-black mist in the lamplight. Percy hooked his arms under him and swam to the surface.

Isolde was there on the pontooned steed, reaching down to pull them out of the water. He was too heavy for her, but Percy hopped on and they lifted up and used the steed to drag him to shore. Percy hopped off as soon as it was shallow and dragged Arthur up the tiny beach as Isolde moved the steed and jumped off. It settled down behind her, cycling back to land mode.

"Jesus Christ, they stabbed him in the heart," Isolde said. Blood seeped around the wound, mixing with pools of water.

"No," Percy said, kneeling down and examining with his pen knife. "It missed his heart, but his lung is punctured."

"Okay, can we focus on getting him breathing?" Isolde knelt down with him.

Percy felt for his pulse. "Yes, his heart is beating. Good pulse, but weak." He put his hands on the wound to seal it.

"CPR," Percy told Isolde. Isolde frowned and gave mouth-to-mouth.

"Lilly, where are you?" Percy said while he worked. "Izz, can you give me your shirt? I can use it as a compress for now."

Isolde pulled off her shirt. "I'm starting to think Arthur likes being a pin cushion. Shot, stabbed, stabbed, shot, lanced, blown up..."

"Let's not get dramatic." Percy worked Arthur's legs to try to drive the water from his lungs. He spat out water and coughed. "Okay, that's better."

"He's not opening his eyes," Isolde said.

"This isn't the movies. People don't instantly wake up and thank—"

"Hey, guys," Arthur whispered. "Took you a while."

"We had a little trouble getting here on time."

"God, I thought Kai's tracker was broken."

"She did say you'd get the equivalent of an ankle bracelet after you kept leaving *Camelot*. You're lucky."

"They stabbed me. Again."

A car approached, slowed, and pulled to the side of the road.

Percy ran up and came back with Lilly, who was carrying a first aid kit.

"Oh, honey, that's way worse than you said it was going to be," Lilly said, opening her kit.

"How bad did you say it was going to be?" Arthur asked Percy.

"I told her you were going to get shot."

"And this is worse? I mean, I've been shot." Arthur's voice was barely above a whisper.

"Does it feel better?"

"Not really."

"You have to stop letting people wound you to prove a point."

Isolde got up and walked away from the group. She went to Lilly's car, where she knew there would be a change of clothes. She stripped and dressed in a new n-suit. The cast gave her trouble, but she worked around it. She pulled on a heavy parka, grabbed the thermos, another kit, and walked back.

"You've lost a lot of blood. Good thing you have a type match here." Lilly eyed Percy.

"You know everyone's blood type?"

"Nurse hobbies one-oh-one."

Arthur chuckled, then coughed. He turned to Isolde. "Where's Anora?"

"She's busy right now."

"You should be—"

"Ellen's with her. She's going to be fine."

Arthur just nodded and lay back. "Fuck, I think I'd rather be deployed..."

Percy rolled up his sleeve. "Finally, a chance to make some jokes about this whole fucked-up situation," he said, lying down.

"How is everyone?" Arthur asked Isolde, who opened the thermos and poured herself some coffee.

"You want to know the truth?"

Arthur nodded.

"We lost two Echoes. Ed is still out of commission for now." She gave him a long stare.

Isolde and Percy exchanged looks. Arthur turned to Percy. "Kai?"

"Gone."

"What? No. That's not possible. That's not supposed to happen." Arthur tried to get up, but Isolde pushed him down. It was strangely easy for her to do. He was in a bad way. "How?"

"She destroyed the bridge with Longinus. Took herself out in the process," Percy said and recounted the rescue attempt.

"Kai . . . ," Arthur said.

Percy watched him and saw the heartbreak for his sister. He thought of Lamar and how lucky he was to have him alive and recovering.

"Not to be, you know, germophobic, but shouldn't we go to a hospital?" Isolde asked Lilly as she set up.

"Just a pint should do it, really," Lilly said, setting out a small hooded lantern. "It won't take long now that I've sealed the wound front and back. You are a lucky man," Lilly said to Arthur.

"Lucky in the company I keep," Arthur said. "Mostly lucky."

From the kit Isolde pulled out and hooked up the heat lamp, and laid it down.

"That feels nice," Arthur said. "'Cause I'm really cold."

"I'm not stripping down naked and giving you my lifesaving body heat," Isolde said, sitting down and watching Lilly work.

"Little thin thing like you might not give much heat," Lilly said, smiling.

"Hey, I'm not that thin. I weigh over a hundred pounds. Maybe," Isolde said. She pulled out her father's M9 from the deep pockets of her coat and checked the chamber. Her father's suicide bullet still remained.

"Thinking of shooting me?" Arthur asked. She looked down at him. She had a faraway look and appeared to have lost track of time. Percy and Lilly stared at her curiously.

"I was just thinking of my father. I wonder how many times he thought of taking his own life but decided not to. What he did for me after Avallach. How much it had been for him to hold on to life, to stay and make sure I was safe." She snapped the slide back and the bullet sprang out. Arthur caught it with a shaky hand. "Many a time, but not today," Isolde said. "It's yours. No one I know will need it."

"Does this mean you stop hating me?"

"Hell no. Just don't want to kill you all the time. Just every time you have a murderous clone."

"Afraid you were getting soft." Arthur examined the bullet, then threw it as hard as he could into the river, where it landed with a plop. "Where we're going, bullets will be useless anyway." He collapsed back, all of his emotions and energy spent.

"I could kill myself with my waveblade," Isolde said.

"About that," he began, but gave up the joke. Percy lay down as the blood transfusion took place. Arthur had that faraway look.

Lilly motioned for Isolde to come sit next to her. "Let me see your face. You look like you got into a fight with a concrete floor."

"Hey, I fight good," Isolde said. "Just give me some concealer."

"Going to need a butt load. How about I just put some Band-Aids on?"

"Depends on what you got."

"I got Hello Kitty."

"Oh, well, let's talk."

Percy nudged Arthur. "Thinking of Kai?"

"Yeah. Did we fight a lot?" Arthur asked.

"Like brother and sister always do. You both worked for the right reasons. You know this isn't a zero-sum game. We're going to lose people."

"I'm glad you didn't lose Lamar."

Percy patted Arthur's shoulder. "Me too, man. But I'd trade him for Kai if you want. Knight for a queen."

Arthur nodded, but Percy knew he'd never take that offer seriously. He was already thinking ahead.

49

MADAM SECRETARY

RLINGTON, VA—
Ellen slowed the steed as they approached the house. "This is it."

Anora nodded to herself. She heard the hint of a question in Ellen's voice but appreciated that she didn't ask.

"She's the last one and the one I'll need to handle with the most care. People like the secretary have a lot of power."

"You could just erase her life," Ellen said. "Get rid of her money holdings, delete her accounts, sell her house, erase her digital life everywhere if you wanted to."

Anora shook her head. "That'd only go about half as far as you think it would. No, this takes delicacy."

"You could just stab her in the heart," Ellen said. "Like you did to Marks."

"Figured that out, huh?" Anora said.

Ellen's broad shoulders shrugged. "He deserved it. What about Isolde?"

"She'll be angry if she finds out, but more than anything she wants to erase the past and move forward with her life. I'll give her that much at least. She's tough."

"That she is."

Anora closed her eyes, laying out all the unspoken cards in her mind.

It was me. When I found out my brother had been murdered, I went to Morgan. I got the technology. I endured the Conditioning that almost killed me. I did it all for the chance to kill him with the technology he stole from my brother. I meant to use it on Arthur, of course.

She opened her eyes. Things had changed, and she'd adapted her plan, but it still had the same endgame. Everyone responsible for the death of her brother would pay. She'd just taken care of the pilot and commanding officer of the squadron who shot down Maven's plane. Morgan's Chevaliers were temporarily crippled. She'd deal with them in other ways, but they hadn't been responsible for Maven. They were just a side effect. And, in a way, she'd gotten revenge for Donna's death as well.

Anora turned to watch the sunrise. "Hell of a show," she said. A front had moved in and flurries drifted down, but that made the sunrise that much more spectacular. Anora thought it was a beautiful, auspicious dawn. She looked down at the secretary. She was on the veranda, watching them. A number of security guards were coming out of the house now.

"Going to be a fight."

"That's just a pretense," Anora said. She seized the waveform. "Are you ready?"

"I'm yours to command," Ellen said.

"Don't get too formal," Anora said. The steed floated down. The blade from Anora's gauntlet flared to life along with Ellen's *Asi*.

Anora watched the secretary, who never moved, but regarded them with cool eyes. *She sees us in a different light now. No longer the baseline human, but something more. A threat? A project gone awry? She controls the Chevalier Corps, but she can't control the Paladins. Demigods on earth.*

EPILOGUE

WASHINGTON, DC—
Special Agent Max Muldoon walked through the crowd of first responders. He found Agent John Atherton sitting alone, sipping coffee with his good arm.

"You look like hell," Max said. "Broken arm?"

"Worse. Clavicle," John replied.

"Shit, and that's your shooting arm," Muldoon said, jamming his hands into his pockets. "Looks like a goddamn war zone. DC's going to be locked down tighter than a virgin's ass—"

"Stop," John said. "How's the home office?"

"Completely fucked up. IT says something's infected the phone lines, but they can't trace the problem. That's why I drove out here to find you myself. I couldn't get anything on their systems."

John smiled and shook his head. "Unassailable, my ass. Someone's getting fired."

"I suspect I'll be on the street soon."

"Nah, there was some serious manipulation going on."

"Do we know what happened?"

"Best guess?"

John nodded through another sip of coffee.

"Infiltration came from the data-extraction group."

John's eyebrows rose. Data extraction were the experts. That meant whatever they were pulling data from infected their systems. Oddly enough they were isolated and used Faraday cages. It had to have been something sophisticated indeed.

"I know, but infiltration is infiltration. Got into all of our systems."

"That's not supposed to be possible."

"I'm a field guy. I don't care to know the details. It just happened. Took months."

"What do we do?"

"Find out who did it."

"No, how do we function?"

"We'll throw a few billion dollars at it and either fix it or just build a new system that will probably be infiltrated as well."

"Guess we picked on the wrong person to piss off. Do we know how DEG was infiltrated?"

"Nope. That's going to take a while."

A gray-uniformed Chevalier walked by, light tape glowing yellow for caution. Her halo creeped John out.

"So, no bullets, huh?"

"Not while they have something called a 'grid' operating."

"We got one of them, right? They can be killed."

John winced at the memory. "A few of them died, mostly at each other's hands. We got the MacGabran sister."

"I heard she had power armor."

"She was like a goddamn machine," John said. "Punched through a car with that armor, but after her brother was killed, she blew up the van, the bridge. Took herself out, really."

"I hope someone picked up the pieces."

"They're dredging the river right now. Maybe we'll find some pieces of the armor."

Max sat down. "I think it might be time to retire."

"You're getting old, man."

"I'm the same age as you. What do you think?"

"When September eleventh happened, we saw the world change.

On the inside, it didn't seem like much, but on the outside, it was a lot. This is another change and I'm not sure where it's going to go."

"So you're retiring?"

John snorted. "Hell no. I'm going to get in the front of the bus. See if I can steer it before it drives humanity off a cliff. The world's going to be really different now, that's for damn sure."

Max kicked at a piece of concrete, still eyeing the Chevalier. Her halo was still visible in the morning light. "I don't much like these Chevaliers if you must know. Seem a bit high and mighty; you know how everyone feels when people like that are around."

"Yeah, I know what you mean." John followed his gaze and got up. "You got a car?"

"Yeah."

"Before you turn in your badge, can you take me back to the office? I got some reports to file and I need to see who wants to fire me over this shit show."

Max chuckled. They threaded their way through the throng of people. "Do you think she had the right?"

"To blow up the bridge? No."

"To cremate her brother, I mean."

"Hell no. But I couldn't stop her. No one could. She called down the wrath of God onto earth and wiped him out of existence."

"I saw the footage."

"It doesn't even come close to what we saw. I'm telling you, the crazies are going to come out of the woodwork, seeing these Chevaliers around. We have to do something about it."

"What're you going to do back at the office?"

"Gonna look over some files for the Avallach case."

"The sinkhole and helicopter last year?"

"Yeah, something about that's bothering me." John put his hands in his pocket and felt the rings. He'd somehow lost MacGabran's rings, but he still had the girl's. There was a label on the evidence bag for the name she'd given them: *Justice.*

ACKNOWLEDGMENTS

Thanks to my family for their support and encouragement. Thanks to Michael Rowley and Aja Pollock for their editorial expertise and to my wife Maria for her proofreading work. Thank you to everyone who endured the rougher drafts of my sequel novel: Maria Britz, L. Canlas, Natalie Root, Prianna Staley, and Elizabeth Mizdail.

ABOUT THE AUTHOR

Ken Britz is an engineer who writes stories working to be a writer who engineers plots. He's an emerging author writing cross genre science fiction and fantasy. He currently lives with his family in Long Island, NY.

Signup for free content and information on upcoming works. Use any of the following methods to reach out and tell me about anything cool you've read recently. I'd love to hear from you!

kenbritz.com
ken@kenbritz.com

ALSO BY KEN BRITZ

Fall to Earth

Made in the USA
Columbia, SC
28 October 2017